WITHDRAWN FROM STOCK

KU-190-195

A WARTIME MARRIAGE

The Kaiser's empire is about to fall and Captain Harry Phillips, a prisoner of war in a Romanian hospital, has had a very hard time of it. Then comes an offer he can't refuse – a ticket home to his beloved England and the arms of his much-missed fiancée Elisabeth. However, the ticket comes with a heavy price; Harry must marry the beautiful, headstrong Princess Irena of Moldova, and risk both their lives by escorting her back to England. As Harry begins to realise that Irena is not only dangerous but extremely precious cargo, will he sacrifice everything for his wartime marriage?

A WARTIME MARRIAGE

A WARTIME MARRIAGE

by

Mary Jane Staples

Magna Large Print Books
Long Preston, North Yorkshire,
BD23 4ND, England.

British Library Cataloguing in Publication Data.

Staples, Mary Jane
A wartime marriage.

A catalogue record of this book is available from the British Library

ISBN 978-0-7505-2956-3

First published in Great Britain in 1977 by Souvenir Press Ltd as *Flight from Bucharest* under the name of Robert Tyler Stevens

Published in Large Print 2009 by arrangement with Transworld Publishers

Magna Large Print is an imprint of Library Magna Books Ltd.

Printed and bound in Great Britain by
T.J. (International) Ltd., Cornwall, PL28 8RW

Chapter One

On a day in October 1918, when the Austrian and German Empires were on their cataclysmic slide into oblivion, the atmosphere in the German-occupied hospital on the north side of Bucharest was orderly and quiet.

Captain Harry Phillips limped along a corridor in his faded woollen dressing gown, his armed German escort behind him. Other walking patients glanced briefly at him or studiously ignored him. He was the acorn in the bag of nuts. They were German, he was British. They were casualties of the battles now raging in Serbia, where the revitalized Serbian Army, supported by British and French divisions, had the Austrians and Germans in escalating retreat. Harry was a casualty of bad luck.

Somewhere in the hospital he heard a gramophone scratchily playing Beethoven's 'Moonlight Sonata'. A nurse, watching his approach, opened a door in the corridor for him. He thanked her in English. She was German, as all the nurses were, but he did not speak her language. Classroom French was his only linguistic achievement, but he had at least managed to improve on the spoken word during his service in France.

The nurse pointed to the grounds outside and said, 'The Herr Major.'

'Thank you,' he said again. She was polite but

did not smile. He understood. She could see defeat staring her country in the face, a defeat so humiliating that the position of Kaiser Wilhelm himself was in the balance.

He walked through the lobby, using his stick, and out into the grounds. The turf was autumn green, the day bright but fresh. He was thankful for the warmth of the hospital dressing gown. His escort marched solidly at his back. A lean figure in the tailored field-grey of a German officer awaited him. The armed escort was dismissed by the gesture of a gloved hand. Harry came to a stop.

'Good morning, Herr Captain,' said Major Carlsen, a man of thirty-five.

'Good morning, Major.' Harry was twenty-seven.

'Shall we sit?' The English was easy, fluent.

'Thanks.'

They were both pleasantly civilized. They seated themselves on a bench. The leaves lay thick in sheltered corners, elsewhere they lifted, rustled and skittered in the breeze. Harry wondered what Major Carlsen was after; he did not think this was a mere social call.

He considered himself a little unlucky to be in German hands, although he had no complaints about the hospital. The Allies had begun their Balkan offensive in September, from Salonika. They had quickly put the Bulgarians out of the war, then driven into Serbia, which had been under Austrian occupation since 1915. The Austrian and German divisions were pushed steadily back, but in one determined counterattack the

Austrians cut out some forward British batteries. Harry was among the prisoners taken. Sent north to an Austrian prisoner-of-war camp, he escaped on the way and began a hazardous trek back through enemy-occupied country in the hope of rejoining his unit.

He had almost broken through the southernmost German lines when he bumped into one of their patrols. In the dusk of evening a young German soldier, nervously reactive to shadows, fired first and enquired later. Harry, a bullet in his thigh, was recaptured muttering and swearing. He was sent for treatment to the Queen Constanza Hospital on the north side of Bucharest. The hospital had been taken over by the Germans, the conquerors of Rumania. He was interrogated by a very correct but very courteous German officer, Major Carlsen, who congratulated him on his initiative and commiserated with his bad luck.

The German doctors and nurses accorded him the same attention they gave to their own wounded and were as courteous as Major Carlsen, who visited him a couple of times. He was fit, his wound was not serious and it healed rapidly. They gave him a stick to help him with the therapeutic exercise of walking about. They did not want to keep him too long. His presence was slightly embarrassing.

'You wished to see me?' said Harry.

'Yes. A cigarette?' Major Carlsen offered his case. Harry took a long white tube with a gold-coloured tip to it. They both lit up. The cigarettes had the strong aroma and distinctive flavour of

Balkan tobacco. 'You are considerably improved, Captain Phillips.'

'Considerably,' said Harry. 'The treatment and attention have been first-class.'

'It was not a complicated matter, I believe, merely a small hole in your leg.'

'Oh, nothing at all,' said Harry.

'You are a very fit man.'

'Am I? Perhaps. The war, of course, hasn't been quite as uncomfortable for the gunners as for the infantry.' But he did look fit, considering his hospitalization. He had no surplus flesh, his dark eyes were clear and alert, and his five-eleven frame was vigorous. True, his auburn-brown hair needed trimming, but it was thick and healthy. The German barber had offered his services but having seen how he cropped the German officers, Harry ducked the operation that would have made him look like an egg. He managed, by being very persuasive, to get one of the nurses to use her scissors on him. She had snipped his tufts quite professionally and Harry left it at that.

'You will be discharged in a day or so,' said Major Carlsen, removing his cigarette and watching the smoke curl before the wind whisked it away.

'I've been expecting that.'

'There is a camp near Bistrita.' Bistrita was in Hungary.

'Is it comfortable there?'

'I doubt it, circumstances being what they are,' said the major, 'but it may be educational. You will meet Russians, Serbians, Poles, French and a few British, I think.'

'Very educational,' said Harry, 'and very crowded, I imagine. However, circumstances being as you say, I may not be there too long.'

Major Carlsen's impassiveness cracked a little. Harry discerned a momentary flicker of sadness, an acknowledgement of coming defeat.

'No, perhaps not too long at all, Captain. Indeed, if you prefer, it can be avoided altogether.'

'I don't suppose you mean I can stay here,' said Harry, 'I'm rather an embarrassment, naturally.'

'Yes. Those who feel a sense of defeat can't communicate with those who wear an air of victory. And you do represent to us a nation whose declaration of war was unnecessary and unjustified.'

'I hope,' said Harry, 'that we're not going to argue about who started it and whose fault it was.' He smiled. 'We shall end up fighting.'

'Those arguments are for the politicians,' said Major Carlsen, his grey eyes observing the caped progress of a hurrying nurse across the grass. 'We are the tools they use to resolve their more intractable differences. But you may be sure they will take no blame for the war. That will be laid at the doors of others. No, I did not mean you could stay here. I meant you might be allowed to make your own way back to your country.'

Harry blew a startled smoke ring. It was picked up by the breeze and carried flirtatiously away.

'Will you say that again, Major?' he said.

'It would not be impossible for you to get to Trieste, and from there to France or Italy, do you think?' It was said in a pleasant, enquiring way.

'You'll turn me loose?' Harry was sceptical.

'From here to Trieste it's your territory. I'd be damned lucky to get halfway.'

'Oh, I don't know.' Major Carlsen sounded casually English. 'I'd say your ingenuity would carry you farther than that.'

'I've nothing to lose, I suppose,' said Harry, 'but there's a catch somewhere, isn't there?'

'There's a little more to it, yes,' said the major. 'You'll need papers. You speak French, I think?'

'Fairly well. It wouldn't deceive the French, but it wouldn't have to, I imagine.'

'I thought the role of a White Russian would do admirably. They are known to speak French.'

Harry regarded the German with curiosity. Major Carlsen's eyes did not waver. He seemed like a man sitting in calm judgement of his own suggestion.

'Pardon me for not falling over myself, Major,' said Harry, 'but I'm wondering why you should do this for me, provide me with fake Russian papers and send me on my way.'

'Because in return,' said the major, 'I thought you might do something for me. I thought you might agree to having a travelling companion.'

'Oh? You don't propose coming, do you?' Harry allowed himself a moment of humour. Major Carlsen did not smile.

'That is a joke?' he said.

'Just a light aside,' said Harry.

'In defeat we can try to joke amongst ourselves, perhaps. It's a little more difficult to joke with others.'

'You concede defeat?' Harry was interested. He knew nothing of the pessimism rife within the

German High Command. 'But you're still fighting.'

Major Carlsen did not sound bitter as he said, 'Yes, I myself concede defeat. There comes a time when hope must give way to reality. Germany will have to sue for peace within the next month or so.' He managed a light rider. 'But we gave you a good run, Captain Phillips, a good long run.'

'Too damned long,' admitted Harry, who had fought in France, Mesopotamia and in the present Salonika campaign. 'Who am I to be saddled with on my wandering journey of hope?'

'I'll come to that in a moment,' said the major, 'but first have I your word as a British officer that whatever you decide you will not speak of our conversation to anyone? I can assure you it's not a matter that will affect the course of the war. It does not even concern the war. It is purely a question of giving help to someone who desperately needs it.'

'You have my word,' said Harry, not disliking the German.

Major Carlsen waited until two patients and a nurse had gone by before going on.

'Captain Phillips,' he said, 'this is not only a bad time for Europe and its peoples, it's a bad time for kings and emperors. The end for many of them is coming. They will be the first scapegoats for the politicians. The Tsar of Russia and his family have already been found guilty and executed. Soon others will be condemned, some because they have been all-powerful or not powerful enough, some for being incompetent or merely patriotic. And some for simply being sons or daughters of the mighty. Do you know Princess Irena of Moldavia?'

'Moldavia? Is that a principality?'

'It was until it became part of Rumania about sixty years ago. Do you know the princess?'

'Personally?' Harry was a little ironic. 'No. I've never moved in exalted circles.'

'I was not expecting you to claim personal acquaintance, of course,' said Major Carlsen with the flicker of a smile. 'I meant, have you heard of her?'

'I've probably heard or read of all of them in my time, without it meaning anything to me.' Harry was not an avid devourer of court circulars but he read his newspapers. 'One European princess is much the same as another as far as I'm concerned.'

The October sun slid behind a grey cloud and the fresh day suddenly became colder.

'Princess Irena isn't quite the same as others,' said Major Carlsen, 'her temperament and character are highly distinctive.'

'I don't know what that means in a princess,' said Harry, 'but in a woman it can mean regular fireworks.'

'It means in Princess Irena a woman of intelligence and spirit.'

'Then I'm pleased for her,' said Harry dryly.

'She is distantly related to King Ferdinand of Rumania, whose Queen is the granddaughter of Queen Victoria.'

'Yes?' For some reason, thought Harry, the major had been doing a little homework.

'Yes.' Major Carlsen was definite. 'Princess

Irena remained here when we occupied Rumania. King Ferdinand and Queen Marie accompanied their government to Jassy. The princess has always been pro-German and was against Rumania going to war with us. Now certain Rumanian Socialists and extremists wish to try her for treason. She has frequently spoken out for Germany and is among those being blamed for many things.'

'Well, for God's sake,' said Harry, 'speaking out on behalf of a country which conquered her own wasn't the most sensible thing to do, was it?'

'All of us hold opinions, Captain, but not all of us are brave enough to continue holding them and speaking them irrespective of circumstances.'

'Where did you learn your English?' asked Harry.

'At Oxford,' said Major Carlsen, 'I spent three years there. Captain Phillips, Princess Irena is still in Bucharest. But when Germany has to sue for peace and leave Rumania, she will no longer be under our protection. She will not be safe in her own country, despite all that King Ferdinand might do for her.'

'Then send her to Germany,' said Harry.

'That is what she wishes, but that is what is denied her. We have been forbidden to help her in that way. Apparently, she would be an embarrassment to the Emperor. He himself is not too safe now, since he will have to take all the blame for the war. His ministers have advised against giving Princess Irena sanctuary. Her presence would be very unwelcome to them.'

Harry drew his dressing gown tighter around his pyjamaed legs.

'That doesn't make sense,' he said, 'not in view of her sympathy for Germany.'

'I think it's a little chilly for you, Captain,' said the major politely.

'Yes,' said Harry, 'can we do a turn around the grounds?'

'You can manage that?' said the major, looking at Harry's stick.

'No trouble at all, and I'm supposed to do more walking than sitting. The bullet hit bone. Walking fends off atrophy, I believe.'

They began to walk, keeping to the paths. There were few other patients about.

'Our ministers require the best possible atmosphere to prevail if they are forced to seek an armistice,' said the major, 'and the princess is notoriously against anything but a continuation of the war. She believes the survival of Germany and Austria absolutely necessary to save Europe from the disaster of Socialism. And she has said so.'

'I see,' said Harry, 'she's pro-German and anti-Socialist. That's consistent, I think.'

'All the same she's being denied entry into Germany. They think she will influence the Kaiser and induce in him a mood of obstinacy that could lead Germany into civil war. No, I am not exaggerating.'

'I should think she's got problems enough in her own country,' said Harry, 'without wanting to get involved with Germany's.'

'That's a good, sound black-and-white comment, Captain,' said Major Carlsen, 'but a little too easy to make, if you'll forgive me.' The sun came out again, sharply outlining the thinning branches of trees. 'Princess Irena is Rumanian first, but has blood ties with almost every European country. In some matters she insists her chief loyalty is to her beliefs and her conscience. She has consistently attacked the policies of the Allies which, she says, will reduce Europe to anarchy. So it's as difficult for her to find refuge in France or England as elsewhere. In your own country several of your politicians have been asking whether certain people in high places are arranging to receive her in England. They have said the British people would not tolerate it, any more than they would tolerate the arrival of Kaiser Wilhelm. However, she cannot stay here. Each day becomes more dangerous for her. Her enemies mean to arrest her, condemn her and shoot her.'

'As a travelling companion,' said Harry, 'she sounds like dynamite with the fuse lit. And where would I take her if nobody wants her?'

'She is headstrong, Captain,' said Major Carlsen, 'but she is worth saving. This is agreeable to you, walking and talking?'

'Oh, agreeable enough,' said Harry, 'but leading to the improbable, I feel.'

'Wars happen and armies engage,' said the major. 'Men blow each other to pieces or shoot each other to death. To sight a rifle for the purpose of killing someone is either an instinctive act of self-preservation or a premeditated act of aggrandizement. However, in the main we have not been so uncivilized as to involve women.'

'Except in wars where they have been considered part of the plunder.'

'An irrelevance, Captain, in these enlightened days,' said the major. 'Would you take a woman out and shoot her?'

'The French shot Mata Hari and you shot Nurse Cavell,' said Harry, 'but no, I'm not in favour of shooting women. Is this really likely to happen to Princess Irena?'

'It will happen the moment Germany withdraws her troops from Rumania.'

'But won't the Austrians or Hungarians give her protection?'

'Out of the question.' The major, hands clasping his short cane behind his back, was dismissive. 'In Austria or Hungary she would be delivered into the hands of Socialists, who would then hand her over to the Rumanian extremists. I am hoping you will try to get her to England, away from the Balkans altogether and safe from the long arms of people determined to execute her. I confess to you, Captain, that I admire her, and I have told her I will do what I can for her.'

'You want me to get her to England?' Harry did not fancy that. 'Ye gods, what a hope! And even if I did manage it, she won't be received, she'll be deported back to Rumania.'

Major Carlsen thought deeply before commenting on that. Then he said, 'Not, perhaps, if she were the wife of a decorated British officer, a man of proven courage. Politicians are capable of things you and I would not consider for a moment. But even the most cynical of them would not stand up and ask for the wife of one of the country's heroes to be taken from him and turned over to people obviously intent on shooting her.'

'Hold on,' said Harry. He stopped on the leaf-strewn path. He was decidedly curious. 'I think I've followed you up till now. Now I think I'm falling behind. Is she married to a British officer?'

'She's married to no one.'

'Oh, by God,' said Harry.

'Yes,' said Major Carlsen impassively, 'I think you have caught up.'

'I still think you'd better put it in plain words.'

Major Carlsen said in his courteous way, 'Captain Phillips, would you consider giving Princess Irena your care and protection by marrying her?'

Chapter Two

A nurse came up and said something to Major Carlsen. He nodded and thanked her. She hesitated, her curiosity aroused by the indefinable, by the strange quiet existing between the politely formal German major and the handsome, resolute British officer. Pointedly, Major Carlsen thanked her again. She flushed slightly and hurried away.

'There's some coffee available, apparently,' said the major, 'we can have it in a private room.'

The private room was someone's small office on the second floor. The coffee was on the desk. The Major poured it. It was not remarkable coffee but it was hot. Harry sipped his with his mind on Elisabeth. Calm, unflappable, her approach to this flight of German fantasy would be endearingly analytical. He thought about the whimsical smile she had given him when, on his last home leave a year ago, he asked her to marry him.

What was it she had said?

'You're being very gallant, Harry.'

'I'm being positive, I hope. Give me your answer, won't you?'

'Yes. Of course yes. You know there's never been anyone else.'

There never had been, for either of them. They had known each other, lived close to each other, for years. He knew no other girl he would rather be married to than Elisabeth. He could not keep her poised on the edge of uncertainty forever just because of the war. They would be married immediately it was over. Their families were delighted with the engagement, especially as they had been waiting in hope for quite some time. Elisabeth wrote him charming letters on his return to the front, telling him in each one to take particular care of himself.

'I must say I'm flattered by your confidence in me, Major,' he said, 'and absolutely bowled over by the princess's willingness, especially as she's never met me. But it's impossible, of course, you must realize that.'

'It's fanciful,' said the major, 'but not impossible. The princess feels that as a British officer you must also be a gentleman, and that therefore it's not necessary to meet you in order to approve or disapprove of you.'

'Oh?' Harry was slightly amused.

'It would put you at risk if you gave her your help and protection. I should not wish to deceive you about that.'

'Major, I'm not free to even consider it.' Harry was firm, decisive. 'I'm engaged to a young lady in England, I've contracted to marry her at the end of the war.'

Major Carlsen did not seem ruffled or discouraged.

'That's a complication,' he conceded, 'but not an insurmountable obstacle. Your marriage to Princess Irena will be annulled as soon as it's tactically and reasonably convenient. The annulment would be on the most unquestionable of grounds, which would make it automatic.'

'I see,' said Harry. The war had made him a little irreverent about proprieties and niceties. 'You mean–?'

'Precisely,' said Major Carlsen with distinct nicety. 'It could be arranged without any publicity after you had spent a little time together in England and any fuss had died down. With luck you might get her into England simply as your wife, and without her true identity coming to light at all. Then there would be no headlines and no fuss of any kind. Your fiancée must be considered, of course, but I am sure she is a sympathetic and intelligent woman. If so, she would understand all you had done for Princess Irena and even admire you for it.'

'A very nice thought, Major,' said Harry, sitting on the edge of the desk, 'but I can't see any woman in a light as angelic as that. We're sometimes inclined to ask of women things we'd never ask of ourselves. And I really can't see myself in the role of Galahad, in any case.'

All the same, he was intrigued, he was interested, and not completely sure he couldn't be persuaded.

Perhaps Major Carlsen sensed this. He said, 'You may have seen newspaper pictures of Princess Irena?'

'I don't know, I may have,' said Harry.

'Let me show you something that does her more justice than a newspaper picture, Herr Captain.' Major Carlsen reached into his pocket, took out a wallet and extracted a postcard-sized photograph. It was a sepia print, a formal portrait of a young woman of about twenty-one, with her expression soft and pensive. Her head was lightly turned to show the graceful line of her neck, a tiara adorned dark hair glossy and beautifully dressed, and she wore earrings, to match the glittering tiara. Her shoulders were bare, her dark lashes long and thick. She was quite lovely. Harry, impressed, smiled wryly. He could not imagine how he would cope with a marriage of convenience to a woman as royal and as beautiful as this. Nor could he picture Elisabeth receiving the news with joy or falling into raptures of admiration for his gallantry. That was too much to ask of any fiancée.

He looked up from his absorbing study of the portrait and caught on the major's face an expression that was almost tender. It told him that the German's concern for the princess was not based on sympathy alone.

'Well?' said the major.

'Frankly,' said Harry, 'I don't think she stands a chance.'

'Captain?' The major raised his eyebrows.

'I mean,' said Harry, 'that with those looks she'll be recognized on every street corner. I wouldn't even get her out of Bucharest.'

'Most men might not. I think you would. You are a man of courage and initiative. And you would receive some necessary co-operation.'

'Look here,' said Harry, 'I've got to have time to think it over.'

'There isn't too much.'

'I'm sorry about that, but you have sprung it on me. And I'd better meet her, don't you think? I appreciate her confidence in me as a gentleman, but I think we need to see each other before any decision is made. I've spent four years firing high explosive at you and the Turks, and it's probably taken some of the polish off me. I wouldn't want the princess to think she's getting Little Lord Fauntleroy.'

'Captain Phillips,' said Major Carlsen, carefully putting the photograph away, 'I will arrange for her to visit the hospital this afternoon. That will arouse no suspicion among those who are watching her, for she visits many hospitals.'

'I'd better have a fresh shave,' said Harry, wondering why the devil he was suddenly halfway to taking on the impossible.

Perhaps it was the photograph.

Perhaps it was that the only alternative was a prisoner-of-war camp. That loomed as unbearably depressing and damned dull.

He was called from the ward later that day. He was taken up to the same small office on the second floor. He knocked. Major Carlsen's voice invited him in. He entered.

She was there, the young woman of the photograph, standing at the window with the major. She turned. She wore a long silver-grey coat trimmed with fur and a matching hat and veil. She put up the veil. Her features were smooth, healthy, her brown eyes inquisitive and alive. She was unarguably lovely, her colour giving her warmth, her hair glossily rich below her hat. But she was cool in her self-possession. He glimpsed teeth immaculately white between her slightly parted lips. She was as curious about Harry as he was about her, and Major Carlsen momentarily delayed the formal introductions.

Harry, lean from campaigns in Flanders and the deserts of Mesopotamia, looked taller than his five feet eleven. In her grey shoes she stood only a few inches shorter. He saw her, aside from her physical beauty, as a problem, a challenge, a rarity. She saw him as a man who might be an invaluable asset or an incalculable liability. She also saw him as a personable British officer whose hospital dressing gown gave him an air of casual charm. His dark eyes were speculative, quizzical.

He smiled. Her response was immediate, a smile of animation and warmth. Major Carlsen coughed.

'Your Highness, may I present Captain Harry Phillips? Captain Phillips, Her Highness Princess Irena of Moldavia.'

Harry bowed. He supposed that was the right

thing to do. She acknowledged the courtesy by extending her hand. He took it. He supposed the next thing to do was to kiss it. He bent his head and put his lips lightly to her fingertips.

'So you are Captain Phillips,' she said in English touched with the soft accent of the Balkans. 'You are the officer Major Carlsen has told me about. Thank you for wishing to meet me.' She had so much charm that Harry wondered how the devil she could upset anyone, politically or otherwise. Well, she was a woman of course. One could never tell which way the most delightful of them would jump.

'I was interested, naturally,' he said.

'I am glad you were,' she smiled, brown eyes soft as they met his.

They were measuring each other, taking stock of whether there were any warts plainly impossible to live with.

'We are establishing a rapport? Good,' said the major.

'I'm in trouble with some people,' said Irena.

'So I'm told,' said Harry, repressing a desire to suggest she might have brought it on herself. She was regarding him without guile, without any hint of guilt, yet he thought there was an air of appeal beneath her calm. Harry, having spent most of his four years of war out of touch with women, had decided that the longer he was away from them the more worthwhile their role in life seemed. Their sense of logic might be a trifle suspect, their tantrums inexplicable, but when one was thinking about them in pools of icy, muddy rain the creatures made a better reason for living than anything else. Princess Irena, for all her highborn status, was vulnerable, her call for help irresistible. There would be nothing about the adventure itself Elisabeth would disapprove of, and the marriage certificate would be torn up at the right time. It would be the relationship that Elisabeth would have suspicions about.

'You are thinking me over?' said Irena in a way that was enchanting.

'I'm thinking how crazy it is,' said Harry.

'I shall be a problem, I know,' she said with a rueful smile, 'but I promise not to be a nuisance as well. Major Carlsen has told me about your fiancée. I should not make the slightest difficulty about that, it is too important to you. I should explain to her how gallant you had been and we would arrange for the annulment to be as quick as possible.'

'That's very important, yes,' said Harry, 'but how can I guarantee I'll ever get you to England?'

'You would be willing to try?' She was softly earnest.

Harry looked hard at her. She had a warmly regal elegance. Quixotic generosity tilted at the windmill of common sense and for once the windmill fell over.

'Yes, I'll try, Your Highness,' he said.

Her eyes became bright, grateful.

'Thank you, you are very gallant, Captain Phillips.'

'I think I'm also slightly off my head,' said Harry.

'Perhaps we all are,' said Irena, 'but sometimes doing the crazy thing is the only answer, isn't it?'

'Sometimes,' said Harry with a smile, 'it leads straight to suicide.'

Her laugh was slightly emotional. Major Carlsen's watchful impassivity was softened by relief. They said goodbye to Harry, the major promising he would return later for a further talk. Harry stood at the window and watched them go. There were three open German cars in the drive. Major Carlsen and Irena took the centre car. The others were full of German soldiers, sitting with rifles upright between their knees. That, thought Harry, had to be a sign of the danger the princess faced in her own capital. The cars moved off, Harry came to. He shook his head at his impulsive idiocy.

He wondered if he'd have said yes had the princess not been so lovely. The advantage women of beauty held over their plainer sisters was typical of the utter unfairness of life.

Major Carlsen was back that evening and again they met in the small office. The German spread a map over the tidied desk.

'First,' he said, 'I am asked by the princess to tell you how grateful she is. She is also very impressed.'

'After a meeting as brief as that? I must say,' said Harry a trifle caustically, 'that I marvel at your willingness to entrust her regal personage to me. You really know nothing about me. At the first sign of trouble I may hand her over to those who want her.'

'Would you do that, Herr Captain?'

'No. But how can you know I wouldn't?'

'Sometimes, Captain Phillips, it isn't necessary to have known a man all his life to decide whether he is a better risk than others.'

'It's a risk right enough. Look here,' said Harry plainly, 'don't make it more difficult for me by trying to convince me I can perform miracles. I can't. I can do my best, but I'm not Jesus Christ and I'm not Hercules. Be logical about our chances and stop making me feel that you think I'm infallible.'

'I shall simply put my trust in your courage and initiative,' said Major Carlsen firmly. 'There shouldn't be too much difficulty getting you and the princess to Belgrade.' He put his finger to the map, tracing the line from Bucharest to Belgrade. 'You will go by train, you will leave her house with her in the evening and travel to the station as a German officer, since the curfew puts restrictions on civilians.'

'German officer?' Harry could not see the sense of that. 'I don't speak a word of German.'

'You won't need to.' The major was crisp, clinical. 'We will have your throat bandaged as if you have been wounded there. The princess will do your talking for you. She will be travelling as an Austrian woman not restricted by the curfew.'

'When will this be?'

'Two evenings from now. You will be even fitter then and it is as much time as we can give you. Once you are out of the city proper and on the train it will be safe for you to change into the civilian clothes I shall get for you. With these you will assume the identity of a White Russian acting as an agent for the German Army Headquarters in Belgrade. I will see you're supplied with the necessary papers. It will be too risky on the train to maintain your pose as a German officer, even with a bandaged throat, for it will be full of troops. As a White Russian you will get by with your French.'

'You sound remarkably confident,' said Harry, 'I feel remarkably nervous.'

The major reflected, not for the first time, on the quality of his man. He was aware of the British habit of underplaying their hand, of the tendency of other people to be taken in by this. There was a slight smile on Captain Phillips' face, but his eyes were as cool as the devil, the line of his mouth and chin firm.

'I am more confident about you than I am about other things,' said the major. 'Plans can go wrong, events take an unexpected turn, but as long as the man in charge is equal to the need for improvisation all will be well. A great general is not one who can make plans but who has the courage, if necessary, to tear them up.'

'Major,' said Harry, 'you're the general in this case, you're making the plans, but I think I'm the one who may be faced with the responsibility of tearing them up.'

'Perhaps,' said the major. He went on to suggest that once in Belgrade, Harry should go into hiding with the princess and wait until the Allied advance forced the Austrians and Germans to evacuate the city. That should only be a matter of days if the Serbian, British and French operations continued to be conducted as aggressively as they were at the moment. Then Harry could come out of hiding, wearing his own uniform, and make his way with the princess across Croatia to Trieste, which would be a most suitable takeoff point for Italy or France. It would not be easy. The princess's enemies would be looking for her the moment they realized she was no longer in Bucharest, and there would probably be a certain amount of civil disorder when the Austrians and Germans began their withdrawal from Serbia. That would not make things easy for anyone, but as a British officer Harry would have some standing, some immunity. The extremists and their agents would look for the princess to be travelling as a peasant or a refugee, anything but what she was. They would not, however, suspect the wife of a British officer to be Irena of Moldavia.

'That wouldn't stop some of them recognizing her,' said Harry.

'True,' agreed the major, 'but she will dress modestly and look as inconspicuous as possible. A little care and thought will be needed.'

'Officially,' said Harry, 'once you've let me go my way I'd be expected to rejoin my unit, providing that was reasonably possible.'

'And if it weren't?'

'Then it would be my duty to try to get back to my country.'

'You will stretch a point?' said the major.

'I suppose I must,' said Harry, 'or it all falls down from the start. I could, I imagine, simply wait for the first British troops to arrive in Belgrade and then hand myself and the princess over to them.'

'Do you think that a good idea?' asked the

major sharply.

'No,' said Harry frankly. 'I should be posted back to my regiment and she, as my wife, would be billeted somewhere. Somewhere fairly decent, of course, but not, from your point of view, very satisfactory.'

'I think we are approaching a point of fine understanding, Captain. It would not be satisfactory at all. She would inevitably be discovered. She must be taken out of the Balkans, out of Europe to England. They will probably be after her all the way. Your problem, when Germany and Austria have sued for peace, will not be with us but with the kind of people who rise to temporary power in towns and villages. There'll be Socialists in some places, ambitious Bolsheviks in others, all demanding the heads of those they consider guilty of crimes against the people. It will last until new law and order is established. You will need steady nerves at times.'

'Really?' Harry was slightly caustic again. 'Frankly, I think my nerves will be jumping about all the time.'

'But you will go through with it?' said the major.

'You say she's worth saving. Perhaps she is. I can only do my best. If I succeed my only concern will be with the quick annulment of this marriage. My fiancée is the best of persons. She too is worth something. When I see her I don't want to be humming and hahing about things, I want to be positive.'

'You may reassure yourself about that.' Major Carlsen allowed himself a slight smile. 'It isn't likely that Her Highness will develop a romantic attachment, she will keep her feet on the ground, as you say.'

'I hope so,' said Harry, 'as I don't think you can rely on every woman to do exactly what men expect her to. Perhaps princesses are different.'

'You're cynical about women?' said the major with a lift of an eyebrow.

'Not at all. They're delightful.' Harry smiled. 'I haven't seen enough of them recently, in the social sense. But I like to be a realist about them. Then one can avoid what I'd call shots in the dark.'

'Captain Phillips,' said the major severely, 'Princess Irena is not likely to wish to remain married to a commoner.'

'Well, damn good,' said Harry fervently.

'Is that realistic enough for you?'

Harry laughed. Major Carlsen smiled. It was a slightly sad smile.

'What else do I need to know?' asked Harry.

'You might care to hear in confidence that certain high personages in your country will be grateful if you manage to arrive safely with Her Highness, but naturally they will not allow their feelings to be made public.'

'With her pro-German background, very naturally.'

'Until recently,' said the major, 'she has refused to believe she was in any real danger from people she has only contempt for. She believes it now because they have been watching her for weeks. They watch her house. They pass to and fro. They watch her when she goes out, they watch to ensure she returns. They slip the curfew to watch her. They make no move but they are always around, day and night. They will arrest her as soon as we Germans go. I am able to see she has adequate protection here in Bucharest and that is all I can do. I could not, for instance, take her to Belgrade myself. I should not get the necessary permission. But if I did our Socialist friends would probably think I was going to take her all the way to Germany, and as likely as not would arrange for a bomb to greet her in Belgrade. I am hopeful, however, that with your help we can get her out of her house at night and on the way to Belgrade without bringing the pack down on you.'

'I don't like the sound of that word,' said Harry.

'What am I achieving, Captain, with all this talk?'

'You're making me nervous,' said Harry.

The major, obviously considering that a satisfactory condition, said, 'Good, it will give you eyes in the back of your head. By the way, don't look for any help from the Serbians in Belgrade. They would do what they could for you as an escaping British prisoner, but they would not lift a finger to help the princess. Almost certainly they would turn her over to Rumanian extremists here.'

'You know,' said Harry thoughtfully, 'with your knowledge of all the political and military implications, you'd make a better protector and guide than I would. Isn't it possible your immediate superior would turn a blind eye if you went off with her to Trieste? I think you'd manage to keep her out of bombing range.'

Major Carlsen began to draw on his gloves.

'My orders, Captain Phillips,' he said, 'are such that I could do nothing of the kind without being placed under arrest on arrival in Belgrade. You as an escaping prisoner of war have much more latitude. May I arrange for you to be brought to her house in two days' time?'

'I should like to think that we're not gambling with her life,' said Harry.

'Her life will be worth nothing if she stays here. She will either be tried and executed, or simply executed. Do you wish to reconsider?'

'No, damn it, I've lit the gas under the pot,' said Harry, 'and it's up to me now to stay with it. Otherwise the porridge will burn. But is it absolutely necessary to marry her?'

'She will not be able to get into England except as your wife. She will be safe there, she will know what to do. I'm afraid you get little out of it, Captain, except your freedom in advance. And that, at times, may be an uncomfortable freedom.'

'Allow me to say,' said Harry dryly, 'that you have a very distinctive way of spreading light and cheer.'

'I am glad I am not the instrument of gloom,' said Major Carlsen gravely.

Chapter Three

Major Carlsen put in his promised reappearance two days later, in the evening. He brought with him the uniform of a German infantry colonel.

'In this,' he said, 'you will be able to enter the princess's house without suspicion. She frequently entertains German officers.'

'I'm not surprised,' said Harry, 'that she's in trouble with her people.'

'She entertains us, she does not collaborate, she has never given us a single piece of information.' The major was stiff in his defence of Irena. 'The house will be watched as usual but no one will stop us. They haven't yet reached the point of being arrogant, of making demands on us. But they are aware of the Allies' advances and they may get bolder any moment. We must have you away with her this evening. The train leaves the station at Chitila, north of Bucharest, just before midnight. It will be mainly carrying troops.'

The uniform was an excellent fit. It turned Harry into a coolly handsome German officer and had Major Carlsen smiling faintly.

'You realize what will happen if I'm caught by your people wearing this?' said Harry.

'Normally, you would be shot.'

'I'd prefer to avoid that.'

'Show them the papers you'll find in the suit of civilian clothes. They establish you as an agent working for us.'

'Yes, a White Russian agent.'

Harry was not regretting his decision, but the uniform did seem to signify a point of no return and he felt he must be quite definitely off his head. He was a man, however, to whom adventure appealed. His father was a bank manager but he had chosen farming as his own career. During breaks from his job as an assistant farm manager he had climbed the Matterhorn, helped to crew a clipper and joined an archaeological dig in France.

He thought about Elisabeth again, and her possible reactions. He smiled a little, he frowned a little. Major Carlsen asked him if he was having second thoughts.

'Mixed ones,' said Harry. At least his wound was no real problem. The bandages could come off tomorrow. He took up a parcel containing his own uniform and accompanied Major Carlsen out of the hospital. They passed a doctor, a nurse, an orderly. They were acknowledged but without second glances. Outside it was dark and fairly cold. There were few lights. They were on the northern fringe of Bucharest. A staff car took them to Princess Irena's house. With the city under curfew from dusk until dawn, German patrols were active most nights, but on this night the area through which the car passed seemed innocuously quiet.

The house, in a long street, was large and square. Harry saw no one about but could well believe there were eyes on his back as he went up the stone steps with the major. The German rang the bell. It was answered by a housemaid dressed in dark blue and crisp white front. She bobbed politely to the major. He stepped into the hall, Harry following. The maid closed the door, led them through the entrance hall into a larger hall and up a wide, carpeted staircase. On the spacious landing she knocked at a door. A woman's voice responded. The maid opened the door, stood aside and the visitors went in.

A small candlelit chandelier illuminated the room. There were shelves full of books, armchairs in a half-circle round a fire in which wood sparked, an Oriental carpet with a fringe and an atmosphere that invited quiet and cosy withdrawal from a world in the final throes of Armageddon.

Irena rose up from a chair. Her dark chestnut hair glinted richly under the light, her brown eyes were warm from the fire and her face glowed a little from its heat. A dress of deep green silk swathed her figure. The shortage of dress materials in wartime, as well as new attitudes to style, had cast from women the voluminous drapery of Edwardian fashions. Harry, who could remember the play and rustle of satin and lace petticoats, and the mystique of frills and furbelows, nevertheless liked the simplicity of the modern styles. Irena's dress enhanced her slender waist and rounded bosom.

He executed a little bow but resisted the impulse to click his heels as she eyed his German uniform, for her expression was cool, as if she disliked this kind of imposture.

'Good evening, Captain Phillips,' she said. Her

English was as fluent as the major's, her soft accent appealing. She did not offer her hand. Major Carlsen glanced at her, obviously asking for a continuation of the rapport established two days ago. She gave the faintest of shrugs, she smiled philosophically and extended her hand. Harry took it, lightly pressed her fingers and relinquished them.

'You must forgive the way I look, Your Highness,' he said with just a suspicion of irony. His front as a German officer was something she and Major Carlsen had undoubtedly cooked up between them.

'It's of no consequence,' she said regally.

Since it was, he thought that remark absurd. He suspected she was in a slightly overwrought state. It was natural. For all her engaging friendliness during their first meeting she had to have some doubts, and she could not be entirely rapturous about a plan which placed her under the protection of a virtual stranger and nominally into his arms. He was an Allied officer and although her country had entered the war on the side of the Allies, it seemed she considered this to have been a mistake. Incurably pro-German, she was bound to dislike the necessity of turning to a British officer for help, and she perhaps believed her sense of obligation would come to feel like a hair shirt. But he liked her pride and the way she held herself. The Germany she admired so much was tottering and her life was in danger. It was not the best time to expect joy and warmth from her.

'I'm jumpy,' he said, 'are you?'

Her smile this time was soft, real.

'Forgive me,' she said, 'I let my own nerves show for a moment.' She turned to indicate a bottle of wine and some glasses on a small, inlaid table. 'Will you please do the honours, Major Carlsen?'

The major poured red wine.

'Your Highness,' he said and she took the glass he offered. She looked at Harry as he accepted his.

'It's a little gesture, you see,' she said. 'Please, shall we drink to being three friends? That is better than drinking to war and to not being friends. That is almost over, the war. We three must lead the way to reconciliation, yes? So, my friends?'

'My friends,' said the major, straight-backed.

Very touching, thought Harry. Brown eyes were warming him, charming him. She was striking, beautiful. He felt the weight of his coming responsibilities. Well, they were a challenge. So was she. So was Major Carlsen.

'My friends,' he said.

They drank. The major looked at his watch. Irena smiled again.

'Shall we be married, Captain Phillips?' she asked.

'That seems to be a very necessary part of the plan,' said Harry.

'Yes,' said Irena, 'but I promise, it will not be a complication for you when we reach England. I shall not forget you have your fiancée to consider, I shall be no trouble, I shall live quietly in London until people become sane again and I can return here. Until then, where else can I go but England?'

'I've no idea,' said Harry, 'I'm not au fait with Balkan politics and I can't keep up sometimes with our own. But as long as you do keep quiet when you get to England, that should help you stay out of trouble there.'

'Oh, you are thinking I'll say things there because I've said things here?' She was a little quick off the mark. 'You believe people should not say what they think?'

'I believe personages should be discreet.' He offered that as a friendly suggestion.

'Personages? Personages?' She was ready to be royally mettlesome.

'Princesses in high places,' said Harry, finishing his wine.

'Really?' Now she was a little fiery. 'Sometimes to be discreet is to be hypocritical, Captain Phillips. Shall we be married or not?'

'Your Highness.' Major Carlsen sounded a soothing note.

Harry smiled. Perhaps she was indiscreet, but she was also fearless and honest. One could not object too much to that.

'I am sorry,' she said, liking his smile, 'perhaps I'm a little on edge, yes? I do not get married every day, you see.'

'Neither do I,' said Harry.

'Or run for my life,' she said ruefully.

That appealed to him. He agreed with Major Carlsen. She was worth saving, worth a little trouble and even the complication of a marriage of convenience. It was still a crazy venture but not as much as it had seemed at first.

'Father Jacobus is ready?' enquired the major.

'I think so,' she said.

'And you two?' Asked of both of them, it offered Harry his last chance to draw back.

'Are we?' she said to Harry.

'I'm told it doesn't actually hurt,' said Harry.

Irena laughed.

'At least I don't think Captain Phillips is going to be dull, Major Carlsen,' she said.

'We are asking a little more of him than that,' said the major.

They were married by Father Jacobus. Sonya Irena Helene Magda Ananescu of Moldavia to Harry Gordon Phillips of Amblestoke, Hampshire, England. It did not take long. Major Carlsen was in attendance and so was the maid who had appeared earlier. Father Jacobus took a small glass of wine before discreetly vanishing, and the maid returned to her duties. The major consulted his watch again.

'You must leave in ten minutes,' he said. 'A cab will be waiting, Her Highness knows where, and our curfew patrols have orders to let it through. You wish to say goodbye to your staff?' he said to Irena. She nodded. 'Please, no longer than ten minutes, Your Highness.'

'I shall not be long,' she said and left the room.

The major produced a bandage, Harry undid the collar of his uniform and the bandage was wound and fastened around his neck like a white stock. Final details were explained to him. His British uniform and the civilian clothes were in a case, the uniform pressed flat under a false bottom. Her Highness would also be taking one case.

She understood it was impracticable to take more. She would be posing as an Austrian woman from the Tyrol, lately widowed and on her way home from Bucharest.

'All in black, you mean?' said Harry. 'Isn't that rather too obvious and too conspicuous a disguise?'

'Not in Central Europe, Captain, and certainly not among Austrian and German women.'

Harry was to dispose of his German uniform as best he could. The civilian clothes contained the faked Russian identity document, together with papers signifying he was a courier for the Germans. Naturally, he was not committed to any rigid course of action except that of getting Her Highness to England, and each step would most likely be governed by circumstances and expediency. For the moment he was Colonel Rupert Wagner.

'Wagner is good enough, I think, Captain? It has a musical ring to it?'

'Has it?' said Harry. 'I thought Wagner went in for thunder and lightning.'

Major Carlsen indulged in one of his rare smiles. He rationed himself strictly.

'Your Russian name will be Sergius Rokossky.'

'My problem,' said Harry, 'will be with making up my mind who I am from day to day.'

'I think you will manage,' said the major calmly. 'Be careful as soon as you reach Belgrade. Once her enemies find the princess has gone the news will travel fast.'

'I'd be obliged,' said Harry, 'if you'd keep them in the dark.'

'I shall do what I can, but they will know eventually. It's even possible the news will come from inside this house. Princess Irena's servants all seem loyal, but who knows how deeply. politics can penetrate domestic loyalty? That is the most contemptible facet of politics. It undermines the most devoted human relationships. I am glad, for all my faults, that I am a soldier.'

'I rather enjoy bringing in a good harvest myself,' said Harry on a practical note.

He and Irena were to leave by the back door, through the gardens and over the wall into the gardens of the house behind the princess's. From there they would make for the adjacent street. A cab would be waiting for them a few minutes' walk away. It would take them to the station at Chitila. On the train they were not to know each other, for if they were seen as a pair at the outset they would be looked for as a pair from then on.

Harry said, 'Major, because of language difficulties, I don't know if I conveyed adequate thanks to your hospital staff. Will you please thank them for me?'

'I shall be happy to. It has been an ugly war, Captain, and a destructive one for my country. But Germany will rise again.'

Harry grimaced.

'I rather wish you hadn't said that, Major.'

'Germany must rise. It will. There are errors to rectify.'

Harry shook his head. Irena came back. She wore a black hat and full veil, with a black coat. She looked like a young widow in mourning. Harry hoped it wasn't an omen.

'Come,' said the major. They went down the rear staircase. The house was solemnly quiet. At the end of a ground-floor passage was a bolted door. A large case stood on the floor. Irena looked at Harry. He perceived a faint smile and a new call for help through the veil. He was carrying his own case. He picked up hers as well. The major unbolted the door and quietly opened it.

'Wait,' said Harry. He put down his case and lowered the wick of the oil lamp fixed to the passage wall. 'Not much sense in lighting up our departure,' he muttered. Carrying the cases, he followed Irena and Major Carlsen out of the house and along a path winding through the dark gardens until they reached a high brick wall. The major moved silently, lifting a ladder and placing it against the wall. Ivy covered the better part of the brickwork.

The major whispered his goodbye to Irena. 'You are the bravest of women. Auf Wiedersehen.' He kissed her gloved fingers.

'And you, I shall not forget you,' she whispered.

He said to Harry, 'You must take good care of her.'

'I'll do my best,' said Harry. His nerves were beginning to jump about and he didn't feel he could safely promise to leap over the moon with her. He rather felt the major was in love with her. Where that would get him with Her Highness was probably nowhere, whatever her own feelings were.

'Goodbye, Captain Phillips. Perhaps we shall meet again.'

'A civilized thought, Major. Goodbye.'

They did not salute. Briefly, they shook hands. Harry went up the ladder and Major Carlsen hefted up the cases to him as he sat astride the ivy-topped wall. He dropped each case to the soft earth on the other side. The night was comfortingly dark and quite moonless. Perfect for cloaks and daggers, he thought. Irena mounted the ladder. He helped her to sit on the wall. She seemed quite cool. Silk stockings glimmered in the night as her coat and dress rucked. He lowered himself and dropped lightly. His thigh twinged just a little. Irena let her legs dangle, let her body go and came plummeting down into his arms. That was damn well done, he thought. No fuss at all. He set her on her feet. She was warm, rounded, her bosom just brushing his chest. He groped for the cases, picked them up, one in each hand, and looked around. The solid block of the other house loomed ahead of them, rising square above the gardens. He saw a faint glow at one heavily curtained window. There were no other lights. Irena began to lead the way over a wide, paved path. He followed. She walked carefully to mute the click of her heels. His tingling nerves kept the cold out.

She still seemed cool, she did not hurry. But the tension was there, mutual and communicative. The night enclosed them and muffled them. They reached another path which led them around the side of the house to a wooden gate. It was bolted. Both bolts were stiff. Harry put the cases down and took the strain off the bolts by pulling on the gate handle. Irena drew them carefully back. She opened the gate as Harry took up the cases again. The gate led to the street. She waited, putting a finger to her mouth and looking back into the solid darkness. A light flashed once, twice.

'That's to say everything is quiet,' she whispered.

Not very brilliant, thought Harry, and not very conclusive, either. It might be all quiet outside the princess's house but how the devil could the major know whether this other street was clear? Any black-bearded Reds who wanted to keep Princess Irena penned up to await the day of judgement weren't going to watch only her front door. They would watch all possible exits. The flash of a signalling torch could kindle a prowling Red eye.

Irena turned into the street, going left. There were no street lamps. Some curtained windows masked domestic lights, that was all. Bucharest seemed in dark, silent abeyance between occupation and deliverance. Harry walked with only a slight limp beside his black-clad companion. He would have preferred her to dye her hair rather than put on widow's weeds. Despite what Major Carlsen had said, he could think of no disguise more obvious. He could only hope that the major's fears concerning the princess's enemies were the exaggerated fears of a man in love.

No one stepped out of dark places to accost them or question them. The curfew seemed to have closed the city down for the night. Irena crossed the street and entered another. Harry was warm from the weight of the cases and the tension. With eyes adjusting to the darkness he saw the outline of a horse-drawn cab not far away. Irena did not quicken her deliberate pace and they walked without haste to the cab. The driver was there, up on his seat. He looked down, his face mistily pale under his hat. He did not get down to offer help. Harry tossed the cases in. He gave Irena a hand and she boarded. He got in after her.

On the other side of the cab a man appeared. His hat was pulled low, the collar of his jacket turned up against the cold. He opened the door and Irena drew a quick breath and squeezed herself back into the dimness of the interior. The man was bearded. Harry thought, by God, there had to be whiskers.

Whiskers spoke to Irena.

'Well met, I think, Your Absconding Highness.' Harry did not understand the language. Irena's response came muffledly from behind her veil, drawn down under her chin to completely cover her face.

'You are mistaken. Go away.' Whatever bitter disappointment she felt was muffled too.

'Who is your fine military friend since he is not the major?' The man was pleased with himself. He leaned in, smiling, his right hand deep in his jacket pocket, his left resting on the open door. Harry did not need to ask what the dialogue was all about.

'Go away, please,' said Irena, veil moving against her mouth.

The man discerned the mourning black of her clothes. 'You've suffered a bereavement? Tck, tck. You're going to the funeral, of course. How sad.

My friend,' he said, turning to Harry, 'who are you? Her Highness's butler or Major Carlsen's influential uncle from Berlin?'

Harry ignored the fact that his bandaged throat was supposed to signify damaged vocal cords. He did not know what Whiskers had said, the moment was one for improvisation, so he put his hand to his ear and barked, 'What, what?' He was belligerent.

'What, what?' The man repeated the words in an amused fashion. He looked more closely at Harry, who sat opposite Irena. 'What, what?' he said again. The repetition enlightened him. He searched for some foreign words. 'English? You are English?'

'Espionage,' said Harry curtly.

'Espionage? What is that?' Whiskers asked the question carefully, as if not so sure of himself.

'Good God,' said Harry, 'I'm working for the Allies, your friends. This is Magda, my comfort, my help and my decoding mistress.'

Irena smothered a little gasp at this outrageous statement. The man chuckled.

'That is good,' he said, 'very good. But not good enough. Take her back, my friend. You understand? Yes? Go back. Tck, tck, a waiting cab in times like these. Not good, eh? Not clever.' He shook his head at the stupidity of it.

Yes, that was another mistake, thought Harry. A waiting cab within any reasonable distance of the princess's house was bound to attract attention and invite questions. He wondered who was sitting up in the driver's seat.

'No, it isn't good,' he said, 'I have to go into the

city and you're holding me up.'

'Ah, so? I am in the way? Of course.' Whiskers chuckled again. 'But she will get out, your Magda, your comfort. It is strange you are English, strange. Ah, I see. They have sent you for her. Not possible. She belongs to us. I, Nicchi Michalides, tell you so. No, do not use that,' he said, nodding at Harry's holstered German revolver, 'it would be silly.' His hand was still in his jacket pocket. 'Very silly.'

'Oh, get in,' said Harry, 'you're damned untidy there. Where the devil do you want us to drive to?'

'That is better,' said Michalides. 'Yes, I will come with you.'

He boarded the cab. Few people board any vehicle with one hand pocketed, and the withdrawal of the hand was instinctive, automatic. It gave Harry, in an atmosphere stiff with tension, the only moment of opportunity he could expect. He thrust his boot between Michalides' legs. The man began to tumble, a curse on his lips. Harry hit him with a gloved right fist smack in the back of his neck. Michalides pitched and sprawled. He opened his mouth to gasp, to shout, but Harry, following up, was on him, kneeling on him, grinding his face into the floor of the cab, Irena staring wide-eyed. Quickly he extracted the stubby revolver from the man's pocket. He chose the spot, measured the distance, weighed up the necessary force and thumped Michalides behind the right ear with the revolver butt. The spitting Rumanian jerked and slumped.

It wasn't good. Harry knew it wasn't. It was the

worst start possible.

'Damn,' he muttered. Irena, a little appalled, thought the atmosphere had not improved. Momentarily they had won themselves respite, but the street, quiet again, now seemed redolent of dark treachery and violent murder. They would not hesitate to assassinate her if they thought she might get away.

Harry got out. The driver was climbing down. Harry, as conscious of the atmosphere as Irena, could take no chances. He pushed the revolver into the man's coat-covered stomach. The man said something. Harry called softly to Irena. She put her head out, looking in her darkly veiled Balkan mystique so much the integral part of it all. Harry asked her what the man was saying.

'Something I could not repeat,' she said.

'Is he a friend of ours or his?'

Irena spoke to the man. His response was hissing, angry. Irena translated it to Harry in plain but acceptable language. The man was not the driver and he was wanting to know what had been done to Michalides.

'Tell him,' said Harry, 'that Michalides hit his head. Tell him to pull him out and do something for him. We'll leave. Tell him we're going into the city, but don't be too obvious about it or he'll know we're not going there at all.'

Irena, her veil as efficacious at night as a mask, spoke to the man again. He pushed the gun away from his stomach with the gesture of a man conceding the advantage for the moment, and he leaned into the cab and pulled out the inert Michalides. He spat in disgust. Irena looked up and down the dark street, shivering a little. She felt as if every shadow must disgorge its anarchist. Harry closed the door on her, looked at the man kneeling beside the now groaning Michalides and heaved himself quickly up into the ledged driving seat, his feet jammed against the angled board. He shook the horse awake and drove off. The man waved a fist after them.

Harry reached behind and knocked on the cab roof. The little flap opened.

'Which way to the city proper?' he asked.

He was terse. She understood that and said, 'Straight on for a while. But it's Chitila we want and we should take the first left turn.'

'Yes, but let's look as if we really are going into the city. Can we turn off later for Chitila?'

It would lengthen their journey, she said, but it could be done. So Harry drove straight on for the moment. He wondered about German patrols. Major Carlsen had said this would be no problem, that the patrols had orders to let this particular cab through. The only danger was that they might become curious or suspicious because it was now being driven by someone who looked like a German colonel. Well, he had to chance it. They were lucky, they met no patrols. And when they did turn off for Chitila it was not long before the urban areas began to seem darkly aloof and disinterested. Development thinned out as they reached the main road that would take them north-west, Irena calling instructions from time to time.

Driving at a smart trot, they left Bucharest behind and at a little after eleven o'clock reached

Chitila without incident. They left the cab in a street, the horse with its head in a sparse bag of oats. They walked to the station, where the train was due in forty minutes. Chitila seemed as much in limbo as Bucharest, as most of Rumania. Elsewhere disintegration proceeded apace. To the east Bessarabia was in chaos, at the mercy of roving bands of Russian deserters, Balkan bandits, scavenging Bolsheviks and mercenaries of every kind. To the west and north-west, the proud but ungainly empire of the Habsburgs was falling apart. In Serbia the Austrian and German garrisons were breaking and retreating as the Serbian, British and French offensive gained momentum. Only Rumania, sleeping under the imposed aegis of its German conquerors, seemed untroubled by the thunder of guns or the anarchy born of disorder. It was a deceptive quietness. But it well suited Harry at this time. There were no massive troop movements to contend with, no columns of field-grey blocking every road to every station, no questions to be answered. At least, not until the station came into view. Here the German soldiers were thick on the ground.

'That looks like trouble,' he said. Irena glanced at him. He had done well so far. But the incident with Michalides had been frightening and she knew he was as tense as she was. She must not let him down. 'I'm a colonel,' he said, and stopped. She stopped with him. 'I can't be seen carrying my own luggage, I'm damn sure I can't. Wait. Call one of those men when we get nearer.'

He gave orders very coolly, she thought, as if he had already decided that however important her escape was, her status meant nothing.

'I'm to shout?' she said as they went on.

'Can princesses shout? I don't think they're trained to, are they? No, just call.'

Trained to? How absurd he was. She glanced at him again. He looked very commanding as a German colonel.

'They're looking,' said Harry, 'no need to call. We'll signal one over. You speak to him.'

'Of course. He is to carry the luggage.'

They halted. Harry signalled. A soldier detached himself from his comrades and approached. He saluted. Harry returned it. He touched his bandaged throat and indicated Irena. The soldier clicked his heels. Irena said to him, 'This luggage. Please take it for the Herr Colonel. It is impossible here, he has had to carry it himself. No one to help, no one to call on, no cabs. But at least there are good soldiers. Thank you.' The infantryman hoisted the cases and they followed him into the station and on to the platform.

The station was as dark as everything else. Four years ago Armageddon had opened, as usual, with colour and song and light. It was coming to its end, as usual, in pallid depression and darkness. There might be a brief flash of rejoicing among the nations claiming to have won, but it would be very brief.

While Harry paced the platform in soldierly fashion, Irena sat on the cases, a dark figure of veiled and unapproachable mourning. Harry, stern and reflective in his pacing, hoped he looked just as unapproachable himself. She was not easily going to give herself away, he thought.

She had kept her head with Michalides, and her pose now as a widow of sadness was touchingly convincing. She sat in quiet, withdrawn isolation and men in field-grey, awaiting the train, did not intrude on her. Something about her affected Harry. He had been given an uncomfortable job in trying to get her to England, and he had a feeling he was completely wrong in principle in helping a pro-German princess to escape justice, suspect though that justice was. But as he slowly paced, as he looked at her, at her air of dark mourning, it seemed as if she were inwardly weeping for what she was about to lose. Her country.

All men, all women, love their own country, he thought, whatever the faults, the wrongs, the shortcomings. Those who praised other countries at the expense of their own, those who deserted their own countries, were called renegades.

She was not a renegade, but she would be called that sometimes when she was in her enforced exile. Harry felt for her as she sat so quietly on this chilly station platform. He could not go and talk to her. He was supposed to be unable to talk. And possibly, at this moment, she wanted no one to try.

The train did not come in at the stated time. Irena suddenly got up and as she approached Harry he saw that her face was pale behind her veil.

'I am suffering,' she said, 'I am cowardly with nerves.'

'So am I,' he said in a sympathetic murmur.

'You do not look nervous.'

'But I am,' he said. There was no one near enough to hear his whisper, but talking was something that could be seen as well as heard.

'The train is late,' she said, and went to an official to complain. If that was her way of fighting cowardice it was worth remembering, thought Harry.

To the official she explained she had just lost her husband in the fighting in Serbia. Was she now to lose her right to see him buried because of a train that should be here but wasn't? The official was a 'dear me' man, who could absorb this kind of punishment all day and often did. He was sorry she had lost her husband and even sorrier to inform her that in these days it was even possible the railway had lost a train. He was grief-stricken to think she might miss her husband's funeral, but then he himself had missed seeing his own mother buried, not because of a lost tram but because she had been blown up by bombs dropped on Belgrade at the beginning of the war, and not even a shoe button had been found.

Irena rejoined Harry and told him, with the glimpse of a smile, that the official was a most diverting man, that she felt much better. Harry, standing immaculate guard over the luggage, appreciated her restored morale. The station became noisy as contingents of soldiers formed and massed. A number of Wehrmacht military police appeared, led by an NCO. They marched crisply to the end of the platform and stood at ease without losing their smartness. They looked as if the night itself could not hide from eyes as alert and well-trained as theirs. Irena was the only civilian on the platform, the only woman. The well-trained eyes regarded her. And the colonel she was with. Harry, becoming aware of the survey, stood with his feet apart, hands behind his back, clasping his stick, and returned the survey with martial severity.

'Oh, that is very good,' whispered Irena in some delight, 'you will make them shuffle their feet in a moment.'

Some began to do just that. The NCO barked at them. Even when standing at ease soldiers should not look untidy or behave sloppily. Harry kept his stern gaze fixed on them.

'No one is going to dare to approach you,' said Irena.

He turned so that no one would see he was talking.

'Look here,' he whispered, 'you realize the apple cart's already upset, don't you? The whiskery gentleman – Michalides, I think he said? – is on to us. They know who to look for now. A German colonel and a widow.'

'Yes, I understand,' she said.

'It was a damned bad start, I thought.'

'Forgive me,' she said quietly, 'but there's to be no swearing or blasphemy. You can explain things at all times without that, for you have the benefit of a language extensive and descriptive.'

Four years in the army had taught him the sharp, brutal distinction between an acceptable adjective and a blasphemous one. He smiled a little.

'Yes, quite so,' he said, still speaking in a murmur. 'Do you mind if I say we'll have to discount your title and status? It has to be put aside, you know. And eventually you'd better call me Harry.'

A slight flush showed behind the veil.

'Certainly not,' she said, 'I would never descend to a specious familiarity.'

'And I'll try to call you Irena.'

'You are not to engage in familiarity of any kind, sir.'

That, he thought, was delicious. He teased her as he said, 'Sometime in the near future it may be necessary or expedient for me to kiss you.'

'How dare you!'

'Or for you to kiss me.'

'Never!'

They were having their dialogue in whispers. His were light, hers indignant.

'When you get on the train,' he said, 'go straight to the toilet and change that hat and coat for anything else you've got in your case.'

'Major Carlsen's instructions–'

'His instructions included leaving nothing to chance. That means we have to act according to circumstances at times, not to the plan. Since we've been spotted we're vulnerable as we are now. So will you please change your clothes? I have to change mine. After that we aren't to know each other. You have your ticket?'

'Yes.' She was newly flushed. 'Captain Phillips–'

'I'm Colonel Wagner at the moment.'

'Oh, puffle.' It came through her veil in an exasperated way.

'Puffle?' He wondered if his light attempts to take her mind off the sadness of exile were doing any good.

'Perhaps it's piffle, I cannot remember exactly, not when I'm so nervous.' She took a breath and steadied herself. 'I was going to argue with you, but no, I will do as you wish because of what you are doing for me. I am sure it's going to be very dangerous for you. We must not have little words about things, must we?'

She propounded common sense with charm and appeal.

'No, of course not,' he said, 'you must excuse my nerves.'

'You had no nerves when you dealt with that man Michalides.' She went on in a quick, cautious voice, 'There's an officer coming, he looks as if he is going to speak to you.'

Harry came to attention, saluted her by touching the peak of his cap with his stick, then turned and resumed his pacing of the platform. A German infantry captain, who had almost reached his elbow, now found himself being passed. He saluted. Harry returned it without really looking at the man and strode on. The officer looked after him, then at Irena, all in black. His heels came together and he gave a stiff little bow of sympathy.

'If you'll forgive me,' said Irena in her effortless German, 'I shouldn't bother him if I were you. Poor man, he was wounded in the neck and is still hardly able to speak.'

'Bad luck, that,' said the German, 'but he seemed to be the senior officer around here and I wanted some information on priorities. I've got a company to get aboard, the transport officer doesn't seem to be available and I thought the Herr Colonel – I'm sorry, it isn't your problem.' He smiled, saluted and went off. That was a little close, she thought. Captain Phillips would not have understood a word, but even accepting he was unable to speak he would have been expected to shake or nod his head or make a few intelligent gestures.

Harry paced his way back. They heard the train then. Within a few minutes it came lumbering in. Shuddering and hissing, it was enormously long and it was armoured. Fiery sparks blew about as the engine passed them. The faces of the driver and fireman were hot, sweaty and sooty, and white teeth gleamed between red lips. The train was carrying troops and guns, the latter lashed on the flat freight cars with soldiers sitting around them, caps jammed down on their heads, great-coat collars turned up. Waggons, with doors half open to admit air, disclosed their complements of men. A series of passenger coaches drew up as the train came to a noisy, clanging halt.

Irena went aboard. With her ticket she had a special pass. Harry pushed her case in. She took it, wincing a little at its weight, and made her way along the corridor. German officers were gazing out of compartment windows. Harry stepped smartly up and in, carrying his case. He remained in the corridor. The troops were piling into the waggons. Irena had disappeared. The train blew steam impatiently and was away as soon as the last soldier was off the platform. An official waved his lamp, brakes undamped and the engine powered slowly forward. The coaches jerked and the movement threw Irena into a heap in the confined space of the toilet. She mentally recorded what she might say to Captain Phillips about that.

The huge iron wheels strained, the long monster plucked itself from the deadness of its own weight and surged forward out of the station. Harry at the door of the coach saw a man burst on to the platform. The official restrained him, shaking his head and wagging his finger. The man pushed him aside but had lost his chance to reach any of the coaches. The waggons were passing him, the train already picking up speed. Harry, carried into darkness, missed whatever happened next but suspected the official was being harried with questions. He had been unable to clearly distinguish the man but felt sure it was Michalides, curfew or no curfew.

He stood by the door for a while, the train clamouring into the night. At the other end of the corridor Irena appeared. She had changed into a costume the colour of ginger-nut brown, with a cream blouse and a brown hat. To the hat was attached a brown half-veil, masking her eyes. Her case sagged heavily from her hand. Ignoring Harry, she slid back a compartment door. Four German officers in comfortable occupation looked up at her, then rose as one man, clicked their heels as one and lifted her case to the rack as one.

'Thank you, gentlemen,' said Irena in their own language. Harry passed by, going on to the toilet to make his own change.

'Fräulein, how good of you to join us,' said a young lieutenant, moving to allow Irena a corner seat. 'You're going to Belgrade?'

'Yes.' She was charming, demure. 'Are things very desperate there? I do so want to be in time to see someone special.'

'Of course, of course.' Empires might be tottering, but not in the presence of such an attractive young woman as this. 'It's not as desperate as that. We are regrouping and–'

'Never mind about that, Schmidt,' said another lieutenant, not so young and not quite so affable.

They talked to her, glad to have her company, although Lieutenant Gruhner, the more formal officer, did not talk as much as he listened. Finally he said to her, 'You're not German, are you?' He had perhaps detected the slightest of flaws in her accent.

'I'm from the Austrian Tyrol,' said Irena.

'Ah.' The women of the Tyrol were the healthiest, shapeliest and most hospitable. This one was also extremely lovely. However, there were few civilians on this train. Those who were had their passes. 'You have your papers and your pass, Fräulein?'

'Now look here, Gruhner,' protested another officer.

'I have them,' said Irena and opened up her handbag. She took out her papers. The pass was in order, the papers faked. She handed them over. Gruhner glanced briefly through them, already satisfied by her unhesitating response. He handed them back. Her heart was beating a little quickly but she looked quite cool.

'Thank you, Fräulein,' he said.

The compartment door slid back. Harry put

his head in. He wore a suit of dark grey over a black jersey with a high neck. A dark blue cap with a peak sat on his head. He had the appearance of a seaman. Gruhner frowned up at him.

'This is reserved,' he said.

Harry looked enquiring but uncomprehending. He mumbled something. He came in and put his case on the rack. Gruhner's frown deepened. Harry sat down in the corner seat opposite Irena. He cleared his throat as if nervous. He decided he was, in fact, very nervous.

'Who are you?' asked Gruhner.

'I don't think he understands German,' said Irena. She tried Italian. Harry shook his head. She tried French. In that language Harry informed her he was a Russian, a refugee from the Bolsheviks.

'Your papers,' said Gruhner, who knew French.

Harry produced them. Gruhner examined them with interest. They named their owner as Sergius Ilyich Rokossky and included the information that he was attached on special duties to the German Headquarters in Belgrade. Gruhner returned them. Harry smiled agreeably and his nerves settled down a little.

The passengers relaxed, easing their limbs. The train would not reach Belgrade until midday tomorrow. It ate slowly into the night, snaking and winding, pulling and jerking, ascending and descending. It denied the comfort necessary for sleep. Heads lolled, eyes closed. Heads snapped, eyes opened. Tiredness seduced Irena; she sat back and cuddled herself. Harry sat upright, looking blankly Russian. The Germans dozed fitfully and Irena twisted and turned.

They crossed the Hungarian border without stopping and pulled into Vrsaac when the sun was up. There the majority of the German troops got off and guns began to be unloaded. Gruhner and his companions rose stiffly to their feet. They said goodbye to Irena and left the compartment. Emptied of field-grey it suddenly seemed spacious.

'Heavenly,' said Irena, stretching her legs. Harry disposed himself along the seat and closed his eyes. He seemed to fall into instant sleep and she could hardly believe it. 'Well,' she breathed almost indignantly, 'for one who is supposed to be living on his nerves, that's too good to be true.'

Outside the noise was deafening, the morning air echoing to shuddering thuds and gigantic clangs as the guns were craned off the freight cars. Irena got to her feet and slid back the door.

'I should stay here if I were you.' Harry's eyes were open, his voice sleepy but insistent.

'I'm going to see if there's coffee somewhere.'

'No, don't show yourself,' he said. She threw him a look that was slightly haughty. 'Your Highness, you're too noticeable in daylight.'

'Not more so than any other person.'

That was hardly true. She was decidedly noticeable, slender and striking despite her night of discomfort.

'You should not look so attractive,' he said, 'someone will give you a second glance and recognize you.'

Her faint blush surprised him. He would have thought her used to compliments and flattery.

'Oh,' she said, not sure whether it was a compliment more than a warning or the other way about. 'Perhaps you are right.' She sat down again. 'But I am dying for coffee or some refreshment, there is nothing on the train. This is what a war does, you see, it even makes it difficult to get a little coffee.'

Harry sighed. The sleepless night had been a strain on limbs and nerves, and he thought he might have snatched five minutes' rest before the train moved off again. Five minutes would be something. But the soft warm voice going on about coffee was impossible to ignore. He got up. Brown eyes smiled at him from under lifted veil.

'Are you going to show yourself?' she asked.

'I'm going to see if I can find anything.'

'If you find nothing you aren't to worry, please,' she said, 'it is the thought that is remembered.'

Princesses, he supposed, were brought up so well that irritability after a sleepless night was something they simply did not indulge in. And if they wanted coffee they beguiled it out of one.

'You must be very tired,' he said.

'Oh, I think we have both survived very well, yes?' she said.

'I won't be long,' he said, leaving the compartment.

The train stood long, solid and hissing as he put his head out of the coach door and surveyed prospects. Both ends of the platform seethed with field-grey. It was clear adjacent the passenger coaches. He got out and walked into the station building. There, refreshments were available and a number of German officers were drinking out of the crested china cups of the Hungarian State Railway. No civilians were in sight, and Harry thought the station was probably temporarily out of bounds to all but the military. A woman behind the buffet looked at him. He sensed he was out of place. He saw Lieutenant Gruhner eyeing him. Harry approached and spoke in French.

'I'm asked to give you the lady's compliments, M'sieu Lieutenant, and to enquire if I may take her some coffee. There is nothing on the train.'

Gruhner nodded briefly, then waved a casual hand.

'You may take her some,' he said. He caught the eye of the woman behind the buffet and pointed to Harry. She nodded.

Harry walked across to the buffet, indicated the orderly array of cups and held up two fingers. He smiled. She smiled back. As she poured the dark brown liquid he saw some fat-looking stone bottles. He peered at the labels. The bottles contained the local brandy, given many certificates of merit. She gave him the cups of coffee. He pointed to the brandy. She put a bottle on the counter. Major Carlsen had supplied him with money and he paid in German marks. She smiled, buxom and beaming. He could see no food. He pointed to his mouth, then his stomach. She responded with a comment that was all Greek to him. He said in French that he did not comprehend, that he was asking for food. He opened his mouth wide to show how yawningly empty it was and that made her giggle, as if she found the cavernous vista entertaining. Magically she produced two dark bread rolls and some fat olives from the depths of a large square biscuit tin. Harry nodded in appreciation and paid for them. She wrapped them in paper, he put them into his left pocket, the bottle into his right. He smiled his thanks, the Hungarian woman beamed, and he carried the coffee back to the train, which had stopped hissing and was standing in huge, elongated apathy.

Irena greeted the coffee with warm cries of ecstasy.

'Oh, how wonderful!' She was even more rapturous when he unwrapped the rolls and olives, and when he showed her the brandy and suggested it would add welcome body to the coffee she was quite overcome, assuring him he was the most admirable husband Major Carlsen could have found for her.

'Cupboard love,' said Harry.

Her knowledge of English did not run to an understanding of its colloquialisms and its peculiar sayings. His mention of love startled her.

'Please?' she said and again he saw the slight pink creeping.

'Oh, it's just a saying,' he said, 'but you must put what you've just told me into writing and I'll show it to Elisabeth.'

'Elisabeth?'

'My fiancée. On second thoughts, no, perhaps you'd better not. It's liable to be misconstrued.'

'It was only a joke,' said Irena.

'I know,' said Harry.

They sat and enjoyed their small, simple repast. Harry suggested a dash of brandy in the coffee and Irena declared it the best thing that could have happened to this particular coffee. Outside the noise gradually abated. The guns were off, the troops beginning to move.

'I hope we aren't simply going to be left here,' said Irena. It was a comment, not an impatience, and Harry was impressed. He supposed she was completely divorced from her normal environment, which he imagined was one of comfort, elegance and sophistication, and she was literally a refugee on the run from extremists. But she was taking everything very coolly, even cheerfully. She represented a problem to him, certainly. It was a help to feel she was not going to lack character or courage.

'Oh, we'll move eventually,' he said, and that coincided with an influx of new troops. They were Austrian. They surged on to the platform and climbed into the waggons, their officers invading the passenger coaches. Three entered the compartment occupied by Irena and Harry. They looked tired and drawn, too tired even to take much notice of Irena. Silently they stretched their legs, sat back and closed their eyes. Harry had a feeling they had been marching through the night.

Fifteen minutes later the train at last began the final stage of its journey to Belgrade. It stopped again, but briefly, at the Serbian frontier to let customs officials aboard, and then went on. The customs men went through the train perfunctorily. Troop trains were not normally their province unless there were special circumstances. When the compartment door slid back and the officials looked in, Harry wondered if there were special circumstances. The officials paid no attention to the Austrians, they looked at Irena, then at him.

'You have passes?' was the question.

They produced them. Irena looked cool but felt terribly apprehensive. Captain Phillips, his case. The German uniform would be in it. For all the fact that his papers proclaimed him an agent for the Germans, that colonel's uniform would be so suspect, for he could not speak German. He was only one spin of fortune's wheel away from inquisition and capture. And did they shoot as spies enemy soldiers who were caught in civilian clothes? She had a terrible feeling they did.

The passes were handed back. Now they would want to see the papers. But no. The officials simply said, 'Thank you,' and left it at that. The door closed and they went on their way.

Irena glanced across at Harry. She thought he gave her the faintest of winks.

When the train drew into Belgrade's main station, they sat still, waiting until the three Austrian officers had left. Then she said on a sudden rush of relieved breath, 'Oh, I thought if those customs men examined your case everything would be lost.'

'You were thinking of that uniform?' he smiled. 'No, I bundled it all up and dropped it out of the coach door window as soon as I'd changed.'

'I wish you had said, I should not have been so near heart failure then.'

'I'm sorry, I thought you'd have guessed,' he said as he watched soldiers streaming along the platform.

'Well, I did not,' she said, a little frosty because of his casualness, 'I am not a mind reader, Captain Phillips. I think it is better that you tell me what you do, not leave me to guess.'

'I'm sorry,' he said again. He supposed she was bound to have her moments of haughtiness. 'I believe Major Carlsen gave you the address of the place where we're to hide up in Belgrade.'

'Yes,' she said. She had memorized it and she told him what it was. He wrote it down on a piece of the paper the rolls had been wrapped in. He lifted the cases from the racks.

'We'll go separately,' he said. 'If any of the comrades here have received word about last night they'll be looking for a woman in black–'

'A woman in black?' She was definitely haughty.

'A lady in black.' He conceded his mistake. 'With a German colonel. Or at least they'll look for a lady and a man together. So go by yourself. I'll follow on with the cases.'

'Go by myself?' She obviously considered this a complete dereliction of his responsibility. Behind the veil her eyes were at their coolest. 'I am to be caught and carried off by my enemies?'

'I hope not,' he said, 'since they won't be able to drag you off kicking and screaming through crowded streets.'

'Captain Phillips, I do not kick and scream, I am not a gipsy.' She was very high on her horse.

'Well, look here, you must if they are waiting for you and do try to carry you off. But I don't think they will. They'll simply follow you. Watch for that. There's a cathedral here, isn't there? So if you think you're being followed don't go to the address, go to the cathedral, go inside. If you're not at the address when I get there I'll come to the cathedral myself and we'll work out a way of slipping them.'

'Very well.'

She left the train. Harry followed a minute so or later.

The station was a massive echo of sound. Contingents of Austrian and German troops imparted urgency to the atmosphere of crisis. Field Marshal von Mackensen, in charge of this theatre of war, was having to make up his mind whether to evacuate the Serbian capital or defend it. But the German High Command was in no position to send him fresh divisions, and the Austrians, who had done so much to help hold back the Russians and the Italians, were now in a state of acute and tired depression. Their empire was about to collapse, and it showed.

Two men, swarthy and keen-eyed, dressed in dark blue serge suits and flat caps, stood at the entrance to the station. But they were not interested in those who were going in, they were scanning everyone coming out. They were there in response to a telephone call from comrades in Bucharest and were looking for a man and a woman. The woman would be wearing black, the man might be in the uniform of a German officer but he was English and therefore likely in his English cunning to have changed into civilian clothes. It was to be assumed that the royalists in London had sent him.

'English, eh?' muttered one man. 'What do the English look like, Palichek?'

'I don't know,' said Palichek, 'except that I've heard they consider themselves on speaking terms with God.'

'What are we looking for, then? An angel? Gabriel?' The first man, called Dimitroff, was heavily sarcastic.

'No, no,' said Palichek, 'simply a man looking superior to everyone else, I should think, with a woman in black. The princess.'

'Well, I may not recognize a man like that, but I'd know her anywhere. She'll have her nose in the air.'

But Irena, in her brown costume and hat with its half-veil, came out of the station with other travellers and in company with an elderly lady whom she had enquiringly approached and who had promised to direct her to the cathedral. They were chatting as they passed under the noses of the two Serbian comrades. Palichek and Dimitroff gave them scarcely a glance.

Harry, lumbered with the cases but not with a lack of caution, was doing some scanning himself. The crowded station was too much of a bedlam and a bustle for anyone to successfully engage in a little private detective work. People looking for other people would almost certainly post someone at the platform exit and someone at the station exit. He scanned the latter, for there had only been a seething mass at the platform exit. Outside there was room for a man to stand and watch the people emerging. He saw two men in caps. His nerves tingled. They might be waiting for friends or relatives but somehow he did not think so. In any case he could lose nothing by being cautious. He found a boy in a huge peaked cap, a boy with bright eager eyes wanting to earn a tip. He showed him the address on the piece of paper and said, 'Cab? Carriage?' The boy screwed up his forehead. 'Taxi?' ventured Harry.

'Ah, taxi, taxi,' said the boy happily at this universal word. He nodded. Harry nodded too. He took the hospital stick which had been strapped to his case, showed the boy the promise of a German banknote and gave him the bags. The boy put the smaller case on his capped head, carried the larger and made his way to the exit. He returned in a few minutes, smiling and beckoning, and Harry, using the stick, a gift from the hospital, hobbled after him like a man crippled. The boy led him out of the station to a waiting horse-drawn cab, both nag and vehicle of ancient lineage. Several people were fighting over it. The boy pushed his way through them, Harry limping at his heels. He gave the boy the banknote, received breathless thanks, then hefted himself into the cab with a show of awkwardness and the cabbie, with a whistle to his horse, took off.

As the vehicle moved away Palichek and Dimitroff stared after it.

'No, not English,' said Palichek.

'You're saying that or meaning it?' said Dimitroff.

'A cripple,' said Palichek.

'You think?'

'I think? What do you think?'

'I think about people when they're running from something,' said Dimitroff, 'they all pretend to be cripples.'

'But there was no woman in black with him, no woman at all. Look some more.'

'We should have been at the platform,' said Dimitroff moodily as they resumed their survey.

'No, no, there's no platform indication about troop trains, we should not have known which one to wait at,' said Palichek, 'and we should have lost them at the start. There, look, what about the woman with that man?'

Dimitroff eyed a woman in black on the arm of a stout man.

'Fifty if she's a day,' he said disgustedly, 'and nothing was said about the Englishman being fat.'

Chapter Four

Harry felt fairly satisfied but not completely. Michalides might have been able to arrange for Belgrade station to be watched and those two men might have been his comradely eyes. They had given the cab a hard, enquiring look as it left the station precinct, but they had made no move. He felt fair satisfaction was as much as he could allow himself, considering everything.

The cab moved slowly through the traffic. The streets seemed full of hurry and urgency. The atmosphere was heady, the undercurrents could be felt. The people and the city itself were excited, expectant, the Austrians and Germans in a mood of dangerous bitterness. A year ago, with Russia virtually out of the war, the Central Powers had pulled back scores of divisions from the Eastern Front to strengthen their armies elsewhere. It had seemed then to the Serbians that it would be years, if ever, before their capital could hope to see the back of its conquerors. Now, suddenly, the Allies had taken command of the war, and the Central Powers were splitting and cracking. Their withdrawal from Belgrade looked so certain that it was difficult for the citizens to hide their elation.

The Austrians and Germans were still very much in evidence, but not in the same way as before. They were not drinking in the cafes or monopolizing the pavements as they had been since 1916. They were, in fact, no longer at play. They were patrolling the city in platoons, they were assembling in their barracks or massing around their headquarters. Or flying about in staff cars. The Serbians kept out of their way. There was no sense in provoking troops about to depart.

Harry was impressed by the wide streets and the imaginativeness of some of the architecture. He saw, from the cab window, the ancient citadel that stood high on the cliff overlooking the meeting place of the two rivers, the Sava and the Danube. The citadel had once been known as the White Castle, from which Belgrade took its name, but age had long since turned it into a mellow russet-maroon.

The cabbie, a Turk – there were Turks in every Balkan town or city – gave way unfailingly to the gliding, clanging trams. His old vehicle creaked loudly as it carried Harry to a modest residential area and stopped outside an apartment block which looked massively Victorian. There was some argument, not unhappy, and conducted mainly in sign language before Harry was able to understand how much the fare was compared with how much the Turk would accept. There were also a few incomprehensible words from the Turk about German marks being offered. He took them when Harry added another, and he also agreed to carry the bags up for a little more. They went up four flights of stone stairs, the concierge in his cubbyhole on the ground floor taking no notice. The cabbie deposited the cases on the landing outside a door numbered 44 and left Harry to it.

Harry knocked. No answer. He could see no bell. He knocked again. Silence. He grimaced. He thought about the cathedral. Then he tried the handle. It was free of the lock. He opened the door and put his head in. The door opened straight on to the living room. The furniture was practical. He brought the cases in and closed the door.

'Anyone home?'

No answer.

Damn it, he thought. A worried feeling took over. Either he was at the wrong address or something had happened to the princess. He crossed the living room and cautiously opened a door. She was there, resting on a bed and sound asleep, shoes off and ankles peeping amid the white froth of petticoats. He smiled. She looked blissfully dreamless, her breathing deep and even.

'Delightful,' he murmured, 'but naughty princess for leaving the door unlocked. The ugly frog might have got you.'

He realized how tired he was himself. The train journey had been nerve-racking and exhausting. Hunger added to the attack on his system. He explored the apartment, first locking the door. The place was about as commodious as a small bachelor flat, with one bedroom, the living room, an adequate kitchen and a tiny bathroom with what Harry thought must be the prototype of the world's first geyser. He tried it, lighting the gas jets. Within seconds the whole contraption began to shake and thunder. It sounded like the prophet's warning of the coming apocalypse. He turned on the water spout. The thunder changed to a frightening, vibrating rumble, water gurgled menacingly, then spurted hot, steaming and the colour of weak cocoa. He let it run but removed himself from a possible explosion. He found a linen cupboard which contained some sheets and blankets and, yes, a towel. But decidedly not a bath towel.

He explored the kitchen cupboards for food. Nothing. The flat was clean but empty of everything except its plain furniture and its minimal amenities. The geyser made a noise like a small, hostile eruption and thudded into silence. He listened to discover whether it had woken up Princess Irena. He heard no sound and went into the bathroom to examine the geyser. The gas had failed. A thin layer of brown water covered the bottom of the bath. He saw the coin meter, its slot a thin hungry maw. He took coins from his pocket and tried them. One went in and the gas hissed. He turned it off. He would need to find a decent-sized towel before he could take a bath.

The apartment door rattled to a sudden knocking.

His nerves reawakened. He walked very quietly to the door, his hand around Michalides' revolver in his jacket pocket.

The door rattled again.

He opened it.

Two German soldiers, one of them a sergeant, looked at him. The other, a private, carried a square, brown-paper parcel tied with string.

'Ah?' said Harry casually.

'Herr Rokossky?' said the sergeant.

'*Oui*,' said Harry, then remembered there was one German word he knew. '*Ja*,' he said.

The sergeant gestured to the private, who thrust the parcel into Harry's arms. He accepted it, his smile masking his distrust of it. They nodded, turned, tramped along the landing with a smart slam of booted feet and descended the stairs. Harry closed the door, took the parcel into the kitchen and unwrapped it gingerly. There were various ways of delivering a bomb. But it contained tinned food, including condensed milk. There was also a packet of tea.

'Tea, by God,' he said. The thought of a steaming cup pulled at him, but heavy eyelids suggested sleep was a more immediate need. He went into the living room, sank into an armchair, put his feet up on another one, and thought satisfyingly about it. Tea. It was there to hand. He would have ten minutes in the chair and then make a cup. He fell asleep.

It was dark when he woke up. Stiffly he felt his way to the door and searched for the light switch. There wasn't one. He struck a match. He saw two gas brackets above the mantelpiece. They were mantled. He lit them. The mantles glowed white. He drew the curtains to cover the window. He looked at his watch. It was ten o'clock. He'd slept for hours. There was still no sound from the bedroom. He boiled a kettle of water on the big, cumbersome gas stove and made tea. He found thick china cups and saucers. He knocked on the bedroom door and looked in. There was sufficient infiltration of light from the living room to reveal that she was still on the bed. He coughed. She turned, opening sleepy eyes. From the shadows she looked up at him in vague, brown-eyed dreaminess.

'Tea, Your Highness?' he suggested.

'Tea?' She was not fully awake.

'Hot from the pot. Well, from the kettle, actually. I couldn't find a pot. In Belgrade, don't they make tea in pots? Perhaps they don't make tea.'

Sleepily she smiled. It was a gracious one. She sat up. She had unpinned her hair and it was loose, spilling around her. He thought her about twenty-one, but in the shadowy half-light she looked younger.

'You are saying there is tea?' she said.

'Yes. Just made. So if you'd like to risk it? I mean, what it's like I haven't the foggiest. Don't get up, I'll bring it.'

'No, I'll come,' she said, 'I'm so thirsty I will risk anything.' She slipped her feet from the bed and into her shoes. She stood up, shook her head, flung back her dark hair and gathered it at the nape of her neck so that it hung thickly fanwise over her back. She fastened it with a narrow tortoiseshell clip. It made her look soft and unsophisticated. She followed him into the kitchen.

He filled both cups, the hot liquid running golden-brown from the iron kettle. She shuddered very delicately when he pierced the tin of condensed milk and she saw the thick liquid ooze.

'There are no lemons?' she asked.

'So sorry, no lemons or sugar,' said Harry, 'just some tinned manna.'

'I will drink mine as it is, then. You aren't going to put that stuff in yours, are you?'

'Well, I prefer cow's milk, of course, but I've been making do with condensed in the army. One can't always find a cow.'

She wrinkled her nose a little at that remark, then positively winced as he upended the tin over his cup and let the liquid run in. It spread like a creamy-brown sludge and when he stirred the mixture with a spoon it was not so much tea in her eyes as a concoction quite undrinkable. He seemed to enjoy it. He looked refreshed and vigorous, but she wondered if he was not poisoning himself.

'How can you? It must be hideous.' She was delicately revolted.

'Hideous? My dear Princess–'

'Captain Phillips.' Quick to remark familiarity, she interrupted him coldly. 'You will please not address me like that.'

He did not seem to think he had been seriously at fault, and he looked quizzically at her over his cup. She considered him at least guilty of condescension.

'I meant nothing,' he said. 'I was going to say that tea comes in various ways, and individual taste has a lot to do with it.'

'In any case,' she said, keeping to what she felt was the more relevant point, 'it is wiser not to call me Princess or Highness. I thought we had agreed on that. What are all these tins?'

'Food, I think,' he said. None of the tins was labelled. Some showed a little rust. 'I opened one. It's a mixture of meat and vegetables. We call it MacConachies. It makes a fairly decent change from bully beef. I rather suspect they've come with the compliments of Major Carlsen, who somehow managed to get the German army to deliver them.'

'Well, he is thoughtful about such things and very competent,' she said, sipping her tea, 'and it is like him to arrange some food supply for us. One must concede the Germans to be the most thorough of people.'

'I'm not in a position to argue about it,' said Harry, 'we've been fighting them on and off for four years.'

'Yes, and see what a dreadful mess it has made of Europe.'

'I'd prefer it if we didn't become involved in these kind of arguments,' said Harry.

'Who is arguing? I am only saying,' she said. Her attitude of slight regal omnipotence was offset by the soft informal look of her hair. 'Shall we take our tea in the other room?'

'Yes, of course,' he said. He might have realized she was not used to drinking tea standing up in a kitchen. In the living room she sat composedly, sipping the beverage. She decided that having been a little on her dignity she could now be gracious, and so she said that her tea, even without lemon, was very refreshing, and he was to be congratulated on being able to prepare a pot.

'I assure you, there's nothing to it,' he said.

'You are too modest,' she said, 'I know I should find the process of making tea in a pot confusing and complicated.'

'You'll manage,' said Harry, 'it's simplicity itself, except that you'll have to make it in the kettle. And the tinned food only needs putting into a saucepan and heating.'

Her brown eyes opened wide, her dark eyebrows lifted.

'Captain Phillips, I am to prepare meals for us?'

'Well, I confess to being a very rough and ready cook myself,' he said. He looked at the glowing gas mantles, and said, 'Ah – um – and a woman's touch, you know, Mrs Phillips?'

She sat up straight.

'Don't be impertinent,' she said.

'Hmm,' said Harry thoughtfully. It was difficult to know exactly how to address her and what footing to try for. 'I think we should agree on a little informality, don't you?'

'That was not a little informality,' she said, and he thought perhaps she might feel slightly vulnerable and that when they were alone she wished to establish an atmosphere of propriety.

The immediate fact was that they were sharing this small apartment. She was probably sensitive about it. It was the last thing a young woman of her status would be used to. On the other hand, she was more responsible for the situation than he was.

'I'll see what I can do in the kitchen,' he said, 'you must be very hungry. I know I am.'

She came impulsively out of her frigidity to say, 'Oh, I am silly. You must forgive me, but I am quite unused to this sort of thing.'

'So am I,' said Harry.

She flushed. It made him wonder if, despite her little bouts of haughtiness, she was not a little shy. They might be in this apartment for days. He had to consider her modesty. And she was stunningly attractive. He had to ignore that. In her eyes, according to Major Carlsen, he was a British officer and therefore a gentleman. She expected him to be understanding and gallant. He gave her a reassuring smile.

'Captain Phillips,' she said, 'you must not let me be ridiculous. We must be informal, of course we must. You should call me Irena, especially when it's necessary for the sake of appearances.'

'It's not necessary here. While we're in Belgrade it's not even wise.'

'Oh,' she said, 'you mean my name. No, of course. You must call me Sonya, then. Sonya is my first name, not Irena. But Irena has always been used. It is agreed, then, we must not stand on ceremony. That is right, not stand on ceremony?'

'Perfectly right.'

'Good,' she said. 'We have our part to play, yes?'

'Including looking married when the time comes?' smiled Harry. 'Well, that wedding was chiefly designed for getting you into England,' he said, 'but since it's not a bad idea to be prepared for the opposition, and since they're looking for a widow I suppose we could try to fox them by presenting them with a picture farthest from widowhood. What I mean is, you could try looking like a bride.'

She was amused by that but just a little suspicious too.

'I'm to go about in a wedding gown?' she said.

'I don't know where we could get you a wedding gown,' said Harry, 'but we could try for the next best thing. Why not go around wearing a few shy blushes?'

'Captain Phillips?'

'With a very nice dress, of course,' he added.

'Oh, you have a very disconcerting sense of humour,' she said, but she put her hand over her mouth to smother a peal of laughter. Then she said, quite demurely, 'Thank you for the dress, now I am sure we shall get used to each other.'

'I'll get something to eat,' he said. He got up and moved towards the kitchen.

'Wait,' she said, 'was it difficult for you, getting away from the station this afternoon? I was quite clever myself, I thought.' She told him how she had left in company with a woman and walked some way with her and then, when she was sure no one was following her, she had made her way to the apartment.

'That was better than clever,' said Harry, 'that was simple and damned original.'

'Very original will do, thank you.'
'Yes, quite so. I did the obvious rather than the ingenious. I realized afterwards it could only have drawn attention.' He explained how he had left the station and his suspicions of the two men he had seen.
'Do you think they might have been looking for us?' She was more interested than perturbed, he thought. She had been dismayed when Michalides appeared last night but she hadn't panicked. Lots of pluck about her.
'I'm not sure,' he said, 'they had a good look at me, yes, but they stayed where they were.' He remembered something. 'Just when the train pulled out from Chitila last night I think our friend Michalides turned up. He was too late to join us but I daresay he had a good idea we were aboard, especially as I don't suppose he missed that cab.'
'Are you sure it was him? There was the curfew, you know.'
'I think Comrade Michalides would work his way round that.'
'And I think you are thinking very well for us, Captain Phillips.'
'I'll heat the food,' he said.
She joined him in the kitchen and looked on with interest as he dealt with the complexities of preparing a meal. She seemed piquantly charmed by the coming together of food, saucepan and lighted gas.
'Well, you see,' she said, 'one is taught codes and ethics and proper behaviour, one is not always taught practical things.'

Harry stirred the mixture of meat, vegetables and gravy with a spoon. The aroma made her feel faint with hunger.

'I suppose saying the right thing at the right time and doing the proper thing at all times is more important to queens and princesses than knowing how to cook,' he said. 'But this isn't cooking, this is only heating food already prepared for the pot.'

'All the same,' she said graciously, 'you are very versatile and much more useful than I am.'

'Charming of you to say so, Your Highness, but on the other hand you would always be a better princess than I would. Ah, I think we're quite hotted up.' The stew was steaming, the gravy bubbling. 'Shall we see if we can eat it?'

They could. They ate at the table in the living room. They did not expect to dine sumptuously while in Belgrade, for the food shortage was as acute here as everywhere else in Europe, and the meat and vegetable mix was as good as they were likely to get. Irena said it was really very nice, especially when one was so hungry.

'Do you know,' said Harry, chewing reminiscently, as if the stew was an old friend, 'damned if I don't think this is our MacConachies. Part of some captured British supplies.'

'How considerate,' said Irena warmly.

'Considerate?'

'Of Major Carlsen,' she said. 'Well, what could be more so than returning some of your own food to you?'

'I won't commit myself on that,' said Harry, 'but I will say that a really considerate man would have included a bottle of wine.'

'One should be thankful for what is provided,' she said primly, 'one shouldn't ask for a banquet, not in these times. But a little wine would have been nice.'

'Ah, that reminds me,' said Harry, remembering the brandy. They drank a little of it at the end of the meal. It produced a warm and friendly glow. The atmosphere between them became more natural. Irena held out her empty glass. Harry peered into her eyes and detected a glimmer of well-being. 'I think not, Princess,' he said.

She smiled.

'You are quite right, I simply cannot drink brandy. Champagne is better, isn't it?'

'For some people,' said Harry. 'May I ask, where are your family?'

'My family? My parents, you mean?'

'Yes. Where are they?'

Her eyes dropped to regard her glass.

'You are talking of Prince Paul and Princess Alexandra of Moldavia?' she said a little sadly. 'He was assassinated in Bulgaria ten years ago, she died two years later. You did not know?'

'I'm sorry,' he said contritely, 'but I didn't know, I was at an agricultural college ten years ago.'

'It's a blissful and oblivious time when one is growing up, isn't it?' She was still a little sad. 'Well, it has been a long day, Captain Phillips.'

'Yes,' he said, 'a long night and a long day. Oh, one thing. It would be wiser, when you're ever alone here, to keep the door locked.'

'Naturally,' she said.

He did not point out she had earlier left it unlocked. He did not want her getting on her high horse again. They separated for the night on their friendly note. They did not discuss the one bedroom and who was to occupy it. The bed and the room were naturally hers. She slept soundly. Harry blanketed himself up on the living-room floor, using a cushion as a pillow. The floor was not as uncomfortable as other resting places he had experienced during the war. He thought about things for a while. He thought about Princess Irena and the menace of Michalides. He thought about Elisabeth. He drifted off with his thoughts confused.

Next morning he suggested he should go out to see if he could buy some fresh food to go with the tinned stuff, and also a bottle of wine.

'Yes, I will come too,' said Irena.

'Wouldn't it be wiser if you stayed here?'

She put on her cool look.

'I shall suffocate,' she said, 'I must have some fresh air.'

That was natural, but Harry wasn't sure whether it was wise.

'I suppose we must run a few risks,' he said.

'We'll go in thirty minutes,' she said.

'I'm ready now.'

'Well, I am not.' It was not said perversely or argumentatively. He accepted she was merely stating her case. As a princess, as a young lady, as a woman, she was simply not prepared to go out until she was satisfied with herself. She confirmed this by saying, 'One does not merely throw a coat on, you know.'

'Quite so,' said Harry agreeably, 'I'll give you half an hour, then. But I assume you're not going to make yourself recognizable?'

'I thought,' she said coolly, 'that the idea was to look as if I had just been married.'

'Well, you have as it happens, haven't you?' he smiled.

'I have not forgotten,' she said. She pointed out that in half an hour there would be more people about, making it easier for them to lose themselves.

He was mildly surprised when she was ready precisely at the agreed time. She came out wearing a warm, plain coat over a dress. A headscarf covered her hair. It gave her a peasant look. It was a look that was not out of keeping with his commonplace grey suit and black jersey. They walked to the centre of the city, which was buzzing. There were rumours that the Austrians and Germans were grouping to the west of the capital, which had to mean they were contemplating a definite withdrawal from Belgrade. Their forces engaged in trying to stem the Allied advance were also retreating to points west of the capital.

Irena said, 'Let us find a cafe. I know the best one. I am dying for some coffee.' They had only had tea for breakfast. They might get a little something to eat at the cafe.

Nicchi Michalides sat down, nodding brusquely to the two men who had been waiting at the riverside cafe for him. He was dark, bearded, thickset and quietly formidable.

'Well, comrades?' He opened on a fairly cordial note, although he knew from their faces that they had failed him.

'They weren't on the train,' said Palichek.

'Or they got off before Belgrade,' said Dimitroff.

'You think so?' said Michalides, scratching his black beard.

'It's a possibility,' said Palichek.

'You were diligent and thorough?'

'That is a question, Comrade Michalides, which you don't need to ask,' said Dimitroff.

'Well, they were coming to Belgrade, you may rely on that,' said Michalides. 'Would you say it was impossible for them to have slipped by you?'

'I'd say so, yes, if they were on that troop train,' said Palichek.

'At least, almost impossible, I'd say,' said Dimitroff.

'So?'

'One could not easily miss her,' said Palichek, 'but an Englishman? Who knows how to pick out that kind of a man? I tell you, I've read about the English. Saxons, Normans, Danes, Vikings, what does a mixture like that make them look like now?'

Michalides dismissed that with a brusque gesture of his hand.

'You saw no German colonel with a woman in black?' he said.

'There were so many women in black, there always are,' said Dimitroff, 'but none came out with any German officer.'

Michalides thought for a moment or two.

'He changed his clothes, of course,' he said. 'The obvious thing to do once he got away from us.' He rubbed a spot behind his right ear. The swelling was still tender. He bore Harry no real malice for that, it was being outwitted that rankled. 'He's a slippery customer, that one. You're sure you saw no one like him, no one who might have been him?'

'The description we received wasn't very detailed,' said Palichek.

'Comrade,' said Michalides, 'I only saw him in the dark.'

'Ah, there are always the little problems,' said Dimitroff.

They sipped brandy, with water added. The day was grey and cold.

'But the princess,' said Michalides, 'there were no problems concerning her appearance. You know what she looks like.'

Palichek shrugged. 'We still didn't see her,' he said.

Dimitroff came out of a thoughtful moment to say, 'But we did see a man who hobbled and a boy who carried two cases for him.'

'Two cases?' A little light glinted in Michalides' dark eyes. 'Yes, there were two. You spoke to him?'

'For myself,' said Dimitroff, 'I thought what reason did we have for speaking to him? And there were idiots in the way, arguing about the cab. But there was something about him that took my eye. What it was I don't know, and I wouldn't swear he looked like an Englishman.'

'What does an Englishman look like to you?'

asked Michalides patiently.

'When they arrive with our Serbian army, we shall see,' said Dimitroff.

'I'm not dealing with fools, am I?' said Michalides not so patiently.

'That's not very friendly, comrade,' said Palichek. His was a hurt protest, not an angry one. Comrade Michalides had a reputation and an influence that extended well beyond his own province of Bucharest.

'Then find the boy,' said the Rumanian, 'and find the cab driver. Ask about the man. You saw how he was dressed?' They described Harry's clothes and Michalides nodded. 'That at least is something,' he said. 'Comrades, where the Englishman is, there she is too. I've been promised help by your party secretary.'

'We are the answer to your cry, comrade,' said Dimitroff.

'Then do this for me, you'll know where to look,' said Michalides. 'Find the boy and the cab driver and ask questions. Ask the driver where he took this man who hobbled. And be quick. I shall be at Grocca's house. They mustn't slip us again. The princess isn't here to enjoy herself. She'll be out of Belgrade as soon as it suits her. Well, it won't suit me if she's already flown. It won't suit any of our comrades.'

Palichek mumbled something and Dimitroff pulled on his ear, but they got up and went.

Chapter Five

The cafe near the cathedral was fairly crowded but they could talk. They sat at a table inside. At an outside table they felt they would be too exposed.

'What are you thinking about?' asked Irena as they drank hot brown liquid said to be coffee. Harry was thoughtfully watching people passing by outside.

'That I don't like sitting around. I'd just as soon chance a train to Trieste today.'

'But you would be at risk all the time,' protested Irena, 'there are Germans on all the trains. Who knows what they would do to you if they caught you? I should feel terrible. We must wait until the Serbians and British get here, then we should only have Socialists to worry about. I am not going to let you get shot. The Germans are in the mood for that and it's natural now that they feel they are losing the war. They are conquerors by nature and to give way to the Serbians is a bitter pill to them.'

'Oh, damn bad luck and all that,' said Harry.

'You do not like them of course.'

'Not quite like you do,' he said.

'Well, you have done enough conquering in your time,' she said.

'I have?'

'The English,' she said coolly. 'It is permissible

for you to go out conquering but as soon as other people try it you are standing on rooftops and shouting how disgraceful. The Germans wish to take nothing from you but all the same you fight them, and it is going to benefit no one but the Bolsheviks. Yes, you will see.'

'Look here,' said Harry, 'I don't know any Germans personally. They may all be quite delightful, and they obviously are to you, but they've been firing damn great shells at my battery for years and all I've felt is a desire to fire back. I don't think we ought to argue about these things, not when we should be trying to get on with each other.'

The slight pink flush that was becoming familiar tinted her cheeks. She seemed to alternate between coolness and confusion.

'There, now you are being cross,' she said, 'and I was only speaking an opinion.'

'I'm not being cross,' he said, 'I'm only sitting around. I think I'll go and buy some wool and learn to knit. One must do something.'

She stared, then laughed.

'Oh, you are quite amusing sometimes,' she said. She looked at her watch. 'Yes, you can do something, you can go and shop now, yes? See, I've written down what you might be able to get, you can go into shops and show it.' She took a piece of paper from her handbag and pushed it across to him. 'There, that is bread,' she said, indicating the first word. 'And that is fish. You aren't likely to get any meat. That is fruit, that is lemons. You will see what wine you can get. I will stay here, it's better not to be together all the time.'

She couldn't cook, thought Harry, and she probably couldn't shop, either. However, that wasn't her fault, that was royal conditioning. He smiled good-temperedly, and glad to have something to do he took the list and rose to his feet.

'I'm not sure how long I'll be,' he said.

'It will take a little time, but I will wait,' she said. Her dark red scarf, tied under her chin, had slipped back a little over her head to reveal a wave of glossy chestnut hair. She looked up at him. He seemed quite confident about things. 'Please be careful,' she said.

'You're more at risk in Belgrade than I am,' he said, 'so stay here under cover and don't wander away.'

At his firmness she flushed again. He smiled to show her he was only being fatherly and left the cafe.

The food shops were sparsely stocked. There were queues at most of them, queues which were more animated than usual. It did not seem so bad now, all this daily searching and patient waiting for the necessities of life when things would soon be much better. Harry found himself having to join more than one line of talkative people. He worked his way through the list, obtaining a small amount of bread, some strips of dried fish, even some pears and olives, all with the help of his piece of paper and some sign language which bemused shopkeepers before it enlightened them. It fascinated many of the female onlookers. Women glanced at each other, smiled or giggled, and wondered was his wife ill that he had to do his own shopping. They supposed he was married, he was too personable not to have a wife. He had been a soldier, of course, he had the look.

'Ah,' said one woman to her friend, 'and there's my Chernik doing nothing all day but clean boots.'

'Well, that's his trade,' said her friend, 'he's a fine bootblack and a good spitter.'

'There's no one who can spit on a German boot better,' said the woman proudly. 'But,' she confessed, 'at everything else he's the world's first incompetent.'

'Everything?' said her friend.

'That's between you and me, of course.'

'Of course. Yet you have six children.'

'Even then he hardly moved a muscle. Woman's work is never done, my dear.'

They watched Harry leave the shop with two bottles of wine and some wrinkled green beans. He caught their glances and winked at them. They blushed to their roots and turned away to giggle breathlessly. With his purchases in a large brown paper bag, he made his way back to Irena. He had been well over an hour. He hoped Irena had not lost patience. He would not put it past her to let the lure of shop windows drag her out of hiding.

When he was some thirty yards from the cafe he saw a man come out, a man in a dark grey coat and hat and brisk in his movements. He walked quickly to the edge of the pavement, sized up the slow-moving traffic and crossed the street as if in command of every vehicle.

It was Major Carlsen.

Harry blinked and said, 'Damn me,' under his

breath. He watched the German, in mufti, merging with people on the other side of the street. He wondered what his mother would think of this development. She liked a good story, well-defined heroes and murky villains. She could not stand what she called the lack of body in the plots and characters of the books she read, nor did she hold with heroes and heroines being burdened with strange social attitudes. Princess Irena, seeking to escape anarchists and assassins, would appeal to her as the perfect heroine, as long as she did not become tiresomely political, while the mysterious metamorphosis of Major Carlsen, the symbol of devious German militarism, into a mere civilian, would be considered utterly intriguing. She would probably tell Harry to follow the major. It was a thought. But there was Irena. If she was still in the cafe she would certainly have been talking to the major. Was that why she had gone there, to meet him? Ah, an assignation with her love? Harry smiled to himself. It was interesting, all the same. She had preferred to stay there rather than to go shopping. Was this a thickening plot?

He went into the cafe. She was still there. She smiled in welcome when she saw him.

'Oh, you've not been long at all,' she said.

'Almost too quick?' said Harry. 'But I've been over an hour.' He put the bag containing the meagre provisions on the table. He sat down. The flat, leather-covered seat of the chair was warm. 'Well?' he said and waited.

'What have you bought?' she asked. She leaned and opened the carrier. She peered into it. 'Oh, how well you've done. But what do we do with these?' She brought out a green bean.

'Cook them and eat them.'

'Naturally, I did not think one smoked them.' She seemed quite vivacious. She and the major must be in love. She had obviously met him and talked to him, and it had left her looking pleased with life. 'Are we to have a banquet or are we to make all this last?'

'It won't last long, there really isn't very much,' he said. Then, after a pause, 'Well, young lady?'

She glanced up from her inspection of the wine he had bought, lifting long dark lashes to regard him in innocent enquiry. Then she frowned a little at the way he had addressed her. Then she smiled.

'I'm hungry,' she said, 'shall we go back to the apartment and have a meal?' He looked at the table. There had been two used cups when he left her. Now there were four. 'Oh, yes, there was nothing to do but drink more coffee while I was waiting,' she said.

'What did Major Carlsen want?' he asked.

'Major Carlsen?' She was so natural in her surprise that one had to place her on the side of the angels. 'Oh, yes, Major Carlsen.'

'Yes.' He was curious, very curious.

'I was so surprised,' she said. A waiter came up. She shook her head. Harry asked for coffee.

'Go on,' he said.

'I had no idea,' she said.

'Go on,' he said.

'Why do you keep saying that?'

'Because I'm waiting for you to say something.'

‘I simply looked up and there he was,’ said Irena, ‘and he was so pleased we were safely here. He knew we had been seen–’

‘I should damn well think we couldn’t have been missed, the way he was flashing light signals.’

Irena put her nose in the air.

‘Really, Captain Phillips, there’s no need to be bad-tempered.’

‘Oh, it’s just my simple inquisitiveness,’ he said. ‘May I ask what he’s doing in Belgrade disguised as a man about town?’

‘It’s something to do with orders, I suppose,’ she said, ‘he did not discuss it with me. He has been very kind, very understanding, but we have never talked about confidential military matters. After all, I am Rumanian.’

‘Really? I’m glad to hear it. How did he know you were here?’

‘But we are supposed to be here, that was the arrangement.’ She was quite composed.

‘I mean in this cafe,’ said Harry, looking her in the eye.

‘He was passing and saw me in here.’ She smiled as if it was all very simple and reasonable. ‘Naturally, he came in. He was delighted about things. We drank coffee together. It’s rather awful, isn’t it?’ Harry had just been served and was trying it for flavour. ‘He told me to tell you how well you had done, because of course I told him about everything that had happened.’

‘I’m flattered,’ said Harry, ‘but I’m not impressed. We didn’t do at all well. We were spotted in the first place, but that was no surprise considering how our departure was advertised. And if your extremist friends are as dedicated as Major Carlsen says they are, then they're going to be on our tail, if they're not already.'

'Major Carlsen said that doesn't matter as long as we are all right now and as long as we stay in hiding.'

'I'm glad he's not worried, because I am,' said Harry, 'and the fact that we're all right at the moment, and not actually on the guillotine, is only half to his credit.'

'I hope,' said Irena, at her coolest, 'that you are not going to turn out to be a rather beastly person.'

'Well, I do have some little failings,' said Harry, 'but I really feel more curious than beastly at this point. What's so odd is why Major Carlsen didn't bring you to Belgrade himself. It would have been easy for him, and he must have known he was going to be here soon after us.'

'Why must he?' Irena was in protest. 'Everyone in uniform is rushing about because of the fighting in the south and I expect he never knows what his next orders might be. Do you think that having seen me he shouldn't have spoken to me? Even though the war is going so badly for Germany he was most concerned about us, and so relieved to know that nothing had happened to us.'

'He might consider Michalides counts for nothing. I don't.'

'Really, you are not very grateful,' said Irena.

'Grateful?'

'Major Carlsen did let you go instead of sending you to a prisoner-of-war camp.'

'Well, if that doesn't beat duck-shooting,' said Harry. She wasn't quite sure what that meant but sensed it was a reflection of his astonishment, and had the grace to blush a little.

'Oh, I am sorry,' she said, 'but I wish you would not be so – so–' She puzzled over the right English word.

'Carping?' suggested Harry.

'No. Grumpy. Yes, that is right, isn't it? Grumpy?'

He restrained a smile. He could not see how in their situation he could talk with anything but frankness. She, being more used to flattery and hand-kissing, no doubt, was not going to take kindly to too much frankness.

'Grumpy will do,' he said, 'and I expect everything will sort itself out. Shall we go and do some cooking?'

They got up. The cafe was full of talkers, all immersed, and the one face that was turned their way was like a bright, round beacon. Harry, immediately aware of it, looked into the alert eyes of youth and experience. They belonged to a boy in a huge peaked cap who stood at the door. The boy glanced over his shoulder at the street, then back at Harry. He looked as if he considered something was up.

'He wants you,' said Irena.

The boy sidled in, keeping his eye on the nearest waiter. The waiter, however, was engrossed, exchanging rumours with customers about which way the Austrians were going to run. The boy reached Harry.

'M'sieu,' he whispered. Like all impecunious hopefuls who piratically competed with porters at railway stations, he had picked up words from many different tongues. Yesterday he had heard Harry produce one or two French words. 'M'sieu?'

In French Harry tried the helpful but non-committal response of, 'My aunt is in the garden.'

The boy looked foxed for a moment, then grinned. The limping man, who had been very generous yesterday, was saying he could understand French. Perhaps he would be generous again. It was surprising what people would pay for information that had no meaning to others.

'M'sieu,' he whispered dramatically, 'they are asking questions.'

'They?' Harry was interested but cautious.

'Two men, m'sieu.' The boy went on in limited French to explain how he had had his ear twisted by these men who wanted to know all about the man with the stick. A man who hobbled. Not liking the pain inflicted, he had only said he carried the man's bags to a cab. He knew he was not likely to be paid for any of the information, so why should he tell them where the man was going?

'No, with your ear hurting,' smiled Harry, 'why should you? Have you been following me?'

'M'sieu?' The boy's bright eyes were clear. 'I see you in here, so I tell you what perhaps you like to know.'

'There,' murmured Irena, 'he saw you just as Major Carlsen saw me.'

'Someone's asking questions,' said Harry. To the boy he said, 'That was all you told him, that you carried my cases to the cab?'

The boy said that was all the men deserved for twisting his ear. Harry gave him the welcome tip. It was received with an engaging smile. Expectancy had been satisfied. One soon got to learn who were the generous people and who were only ear-twisters. He sidled towards the door. The waiter spotted him at last and moved, aiming a cuff at him to help him on his way through the door. It missed by a yard.

'We'd better go,' said Harry.

'In a cab, perhaps?' said Irena.

It was impossible. Every moving vehicle was full. It was not only the Austrian and German troops who were preparing to leave Belgrade. Numbers of officials and civilians who had collaborated with the occupying powers were also trying to get away. They did not want to be around when their protectors had gone. In the eyes of Rumanian patriots, Princess Irena was in this category.

The atmosphere was electric. Irena and Harry walked swiftly, Harry bothered by no more than a twinge or two in his leg. From time to time he turned to look for an available cab. He felt impeded on the pavements. People were moving slowly, watching the traffic, or clustering in talkative knots. Only the Turkish citizens seemed unaffected by events. The men in their blue jackets, white trousers and red fezzes, followed by their veiled women, accepted that all things were the will of Allah, and their calm eyes said so.

Harry obtained a cab at last. The driver took them only because their address was on the way to the stables. He had been working night and day for the past week and now he was going to sleep for two days, and so was his horse. He dropped his passengers off at the apartment block. The area was quiet, the street itself very quiet except for the sound of the departing cab as Irena entered the block. Harry, on edge again, stood listening.

'What are you waiting for?' called Irena.

'It's my nerves,' he said. He heard more clearly then what his ears had faintly picked up a moment ago. Breaking into the lessening sound of one cab was the rhythmic creaking and clip-clop of another. Harry took a step forward. Away down the street an ancient vehicle was advancing, rolling along with a sway, and with old springs shuddering. Harry knew it. He ran to the entrance. 'Quick!' Irena did not argue, she raced up the stone flights with him. He noticed with relief that the resident caretaker, the concierge, was not around. That meant the man would be unable to answer questions. They reached the fourth floor, unlocked the apartment door, burst in. Harry put the bag of groceries in the kitchen, ran into the bedroom, opened up the wardrobe and flung all Irena's clothes back into her case. 'You must go to the top flight and stay there,' he said. 'Take everything that belongs to you.'

She pulled open drawers in the tallboy, swept undergarments into the case, threw in brushes, combs, hand mirror and everything else.

'Your uniform!' she cried. His British khaki

hung there in the wardrobe.

'Leave it,' he said, 'it'll prove to Michalides that I am a British officer, if he is paying a call on us. They found the cab driver, damn it, of course! Can you manage that case?'

He took it out for her, thrust it into her arms. She gasped. But she went up the remaining flights of stairs with it. She disappeared. He waited until the sound of her footsteps ceased, then closed the door, took his own case from the living room into the bedroom and put it in the wardrobe. He looked around the apartment, checking quickly.

Someone knocked on the door. Unless he answered they would prowl around the block, inside and out, up and down. And they would wait.

He answered.

Michalides smiled, white teeth gleaming amid his black beard. Behind him were Palichek and Dimitroff.

'Ah,' said Michalides. He sounded amiable but his eyes were glinting.

'M'sieu?' enquired Harry.

'What, French today, my friend?' said Michalides. 'First you are German, next English, now French. That is good, very good.'

'Who are you?' Harry peered into the whiskers. 'Oh, it's you,' he said casually. 'Well, you'd better come in, I suppose.'

This slightly disconcerted Michalides. He had expected anything but an invitation, and his foot had been thrust forward to prevent the door being closed. Harry, however, was now opening it wider and standing politely aside.

'You may bring your friends in with you,' he said.

They all entered. Michalides looked around. Palichek and Dimitroff looked at Harry.

'He is English?' said Palichek.

'Who'd have known? It shows how cunning they are,' said Dimitroff.

'Gentlemen?' said Harry.

'My friends are saying you look the same as other people,' said Michalides, eyes darting.

'What did they think, that I'd only have one eye?' said Harry.

Michalides caressed his beard. He smiled in a way that made him look genially willing to come to terms. Harry was not deceived.

'It was a lesson for both of us, our first meeting,' said the Rumanian. 'Each thought too little of the other. You left me with a sore head and a setback. That was my lesson. But I am here, you see. I am not easily put off. That is your lesson.'

'Accept my apologies for being rough,' said Harry, 'but I had to get to Belgrade.'

Michalides gently adjusted his wide-brimmed black hat. It was a hat which was sinisterly traditional among anarchists. The flat caps of the two Serbians were indicative of followers who had yet to climb the heights to greatness.

'One accepts the blows as well as the blessings of life,' said Michalides. 'Of course, I do have a proverb. It says that a man who sets fire to his neighbour's house will have his own fall in on him.'

'Oh, we say what's sauce for the goose is sauce for the gander.'

‘Ah?’ Michalides, hands in his jacket pockets, began to wander about.

‘Have you come to pull my house in on me?’ asked Harry.

Michalides waved that aside. ‘Not important. Justice is important.’

‘I know, my dear chap,’ said Harry, ‘it’s only the condemned man who argues about it.’

‘Where is she?’ asked Michalides abruptly.

‘I’m sorry?’ Harry looked mystified.

‘The woman, the royal swan with the long neck, where is she?’

‘I’m afraid I’m riddled with ignorance,’ said Harry. ‘Who are you talking about?’

Michalides showed a glimmer of white teeth. He was a man who had learned to contain his temper and to use his patience and persistence, so that when the right moment was reached he could strike with a great deal of self-satisfaction. One showed one’s teeth but one did not bite precipitately. Undisciplined hunger could lead one into biting off the wrong head. The Englishman was cool enough, but so he would be. He had already shown his mettle. But undoubtedly the princess was here. She had to be. She was the one he, Michalides, had come for. And he would take her and escort her to the house of Serbian comrades, where she would receive civilized comfort but be held until the war was over and trials began. Then she would be sent back to Rumania for her own trial.

Michalides nodded to his friends. Palichek and Dimitroff searched the bedroom, investigated the kitchen and tried the bathroom. The blanks they drew nettled them. They returned to the living room on the verge of bad temper. Michalides, seeing their faces, took off his hat, carefully brushed the nap with the sleeve of his jacket, and put it on again.

'Comrades?' he said.

They shrugged and spread their hands. Michalides searched the bedroom for himself. He did not make much noise. He was quietly systematic. He came out carrying the jacket of Harry's uniform.

'So? What is this?' he asked.

'Mine,' said Harry, 'I told you I'm a British officer. I'm on a mission. And I'm waiting now for the British to arrive with the Serbians. That's all I can say. Except that we're on the same side.'

'Are we?' Michalides pursed his full lips. He thought. Light came. 'Ah, yes, we talked about it before. Your government sent you for her.'

'What you're talking about I didn't know then and I don't know now,' said Harry. 'I don't even know why I let you in here, except to apologize for hitting you over the head. But that sort of thing sometimes can't be helped.'

'Naturally, you must lie about her,' said Michalides, 'but, my friend, Princess Irena was with you when we first met. You came from her house with her. Your mission is to take her from us. Yes? Come, if as you say we are on the same side, you can say so.'

'Who the devil is Princess Irena?' Harry sounded irritable.

'Come,' said Michalides again, 'I am not a fool.'

Palichek and Dimitroff, understanding not a

word of English, shifted about impatiently.

'If you care to check,' said Harry, 'you'll find I was captured after we began our advance from Salonika. I escaped, got a bullet in my leg and was treated at the Queen Constanza Hospital in Bucharest. I met a German officer, Major Carlsen.'

'Your mission was to get a bullet in your leg?' Michalides was ironical.

'No, to make contact with certain people in Belgrade. I can't discuss it, or the ways and means. However, the bullet in the leg spoiled things for a while. Then Major Carlsen suggested there was little point in sending me off to a prison camp since he considered the war nearly over. Rather a civilized man, the major. There aren't many of them around.'

'Only a mirror reflects the true face of each man,' said Michalides sententiously, 'only in a mirror does a fox see himself. What a fox is Major Carlsen. And you are his first cousin.'

'My dear chap,' said Harry, 'he offered me a ticket to Belgrade. Nothing could have suited me better. I was asked only a small favour in return. That of escorting a young lady recently widowed. I agreed. I parted from her at Belgrade station.'

'That is good, that is very good,' said Michalides. 'So, you are given your freedom, a German uniform, a ticket and a widow. Tck, tck.'

'She was a distressed soul, poor woman, and rather mournful company,' said Harry reflectively. 'I thought Major Carlsen quite decent about it all. But there are occasions when a unique camaraderie arises between friend and foe, which makes up in an odd way for all the other occasions when we're shooting at each other.'

'Do you take me for an idiot?' Michalides was insulted. 'I ask you again, where is Princess Irena of Moldavia?'

'Good God, is that it?' said Harry. 'Is that what you're trying to tell me, that the lady was no widow but a princess? Not that it means much to me, I've never heard of any Princess Irena.'

'My friend,' said Michalides, 'you are making me tremble. Do you understand?' He stuck a thick forefinger into Harry's chest. Harry removed it and picked up his uniform jacket which Michalides had thrown on to a chair. Palichek sucked his teeth and Dimitroff cleaned out an ear.

'Mr Michalides,' said Harry, 'please look carefully at this jacket. It was tailored to fit me, not some mountain goat. It signifies I'm commissioned to serve my King and country. My country has a long arm. I'm not concerned with your problems, with the whereabouts of some person you say is Princess Irena of Moldavia, and you should not concern yourself in any way with me. In any way. Now, do *you* understand?'

Michalides, his cold eyes at variance with his smile, shrugged.

'You have made a point,' he said. 'May I ask who you are?'

'Phillips. Harry Phillips. Captain.' He pointed to the three pips.

'Captain?'

'Quite so.'

'One can be reasonable,' said the Rumanian, 'and I am very reasonable. I will tell you, no, I do not concern myself with you. Only with the princess. So you see, tell me where she is and you and I will be good friends. It is right, we are on the same side. Against Germans and against traitors, yes?'

'I still can't help you with the princess,' said Harry. 'What do you want her for, what has she done?'

'She loves Germans,' said Michalides.

'Unwise at the moment, perhaps, but hardly a crime, and when the war's over what will it matter?'

'It will matter to us.' Michalides stroked his beard again. Softly he said, 'Where is the other case?'

Damn, thought Harry. He had slipped up there. But then this kind of thing was new to him.

'What other case? I've only one, and that was given to me by Major Carlsen.'

'Yes, there is only one here,' said Michalides, 'but at the station you had two. A boy carried them to a cab for you. The other one, you have eaten it?'

Harry laughed heartily and thought rapidly.

'Well, I must say,' he said, 'you are a suspicious chap. The other case was hers, the lady I escorted as far as Belgrade station. So of course it isn't here. She wasn't only in a distressed state, she was unhappy about all kinds of things, it seemed. Perhaps she is the person you want, I don't know. She asked me to look after the case for a few hours and to take it to a cafe for her in the evening. Well, damn it, whoever she is, could I say no? Would you refuse a young widow with tears in her eyes?'

'Ah, the tears of a young widow are sadder than the cries of a lost lamb,' said Michalides. 'You took the case? To which cafe?'

'The one almost opposite the cathedral, there's a white cross over the door. I met her there, gave it to her, we parted and that's all. You realize, do you, that in answering all these questions I'm being very accommodating?'

'I am not sure, Captain, if you are answering questions or merely talking,' said Michalides. 'I am thinking you are a great one for talking.'

'Well, I've got time to spare for that,' said Harry, 'while I'm waiting for the advance British forces to arrive. However, I don't want to be drawn into what I think is a local political matter. I don't care for that at all, and my superiors would be against it. Your princess is probably on her way to somewhere else by now. I've time to spare, as I said, but I think you're wasting yours.'

'Tell me about the cafe again,' said Michalides.

Harry repeated what he had said about the cafe with a white cross over its door. Michalides spoke to Dimitroff. Dimitroff answered, nodded. Palichek, who had wandered into the kitchen, came out again. He was not so sour-faced. He was grinning. Harry felt a little alarm bell ring in his mind. It was smothered by relief when the man brought a bottle of wine out from behind his back.

'It's been a thirsty morning, Comrade Michalides,' said Palichek.

Dimitroff brightened and said, 'It's not much to ask of your English friend, a glass of his wine.'

'He's not my friend,' said Michalides, 'he's like a woman with all his devious talk.'

Harry, guessing the wine was the subject, said, 'Do they want a drink? Tell them to help themselves.'

'Bring it with you,' said Michalides to the Serbians, 'we're going to the White Cross cafe.' To Harry he said, 'Well, we shall do some looking and ask some more questions. We shall find her.'

'I can't wish you luck, I'm impartial,' said Harry. Politely he saw them out. Michalides looked around the landing and at the upward flight of stairs. He glanced back at Harry, standing in the open doorway. He smiled and went up the stairs, to the fifth floor and the sixth, the last. They heard his footsteps on the stone flights. Harry waited for a cry, a scuffle. He knew for certain now that Major Carlsen was right. These men wanted the princess, and badly. He slipped his hand into his jacket pocket. The revolver was still there. He could not let them take her. Michalides would cheerfully hang her.

There was silence at the top. Palichek fiddled with the bottle of wine. Dimitroff leaned against the wall. Footsteps sounded again. Michalides came down. He looked at Harry, gave him a cold-eyed smile and took Palichek and Dimitroff down to the street with him. Harry went quietly to the head of the stairs and heard them cross the tiled hall. Was the cab still there? He went to the landing window which overlooked the street. They were getting into the cab. He waited until it drove off, then ran to the top floor, taking the stairs two at a time. The top-floor landing was deserted, the doors of each apartment closed. Irena had gone, and her case.

Chapter Six

Somewhere, faintly, Harry heard a child crying. The apartment block was solidly built and closed doors shut out most of the ordinary sounds of life and living. The silence left by Irena's disappearance was an uneasy one. He disliked it intensely. Where the devil was she? Obviously, she had not been here when Michalides had come nosing up. Had she decided the landing was too exposed? If so, and she had gone creeping down to the street, she had taken a terrible risk. She could not have known whether Michalides had a man waiting.

The child cried again. Had that panicked her, a child's cry and the thought that a door would open and someone see her and ask her questions? No, she would think quickly and act coolly, he was sure. The fire escape. He paced across the landing and looked out of a cold, high doorway at the iron staircase. He saw one or two people walking down below, he did not see Irena.

An apartment door opened. He turned, closing the fire exit. A woman was looking at him. She shut the door. It opened again a few seconds later and there was Irena, her hopeful smile asking if everything was all right. The woman appeared beside her and regarded Harry with feminine interest. Irena turned to her.

'See, he's here. Now I've no more worries. But I'm sure this was the apartment number he gave me. Love makes some men get little things wrong. You've been so kind. Thank you.'

She pulled out her large case, slithering it along the floor. The woman remained there, intrigued, wondering how a young married couple would reunite after having lost each other. Harry did not understand what Irena had said, but her look of simulated relief and pleasure gave him a clue. She was a resourceful young woman.

In French he said ecstatically, 'Sonya! My love!' He swept her into his arms and kissed her resoundingly on both cheeks. She had not expected him to play up as demonstratively as that, and the vibrations that ran through her body were of indignation and shock. The woman smiled to see that the war had not spoiled love for some people, then closed the door. Irena, face burning, retreated in hot confusion from Harry's arms. He picked up her case and they went down to their apartment. Inside it she faced up to him.

'How dared you!' she said.

'Please, not now, Your Highness.'

'Not now? What do you mean?' The inference she drew turned her pinker. 'You are a cad, sir!'

'No, it was all for the benefit of the lady upstairs. I'm right, aren't I, in thinking you knocked on her door and told her you were looking for your husband? And that she invited you in to hear your story?'

'Yes. But even so–'

'You can tell me later.' He was brisk, urgent,

treating her sensitivity as an irrelevance. 'They're on to us. You must go. Leave your case, I'll pack as many of your things into mine as I can. Leave by the rear exit on the ground floor, you can get through to the adjacent street from there. For God's sake be careful. They've gone off in that cab but they won't go far. Michalides will give me just enough time to make me think he's going to the cafe in the cathedral square, then he'll be back, hoping to catch you here. He's convinced you're around. And the least he'll do is have someone watch this place.'

Irena looked haughtily obstinate.

'We are staying here,' she said, 'Major Carlsen–'

'Oh, you'd rather wait for Belgrade to be relieved, would you? I doubt if it'll be like Mafeking night for you. They'll pick you up before then. I might be able to stall them for a while but I can't shoot their heads off. We'll leave tonight. Go to the station, find out if there's a train leaving for Trieste this evening and if so, get tickets. I'll meet you there just after dark.'

'But that is not the plan!' She pulled her headscarf off and flung her hair about in a spasm of temperament.

'I know it isn't,' he said, 'and you must know that the original plan, such as it is, has fallen down dead. Now there's no plan at all. We've just got to cut and run for it.'

She calmed down and said in her cool way, 'Major Carlsen said we were to wait here until the war was over, because then it would be safer and easier for us to get to Trieste. I don't think we should run just because those men have found you. They have not found me.'

'My dear young lady–'

'You are forgetting yourself, Captain Phillips.'

'Your Highness,' he said firmly, 'wayward princesses are out of place at the moment.'

'Oh!' She stamped her foot.

'Listen, please. They aren't idiots, they'll be back. Now despite my lack of qualifications for this job and my limitations as a lord chamberlain or grand vizier or royal paperweight–'

'Oh!'

'I'm going to get you to Trieste, and then to England, even if I have to launch you on a raft.'

'You are a bully, sir! Do you hear? A bully!'

'Yes, but I happen to agree with Major Carlsen now,' he said, 'I think you're worth saving from the hangmen of Michalides. But can we be more agreeable about the ways and means?'

Irena stared at him, at his dark, uncompromising eyes and at his expression, which was almost grim. Her hot resentment melted. Her lashes drooped as angry eyes softened.

'May I put on a hat and veil?' she asked quietly. He opened up her case. She found her brown hat, with its half-veil. She put it on. He frowned a little because she looked so chastened by his bullying, so vulnerable to a man like Michalides. His frown was at himself. 'Please,' she said, 'will you make sure that whatever else you leave behind you will pack my brown costume?'

'Yes,' he said.

'I will stay and pack the things I want if you like.'

'No. You must go. Please.'

‘There are some things–’ She blushed.

‘Yes, I understand.’ He knew she would want him to include as much fresh underwear as could be managed.

‘I’ll try to get something to eat at a cafe,’ she said.

‘I’m sorry,’ said Harry, ‘I know how hungry you must be again, but I’ll bring some of the food we’ve got here. Wait.’ He fetched two of the pears and gave them to her. She put one into her handbag and bit into the other without ceremony. It was a crisp, hard fruit. ‘Good,’ he said, ‘eat them on the way.’ He opened the door for her. She looked at the pear in her gloved hand.

‘You will meet me later?’ she said.

‘Of course. Keep yourself out of sight and watch for me soon after dark.’

‘I know you will come,’ she said, ‘but I shan’t go on any train until you do arrive. You will remember my brown costume, please? I must have that.’

‘Yes,’ he said. She left quietly. He followed her down, watched her leave the building by a rear exit, then he slipped out through the front door. He looked around but saw no sign of the men or the cab and sped back upstairs.

Irena’s case had to be got out of sight. If Michalides did return he had to be let in again. Harry sensed he had a certain immunity in the eyes of the Rumanian, but only as long as Michalides remained a little unsure of his ground. Once he was convinced of Harry’s complete involvement with the princess, that immunity would cease to exist. Politics were more important to men like Michalides than the war – when he spoke of which side people were on, he had politics in mind, not armies. Well, the man had rummaged around and searched the bedroom himself, and had found nothing he could associate with the presence of Irena. If he came back it would be in the hope of bursting in on her.

The case. There was only one place for it. Under the bed. They would have already looked there. If they came back and there was no sign of her, they would not rummage around again. He must chance that they wouldn't. He took the case in and shoved it under the bed, tightly up against the wall, where it was darkest. In the kitchen he turned the beans out of the bag and into a bowl. He put some water into a saucepan. He poured himself a measure of brandy. Then, with his jacket off and the sleeves of his jersey rolled up, he simply waited. He nipped off the tops and stripped the spines of a couple of beans as an afterthought, putting them into the saucepan.

He felt Michalides had swallowed nothing of his story. He had lied on a first-class note – well, one either performed well or not at all – but Michalides had not been convinced. He would not have checked the upper landings otherwise. And if he intended to return the knock would happen any moment now.

It came five minutes later. Harry lit a low gas under the saucepan and answered the summons with a peeling knife in his hand. Michalides had only one man with him this time. The other one, obviously, would be holding a watching brief downstairs. Michalides looked ready for trouble.

'Oh, damn it,' said Harry in reasonable exasperation, 'what the devil is it this time?' In his right hand the blade of the peeling knife glinted.

'What is that for?' The Rumanian's voice was soft.

'Beans,' said Harry, 'I'm trying to get myself a meal.'

'Excuse.' Michalides thrust the door back and brushed by, Dimitroff on his heels. Harry shut the door, called Michalides a time-wasting idiot and returned to the kitchen. Michalides flashed in after him like a black shadow and caught him using the knife on the beans. He plopped each one into the saucepan of water. Michalides looked almost outraged. Dimitroff appeared at his shoulder.

'You're wasting your time, you know,' said Harry shortly.

'I am not satisfied,' said Michalides.

'Neither am I,' said Harry, 'you're turning this place into a railway station.' He took a sip of the brandy he had poured himself. Michalides turned abruptly, shouldered past Dimitroff and strode through the living room to the bedroom. Dimitroff put his head into the bathroom, into cupboards, then joined Michalides in the bedroom. Harry finished preparing his beans, listening to the sound of their voices. Carrying his brandy he sauntered casually in on them after a while. They had opened up the wardrobe again and this time had stripped off the bedclothes, which lay in a tumbled heap on the floor beside the bed. That could be a help, thought Harry. It restricted the view under the bed. Michalides looked the picture of black frustration.

'Good God,' said Harry irritably, 'what the devil are you doing now? Do you think I've got her sewn up in the mattress? Or perhaps in a sack under the bed?'

Michalides showed his teeth. They were grinding.

'I am not satisfied, I tell you,' he said.

'That's damned obvious,' said Harry. He took a mouthful of brandy. He sensed the menace of the Rumanian's henchman standing close by, the temptation Michalides felt to try more primitive methods of persuasion. 'If you wreck the place you'll pay for it, I tell you that. I'll be in the kitchen when you've come to your senses. There's some brandy if you want it. You're having a tiring day. So am I.'

It worked. They followed him into the kitchen. He pointed to the brandy bottle. Dimitroff was not a man to worry about losing face. He helped himself. He poured some for Michalides. Michalides took it, scowled at it and tossed it down his throat. Harry put salt in the beans. The water was steaming.

'What's he doing, drowning them in hot water?' asked Dimitroff.

Michalides, giving himself time to think, put the question to Harry.

'I don't like oily beans, I like them cooked clean and slightly salted,' said Harry. 'Look here, if you're convinced your elusive princess is still in Belgrade, why don't you try the cathedral? Royal personages are known to be very devout and you can be very devout in a cathedral and keep your face hidden at the same time. After all, it was in that cafe near the cathedral where I last saw her.'

'Talk,' said Michalides and ground his teeth. 'I have never heard any talk which said as little as yours. No, I am still not satisfied. She is here somewhere.' He walked out. Dimitroff finished his brandy and went after him. Harry heard the apartment door close. He went to the door and stood with his ear against it. He caught the faint sounds the two men made. They were going up and down flights, searching, looking. He heard the hollow sound of a fire-exit door slam. He had thought about putting the case somewhere out on that iron staircase. He stayed at the door, listening, until finally he heard them descending to the ground floor. Then he returned to the kitchen.

The beans simmered and cooked. He ate them with a piece of dark bread, which tasted of chaff. He hoped Irena would forgive him for having this minor meal. He ate one of the hard pears for dessert. He saved the wine and the rest of the food. He retrieved her case from beneath the bed and opened it up. A tumbled array of clothes looked up at him.

'Something has to be sacrificed for the cause,' he said. His own case was smaller. His British uniform must go in, plus his razor and toothbrush. The rest of the space had to take what it could of her things. She had the clothes she was wearing. He would include her brown costume, as promised, and as many of her undergarments as possible. With her royal background she might endure the prospect of only one change of outer clothes, but would consider life an outrage if she did not have a sufficiency of fresh underwear. He packed his uniform first, then her undergarments en masse, thus avoiding the delicate responsibility of having to make a selection of what she might consider the utter necessities and the do-withouts. He stowed in all her toilet articles. Lastly he put in her costume.

Yet there was always the possibility that he might have to get rid of the case and all its contents in an emergency. If he was literally going to have to run for it the case would have to be dumped. She had been very insistent about her costume, the brown one. He wondered why. He was having to leave dresses and another costume behind, but had to take the brown jacket and skirt, with the cream blouse. He thought about it. It came to him that she was wearing no jewellery. That was wise. But as she was going into exile it was also improvident. What was she going to live on unless she had funds salted away somewhere?

He took the costume out. He examined it. He ran his fingers over the closely woven material. Around the hem of the skirt he felt the presence of hard, small stones. With a sharp-pointed kitchen knife he carefully snipped some of the neat stitching. A minute later a tiny cataract of brilliance spilled into his hand, forming a small pyramid that flashed with iridescent light. Fifty matching diamonds at least, fifty.

'Ye gods,' he said.

He wrapped them carefully in one of her tiny, lace-edged handkerchiefs, then sat down to think about Michalides. He had no doubt the apartment block was being watched. One man at least would be lurking somewhere around. Michalides himself was probably on his way to that cafe. He would get no satisfaction, but he would ask his questions, be suspicious of every answer, roam about and ask again. Then sooner or later he would be back here.

Harry knew he could not leave before dusk. If he were spotted, and with his case, there would be no more politeness, no more patient probing. They would have the case off him, open it, see her clothes and know for sure that he knew where she was. Therefore, if he were spotted, he would have to run for it before they laid hands on him. That was when the case would have to be dumped. 'Ye gods,' he said again. If he hadn't examined her costume he would have been in danger of dumping a fortune. The thought made him take another look at the costume, and at the clothes he was leaving behind. He found nothing more. He repacked the costume. He pushed in the wine, the brandy and the small amount of wrapped food.

At the first sign of dusk he went out on to the landing and peered through the window into the street below. He knew why it was so quiet. Almost everyone was in the city centre, unable to keep away from the hub of news, rumour and excitement.

If Michalides had a man on watch he wasn't visible from the window.

When darkness swam to submerge dusk Harry left the apartment. Going down the flights a man and a woman passed him on their way up. They were both talking at once. They glanced at him and went on talking and ascending. He continued quietly down. On the ground floor the single economic light in the hall scarcely fingered him as he skirted it and faded into the darkness by the rear door. Cautiously he opened it, staying close to the wall. He looked and listened. Somewhere he thought he could smell cooking. The quadrangle at the rear of the block, its paved surface slightly crumbling, was dark. He counted himself invisible against the wall. He put the case down, reached into his pocket and drew out a paper-wrapped ball of bean strips. He tossed it upwards and outwards. It fell into the quadrangle with a small rustling noise. The sound drew an immediate and perceptible reaction. Harry heard the soft slither of feet. A torch suddenly beamed, sweeping to and fro as Harry closed the rear door. It picked up nothing, rushed back on itself and was swallowed by its source. Darkness reclaimed the quadrangle and its gate, the gate through which Irena would have gone earlier, but which was denied to Harry now.

He left by the front entrance. His emergence was fast and in socked feet, his tied boots around his neck. He turned eastward, away from the city centre, carrying the case in his arms and against his chest, camouflaging it. There were no street lights and in the cold darkness his deep grey suit, black jersey and peaked cap made of him a moving shadow. But Dimitroff, inconspicuously posted on the west side of the block, was sharp of eye and adjusted of vision. He came out from cover and began to walk in long-striding pursuit, signalling to Palichek with a low whistle as he did so. Harry, silent in his socks, heard him before he whistled, heard him the moment he moved, and immediately vaulted the yard-high wall fronting the house next to the block. He stretched himself flat on the ground beside it, the case pushed out in front of him. He lay in the chill well of darkness, grateful for the wartime fuel shortage which denied all but essential light to a city.

He heard the man go by. He waited as he caught the sound of another man, a man running, who passed by quickly. Harry did not wait for a second chance, a better chance, or a longer interval. He was over the low wall at once, speeding silently back past the apartment block and going westward. He ran, softly padding, risking his socked feet as he kept close to the line of houses, the case swinging heavily in his hand. If he trod on a stone it would be murder. But he ran faster. He stopped abruptly at the sound of people ahead. He turned and flitted across the street, avoiding them. He heard them pass. He went on, entered a street on his right and began to run once more. He stopped again after a few minutes and put his boots on. Then he strode on quickly, making for the railway station. How long he had before Michalides decided he was on his way out of Belgrade he did not know.

In a little while he was in streets that were crowded. Shop fronts showed a few lights. To the Serbians the excitement was of the kind that kept a tongue buzzing or grew like a knot in the stomach. They were watching their conquerors departing. Down the main street they came, battalions of German troops, marching in long columns. At the head of each company rode the commanding officer.

Harry had to stop. He could not cross until the columns had passed by. His impatience was of an eruptive quality. Princess Irena had been alone for hours and God knows who might have recognized her if she had been wandering about. She would be waiting for him now, looking for him. He stood on the pavement, hemmed in by the people of Belgrade, and the Germans, their faces expressionless, came marching through. Momentarily, Harry's impatience was mitigated by the drama of the spectacle.

They marched down the Balkanska with precision, still governed by years of incomparable discipline. They were great-coated, their rifles slung. Beneath their steel helmets their eyes were like dark shadows. They marched in faultless step, each battalion going by in companies, and towards the west. As soldiers, thought Harry, they had no superiors. Their officers rode looking straight ahead, aloof to the citizens of Belgrade and to the implications of their retreat from this Serbian capital. They had helped the Austrians to capture it and hold it. It could be held no longer.

The people became silent. It was a silence that was impressive, that was almost a tribute to the soldiers of Kaiser Wilhelm. The Germans did not look like defeated men, they were not departing like defeated men, and no Serbian with any sense would spit at even the most insignificant of them. The company machine-gunners would execute a streetful of people in return.

A number of policemen lined the route of the march, but except for the steady, rhythmic tramp of booted feet it was a silent and completely undemonstrative event on both sides. Harry looked on with emotions of his own. In one way or another he had been up against men of this kind for four years. He knew what they were like. More or less, they were all like Major Carlsen.

There was a break as the rearguard of a column passed him. Horse-drawn transport was following on, but fifty yards away. He heard the sound most familiar to him, that of rolling gun carriages. There were no policemen to hold him back and he slipped across the road while it was clear. The station was not far and he reached it without incident. After the quietness the noise here was deafening. Standing trains were letting off steam and most of the platforms seemed to be choked with Austrian or German troops. Not every soldier was marching. Civilians were besieging booking offices and station officials. Hundreds of people had been slipping out of the city for days. This evening it looked as if hundreds more had decided to follow. Serbian women who had married Austrian or German soldiers were waving papers at clerks, officials and even porters, demanding their right to a place on a train.

Harry thought the prospects of getting to Trieste must be pretty slim. He thought the prospects of making the journey by road even slimmer. Transport of any kind would be at a premium, many of the roads would be swarming, and he frankly did not fancy the wildness of Croatia, or some of its more medieval reception committees, except from the security of the railroad. The greater part of the journey to Trieste would be through the country of the Croats, and although it was under the administration of Austria, the crumbling nature of the Habsburg Empire now was an encouragement to Croatian insurgents and irregulars.

He detached himself from the worst of the press. Irena had to be able to see him. He prepared himself for the possibility of having to search for her, feeling that after all these hours she might have engaged herself in a tête-à-tête situation with someone simply to relieve her boredom. There were times when nothing could hold a woman back from a companionable dialogue.

As he scoured the eastern side of the station with slightly anxious eyes a gloved hand touched his arm.

'Thank goodness,' said a soft, warm voice, 'I've been looking for you until my eyes hurt.'

He felt immensely relieved to see her. His responsibility to get her safely to England was not a risky adventure any more, it was, because of Michalides, something that had become a compulsive necessity. There she was in her brown hat, half-veil and dark coat, looking quite cool and lovely against the shuffling, surging background of the noisy station. He drew her into the entrance of a closed station shop.

'I couldn't leave before dark,' he said, 'Michalides and his men had their noses all over the place.'

'They came back?'

'Yes. And then they were prowling about.'

'But you have given them the slip?' She was earnest.'

'I hope so.'

'You are very clever,' she said. Then came a soft rush of words. 'Oh, I'm so glad you're here, it's been hours, and I did not like feeling so alone after being so well protected.'

'Well, I swore all those oaths,' smiled Harry, 'so I had to get here. Otherwise you'd have thought me an advertisement for hot air.'

'Oh? What is an advertisement for hot air?' She was sure it was amusing, she wished to be amused. It had been such a long wait, such a relief to see him in the end. She did not want to be responsible for something terrible happening to him.

'Oh, hot air just means talking for the sake of it,' said Harry. 'You haven't said, is there a train to Trieste?'

'Yes. It's supposed to leave in an hour. I have tickets. Do you know, I have been quite clever again, I think. I have been hiding myself in the office of the senior Austrian transport officer here. He was very charming but a little curious. I think perhaps he felt my face was familiar in some way.' She did not look as if that had worried her. She laughed a little, her mood reflecting her relief. Her qualities of courage and resilience, her charm, her vulnerability and her little lapses into hauteur, were growing on him. She looked warm and alive at this moment. 'You are listening?' she said.

'Of course. About how clever you've been.'

'Yes? It was, don't you think, to keep out of the way in the railway offices with the Austrians? And although the officer thought my face was familiar, he did not hold it against me. So we have tickets, you see, and he will see that we have seats too.'

'Well done,' said Harry.

'Yes?' She was pleased. She looked at the case he held. 'Oh, that is smaller than I thought it was, but you have most of my clothes in it?'

'I'm sorry, no,' he said, 'I managed all your undergarments but–'

'But my clothes, my brown costume!' She was agitated. 'You have never dared to leave me with only the things I stand up in!'

'I put your costume in,' he said.

'Oh,' she said and sighed with new relief.

'And these,' he said. In the recess of the shop entrance they were apart from the mob and he pulled a small knotted handkerchief from his pocket. It was one of her own and the knot was tight and secure. He handed it to her. She felt the small shifting heap of stones it contained. Her eyes widened and she flushed.

'Captain Phillips–'

'I felt you were worried about that costume,' he said, 'and as I might have had to get rid of the case I thought I'd better investigate. They were sewn into the skirt hem, they're all there, as far as I know, fifty-two of them. Is that the right number?'

'Yes,' she said, closing her gloved hand over the tiny bundle.

'You must keep them with you, don't sew them back unless you're going to wear the costume permanently. You never know when we might have to run for it and leave everything behind. Are there any other stones?'

She did not know what to say for a moment.

'Oh, I'm sorry,' she said, 'I should have trusted you and told you about them. But I was not to know you would be as intelligent as that, was I? I've not always heard the most flattering things about British officers. You are quite a pleasant surprise.'

'Really?' Under his peaked blue cap Harry raised his eyebrows. 'I never apply generalizations to individuals myself. If I did I'd never have taken this job on.'

'Please?' She wanted clarification.

'Well, I've always heard that Balkan princesses spend most of their time screaming their heads off and scratching their maids into shreds. I thought this simply couldn't be true of all of them and it isn't.'

'I should think not,' said Irena hotly, 'it's a shameful lie, an odious slander and it isn't true of any of them.'

'Are there any other stones?' asked Harry again.

'Yes.' She put the knotted handkerchief deep into her handbag. 'But not in any of my other clothes, only some sewn into the hem of this coat I have on. And I have one or two pearls in a little pot of face cream in my handbag. They–'

'I'm only concerned to know I left none behind,' said Harry.

'But I am concerned to tell you what I have,' she said, a little distressed. 'They are all I've brought, everything else I've had to leave.'

'I don't think you'll be poor,' said Harry and smiled. 'Have you had something to eat?'

'Yes, I went to that cafe where we had coffee this morning, they were serving *riblja corba* and there was a little bread to eat with it. Something is wrong?' She was aware that he wasn't looking at all pleased with her. 'Oh, you're wondering about *riblja corba?* That is only fish soup, it isn't dangerous–'

'You went wandering about, and to that cafe of all places? When? How long ago?' The station was a hubbub of sound and movement. Harry was oblivious of it.

'About an hour,' said Irena, 'but what does it matter? Why are you looking so fierce?'

'Why? Why?' Harry wondered almost helplessly if she knew what she was saying. Her casual indifference to the threat posed by Michalides would have been admirable if it hadn't been suicidal. She knew flight from her enemies was necessary, but apparently she wasn't going to realize just how necessary until they were standing her up against the wall on a cold dawn. 'Were you trying to walk into their arms?' he asked. 'Didn't I tell you Michalides would be going to that cafe?'

'You did say something but not quite that,' she said. She became cool, as she always did when he was treating her like this. 'I wish you would not speak to me as if I were ten years old.'

He wanted to tell her not to behave as if she were, but he didn't. He knew he would sound arrogant and presumptuous, and he probably would be. She was not an ordinary young woman. In her position the cold hard facts of life would be kept from her. Now she was out in the cold hard world. No one could expect her to behave as ordinary people would.

'I'm sorry,' he said, 'but I didn't have time to give you the full story, although I thought I did say enough to make you understand you weren't to go wandering about, you were to stay here.'

'I was not wandering about, I went to find something to eat.'

'Yes. All right,' he said. 'Anyway, it's done now, and obviously you didn't see Michalides. But I wonder if he saw you?'

'Of course not.' Her eyes flashed at him through her veil. 'He would have dragged me off if he had.'

'Yes, if he could have got away with it. Well, we can't be sure he didn't spot you and follow you.' Harry regarded her with a little severity. 'You do realize that, don't you?'

'Oh, you are an old fuss,' said Irena. Then she smiled. 'I suppose you are right, but are you sure we must leave? It's going to be crowded on the train and whether it will ever get to Trieste no one knows. Really, I should not at all mind taking the risk of staying here for a few days longer and leaving when things are quieter.'

Harry surveyed the teeming station. The roar of steam and the din of troops and civilians rose like shock waves to rebound from the vaulted roof.

'Things aren't going to get quieter for weeks,' he said, 'and if we stay here a mountain of trouble will fall on you. We must catch that train.'

She hesitated, then gave the slightest of shrugs.

'Very well. You are in command, Captain Phillips.'

'Look here, I don't mean to be bumptious,' said Harry.

'What is bumptious? You are very firm, that's all. Firmness is necessary with funny Balkan princesses, isn't it? I should not think much of you if you dithered and dallied. That is right, dithered and dallied?'

'Nearly right. You should say dillied, not dithered.'

'Well, nearly right is quite good, isn't it?' She was smiling again. 'Shall we see if the train is in?'

'Idiots,' said Michalides, and not for the first time. His mood was blacker than his beard. It was cold outside the apartment block and they had already spent a chilly time on the fourth floor trying to break into the vacated flat.

'I protest,' said Palichek.

'I share his protest,' said Dimitroff, 'and you have done all the talking, you have sown all the seed. Now you blame us for a barren harvest.'

'But to let him get away when there were two of you, what could have been more idiotic?' said Michalides coldly.

'Bad luck is an impartial pest,' said Palichek, 'it attacks the wise as well as the foolish. It's no good using hard words, comrade. You did no better than we did, going all the way to that cafe and finding nothing.'

'That was a stone that couldn't be left unturned,' said Michalides. 'But a moment, my friends, before we quarrel. Let me think.' He did think. He was capable of very clinical analyses. He came to a conclusion with a gleam in his eye. 'Of course! He has run, and in running he's confirmed what we all suspect.'

'What do we all suspect?' asked Dimitroff, hands in his pockets and his jacket collar turned up.

'Why, that Irena of Moldavia, the she-puppet of the Kaiser, is running with him. Ah, that slippery fox. Why else did he go? To get to her before we did. To go off with her. To cheat us of her. We were making life too uncomfortable for him, we were getting too close to her. He'll not come back here. He's acting for others, my friends. He'll get her out of Belgrade, take her to England and deposit her in the comforting laps of the royal family there. Ah, these cursed royals, thinking more of each other than their countries. It's burglary, I tell you. They're robbing the Rumanian people of their right to hang her.'

'If we catch her,' said Palichek, 'we Serbians will be proud to hang her for you. No one can say we're given to fiddling about when there's a people's account to be squared.'

'Ah, the flames of justice,' said Dimitroff.

'No, that might cause unnecessary dissatisfaction,' said Michalides. 'We Rumanians are a jealous people and like to square our own accounts.'

'It's good to know you're not too jealous to allow us to help,' said Dimitroff with his tongue in his cheek.

'Believe me,' said Michalides generously, 'we couldn't do without it.' He said nothing about their lack of imagination. They were Serbian gift horses and he had to make the best use of them he could. 'Now, my friends, our slippery pair won't go back to Bucharest, that's certain. They'll head west, with the retreating Germans. Our talkative Englishman will risk the Germans rather than us. You may rely on it, he's been ordered to help our plump royal partridge escape us, and if I know her she's already twisting him around her little finger.'

'I'd not call her plump,' said Palichek, 'not from her pictures.'

'From her pictures,' said Dimitroff, 'I'd say she was so-so.' And he used his hands to describe a rounded figure and a slender waist.

'Well, she'll hang as good as the plump ones and dance better than most,' said Michalides. 'No more time must be lost. Get your friends to watch every road and every train. They'll try to get out of Belgrade tonight or, at the latest, tomorrow. Trains are difficult, but he'll use that slippery talk of his and she'll use her sugary smile. Every station must be visited.'

'This is work for our comrades,' said Palichek, 'but many of them have their own pigeons to trap, their own business to see to. We are after our own traitors, Comrade Michalides. It's not possible to find enough of our friends to watch every road and every station.'

'We shall lose her!' Michalides, about to jump into the cab that had been standing by, turned fiercely on the Serbians. His beard bristled.

'No, we shall get her,' said Dimitroff, 'there'll be enough of us, comrade. We have friends who'll be glad to stay up all night looking for her. I know someone who could find a lost leaf in an autumn forest.'

'Ah, that's what makes good comrades of some friends,' said Michalides as they settled themselves in the swaying cab.

'We're all ready to serve,' said Palichek. He produced, in the most natural way, a long-bladed knife with a finely tapered point. He caressed it. 'If there is trouble in bringing her back, comrade?'

'Naturally, she must not be spoiled,' said Michalides, 'but you may slice him up if it's necessary. Forgive me for raising my voice a moment ago, but we Rumanians are a serious people in matters of this kind.'

'We Serbians don't joke much, either,' said Dimitroff.

Chapter Seven

There was only one passenger coach available to civilians on the Trieste train. The other two coaches were for German officers. The rest of the train was made up of freight cars and waggons, carrying German troops, stores, horses and guns. Harry and Irena were in a compartment managing to seat ten. As she had suspected, the journey was not going to be one of comfort and joy. She resigned herself to it without complaint, however, which Harry thought both sensible and advisable. An uncomfortable train ride was preferable to the uncompromising finality of losing her lovely head.

As railway officials channelled privileged ticket-holders into the right coach and right compartments, Irena sat in squashed contact with a window. Next to her was a large man with a hot body and a worried frown. Troubled by the circumstances which were forcing him to leave Belgrade, he sat brooding and overweight, his right side compressing Irena, his left burdening his small wife. Irena's eyes sought Harry's in appeal. Discomfort was one thing, smothering was another. Harry saw her crushed look. It was not what she was used to at all. He smiled a little. Irena could hardly believe it. He was laughing at the way she was being squeezed to death? She flashed a withering look. He leaned forward from his seat opposite her and tapped the man on the knee. The man gave a start of heavy flesh and his jowls quivered. His little wife stared anxiously.

'*Ja?*' he said.

Irena took it up.

'Do you mind if places are changed?' she said. An irresistible smile followed.

'Changed?' The large man had other things on his mind.

'Please, everyone stand,' said Irena as if she had been rearranging crowded train compartments all her life, and nine people rose to their feet, including Harry, who wanted to laugh at her audacity. She herself remained seated. The door slid back at that moment, an official said, 'There, this is the best I can do for you,' and a girl appeared. She had a mass of black hair, a breathless, eager look, and was dressed in a warm woollen costume of dark red with a matching hat.

'Go away, we are full!' cried the large man's wife. But the girl was like a quick cat among shuffling pigeons. She was darting while others were trying, for no reason at all, to change seats. Irena seized Harry's wrist and jerked him down beside her.

'Where is your initiative?' she hissed in French.

'I rarely use it on mere social occasions,' murmured Harry.

The girl had whipped into the seat he had vacated opposite Irena, and other people, quickly recovering from their moment of induced hypnosis, were falling back into theirs. This alleviated the confusion but did not cure it completely. The little wife was kicking and scratching on behalf of her large husband, who was doing his slow, bear-like best for her and his ponderous best for himself. No one said a word, muttered exclamations of incomprehension were as far as anyone went. It was all over quite soon, a brief Slavonic dance which never achieved rhythm. It left the large man seatless. The cause of the dance, Irena, had not moved at all. She now sat with a cool, pleased look on her face. Harry next to her was far more acceptable than the big man, far less overwhelming. The latter now loomed enormously out of place, and was embarrassed as well as worried. His wife sighed in sympathy for him. There was simply nowhere he could sit, it was impossible to make room for his bulk. He mumbled, accepted defeat, slid back the door and took up a position in the corridor.

'He'll be better there,' said his wife sagely, 'he can walk up and down. He has all his worries.'

Other passengers nodded. Everyone had their worries, including three young Serbian women married to Austrian soldiers. They were going to Zagreb and then north to Austria. There were two hard-faced men who had policed Belgrade for the Austrians and wished to put as much distance as possible between themselves and Serbia. And there was a quiet-looking man who used his eyes more than his tongue.

'It's a bad time,' said one of the Serbian women, and they all began to talk then, the women. Women have an exceptional ability to communicate. It is often better, as poets of old imply, not to silence a woman with kisses but to let her talk on until man's love and woman's conversation achieve a confluence, flowing and uninterrupted.

Harry thought about it and smiled, then let it go over his head. He sat back. A gloved hand slid inside his arm.

'This is much better,' whispered Irena, 'I should have suffocated or caught fire with that stout man next to me.'

'Well, you've very successfully resolved that problem,' said Harry. He could not afford to play any role but the accepted one with Irena. Anything not strictly related to the object of the exercise was to be avoided. Not that he was likely to fall in love with her. Princesses who had haughty moods would make errand boys of any men senseless enough to fall in love with them. And he wanted to have an absolutely straightforward story to tell Elisabeth. Elisabeth deserved straightforwardness. 'I wonder if we'll get to Trieste?' he murmured. The train, full of noises, thumps and bangs, seemed in no hurry even to start.

'Oh, nothing is easier to you,' she said a little coolly, for she was quite aware of his lack of response to her friendliness, 'you would get a three-legged elephant to the top of Everest as long as it didn't argue with you.'

Harry wondered if a three-legged elephant would be any more manageable than a highly individualistic princess. He did not put the question but the thought of doing so made him smile.

'You beast,' she whispered, 'you have just thought of something horrid to say.'

'No, I've just thought I shan't feel comfortable until this train has taken us out of Belgrade. I feel it's standing around waiting for our friends to jump aboard. We're doing the obvious thing, being aboard ourselves.'

'Well, it is your idea,' she said. They were whispering in French.

The girl in the dark red costume and woollen hat was giving Harry shy, quick glances. Irena did not miss this or the fact that the girl had decided Harry was the one with whom she would most like to converse. Was he the best-looking? She glanced at the other men, then at Harry in profile. He had a good profile, firm mouth and thick lashes for a man. Irena felt a strange little tug at her heart. The girl was waiting to pounce, to engage him. Breathless, eager girls, once they pounced and attached themselves to a man, clung like rustling ivy. Irena's gloved hand was still inside Harry's arm and she kept it there to discourage any outside overtures. They could not afford to pick up unshakeable acquaintances.

Suddenly whistles shrilled. The loaded train vibrated and began to pull slowly out of the station. At which the girl said excitedly to Harry, 'Are we going, do you think?' She spoke in Serbo-Croatian, which sounded like garbled Greek to him. The silent man looked across at her, mildly disgusted that anyone could ask so unnecessary a question.

Harry said, 'Pardon, mademoiselle?'

'Oh, you are French?' Leaning forward, whispering the words in French, she invited his confidential response. A Slav, she seemed like all of them to have a natural interest in anything remotely conspiratorial or out of the ordinary. A Frenchman on a train full of German soldiers was very out of the ordinary.

Harry leaned forward too and just as earnestly whispered, 'I am Russian.'

'Russian?' She breathed in little intakes. 'Oh, you have been through the fire of revolution and felt its heat? It was awesome?'

'Hot,' whispered Harry in confidence, while Irena from behind her veil eyed the girl extremely coolly. 'And noisy. People running about, and everyone shouting and shooting night and day. One could not get to sleep.'

'Oh?' The girl seemed a trifle perplexed, as if a mundane complaint instead of a great revelation would hardly make sense to anybody. Then she became very shy and confused, for no one else was saying a word now, all eyes were on her and this resolute-looking Russian. She sat back. Irena applied a pinch to Harry's arm, a warning not to get involved with an obvious chatterbox. The girl, aware that everyone was looking and waiting for more, said breathlessly, 'Well, he's a Russian, think of it.'

'A Bolshevik?' gasped the little wife, turning pale. 'You are a Bolshevik?' the girl asked Harry.

'Certainly not.' Irena interrupted coldly. 'He's a friend of some relatives of mine in Galicia. Do you think a friend of relatives of mine would be a Bolshevik?'

'Oh, no,' said the girl. 'He's not a Bolshevik,' she informed the little wife. There were sighs. Things were bad enough as it was without the problem posed by the presence of a Russian Red. The girl remarked that she had heard the worst Bolsheviks ate babies.

'Not their own?' cried the little wife, eyes dilated.

'Oh, no,' said the girl reassuringly, 'it would only be aristocratic ones.'

'Rubbish,' said the mostly silent man.

'It's not rubbish,' said the girl.

Contemptuously the man said, 'What are you saying, that the aristocratic ones taste better?' He turned away, obviously impatient of the foolishness of people.

Arguments began, arguments about the character of Bolsheviks, about their aims and whether any political party had the right to take a people into civil war. The girl leaned forward to talk to Harry again.

'They're discussing Russian revolutionaries,'

she said with an air of intimacy.

'Not a peaceful subject, mademoiselle,' said Harry.

Irena was icy. The girl was blatantly making up to Harry, her shy eagerness a foil for her boldness. An utter minx, thought Irena. The girl smiled at her. Irena responded with a glint of white teeth. The three Serbian women resumed their own kind of conversation. The quiet man's slightly moody eyes contemplated them with dislike. The train rattled, running slowly out of the western environs of Belgrade to feel its way into the night. The girl said she was glad it was making up its mind.

Irena glanced at Harry again. He seemed relaxed, a half-smile on his face as the girl fed him trivial comments. It was obvious to Irena that the creature was dying to become his best friend. The world was growing up but surely it would never be proper for an unchaperoned girl on a train to behave with anything but modesty.

The coaches and waggons gathered momentum behind the engine, couplings rattled and wheels bit firmly as the train stretched to run at speed. It passed over the last series of points and steamed into the dark mouth of the night. It entered Croatia-Slovenia, annexed by the Habsburg Empire decades ago. The three Serbian women were visibly relaxed, glad to feel they were well on their way and leaving the mounting hostility of relatives in Belgrade, for in marrying Austrian soldiers they had committed the unforgivable social sin. They chattered freely. The two ex-policemen smoked and disappeared behind the clouds they emitted, the little woman made fluttering signals to her husband outside the door and the quiet man behaved himself, closing his eyes to rest in peace.

No one expected the train to stop at St Pazova, only at Zagreb. But it did stop, pulling up with a smooth application of the brakes and the sound of metal yielding to stern compulsion. Waiting to board were about fifty German soldiers, an officer and, it seemed, several black-clad peasant women. Harry leaned and peered. Under the light of makeshift oil lamps the soldiers began to move, gestured on by the officer. He was immaculate in greatcoat and cap. He was a man easy to recognize, despite the inadequacy of the station lamps. He was Major Carlsen. Harry looked at Irena, sitting next to the window. She had seen the major too. She met Harry's glance, gave him the faintest of smiles and a little shrug. Behind the veil her eyes were darkly brown.

The German soldiers boarded. Major Carlsen waited by the door of the second coach. The peasant women edged nervously and anxiously forward. The major turned and with a gesture of finely edged mockery bowed slightly to indicate they should precede him. They rushed past him, his presence and his manner agitating and confusing them, and climbed up into the coach. Harry got up and went into the corridor. There were several people sitting on their belongings. The large man was sitting on the floor, still brooding. Major Carlsen entered the corridor from the other coach, wrinkling his nose a little at the earthy odour of the peasant women preceding him. He was ushering them forward. They were all in thick black dresses, black headscarves covered their hair and their black boots were tarnished and streaked with the dried grey earth of their fields. They looked confused and lost, the more so when confronted with the obstacle of people. Major Carlsen called to them and they stopped their rustling, crowded advance. He slid back the door of the first compartment, occupied by a senior Austrian railway official who was dining alone and in comfort on a bottle of wine and a precious piece of cold sausage.

Harry, at his end of the corridor, heard the major say something, then he saw him turn to the peasant women, who looked from behind a little like elongated crows with broad beams. The major's courtesy was still edged with a subtle shade of mockery as he gestured them into the compartment. They sidled in awkwardly, six of them, eyes lowered, simple women whose existence was governed by the basic tenets of survival. They filled the compartment, they overflowed as they sat with their clothes voluminously occupying space their bodies did not require. The Austrian official, discomfited and disgusted, took his wine and sausage and beat a retreat under the uncompromising grey eyes of Major Carlsen. The major bowed to the women, closed the door and turned his attention on the people littering the corridor. He saw Harry then. The two observed each other from the opposite ends of the corridor. The major stared in surprise and cold disapproval. He moved, stopping to ask abrupt questions of the human obstacles. Answers came nervously, were received expressionlessly. He reached Harry as the train gathered speed again. He glanced into the compartment before speaking. He saw Irena. She made no sign.

'Who are you?' He asked the question of Harry in German.

Harry, understanding it was for local consumption, asked in French what was required of him. The large man had got up and was trying bulkily to make little of himself.

'Your papers.' The major's French was crisp. Harry produced his documents and the major inspected them. 'Come with me,' he said. Harry followed him back down the swaying corridor, stepping over legs. The major passed the compartment full of black-clad peasant women and went through to the next coach. Two German soldiers stood outside the first compartment. They saluted the major and stepped aside. He slid back the door and entered. Harry walked in after him. The major closed the door. He turned to Harry.

'Are you disobeying orders, Captain Phillips?'

'Orders?'

'You understand me, I think.' The major was frowning, dissatisfied. 'What are you doing here?'

'Going to Trieste,' said Harry, 'it's pressure of circumstances. And look here, I'd like to know what you're up to, Major. I've had the devil of a job getting as far as this, and it seems to me you could have done just as well with no bother at all. Damn it, you were in Belgrade this morning taking coffee with your problem princess–'

'You will oblige me, Captain, by not referring

to Her Highness in your music-hall terms.'

'I can't not call her a problem,' said Harry. 'You were in mufti, by the way. Is there anything you think you should tell me?'

'Sit down,' said the major. They both sat. 'Yes, I saw Her Highness and naturally I spoke to her. The fact that I was not in uniform was merely to do with confidential orders I received. They did not concern you or Her Highness. You must remember I was able to control events only up to a certain point, I told you that you were more of a free agent than I was. It was impossible because of that for me to accompany Princess Irena to Belgrade or anywhere else. I'm on my way to Zagreb now because of new orders and our meeting on this train is a coincidence.'

'But very fortuitous,' said Harry, watching his man with interest, 'you can take her over now, can't you?'

'Impossible,' said the major flatly, 'and outside the terms of our agreement. Are you forgetting those terms? You are on your honour, I think, to look after the princess and get her to England. I could not accomplish that. May I now point out that you were advised to stay in Belgrade?'

'I was also advised to use my initiative,' said Harry. The compartment shook a little as the train rattled and swayed. 'A man called Michalides and a couple of his comrades were squeezing us in Belgrade. Do you know Michalides?'

The major's eyes flickered. 'I know him,' he said.

'He traced us to that apartment, he was on to us from the moment we left you.' Harry was as crisp as the major. 'That was rather too obvious, that waiting cab, wasn't it? Michalides was waiting with it. But you know all about that, the princess told you when you spoke to her at the cafe this morning.'

'I was not aware they had traced you to the apartment.' Major Carlsen showed a faint line of worry.

'No, that happened later.'

'I am concerned. This man Michalides, he saw her there?'

'No. We knew he was on his way and I had her out of the place before he arrived.'

'Captain Phillips,' said the major with relief, 'it is good to know you can make your moves quickly.'

'You make yours mysteriously,' said Harry.

'No.' The major shook his head. 'My moves are entirely governed by the decisions of my superiors. We agreed you might have to act according to developments. Had you remained undiscovered in Belgrade you could have waited until we had evacuated Serbia and withdrawn from Croatia. Then you could have travelled to Trieste. Instead you are travelling with our troops all round you and that is dangerous, Captain. The slightest suspicion that you aren't what you claim to be and they will shoot you. I should regret that.'

'No more than I would,' said Harry.

'However, the princess's one chance is still with you,' said Major Carlsen emphatically, 'therefore kindly remain alive. She is taking things well?'

'Remarkably well. She's the coolest young lady

I've ever met. I suppose she's conditioned to present a calm royal front whatever the circumstances. Even so, she's still remarkable. Personally, when I'm in a blue funk I want to go and lie down.'

Major Carlsen smiled.

'I think you will survive,' he said.

'Will I? I had to face up to Michalides and two of his cut-throats in that apartment, and I've a feeling they were measuring my neck for the same rope they're saving for her. I told Michalides I knew nothing about her. He knew I was lying. We had to get out. That's why we're here.'

'We must hope,' said the major, 'that you've left him foxed.'

'Let's hope he's not on this train,' said Harry, 'because I'm damn sure he isn't foxed. All we've done is to slip him for the time being.'

'I still have confidence in you,' said Major Carlsen, 'and so, I'm sure, has Her Royal Highness.'

'I haven't lost her yet,' said Harry, 'but there's still time. Tell me, who are all those women who came on the train with you?'

'Unfortunately,' said the major, 'they were foolish enough to appear on the roads in their market cart, and the roads are full of our troops, who are short of transport and food. The carts contained fruit and vegetables. Everything was commandeered. It's a conventional necessity of war. The women came wailing to the station hours ago, not wishing to walk many miles home. I did what I could for them, as you saw. I even gave them seats which some of my men should have had. I hope, when you reach England, you will feel able to tell your newspapers that not all Germans cook peasant women and eat them.'

'Oh, glad to, Major,' said Harry. 'Are they going all the way to Zagreb?'

'No. We shall stop at Vrycho. You had better rejoin Her Highness. I will do what I can to look after you while I'm on the train, but my orders take me only as far as Zagreb. Now that you are on the train I advise you to stay on it.'

They stood up. Harry said, 'I wonder why the devil I let you get me into this?'

The major said, 'In times like these, Captain Phillips, would you really prefer to be sitting on your backside? No. Please give my felicitations to Her Highness.'

When Harry returned to the compartment everyone began asking questions, except Irena. Irena knew she could not get the right answers until they were alone. And the quiet man dourly asked only for a little peace.

The girl in dark red was eager to know what had happened.

'It was all because I'm a Russian,' explained Harry in his correct French, 'and the German officer wanted to know whether I was a good one or a bad one.'

'He thought perhaps you were a bad one, a Bolshevik?' she asked excitedly.

Harry laughed and shook his head, and the girl informed the other passengers that he had safely survived severe interrogation.

Irena wondered if the age of naivety was not for

a girl the sweetest and most satisfying. The innocence and faith and hope of youth filled one's life with perfect images, everything was beautiful or could be made beautiful. When one was twenty-one, as she was, one had grown up and could no longer run barefooted through the grass and dance in the dew. There was decorum to be considered. And at sixteen one did not mind wet feet as one minded them at twenty-one.

She sighed. Really, she had accomplished nothing beyond her climb out of blissful adolescence. Except that she had met Major Helmut Carlsen, an ingenious and fearless German officer, and Captain Harry Phillips of the British army, in the strangest possible circumstances. She did not think that Major Carlsen had ever suffered the awkwardness of boyish adolescence, and Captain Phillips had come of age long ago as far as attitudes were concerned, she thought. But he wasn't cynical, even though he had fought in this terrible war. It was making so many other people very cynical and intolerant, willing to listen to no views which did not coincide with their own. She thought Captain Phillips still had faith in some things, even if only in the ridiculousness of people. Of course, he was as masculine as most men, thinking that making women do as they were told was the same thing as protecting them. She must not let him speak to her as if she were not a princess. That would never do. It would make Major Carlsen frown.

It was frustrating not to be able to talk to him about the major, but nothing serious could have come up between him and the German or he would have communicated a warning note of some kind to her.

The night passed slowly, the train chugging over its iron road, surmounting gorge and river and snaking around the hills of Slavonia. People brought out what food they had. The little wife went out to join her worried husband in the corridor. Harry extracted the food he had packed. It wasn't much. Too hungry to ration the small amount, he and Irena finished it up. They drank wine from the bottle, then passed it round.

Heads began to nod. The steamed-up windows hid the night. The dour man went to sleep. The Serbian women dozed off. Irena's head tipped slowly sideways and came to rest on Harry's shoulder. A small tired sigh escaped her. She moved and cuddled his arm, tucking herself close, and drifted into a series of catnaps. The girl in the dark red suit smiled a little enviously, closed her eyes and relaxed. The petite wife shared the discomfort of the corridor for a while with her husband, then sneaked back into the compartment to leave him wondering what had gone wrong with his life when he had been such a good servant to the Austrian authorities in Belgrade.

Dawn came greyly, fingering the windows uncertainly until the shadows left by night had cleared from the sky and slipped from the clouds. The train was steaming through the wild and rugged terrain of Croatia. The valleys, the gorges and the heights created a spectacular extravagance of nature in its most bizarre mood. Neither road nor track could be seen, neither sheep nor goats.

Passengers got up to exercise stiff limbs in the corridors. The train began to slow down. It was moving over the tracked road cut from the face of the hill, which rose on the left and sloped down on the right. Climbing the long gentle gradient, it did not take long to come to a stop. The contact of buffers between coaches and waggons produced a harsh, grinding ripple of noise that startled the silence of the thickly wooded slopes. Hollow echoes rolled around the cloudy sky. Steam hissed.

Harry wondered if the stop was to allow the peasant women to alight, but it was hardly likely in country as wild as this. Major Carlsen had mentioned a place called Vrycho. This wasn't Vrycho, this was nowhere. God had made it and then forgotten it. To the right, on the other side of the green and brown canyon, hills rose, bleakly forbidding. The quietness, the lack of any sound apart from the hiss of steam, was uncanny.

'Why are we stopping?' The girl who liked to ask questions and exchange glances made the enquiry of Harry. Really, thought Irena, why doesn't she ask me? I am as wise about it as he is.

'Yes, why, I wonder?' said Harry.

'I am Nadia,' said the girl, smiling. The moody man came to and gave her a look which plainly told her there had been far more earth-shattering news items than that during the course of history.

'I'm Sergius,' said Harry, 'and my friend is Helga.' That was the name, Helga Strasser, which Major Carlsen had given to her in her faked Austrian documents.

The girl seemed enchanted. Irena smiled. The train stayed locked to the hillside.

'If you'll excuse us,' said Irena, 'Sergius and I will go and find out what is happening.'

'I'll go with him if you like,' offered the girl, 'there's no need for you to trouble.'

'It's no trouble,' said Irena sweetly, 'and you must rest, you look tired. One can have a bad night on trains.' She got up, saying to Harry, 'Let's go and ask some questions.' They left the compartment, the quiet man looking as if peace would never happen unless people stopped walking and talking.

The train was a motionless, grey-coated centipede of iron, the slopes thick with trees and bush that never stirred. Irena thought the moment justified a call on Major Carlsen, and since Harry thought that if anyone knew the reason for stopping at such a spot as this it would be the German, he accompanied her along the corridor. It wasn't easy. They had to step over huddled bodies, Irena not wanting to ask tired people to move. She whispered to Harry.

'That girl, don't encourage her, she's the kind one never gets rid of.'

'I know,' he said, 'but it might be useful to make a few friends here and there.'

Major Carlsen appeared, frowning. He looked into the compartment housing the peasant women, then glanced up to see Irena and Harry. He turned abruptly and returned to the next coach. The two German soldiers were still policing the corridor. The major held back the door of his compartment, nodded to Irena and Harry and joined them as they went in and sat down. He gave Irena a courteous but formal smile, as much as he would concede in acknowledgement of her under these circumstances.

'What's holding us up?' asked Harry.

'I've sent some men forward to find out,' said the major. He peered through the window at the tree-infested slopes that rose on the left of the train. It was then that hidden rifles opened up. The unchallengeable silence broke. Whining bullets began to pepper the coaches and waggons. Lead thudded into woodwork, smashed through glass and smacked against steel. Windows splintered and shattered. Women shrieked. In every compartment passengers flung themselves to the floor or threw themselves into the corridor, which overlooked the descent to the foothills. Irena heard Harry shout and she tumbled from her seat and went to ground with him, Major Carlsen flat beside her.

'We're ambushed,' said the major in cold fury. The enfilading rifle fire lessened and he cautiously lifted his head. He saw some of them, dark figures flitting from tree to tree, moving downwards.

'Who the devil would ambush us?' asked Harry, taking a look for himself.

'Croatian irregulars, brigands and thieves,' said Major Carlsen. 'The beginning of our retreat from Serbia is one of the moments they've been waiting for.' He ducked down as bullets whistled and struck the outside coachwork with sharp coughs. 'They're after whatever they can get, booty, ammunition, weapons and lives. Any lives.

Everyone on this train is expendable, Captain. Everyone. And the train itself, they will ransom it or blow it up.'

'You mentioned nothing like this,' said Harry grimly.

'A hazard of the times, Captain. You should have stayed in Belgrade.'

'We had our own hazards there – look out!' Harry pushed Irena down as the corner window smashed and splinters rained. Two soldiers appeared, thrusting back the door and crouching low. Bullets were screaming into and through the train. One man spoke to Major Carlsen. They had been investigating up front. The engine was unattended, driver and fireman missing. There was no obstacle on the line, no track damage. It looked as if driver and fireman had simply brought the train to a stop and vanished.

'Frightened off or damn well bought off,' said the major, having explained to Harry.

Harry did not like the sound of the rifle fire as it reached a crescendo. It was not the sound of a few rifles, but hundreds. He heard the rumbling sound of heavy waggon doors sliding back, followed by the consoling sound of German troops returning the fire. German officers, trapped in compartments farther down, were shouting orders. Major Carlsen's small complement of troops in this second passenger coach were clearing glass from smashed windows and poking rifles through. But the sweep of bullets, constant now from the hillside, made it risky for a defender to show even the top of his head.

'They're up to something,' said Harry.

'Thank you for that information,' said the major, his sarcasm coldly savage.

'It's a hackneyed old tactic,' said Harry, 'but with enough firepower it always works. They're using a ton of ammunition to pin us down. I think that means a piece of sly old trickery is in the offing. What? I think they're after the engine. They'll uncouple it and immobilize us.'

'Without a driver we are immobilized,' said the major.

'Then somebody please do something,' said Irena, hating the noisy impact of bullets and her proximity to the dusty floor. 'Major Carlsen, you must do something.'

'Yes, I know that,' said the major grimly.

'Go and see,' said Irena, then shuddered as coachwork was gouged and splintered, bullets ripping into the train from end to end.

'I'll go,' said Harry, 'I was once seconded to the Royal Engineers. I can handle a locomotive. But I'll need someone to shovel coal for me. And I think we'll have to hurry.'

Major Carlsen scrambled from the compartment, Harry after him. Irena turned.

'Stay down,' said Harry.

'On this filthy floor? Never,' she said bravely. She thought the noise hideous as the three of them scrambled along the corridor, almost on all fours.

'Go back,' ordered Harry.

Breathless, shaken by the murderous hostility of the constant rifle fire, she gasped, 'What does it matter?'

'Leave her with me,' said the major brusquely,

'take two of my men.' He slid open a compartment door. The peasant women lay in black, shapeless heaps on the floor. The Major went in, flinging himself face down over a seat. He called to a soldier, who tossed his rifle in. The major caught it. He nodded to Harry, he spoke to two of his men. Irena crouched outside the compartment. German troops appeared, pounding down the corridors, thudding an accompaniment to the whining, pulverizing din of bullets. They hurled themselves into compartments and over seats, over huddled passengers, and sighted rifles through shattered windows. Harry kicked, crouched and struggled his way down the corridor.

From the side of the hill, from the trees, the Croats kept up their rain of fire. A man slithered out from behind a tree and came hurtling down the slope. His arm swept back and he flung the stick grenade as he bounded. It came flying and twisting, exploding as it bounced off the roof of the coach. A German sighted. Unhurriedly he picked out the man, now scrambling for cover. He fired twice in rapid succession. The man jerked from the impact of the second bullet and fell back, sliding and tumbling until he plunged into the embrace of a bush. Shots came screaming from his comrades in angry reprisal.

The peasant women were moaning and praying, Major Carlsen was firing and barking orders with every shot. At Harry's heels were two soldiers, one of whom passed him a rifle. He worked his way towards the front of the train. As he passed his own compartment the silent man lifted his head from the floor and looked at him, his expression indicative of his complete disgust with life and people. Harry, ape-like in his crouching advance, went on. The train vibrated with noise, screams mingling with the smack of Croatian bullets and the unequivocal crack of German rifle fire. The subtly confusing sound of muffled lead entering upholstery induced cries and prayers as reverberations rushed through the train like hollow hammerings. The Croatians kept the Germans penned in the waggons and lying flat on the freight cars. Another man chanced his arm, emerging from shelter to leap down the slope and to hurl a grenade. Of the German stick variety, it arced high and fell fast, exploding against the side of a half-open waggon door. Smoke and fragmented metal split and polluted the air.

Harry emerged from the front coach on the far side. He shot back up again as a rifle spat from a point in advance of the engine. A number of men were weaving their way down the line towards the locomotive, and it did not need a psychic genius to pronounce on their intentions. The Germans might have a substitute driver available. Therefore, take away the engine and the immobilized train became a sitting duck.

Harry turned to the two Germans, efficient-looking professionals. Well, for once, he and they were on the same side. He leaned out of the open coach door and pointed. The soldiers leaned out with him and saw the Croats. There were six of them, all carrying rifles and wearing bandoliers of Croatian insurgents. They were advancing along the track, which curved in from the right. There was a seventh man by the side of the track acting as look-out and sniper. He had already had a crack at Harry.

'I'll have to make a dash for it,' said Harry, 'can you keep me covered?' He was too pent-up, too involved with the highly problematical, to think or speak in any language but his own. The Germans looked stumped.

'He's asking you to give him protection so that he can get to the engine,' said a calm, soft voice. Irena was there, speaking in German. 'He will drive the train then. Your officer says he's not to get shot as that would be no help to anyone.'

Harry gave her a look that was grim but admiring. The Germans, impressed by her composure, nodded and moved. One took up a sitting position in the open doorway, the other leaned. Their line of fire was helped by the long bend in the track ahead, which would keep the advancing Croats in view until they were close to the engine. They were coming on cautiously. The lookout man was clearly visible, down on his stomach by the side of the rail. Harry got ready to go and the sitting German opened up. The moving Croats scattered, plunging face down and digging in with teeth and feet. The sniper squinted along his rifle, but a German bullet smacked into a sleeper close by and he dug in too. Harry leapt from the coach and hared towards the engine, the leaning German opening fire now while his comrade reloaded.

The Croats saw Harry and slid their rifles forward. The second German emptied his magazine at them. Harry received cover just long enough to reach the footplate and scramble up. The look-out man had an instant to achieve something. He fired. His bullet pinged against smoke-grimed steel a fraction of a second too late to do more than scorch the cloth of Harry's jacket. He was in the cab, the engine bulk protecting him.

All hell was erupting on his left, the hillside alive with a drumming cannonade of rifle fire, the streams of lead rattling against the train, the returning fire of the Germans from coaches and waggons smacking into hill and trees. The clouds, dark grey now, dulled the scene but enhanced the tiny flashes of fire.

Through the thick glass of the cab window Harry saw the Croats flat on the track some fifty yards away. He heard the whip and crack of bullets from the two Germans, but the Croats were squirming to the left, removing themselves from the line of fire. The lookout, too exposed now, made a dash for cover. A bullet took him in the leg and he pitched beside the track. Harry knew his two Germans could not show themselves on the left side of the train, they would be shot to pieces from the hill. He ran his eyes over the engine controls, over smeared brass and steel. The cab was hot, the fire rumbling. He looked up, saw the six Croats moving well to the left of the track. He leaned out, drew a bead on the foremost man and squeezed the trigger. The rifle cracked, the stock jerking against his shoulder and the sound creating a small, booming echo around the cab. The leading Croat pulled up with a crazy flip of his hips, rolled like a drunk and fell twitching. The others, without cover, fell flat on their faces again.

Harry, resighting, heard someone on the footplate to his right. He swung round. Irena stared at the glinting rifle barrel with enormous eyes.

'My God,' hissed Harry, 'are you mad?'

She came up into the cab and pushed the rifle aside.

'Mad? I? What a thing to say when you were about to blow my head off.' She was a little pale but very self-possessed. 'Give me the rifle. You are to drive the engine and get the train moving.'

Her veil was turned up. He agreed, it did not seem important to hide her face now. Her eyes were dark with obstinacy, her mouth cool but set. The two Germans were still doing their best but the grounded Croats were wriggling closer. They would not stay grounded for long. Whoever was directing the ambush would do something to help them. Insurgents lodged in trees were already turning more attention on the leading coach. Irena put her hand on the rifle.

'Get down,' said Harry, appalled at her presence. The Croats would blast the engine to kingdom come, with her in it, rather than give it up. 'Get down, for God's sake.'

'No, we are sheltered here,' she said, 'and if they do try to hit us they are just as likely to hit their own men. Please, do be practical.' She took the rifle from him. The hills threw back the rattling, cracking cacophony of war. 'I can use this, I am not quite helpless. Please start the engine and leave me to do the shooting.' She moved to the footplate, rested the rifle over iron and sighted it on the men making ground in quick, surging darts. She fired. They plunged flat.

Harry studied the controls again in sweating urgency. The steam was hissing at a reduced rate.

'How the devil does it all work?' he muttered.

Irena, watching the Croats inching forward, said in shock, 'You are saying it's a mystery to you?'

'I took a ride once when I was a boy. Well, damn it, someone has to have a go at it now, it's our only chance. I know there's a valve somewhere and I think the fire's going dead. Ah, what's this?' He pulled out the damper and the fire glowed and leapt into flame. It was a wood-burner. 'Now I'll burst the damn boiler, I suppose.' He fiddled with a brass wheel. He muttered fiercely. Irena closed her ears to his muttering and prayed for a miracle. Bullets began to fly around the engine, pinging and ringing as they struck iron. But she kept her eyes on the Croats. One of the German soldiers appeared, down on the track, using a huge wheel as cover. He fired. She fired. The Croats flattened again but came on, wriggling forward and always farther to the left. Soon she and the German would not be able to see them.

Aware that the engine was coming under fire, Major Carlsen sent more men forward, ordering them to give what cover they could to the man trying to get the train moving. It had to be moved, for there were four or five hundred insurgents in those wooded slopes and they were pressing their attack insistently and savagely. They surged downwards in little rushes, from one belt of trees to the next, in ones and twos, in little groups, coming closer. They had a few grenades, and periodically one rose in a high lob to pitch at an open waggon door, which was promptly slammed shut by the Germans. The explosions as the grenades bounced off the massive sides were shuddering. The threat they posed, together with the sustained rifle fire, bottled the Germans up. Nevertheless, their return fire, spitting from smashed coach windows and half-open waggons, contained the ambush to some extent. The Croats suffered casualties. Dead and wounded lay around trees.

Major Carlsen, icy in his fury, used his borrowed rifle with telling precision, while on the floor the peasant women were moaning, grumbling.

'Mother of God, what of my little ones?' groaned a frightened soul.

'Your little ones aren't here,' said a calmer woman, 'you're in enough trouble without inventing more.'

In her position on the footplate Irena felt like a woman deceived as Harry muttered and fiddled. What was he doing there at all if he couldn't drive the thing? And what was she doing here with him? She squeezed the trigger of the German rifle in a spasm of disgust. The bullet ricocheted off the rail into the arm of a Croat. That, she thought, was not bad for a shot aimed in temper, and hitting a man's arm was better than killing him.

The fire was eating up its fuel. The tender was loaded with logs and there was a supply at the rear of the cab. Harry, imprecations hissing between his teeth, found the brake wheel. That was something. Bullets screamed thick and fast, smacking into steel and rushing overhead. The Croats in front of the train were so close now, getting cover from the hillside, and from the right side of the engine Irena knew the iron monster was about to block them from view. She fixed her last round. The German crouching beside the wheel flung himself forward beside the track.

'Reload!' shouted Harry, wrenching at the brake wheel. Nothing had happened in response to his manipulation of other controls.

'What with?' she shouted back.

The other German was out of the coach. He climbed into the cab and dropped ammunition on the floor. Irena crouched and reloaded while he took on the closing Croats from the exposed side of the engine. Three of them were wounded, four were coming on. The covering fire from the hillside bit into the air around them, and one lifted himself from his worming position and shook his fist at the slopes. Harry saw a stick grenade hanging from the belt of the German soldier. He tapped him on the shoulder and pointed. The man said, *'Ach!'* He grounded his rifle, slipped the grenade free, set the pin and stepped back to lob it over the engine. Whistling bullets rushed. He was struck in the leg. He fell, so did his grenade. Harry went into mad action, ducking and diving to retrieve the live stick bomb. He seized it and swung it loopingly upwards over the roof of the cab. It dropped, keeling and twisting, hitting the earth on the side of the track and bursting like an obscenely giant flower with a red heart and pitted grey-black petals. Shrapnel sprayed. The four Croats, scrambling forward, lunged for the protection of mother earth. The explosion swept them and left one jerking and another shuddering and bloody.

'Oh, this is terrible,' gasped Irena.

'It isn't yet, it could be,' panted Harry and chanced his arm. The hissing steam shrieked. He had found the valve. There was the vibrating sensation of an engine throbbing and alive. Irena turned. He looked at her, the faintest glimmer of hope in his eyes. He manipulated the valve – it did things with the power of the steam. The Croats on the hillside were closer, a swarming barrage of men slipping from cover to cover. The Germans on the train maintained a steady fire and on one flat freight car they were trying to mount a machine gun. Bullets slammed around them and into them.

Irena wondered how long it would be before she and Major Carlsen and Captain Phillips and everyone else on the train were all dead.

She jerked and slewed as the engine suddenly lurched. She gasped. Harry was beginning to smile, his hand on a brass wheel. From the cab floor the wounded German said something. He was obviously living in hope too. Engine wheels began to turn.

'Oh, Harry!' Irena was ecstatic. 'Oh, you wonderful man!'

'Wait,' said Harry, his fixed grin a little fiendish. The engine howled, jerked in tremendous outrage under the hand of a novice, then pulled and strained. Germans crouching behind wheels far down the train sprang to their feet as they felt the vibrations of iron movement. The wheels were turning, slowly, slowly, hideous skids and clashes taking place as Harry manipulated the throttle.

The enormous driving power of steam was awesome.

'God,' he said suddenly. Those Croats, staggering up from the grenade explosion, would be aboard as soon as he drew level with them, and there were others scrambling down the hillside, ignoring the German bullets as they raced towards the slipping, shuddering engine. Harry found the reverse lever. He flung everything to the wind. Brakes were off, wheels in reverse, and the throttle open wide as the Croats charged. The whole train screamed, clanged, boomed and buffeted, but it began to run back down the track. Irena saw the running insurgents recede. From death in close-up they changed to faraway faces of frustration. She sprang up from where she had been clinging and found the shelter of the cab. She laughed in exhilaration.

'We are going, going!' she cried.

'I hope we can stop,' said Harry.

The train thundered back down the gradient in unchecked reverse, the Croats on the hillside pouring fire after it, but it was quickly out of range. It rushed backwards round a long bend, swaying and lurching, and the wounded German skidded over the cab floor. Harry stuck out a leg and brought him to a halt. He apologized in French for his abominable driving.

'*Wunderbar*,' said the German, happy despite his wound.

'We're going rather fast,' said Irena unsteadily as she clung to the rail.

'Well, that'll get us back to a new starting point in nice quick time,' said Harry hopefully.

'You are not going to drive us all back through that ambush again?'

'There's no other way to get to Zagreb,' said Harry. He eased the throttle and felt a little surge of triumph as the revolutions decreased. The gradient became kinder as the hill receded, and the speed decreased as waggons led a rumbling, rolling way on to a long straight track. 'We'll have to work up a fast run and charge like a column of tigers,' said Harry.

'Don't be silly,' said Irena.

The wounded German, a little cloudy with pain, wondered what language these two were using. He would like to have known what the remarkable woman and the seamanlike man were saying to each other.

'Do you think,' said Harry, leaning over the side but keeping his hand on the throttle, 'that you could put some coal on the fire? Well, wood, actually.'

'I will surprise you,' said Irena. She took the long iron bar and opened up the fire. The German, sitting with his back against the pile of logs, guessed what was wanted. He began to hand the split timber to Irena. She took the logs one at a time and fed the fire. Harry began gradually to close the throttle, looking back down the line. The train was running at a controllable speed and he felt things could have been a lot worse. They had one wounded leg between them. The other German had scrambled safely back into the leading coach. One wounded leg was damned hard luck on the sufferer but not bad under the circumstances.

He began his tug on the brake wheel. Immediately everything shrieked in iron protest.

'I'm not as good as I thought,' he muttered. He eased the brakes, the juddering and shrieking ceased and with the throttle closed he let the train glide.

'You are very good,' said Irena, who had heard him mutter. She was looking at him with a faint smile, her brown eyes bright with admiration. 'Yes, very good.'

'I think we'll save the compliments until we've made our charge.'

'Don't be silly,' she said again.

'All the same,' said Harry, the wind tugging at him as he leaned out to watch the gliding train, 'you deserve an unqualified vote of thanks. You're the coolest young lady. When we stop you can take a well-earned rest. We'll transfer you to the care of Major Carlsen and I'll get someone else to help me up here.'

'You will not.' She was proudly decisive. 'That is a fine thing, thanking me one moment and trying to get rid of me the next. Do you think I will be useless?'

'Far from it, but–'

'Then I am not going to be ordered about. You have done enough of that. I am going to be your fireman.'

'It's a brave thought, but you're not,' said Harry. The train was slowing. Hills on both sides opened out in rugged colour as the track began to ascend into a green and brown landscape. Spots of chill rain began to fall. 'You know you're not,' he added.

'You are like all men,' she said, 'you wish to have all the fun.'

'I'm not thinking of having fun,' said Harry, 'I'm thinking it might get rather noisy again and you're too valuable to be put at more risk. And too nice.'

She looked at him. He was speculating on the finer points of brake manipulation. He was a little sooty. She supposed she might be too. She hoped not.

'Harry, please let me stay,' she said, 'I shall be as safe here as in the compartment. Safer if I'm with you. I could not have a better protector.'

'Oh, look here,' said Harry, 'I can't deliberately put you in the firing line.'

'Then I shall volunteer. That is right, volunteer? We shall charge them together.'

Harry said something about demon princesses.

'We'll see,' he said, 'but I don't think Major Carlsen is going to approve. Wouldn't you rather join him for a while?'

'That is not the point.' She was cool, obstinate. 'I am going to do what I wish for once and not be ordered about.'

'I didn't hear that,' said Harry. 'Well, let's try the brakes again and see if we can stop this thing without breaking it in half.'

She came out of haughtiness then and laughed. She was in a state of high excitement. War was terrible, killing unforgivable, but because the wrong kind of men took up the wrong kind of positions and governments were so unyielding, war and killing became inevitable. But sometimes even in war something splendid happened, something exhilarating and pulse-quickening, and for a moment it made the war seem like the heroic background to glorious adventure. Harry would not really take the train back again, would he? Major Carlsen would never allow him to. There was too much at stake.

Harry braked. The engine juddered, the train pulled at it then seemed to squeeze and strain through the cold, moist air, to concertina, to unfold and concertina again. Noisy shocks ran from the locomotive to the farthest waggon and back again. The wounded German braced himself against the timber stack, Irena hung on and Harry looked as if he was grinning. When the jarring violence abated and the monster stood quite still, Irena said, 'I think you should be decorated, even if only for not breaking it in half.'

'You too deserve meritorious mention,' said Harry, letting steam escape, 'and I might just put it to the King of Rumania that you be made a railway admiral first-class.'

'I hope the uniform will be ravishing,' said Irena, and bent to speak to the German soldier, whose hands were tight around his wounded leg. His trousers were wet with blood. But he was quite cheerful.

German troops hastened down the track and climbed into the cab. They clapped Harry on the back. They carried the wounded man away. Major Carlsen arrived, spoke to a couple of officers standing by the track and then swung himself up. He waited until all troops and officers had gone before speaking. Then he saluted Harry and said, 'Thank you, Captain. Well played. May I say that?' His smile was almost warm. 'It was the thing to say at Oxford.'

'Frankly, Major,' said Harry, 'it was all a gigantic fluke. I–'

'He is going to be overbearingly modest,' said Irena, straightening her hat, 'he is going to tell you something quite unnecessary and ridiculous. I am going to tell you it wasn't a fluke, it was splendid, a miracle.'

'Same thing,' said Harry.

'Major Carlsen,' she said, 'are there many people hurt?'

'There are a few casualties among the troops,' he said, 'and some passengers are hurt. But no, not many.'

'Everyone else is all right?' She was quietly anxious.

'Everyone,' he said, 'you need not worry. Our only problem now is to make a decision. If we stay as we are we take the risk of being attacked again, if we go forward we take the same risk. But all units aboard have been ordered to reach Zagreb and unless we can get those orders changed–'

'But, Major Carlsen,' said Irena, her immaculate look not what it had been, 'it is not quite like that now. Captain Phillips says we are going to take the train on again, that we are going to mix up an immense amount of steam and charge on to Zagreb like galloping tigers.'

'It can be done?' said Major Carlsen.

'Well, as you say, we can't stay here,' said Harry, 'and it's just as easy to go forward as backwards. Easy needs to be qualified, of course. And we want to get Her Highness to Trieste, not run her all the way back to Belgrade.'

'You can see about Trieste when you reach Zagreb,' said the major.

'Major Carlsen, you will let him do it?' said Irena, the air cold and fresh in her face.

'I would prefer to go on myself,' he said.

'But the risk,' said Irena.

'We will all take the same risk together,' said Major Carlsen. 'Captain Phillips, I'll send you two men and take Princess Irena back into the train.'

'That is not necessary,' said Irena firmly. In her hat, which had turned smoky, and her coat, which was patterned with smuts, she looked as if she was not unused to stoking fires. Her face was slightly smudged. Neither man dared to mention it. 'I am to be the fireman. Captain Phillips and I can manage very well on our own.'

'I think she'd better go with you, Major,' said Harry, hefting wood into the fire.

'I am staying here,' said Irena, 'I wish to correct the strange idea Captain Phillips has that women are weak and helpless and men should have all the fun. I should also like to say he has protected me very well, and I am extremely grateful, but he is to stop giving me orders.'

'Good God,' said Harry, watching sparks burst and fly as he threw in a split log.

'I think Her Highness will be as safe inside this cab as anywhere,' said Major Carlsen.

'Rubbish,' said Harry. Irena stared fiercely at him.

'He is very trying,' she said to the major.

'One grenade will blow both of us and the cab to bits,' said Harry.

'You see?' said Irena to the major. 'The way he speaks you would think I was a peasant.'

The major regarded her keenly, his grey eyes taking in her pride, her determination and her look of smudged wear and tear. She lifted her chin and turned away. He saw the faint blush that mantled her in the grey, cloudy light.

'The Croats may have dispersed by now,' he said, 'and if you really feel the train can be taken on, Captain, then take it on. The two of you may as well stay together. Separated, you are no help to each other. When you reach Zagreb you will have to change trains. They will not let this one continue. We have some wounded aboard and the sooner you can make your run the better. Do you say you can manage? You can have some help if you wish.'

'Two men could ride the tender,' said Harry, 'they'd be near enough to us then to give us any necessary help.'

'But not near enough to overhear you.' The major's smile was his bleak one. 'Yes, it must be difficult, always having to be careful what you say and what language to use.' He looked at the countryside, wild and gloomy under the lowering clouds, then turned his eyes on the red, roaring fire Harry was building. 'You are ready?' he said.

'Almost,' said Harry, 'but I'd still feel happier if you took charge of Her Highness for the time being.'

'Oh!' She stamped her foot.

'I think we'll need to be running at thirty,'

Harry went on, 'at that speed we should run through them if they're still there. That means we'll have to rush at the gradient like runaway elephants–'

'Tigers,' said Irena.

'Yes.' Harry wiped oil and soot from his hands with a rag. 'If we lose too much speed when we start climbing and the Croats are still around, we'll have to run into reverse again. Will you explain that to everyone, Major?'

'I will,' said Major Carlsen, 'and we shall do our part, I assure you. I am happy to leave you to do yours.' He descended to the track. He called up. 'Will you remember to stop at Vrycho? It's about five miles on and those women are to be put off there.'

'I can't guarantee I can coincide the train with the station,' muttered Harry.

'What?' The major cupped his ear.

'He is muttering,' said Irena, looking down from the cab, 'but he will do as you wish.'

The Major returned to his coach. He sent up two men to ride on the tender. They ensconced themselves firmly amid the piled timber. The fire was roaring. Harry, aware of the vibrations of power, let steam escape. It blew fiercely and frighteningly.

'It's all right?' asked Irena a little uncertainly.

'It's what they call a good head, I hope,' said Harry. He knew he was walking in the dark, but circumstances being what they were he thought he might as well run as walk. He couldn't see himself driving the train in reverse all the way back to civilization without either cannoning into some other wandering iron monster or piling his train into a heap because of some unseen hazard. He put his trust in luck, in the feeling that the Croats would have gone, and he released the brakes and reached for the throttle.

'It is all right, isn't it?' said Irena, as conscious as Harry of heat and power.

'Confidentially,' he said, 'I think there's a chance that through sheer ignorance we can burst the boiler. I mean, exactly what is a good head of steam? See that gauge? I think it indicates the temperature. What's the danger mark, that fat-looking line? I don't know. Well, let's try hitting the thing for six.'

He opened the throttle and the engine jerked and pulled, the wheels gripped and turned, and the train followed. Familiar bangs and clangs smote their ears. Irena laughed a little hysterically. Harry gave the engine more throttle, the pistons responded and the locomotive bore down the track in chugging mastery.

'Oh, how wonderful,' cried Irena.

It was hot in the cab, although cold outside it. She took off her coat. Her gloved hands pushed her veil farther up and left smudges on her forehead.

'Keep your eye on the fire,' said Harry. It was a roarer at the moment, devouring the timber, and Irena kept it roaring, bringing the fuel log by log and plunging the timber in. Harry opened the throttle wider still and the engine began to thump and thunder. The heat of the fire turned Irena a flushed pink. The train gathered speed, running fast over the long level stretch, Harry hazarding all on the first two miles of their return to the place of ambush. He had to use those two miles to achieve the speed he thought necessary to carry the train up the gradient at a pace that would see them safely through. In short bursts men could run at fifteen miles an hour. If the Croats were still there they would either have blocked the line or be waiting to blow the engine off the track with grenades tossed into the cab. He knew nothing about the capacity of a locomotive on an upward gradient, except that he did not think he had ever seen one racing when it was climbing. Not that the approaching gradient was steep, it was kindness itself. If they did not drop below a speed of twenty-five he thought they would get through any new ambush.

The fire was a blazing furnace. Irena had fed it to its limit. They had a boiling head of steam. If anything blew up he felt neither of them would know very much about it. That gauge was pulsating. And she was amazing. He had never envisaged her in this kind of role. Few princesses would care to stagger about pitching heavy logs into the red-hot fire of a pounding locomotive cab.

'There,' she panted, and used the long iron bar to close the fire. She was covered with tiny grey smuts of wood ash.

'Well done, Princess,' he said.

She laughed excitedly, holding on as she leaned outwards to look at what was ahead of them. The cold air rushed bitingly into her face, plucked at her hat and almost dislodged it. The hatpin held it. She put a hand to it, the wind taking her breath. The dully gleaming rails ran at them and were swallowed by the ravenous iron wheels, track and bush and landscape hurtled at them and swept past. On the left the line of hills began to close in, and somewhere ahead was the point where the track had been cut out of the hillside. She drew back into the shelter of the cab, out of the wind, her face tingling.

There was a bend in the distance. Harry, peering through the thick glass lookout window, saw it. They were thundering at it. God, he thought, we'll run straight off the line. He throttled down and opened the steam outlet. It rushed white and noisy into the moist air. Heat and vibrations enveloped them. The train pounded on, vast and weighty, its small front guiding wheels grinding against the rails as the bend swooped towards them. The engine lurched, ploughed on, the whole train screaming, rocking and clattering. The Germans lodged in the timber pile clung grimly. Irena staggered, Harry flung an arm around her waist and held her until she found purchase. Her teeth clenched as the engine seemed to keel, careering into the long line of the bend, its gigantic impetus threatening to tear it from the rails. The wheels shrieked, the iron monster shuddered and Irena prayed. The wheels gripped, touched down and ran true, the locomotive steaming powerfully on and pulling swaying coaches and waggons with it.

They cleared the bend. The track ran straight again, Harry opened up and they hammered on towards the gentle ascent. The hill rose on their left, dropped away on their right. Harry gave the engine more throttle and the vibrations turned into a thumping, frightening protest of straining power.

'Go, old lady, go,' he breathed.

They were powering their way up to the scene of the ambush, the train a roar of steam and smoke. The ascent burdened the engine with the deadening weight of coaches, cars and waggons. It began to lose speed. And the Croats were still there, with their dead and wounded. The hillside, dark under the grey sky, flickered with a hundred tiny flashes of light as rifles opened up. They had heard the train coming. The bullets began to whack and whistle. Train windows already smashed suffered disintegration, and flying lead played its deadly tattoo on the iron. The Germans high on the tender flattened themselves. Those stationed in coaches and waggons opened up a retaliatory fire.

Harry glimpsed men slithering and sliding down the hill ahead. Bullets whined through the open end of the cab. Irena pressed herself tightly under cover close to him. Harry muttered something about hell and the devil and flung the throttle wide open. He waited for the blinding cataclysm of an engine blowing up, but instead pistons thumped and the fire roared. The train charged on, running on boiling, hissing steam, and Irena in wild exhilaration pulled on a cord and the whistle shrieked. Dust, smoke and vapour burst into the air. Harry watched the track, straining to sight obstacle or opposition. It was the two Germans, flat on the tender, who saw the Croats surging beside the line a little way on, stick grenades in their hands. They dug in over the timber and opened fire. It warned Harry – he brought Irena closer to him. The Croats tumbled under the rapid fire and the locomotive, pulling and straining, roared up to them. The ascent was draining it of power and Harry sweated at the loss of speed. A man lobbed, the grenade thumped over the cab floor and he kicked it wildly out over the footplate. It exploded seconds later as the tender passed it, flame and shrapnel fierily kissing a wheel.

Croats reeled back from the charging train, which thumped and belched on as the two Germans emptied their magazines. The hillside flashes increased to give the effect of insurgency suffering the fiery frustrations of rage. The train ran on with the useless crack of bullets signalling its escape and departure. Harry looked back, gesturing his thanks to the two soldiers. They gave him the international thumbs-up response.

Irena, free of apprehension, laughed aloud. They were clear. They had done it. They had made the charge and sustained it.

'Oh, Harry!' Her eyes were shining. She flung her arms around him and hugged him.

'Steady, old girl,' he said, watching the jerking temperature gauge.

'Old? Who is old? What a cheek!'

'No, no, not meant like that,' said Harry, 'it's just a bit of quaint English.'

'It is hardly quaint.' But she was laughing and just a little pink from her demonstrative impulse. She had never known such excitement, such splendid endeavour. 'Oh, you did it,' she said happily, 'how marvellous.'

'We all did it,' said Harry, wiping sweat away. They were running on level track again. He pushed back his peaked cap and wiped at more sweat. He eased the power, feeling safer on steadier revolutions. He did not want to career around any other bends.

'What a game old galloper,' he said, patting smeared brass. 'Sorry if we were a little rough, old thing. It's our nerves.'

'Oh, no one is going to complain about your nerves,' said Irena.

'Or yours,' said Harry. 'You have my warmest admiration, Princess.'

'How kind,' she said.

'Put some more wood on the fire,' said Harry.

He was sooty. He peered at her as she laughed. She was flushed and she looked lovely through her soot. She had dancing lights in her brown eyes.

They both laughed. They felt bravely free and triumphant.

Chapter Eight

Vrycho was a halt. What for and why, Harry had no idea. The countryside looked as uninhabitable as ever, although not so hilly. He could see no village, no signs of cultivation. He applied the brakes tentatively, turning the wheel slowly, realizing this was an art in itself. But despite his care the engine wheels took their incurable umbrage, and grinding shudders of protest ran the length of the train. He did not have the heart to ask more of it than it was prepared to give to an unknown hand. He let it take its time to pull up. Hissing, grinding, the train ran slowly on past the halt and came to a stop with its tail looking back at the landing point.

Harry leaned out of the cab. He saw the six peasant women descending to the side of the track. It was a long way down for them. They accomplished it by sitting on the step of the open coach door, dangling their legs and launching themselves. The ubiquitous Major Carlsen, enigmatic to the last, was there to help them. He stood while each woman launched herself down into his arms.

'Good God,' said Harry, 'never thought him that kind of ladies' man.'

The women formed into a tight little cluster of shapeless black. Seeing Harry, they bobbed and smiled at him. Harry gave them a wave. Major Carlsen, a bottle having magically appeared in his hand, walked up to the cab.

'Captain Phillips, I'm honoured to have discovered you,' he said. 'I will,' he added with a slightly bleak smile, 'take some of the credit in that having discovered you I made the right decision about you. This is from the women, with their thanks. It was something that escaped being commandeered.' He held up a bottle of rough white wine. Harry bent and took it with a smile, giving the women another wave. They giggled. Irena appeared at his elbow. Major Carlsen blinked at her sootiness.

'*Himmel*,' he breathed.

'What is wrong?' asked Irena. 'We have done well, haven't we? So what is wrong?'

The major climbed up into the cab. The Germans on the tender watched, as much interested in the bottle of wine as the conversation they could not hear. The major murmured his next words.

'Your Highness, everything is very much better than it was.'

It seemed as if he did not dare to look her in the eye. She turned to Harry.

'Captain Phillips,' she demanded, 'what is wrong?'

'Do you see me?' said Harry, while the locomotive stood and steam rose.

His face was streaked and smudged, his hands dirty and oily. She looked at her gloves. They were disgraceful. She looked at her dress. It was deplorable. The awful truth began to dawn. The heady excitement which had lifted her out of the realms of convention, which had sustained her in her hour of glorious endeavour, sank to cold zero. Her handbag was tucked into a corner of the cab with her coat. She picked it up, took out a mirror and looked into it. Her gasp was like a tragic moan. Her face was covered with smuts.

'That is me?' Her eyes regarded her reflection in glazed horror. 'That is me? Oh! I am disgusting!'

'You are not,' said Major Carlsen, 'you are brave and beautiful. I salute you.' He took her gloved hand and raised it to his lips.

'She's also a very good fireman,' said Harry.

'I am filthy,' she cried in despair.

'It's very honest filth, you know,' said Harry, trying not to smile. 'But go back into the train and Major Carlsen will–'

'No.' She rose above despair. The damage was done. She was hideous and it was as much his fault as anybody's. Therefore he would have to put up with her state. Moreover, she was not going to be robbed of completing the adventure. 'After all, I am no more filthy than you. And nobody at Zagreb will recognize me now. They will think I am a woman who sweeps roads. That is something, isn't it? And you need not look at me while you are driving.'

'Very well,' said Harry gravely.

'Captain Phillips,' said Major Carlsen, keeping his face just as straight, 'I think that after all this you will have no trouble reaching Trieste. I shall expect to hear sometime in the future that you have Her Highness safely in England. I have your address and when the war is over I hope to be able to land in England myself, to call on Her Highness and to see you.'

'I don't like the way you make it all sound simple,' said Harry, 'it's shooting an arrow at providence.'

'I am very confident, Captain. I am also grateful.' The major saluted them both, then descended to the track. Irena leaned from the cab, watched him in his progress and gave Harry the all-clear.

Harry handed her the bottle of wine. The cork was loose. She pulled it out and drank thirstily from the bottle. The wine was new. It stimulated her, took the edge off her mortification. Harry had several mouthfuls, then put the cork back and tossed the bottle up to the Germans on the tender. They received it gratefully.

Irena, resigned to the fact that she could not look any worse, fed the fire and Harry drove the train on to Zagreb. His abysmal ignorance of railway systems was hardly conducive to bliss and all he could do was to keep the speed controllable. He could at least rely on the fact that the train was expected, that the line would accordingly be clear. But as the comparative simplicity of the track began to spawn a complexity of urban tracks, he wondered whether it wouldn't be wiser to stop and to get out and walk. How the devil could he successfully take the train into a main station like Zagreb?

Irena, reading his thoughts, said, 'It is going to be difficult?'

'I don't know, I suppose we could end up with a collection of old iron and a badly mangled station,' said Harry. He caressed the engine with a tender, cautious hand. 'But look here, I don't see why we shouldn't try to make a go of it. They might make a fuss of us then. The Austrian authorities aren't going to be small-minded about two people who brought home a train for them. And not just the train, but people and troops. Which reminds me, what am I doing, saving German troops? I could be court-martialled.'

'What is wrong with saving German troops? They have helped to save us, haven't they?' Irena was slightly militant.

'My dear girl–'

'Don't call me that!' Again came that stamp of

her foot. 'First you say I am old, now you say I am not grown-up.'

'It's my careless English,' said Harry, watching the multiple tracks as the train clattered over points. 'Nothing meant, I assure you.' He looked at her. She had her chin in the air. 'Well, what do you say, Princess, shall we risk Zagreb? We don't want to walk from here to Trieste, do we? Let's take our iron maiden in. Why not? In return, we won't ask for any decorations, only a comfortable first-class compartment on a train to Trieste.'

Irena turned forgiving brown eyes on him. She glowed.

'Oh, yes, let us do it, let us steam beautifully into Zagreb.'

'Do you mind if we creep in? I think it'll be safer. We can't really expect to be beautiful, we're too knocked about. And I don't know what the devil is going to happen if we meet a train coming the other way. Keep your eye open for signals.'

'What do I look for?' she asked.

'Oh, ups and downs,' said Harry. He had the engine chugging comfortably, the coaches and waggons winding steadily along behind it. 'I think you stop if it's down. But they must be expecting us. We're hours late and I suppose all the points are being attended to. We'll just–'

'Harry, a train!' she screamed.

They saw it, majestically steaming towards them in the rain-cloudy light. It seemed magnificently capable of tossing them aside and Harry thought of the irresistible force running smack into an extremely movable object, except that he knew they weren't as movable as that. Their train was steaming slowly, the oncoming locomotive running fast.

'It's on the other line,' he said.

It was. From out of the bewildering array of shining steel rails it sheered past them and the air vibrated to the impact of its going. They went on, the system beginning to look like an impossible confusion of rails and points. They rattled as points channelled them from one track to the next. Signals stood like an array of tall, slender sentinels. As far as Harry could see or guess, none commanded him to stop. He crept on. Irena clutched his arm as the leading wheels forked. She saw men in signal boxes staring down at her, and at smashed and splintered coach windows. Harry took out his khaki silk handkerchief and gave it to her. She cleaned the worst of the soot from her face.

He shut off power and let the train glide under the impetus of its own weight. He put his hand on the brake wheel.

She saw the station ahead.

'There, you will do it, Harry,' she said, but prayed a little under her breath.

'I hope there are no buffers,' said Harry, 'just a clear line. What a fool if I end up in the street.'

'Oh, a buffer or two will be nothing,' she said, 'you will only give them a kiss.'

He began to apply the brakes. They slowly clamped and the gliding train groaned. It crept in frictioned resistance into Zagreb station. They saw the crowds, uniformed officials, Austrian officers and gaping railwaymen. Irena stood by the footplate, watching the platform and smiling in proud delight as Harry brought their game old iron maiden to a shuddering stop beneath the high station roof.

He wiped his hands. He smiled at her, liking her for her aptitude, her courage, her soot.

'Thank you, Your Highness,' he said. She made a little face at him for such formality at such a triumphant moment.

The noise of the station was deafening. But it was almost comforting after the noise of violent ambush. Irena's smudged look yielded to her feeling of victory and she smiled in pleasure of their shared achievement. As bemused and astonished officials converged on the engine she laughed a little breathlessly.

'Oh, it was nothing,' she said, 'I would do it again any time.'

'Would you?'

'With you I would.'

The train was besieged. German officers were calling for ambulances to hospitalize wounded men. Passengers began to exchange excited comments with people on the platform. Two station officials, gold-braided, clambered up into the cab. A slim, slightly stooping Austrian army officer of middle age also ventured up. They stared at Harry, looked in astonishment at Irena, and broke into incredulous speech, but all at once.

'Please, gentlemen,' said Irena, and when they had quietened down she began to explain in her fluent German. She was very descriptive concerning their arrival at the point of ambush and how the driver and the fireman had vanished.

'Vanished?' One official did not know how that

shameful fact could be put down in the report.

'Yes. However,' said Irena comfortingly, 'with exemplary courage, a Russian friend of mine–'

'Russian? Russian?'

'Yes. Sergius Rokossky.' Irena cordially drew their attention to the exemplary one, who smiled modestly and wondered what the devil she was telling them. 'I am Austrian, he's a White Russian. Now, the driver and the fireman having deserted the train–'

'What scoundrels.' The official shook his head sadly and a seething mass of people on the platform stared and chattered excitedly.

'Please, let her proceed,' said the Austrian officer, his astonishment giving way to intrigued interest. A colonel, he was the senior transport officer of the area. He was involved now in the shattering consequences of the grand failure of the Habsburg Empire, at his wits' end to find transport for the retreating divisions of Austria and Germany. But for a brief moment, this young woman and her male companion, and the implications of their presence in this cab, made Colonel Oscar Gebert forget the harrowing hours. They were quite dirty, both of them, but he thought them singularly impressive.

'Everyone was ducking or lying down,' continued Irena, 'and the firing made it terribly difficult for anyone to get up to the engine. But as my friend Sergius was the only one who thought he could drive it, he did what he could and I gave him a little help.' She smiled demurely, hoping no one would be ungallant enough to think her sootiness was more distracting than her story. 'What else could we do but get the train moving? We had no choice but to brave the rigours and the dangers for the sake of the soldiers and passengers on board.'

'Fräulein, it was brave indeed,' said one of the officials.

'Oh, it was nothing, nothing,' said Irena. The officials and Colonel Gebert were fascinated, quite unable to leave the cab until they had heard all. Harry looked on, all too aware of Irena's occupation of the stage without understanding a word she said. He smiled at her gestures, the way she used her eyes, the life and animation she conveyed. She described the trials and terrors of the ambush with slightly more than poetic licence, so intent was she on making Harry's part loom larger than a mere basket of eggs. She told how he had run the train in reverse while under heavy fire and the magnificence of his charge to freedom. She had been more than happy to act as his fireman and she did not think she had been altogether hopeless at the job. Her listeners were both impressed and enchanted. The officials were also expressively grateful, for there was no asset more valuable these days than rolling stock. The train was damaged, but it had been saved.

The platform meanwhile hummed with excitement. Passengers were helped from bullet-scarred coaches and the German troops vacated the waggons with their wounded. Two of their officers pushed their way through the mob to climb into the cab, where they saluted Irena and Harry and congratulated them. They spoke to the Austrian officer, Colonel Gebert. It was a pity, thought

Irena, that Harry could not understand German, for he would feel very flattered at what was being said. How very funny if the Germans and Austrians decided to decorate him, if he returned to England wearing a German medal.

The two railway officials, while enthralled, did not know how it could all be translated into a cogent report, for there had been phrases from the charming woman like '...and then my gallant Russian friend burst into the bend like a rocket so that for unimaginable seconds we hung over bottomless space with our wings folded.' As for her sooty state, they were distressed for her. She had been so courageous. It was a deplorable indication of the railway's fall from grace, but then everything had suffered so much from this terrible war.

Harry, while getting an honourable mention, understood none of it. But as long as Irena was making a good case for them, he did not mind. All they wanted was a decently comfortable passage to Trieste. He was cooling down now. The nerve-racking encounter with the unpleasant and the unknown had been prolonged. He felt hungry, thirsty, dirty and tired.

'Is it possible to get a meal somewhere?' he asked Irena in French.

'Oh, that would be heaven, I am starving myself,' she said.

Colonel Gebert introduced himself. French, the language of diplomacy, culture and intrigue, was the second tongue of most European countries.

'Allow me, please,' he said, 'I am Colonel

Gebert, senior officer here. We owe you much more than a meal.'

'Perhaps a bath and some comfortable rooms? We are so dirty,' said Irena.

'Please, come with me,' said the middle-aged Austrian.

They accompanied him down to the platform. Stretchers had appeared and wounded troops and civilians were let through the buzzing throng. Harry clapped a hand to his head.

'The case,' he said.

'Oh,' said Irena. She knew his British uniform was carefully packed in that case. It could be important to them at a stage in the immediate future, it represented a dangerous unmasking of his identity if discovered before then. It was a risk to have brought it at all.

They investigated, Colonel Gebert assuring them he would wait. Outside the passenger coach, with its every window smashed, was the girl in the dark red suit. She saw them and almost rushed at them in breathless wonder and admiration.

'Oh, how brave, m'sieu,' she cried to Harry, 'it was magnificent, everyone says so.'

'Thank you, mademoiselle,' said Harry, lightly fending off what looked like the promise of a heartfelt cuddle from the adoring girl, 'but I rather think I jerked everything about a little too much for your comfort. Never mind. Has the compartment been emptied? My case was there.'

'Your case, m'sieu?' Nadia was eager to help. 'It was brown and so big?' She used her hands. The little group was being bustled a bit by a cosmopolitan crowd wanting to see the man and woman rumoured to have rescued a train from rebels and robbers. Nadia took no notice, she was proud and happy to concentrate on what she knew about Harry's case. Yes, she thought it was still in the compartment but she was sorry to say everyone had used it to help ward off bullets, especially that man who had sat in a corner glowering at people. Harry remembered the man, quiet and rather moody. 'See, there he is,' said Nadia, pointing.

The man was standing aside from the bustle, leaning against a wall, his hands in his pockets. He still looked dourly disapproving of humanity, and as he met Harry's eye he gave a shrug as if to say he did not know why Harry had bothered.

'Yes, I see him,' said Harry, 'but it's my case I want.'

And the case, as Nadia had said, was still in the compartment. On the seat. Someone went in for it and handed it out to Harry through the gaping window. The leather strap that had been around it was gone, it was pitted front and back, and the lid gaped at one end where a catch had broken.

Colonel Gebert came up and regretfully said, 'Hm.'

'Full of bullets. Oh, *sacré bleu*,' said Harry with Gallic realism. But it could not be helped, he said, and he thanked the girl, Nadia, for her kindness. Then he and Irena went through the station with Colonel Gebert. Nadia looked after them and sighed.

Zagreb was not buzzing in the same way as Belgrade. It had known Austrian administration for many years, and while its Croatian citizens were aggressive in their demands for independence the solid German and Magyar minorities, who formed the greater part of the aristocracy, knew they had no future in any kind of independent Croatia. Feelings in Zagreb were therefore polarized. They were triumphantly overt on one side, defiant but pessimistic on the other. The Austrian authorities, lacking now a directive of strength and purpose from Vienna, were beginning to feel they were standing on a castle of sand which was slipping from under them with every new setback.

It did not strain the resources of Colonel Gebert, however, to have rooms made available for Irena and Harry in the private building backing on to the ornate station hotel. The building, owned by the railway, was used for receptions and conferences. The colonel also saw to the question of having food prepared for the guests. He forgot the mountainous worries of his work for the moment. It was a time for temporarily putting despondency aside and doing something for two young people who he thought were among those a little out of the ordinary. She said she was Helga Strasser from the Tyrol, he said he was Sergius Rokossky, a White Russian from Petrograd. Perhaps this was so, perhaps not. At this stage of the declining war it did not matter. They were courageous young people.

The Austrian, full of the charm and courtesy of a bygone age, even assured Irena that since her clothes had been ruined he would arrange for his wife to do something about this. Irena, the sound of a running bath beautiful in her ears, said he was extremely kind but he was not to bother his wife. Because of the war they had enough worries of their own. And she had a costume she could wear.

'Very well,' said Colonel Gebert, 'but tomorrow, Fräulein Strasser, you may draw on railway funds to buy what you wish from the shops. I will see to that. Perhaps I should tell you, however, that because of things being so bad the shops aren't offering an abundance of fashions.'

'Oh, anything will do,' she said, 'and this is not really the time to dress as if one were going to a concert or ball.'

He seemed in gentle agreement with that. She thanked him for his thoughtfulness, his generosity, and when he had gone she knocked on the communicating door. Harry opened it. He was wearing only his trousers and vest. He still looked sooty. She could hear his own bath running.

'Oh, I'm sorry,' she said and turned away in modesty.

'I'm not actually undressed,' said Harry. She was quite pink and he thought that rather sweet. He had once looked up from a naked bathe in a French river to see a group of French housewives staring fascinatedly and without a blush between them.

'I was simply going to ask how you were feeling now,' she said, 'and to tell you that Colonel Gebert will arrange for me to buy some clothes at the railway's expense. That is kind, isn't it?'

'No more than you deserve,' said Harry. What a strange girl she was. She resolutely refused to turn her head. She was either shy or prim. She would, as a princess, certainly be correct. Even so, they were not living in Victorian times. Edward and Alexandra had brought the whole world out of its laced-up Puritanism. 'You've washed your face,' he said.

'Of course I have,' she said, 'and now I am going to take a bath.'

'What I mean,' said Harry from the discreet side of the open door, 'is that you took a risk, didn't you, in showing an utterly clean and uncovered face to an Austrian officer who may be familiar with royal countenances?'

'Oh, how silly,' she said but looked a little guilty. 'Are you saying I must go about with soot all over me?'

'Well, it was a good disguise,' said Harry, 'and not unappealing.'

She took a quick glance. He was laughing.

'Oh, that isn't a bit funny! Go away, you beast.' She turned and shut the door on him. She heard him give a cry of pain. Aghast, she pulled the door open again. He was standing there with his hand over his nose. 'Oh, I have hurt you?' she said in distress. He uncovered his nose. It was quite unmarked.

'I think you missed, Your Highness,' he said, 'but it was fearfully close.'

'Idiot!' she cried. She would not be treated so lightly, as if she had become part of a circus. She slammed the door.

But when she was in the bath she began to laugh. The bath, sheer heaven, was conducive to divine well-being and put her into a mood where she was able to forgive all men for their imperfections, including Harry.

The case had been unpacked. There actually were bullets in it. But she was able to put on clean and untouched undergarments after her bath, and that was heaven too. She had hung up her brown costume. It was all she had to wear in the way of outer garments, that and her cream blouse which Harry had had the sense to include. A spent bullet fell from the blouse when she unfolded it. The lead had left a tiny mark but fortunately the costume jacket hid it. She had washed her hair and it was still damp as she braided it. She finished with a crown of rich chestnut that gleamed.

A meal was served to them in a small, private dining room. They were ravenous and Irena delightedly plunged a large ladle into a miniature cauldron that was placed on the table. It steamed. Harry sniffed adventurously.

'Fish stew,' he said.

'Oh, a little better than that,' she said, 'it's *brodetto*. Fish ragout.'

'Yes, I said that, fish stew. Well, anything outside of a crust is a banquet to a starving man.' He let her fill his plate. He thought she looked better than refreshed from her bath and make-up. Her hair was superb, her eyes clear and healthy and quite absorbed in seeing that she had given him enough. He tried the dish. 'Delicious,' he said.

'Yes?' she said.

'Yes.'

She helped herself. He thought her aptitude for survival quite admirable. Life neither frightened her nor intimidated her. She had no maid, no lady-in-waiting, and had not once complained about the lack of either.

She was enjoying herself, eating her meal with relish and no fine or finicky airs. They were given a bottle of wine from the vineyards of Slovenia, a clear and exhilarating Ljutomer Riesling. She drank that with relish too.

'I'm ashamed,' she said a little later. 'Look, we have eaten it all.'

'Your Highness,' said Harry, who thought that from time to time she did not object to the right form of address, 'you don't think we were supposed to save some, do you?'

'Do you think we were?' Irena looked as if she was sure they had deprived other hungry people. 'Oh, how awful.'

A man in a blue, sleeveless jacket, black trousers and red waist sash, came in and ventured a glance at the pot. It was empty. He smiled delightedly.

'It was good?' he said.

'Oh, delicious,' said Irena.

He asked if they wanted anything else. Irena translated this to Harry. Harry rather suspected the generous dish of fish ragout had strained the thin wartime resources of the larder and it was a pleasure, therefore, to truthfully declare he wanted nothing more. Neither did Irena, except for coffee. Could they have coffee? It was brought to them and was as near to genuine coffee as any they had had for some time.

'You know,' said Harry, 'you haven't said a word about Major Carlsen.'

'Oh, should I have done?' She did not sound worried. 'But why?'

Harry leaned back, looking thoughtfully at a large oil painting on the wall behind her. It depicted a standing group of magnificently attired railway officials.

'He didn't appear when we got here,' said Harry. 'Odd, don't you think? I thought he'd be the first to show himself. In his more Machiavellian pose, of course.'

Her flush was instant and marked.

'What do you wish me to say to that?' she said, sitting up straight-backed and defiant.

'I simply said–'

'Well, I will tell you what I will say.' Her defiance became cold hostility. 'That Major Carlsen is a gentleman. That you are odious.'

'You're misjudging me,' said Harry. He understood why she was so sensitive about the major. They held each other in mutual affection and regard. 'Why didn't he show up, I wonder?'

'You forget how late the train was,' said Irena icily, 'and that he doesn't have the time we do. We can come to these rooms and have a bath and a meal. We can take time to talk. Do you think, with the days so critical for the Germans, that Major Carlsen can step airily off a train; saunter about, say hello and wave goodbye as if he had no worry in the world except us?'

'The days are critical for everyone, including Rumania,' said Harry. He looked cleanly admonishing. His suit and jersey had been taken away while he was in the bath and returned dry-cleaned an hour later.

'How dare you say it like that!' Irena stared fiercely at him. 'Do you suppose I am not concerned about my country? I am as much concerned as you are about yours. But I am not blindly prejudiced.'

'Prejudiced?' He was quite calm, thinking it all a storm in a teacup. This did her no good at all. They were quarrelling and therefore he simply had no right not to be as passionate about it as she was.

'Yes, that is what I said. You are fighting the Germans, so of course they must all be hateful or sinister or Machi – or Macha–' She was groping because of hot resentment.

'Machiavellian.' He helped her out. 'Which means devious.'

She left hot resentment behind and became coldly furious.

'You are speaking of my grandmother, sir!'

'Your grandmother was Machiavellian?' he said interestedly.

Oh, the cool beast!

'How dare you!' she flamed.

'You mean she was German? Mmm,' said Harry.

'I see! You are saying I am sinister and devious because I have some German blood?'

'I'm not saying anything of the sort.'

'But you are looking down your nose!'

He laughed. She regarded him freezingly. He coughed. She was quite different from Elisabeth. Elisabeth was fair and tranquil. Princess Irena was dark and sensitive.

'Your Highness, you're really getting worked up

about nothing at all,' he said.

'I am not! Major Carlsen is a fine man. And that is what this is all about.' She bent her head over her coffee.

'Well, I'm sorry if I wonder about him sometimes. By the way, I think someone opened our case. The strap was gone and the catches had been forced.'

'Oh,' she said, calming down.

'Nothing had been taken, as far as I could see.'

'But your uniform, if someone saw that?'

'No, that was in the false bottom,' he said. 'The case had certainly been used to stop bullets. I found six or seven.'

'You missed one. It was in my blouse.' She looked at him a little hesitantly. He smiled. 'Oh, I am sorry,' she said, 'we should not quarrel, should we?'

'Have we quarrelled? I don't think so.'

'You will think me very ungracious, you are taking such risks for me. Oh, I am sorry,' she said again.

'I think you very courageous,' he said.

'Oh, it was splendid today, wasn't it?'

'Frightening?' he suggested.

'Terrifying. But splendid all the same. Perhaps,' she said, 'someone thought there were valuables to steal in the case. Yes, I think so. I have been keeping all the jewels close to me.'

There was a knock. A door opened and Colonel Gebert looked in.

'Ah, that is good,' he smiled. He came in and enquired if the food had been to their satisfaction. Irena assured him it had.

'Will you have some coffee with us, Colonel?' Harry asked the question in French. Colonel Gebert said he would. He was happy to sit down with them for a while. He apologized for the quality of the coffee and became a little sad about so many things not being as they had in the past. He spoke of the war rushing to a finish of tragic proportions, politically and economically. What was to happen to Austria and her empire he did not know. It was falling apart, thought Harry, but did not say so.

Colonel Gebert recounted how he had lived for many years in Zagreb, as an officer in the Austrian garrison. It was a city which over a long period had acquired a look of Viennese charm, with its own nucleus of intellectuals, artists, writers, and poets. It was perhaps considered a backwater by the more sophisticated European capitals, but Colonel Gebert was sure that people could live as graciously in Zagreb as anywhere. It had prospered under the protection of Imperial Austria. Now there were incredible rumours that the Emperor Charles was being forced to abdicate, of the empire being piecemealed. What good would that do?

'No good at all,' declared Irena, 'and those who are thinking of doing such an insensible thing aren't thinking of tomorrow.'

Colonel Gebert said, 'One doesn't tell children they must look after themselves, one doesn't remove from them the wisdom and protection of their parents and leave them to fend for themselves. Let us hope that if the Allies win this war they won't be short-sighted enough to create a number of little nations. These would only be swallowed up eventually by a power far less benevolent than Austria.' He looked sad, introspective, then said, 'But there's still hope for the future when there are young people like you around. Is there anything more we can do for you?'

'There's one small favour,' said Harry, 'we want to get to Trieste. Is there a train tomorrow?'

'Perhaps the day after tomorrow we may only be able to shrug our shoulders,' said the colonel, 'but tomorrow there will still be trains, even if they don't arrive or depart at stated times. And Trieste, you say? Yes. But no one these days seems to want to stay in one place. Everyone is either going somewhere or returning from somewhere, infected merely by the mood of a moment or the rumour of the day. Some are in a state of constant panic, others are uneasy and others either running from trouble or looking for it. There are so many different nationalities, so many minorities. You wish to go to Trieste. What I am trying to say, my young friends, is that you will probably find a thousand others who wish to go at the same time.'

'In other words,' said Harry, 'all trains to Trieste are crowded.'

'All trains to anywhere are crowded.'

'We were hoping for a quiet ride this time,' said Harry.

'It isn't possible to have a reserved compartment?' said Irena. 'No, of course not, that is a little selfish, isn't it?'

'If that's all you're asking for after all you have

done today,' smiled Colonel Gebert, 'that is remarkably modest. For you, one must attempt the impossible. No, one must achieve it. My dear young lady, you remind me of prouder days. Have I seen you before, on some grand occasion?'

Harry felt his nerves quicken. But Irena was equal to the moment.

'Oh,' she said lightly, 'on any grand occasion I should only have been one more face among thousands, Colonel Gebert.'

'I should not put it quite like that myself,' said the colonel, quite taken by her looks and her vitality. 'Well, if it's Trieste you want there's a train timed to leave at noon tomorrow. I will see that you are accommodated. Perhaps you will meet me in my station office at eleven thirty. But then there are the clothes you wish to shop for. Please call on me earlier concerning funds.'

'Oh, that isn't–'

'I insist,' smiled the colonel, 'and the railway board will insist. Now, if you'll excuse me, I must go home to my wife. It has been good to meet you both and to talk to you.'

In Belgrade, Dimitroff took the telephone call from his comrade in Zagreb. He listened carefully to what was said. It was necessary to communicate the exact details to Comrade Michalides, who had a critical mind and cold eyes.

'Amazing,' he murmured, 'and you're sure the man is the Englishman?'

'From your description, I have no doubt. Also, he has a British army uniform hidden in his case.

I was able to open it when everyone else had left the compartment.'

'Ah, what fine eyes you have,' said Dimitroff warmly, 'I knew you would use them, comrade. He was with the woman all the time?'

'They were inseparable. One must admire them for their work.'

'It was merely concern for their own shifty lives,' said Dimitroff, 'and what a liar the Englishman is. He's told our friend Michalides a hundred different fairy stories. But you have your finger on him now and her too. She is the person Comrade Michalides is looking for?'

'I've never seen her in her parasitical trappings, comrade, but yes, she has all the characteristics, together with a fine nose she puts in the air at times.'

'That's something they're born with,' said Dimitroff. 'Now, you're sure you know where they are?'

'I am sure.'

'Good. But watch them, they're slippery, both of them. Wait now, let me talk to Comrade Michalides.' Dimitroff talked to the Rumanian and came back. 'Listen, here is what you must do. First, go to see our friends in Zagreb.'

'I can't do that and also keep watch.'

'They're nesting for the moment, aren't they? Michalides says they won't make a fresh move until morning. So. Listen, Comrade Jovanovic.'

Dimitroff outlined the plan.

Chapter Nine

At breakfast the next morning in the same private room, Irena told Harry he must see that nothing made her feel more destitute than having to go about in worn rags.

'Rags?' He concealed his amusement, passing a hand over his mouth. She was wearing her ginger-nut-brown costume, which he thought very stylish. Almost too stylish. 'But that costume?'

'I have worn this three times already,' she said.

'But you're not on a royal tour,' he said.

'I am not going to turn into a gipsy,' she said. Therefore she would go to the shops and buy new clothes. Also a few other things and a new case.

Harry demurred. Her dress and coat had been cleaned overnight and were as good as new. He did not feel the need for either of them to encumber themselves with further clothes.

'But, Harry, please,' she said, 'we aren't having to run from those men now, we have lost them.'

He was a little uneasy. Not on account of what the frustrated Michalides might be up to, but because he was unable to resist her. They were still on the run and unnecessary luggage was an encumbering luxury. He ought to put his foot down. He had tried that once or twice. She did not like it. He felt less inclined to now.

'Please buy only what you really need,' he said

abruptly, 'and make sure the case is small, not enormous. I'm not even certain it's wise for you to go shopping.'

'But I'm not to shop alone, am I? You are coming, aren't you?' She was fresh and lovely after her night's sleep and quite vivid with colour.

'Yes, I'd better,' he said, 'I can keep an eye on quantity then.'

She laughed.

'You are going to behave like a husband? Oh, dear.' She cast her lashes demurely. Witch, he thought. 'Harry, why are you looking so Russian this morning?'

'I had no shaving soap, it's hard to get here, I suppose,' he said, rubbing his bristly chin. 'But I made signs and I think there'll be something in my room now. I hope it'll lather.'

'No,' she said, 'I meant you were looking pokey-faced.'

'Poker-faced.'

'Yes, I said that.' She laughed again. She was vivacious this morning. 'Well, while you are shaving I'll go down to the station and see Colonel Gebert. He will insist on giving me funds and I have no local money.'

'I think he wishes well of you. I'll meet you in his office as soon as I've shaved.' He looked hard at her. 'Put your hat and veil on.'

She put her nose up a little.

'But they are so sooty,' she said.

'Put them on all the same,' said Harry.

Her brown eyes were challenging.

'I wish you would not–'

'I'm sorry,' he said, 'I sometimes forget who

you are. I shouldn't give you orders. Forgive me.'

'Oh, no, I don't want you to be always thinking of that,' she said, 'it's so different now. We are friends now, aren't we?'

'Companions in distress,' he smiled. 'I'm escaping Germans, you're escaping Michalides. Would you put your hat and veil on, please?'

'Yes, of course,' she said.

'Why didn't you have them cleaned with your other things?'

'Because all the jewels are inside my hat. I have very cleverly sewn them inside the lining.'

'Well played,' said Harry. 'Your Highness, I should hate to lose you now to Michalides.'

Her dark lashes flickered, a faint flush warmed her face.

Harry left the building as soon as he had shaved. He made his way to the railway transport officer's enclave. The station was full, the tide of people enveloping porters, officials and platforms. Harry spotted Colonel Gebert outside his office, talking to a German captain. He waited until the German had saluted and gone, then approached the colonel.

'Colonel Gebert?'

'Ah, good morning,' said the colonel warmly.

'Is my friend Helga in your office?'

'Not as far as I'm aware.'

'But she's been to see you?'

'Not this morning, not yet.'

Harry's built-in alarm bell was touched off. Irena had knocked on his door five minutes ago to tell him she was on her way down.

'She's not the kind of person to lose herself in a station,' said Harry.

'No, I'm sure she isn't.' Colonel Gebert spoke on a pleasant conversational note. He had no reason to feel Harry's concern. 'Well, she has stopped somewhere amongst all these restless people.' A corporal came out from the office and spoke to him. The colonel nodded. 'Excuse me, please,' he said to Harry and went into his office to deal with one more impossible worry.

Harry stood anxiously surveying the crowded station, seeing faces move like heads on a roundabout. His alarm increased. She was so infernally cool, so casual about the dangers she ran. He could well imagine her fearlessly speaking up for the Germans she admired, no matter who was listening. Or strolling blithely around looking into the station shops. Harry turned a little grim. Wait until she condescended to appear. Highness or not, there would be things to say to her.

But he knew he was not convincing himself. She was not strolling around. She was cool, she was not thoughtless or stupid. If she had walked into the waiting arms of her enemies, what chance would he have of getting her back? Without any knowledge of the country, with his ignorance of any of the Balkan languages and his further ignorance of their hot-tempered politics, he would be like a blind cockerel in a den of foxes.

Perhaps for some reason she had gone back to her room? The hope of that was like a rush of light. Hurriedly he returned to the building. She was not there.

'Damn everything,' he muttered. 'God, it's my own fault, I should never have let her out of my sight.'

He went back to the transport officer. Colonel Gebert was in evidence again and curtailed a conversation he was having with one of his staff to spare Harry some time.

'You have found her?' he asked.

'No. Colonel Gebert, I'm worried.'

The courteous Austrian looked at him. Harry was dark and grim.

'Come into my office,' said Colonel Gebert. Harry went with him through a room full of desks, papers, telephones and military personnel, and into the colonel's own sanctum. 'We may get interruptions, but let us do the best we can. M'sieu Rokossky, why are you worried?'

Harry considered his position carefully. Helpful and considerate though the Austrian was, he would not be overjoyed to find Sergius Rokossky was actually an escaping British officer. Since the British were as responsible as any of the Allies for the impending collapse of the Austrian Empire, Colonel Gebert was more likely to become coldly correct. And highly suspicious of Helga Strasser.

Phrasing his French with care, Harry said, 'The fact is, Colonel Gebert, I am running from the Bolsheviks and Fräulein Strasser is running from the International Socialists.' He did not know if there was such an organization but it sounded credible enough. And perhaps disagreeable enough to the aristocratic Austrian army officer.

Colonel Gebert rubbed his chin. The lines under his eyes signified harassment, weariness, but there was a smile on his mouth. He did not seem surprised.

'You are political creatures, you and Fräulein Strasser? Agents, perhaps?'

'There's only one conclusive way of fighting battles, Colonel, but there are various ways of fighting political systems.'

'Bolshevism and Socialism, yes,' said the colonel, 'these are our new enemies. The difficulty is in persuading people to see it.' He regarded Harry shrewdly. 'I'm not sure what you are or who Fräulein Strasser really is, but I do know you saved an ambushed train and everyone on it. My world, I think, is finished. My wife and I will only have our memories to live on soon. But your world is about to begin and you and Fräulein Strasser will be needed in it to fight for it. I will ask only two questions. Do you assure me that Fräulein Strasser's enemies are these Socialists? And if she has disappeared are they the people most likely to be holding her?'

'Yes,' said Harry, 'and I further assure you they will have her head if they can. She wished to go shopping, to see you first, and I was to meet her here. I know her. The only reason why she would not be here would be because she'd been taken.'

'Well, we still administer Zagreb,' said the colonel, 'and we know where the political extremists are to be found, the ones who would shoot their own mothers if they got in their way. They are unusually quiet at the moment. They are waiting for Austria to sue for peace. They will be very noisy then. But today there are things we can still do. Let us go straight to the most likely point, a house in Javoga Square.' He picked up a telephone, asked for a number, was connected and spoke rapidly to someone at the other end. He replaced the receiver. 'Come, my Russian friend,' he said.

'Colonel Gebert, do you have time for this?'

'No,' said the colonel, 'but I have even less time for extremists and anarchists, and I do have an admiration for your colleague, a most remarkable and lovely young lady. It would be a pity not to spare a little time for her.'

Harry recognized a man coming to terms with his feelings, not with facts. Colonel Gebert preferred to help rather than ask questions. Questions might produce the wrong answers. Harry judged his man to be in his middle fifties, but he was neither dilatory in his decisions nor slow in his actions. Five minutes later he had Harry motoring with him through the district north of the station. Harry thought the place looked mellow, charming. They passed the King Tomislav monument and the Academy of Science and Art, founded by Bishop Strossmayer, long-living champion of Croatian independence and therefore a slight thorn in the side of the Emperor Franz Josef and a misguided man in the eyes of Colonel Gebert.

Harry, however, was far too tense to take on the role of a normal sightseer. He was savage with himself, he knew he had slipped up in letting Irena leave the building by herself. He could not believe that Colonel Gebert would merely drive up to some house and have her handed over to him. It could not be as simple as that. And the colonel did not know the value of the hostage, did not know it was Princess Irena of Moldavia the extremists were holding, if she was indeed in their hands.

The car pulled up at the end of a street, just before a large square. The centre of the square was a green garden, slightly neglected because with the gathering crisis the authorities could not get the ordinary things done in the usual way. Colonel Gebert, who had said nothing during the drive, possibly because of the ears of the corporal at the wheel, alighted and took Harry with him. Few people took much notice of them. Austrian troops here were not under the same pressure as those in Belgrade, threatened by the advancing Allies, and they maintained a numerically strong if tactically uneasy command of Zagreb.

Colonel Gebert looked across the square from the street corner. On the far side a man in a hat and coat put his hands into his coat pockets.

'This way,' said the colonel and turned around to lead Harry down a paved walk running adjacent to the near side of the square. The houses on this side of the square backed on to the walk. There were neat, painted tradesmen's doors let into the high boundary wall that ran the length of the walk. Three men ambling over the flagstones approached as the colonel stopped outside a dark green door. It was latched but not locked. He opened it and went through with Harry, the three men following. They were in the paved garden of a house. Shrubs and fruit trees grew in round beds, which were overgrown with weeds, and moss crept along cracks in the paving.

'Bolsheviks and Socialists,' murmured the colonel, 'leave gardening to the people. It's a fine point, M'sieu Rokossky, but a true one. This will do,' he added and took up a waiting position by some shrubs. They all waited there, the shrubs and the wintry-looking trees camouflaging their presence. It was a dull, moist November day, with the fallen leaves of autumn looking dead and wet. The windows of the three-storey house seemed just as dead. Steps led down to the garden from the ground floor and up to it from the basement. There was no sign of life.

In the square another plain-clothes man climbed the front steps of the house and knocked on the door. It was opened after a minute or two by a balding man. The policeman pushed him back and immediately other men, loitering nearby, rushed up the steps and surged into the house, where they began a thorough search. One man went to a back window, showed himself and signalled.

'Well, we shall see now,' said Colonel Gebert. He was quite restrained, quite calm, but he was aware that Harry was tense with acute worry and he hoped very much that the raid would be successful. But no one emerged from the back of the house, there was no sudden flight of men from the basement. Except for the man who had answered the door, and his wife, the house was empty. Colonel Gebert and Harry went in. They walked from room to room while a second search was made. Harry felt there was nothing here but the transient echoes of people who had slipped away. The balding man and his wife knew nothing of any woman. He walked back to the car with Colonel Gebert, his mood fierce, his anxiety mounting. The man in charge of the plainclothes police detachment walked with them, talking to the colonel.

The colonel said to Harry after a while, 'Is it possible you were so closely watched by the agents of these people that they might have known you were in contact with me?'

'Very possible,' said Harry.

'Then, my friend, it's also possible they would not have taken her to that house. That house is their daily rendezvous, where they talk about putting one half of the world to death. We know this house and they are aware we know.'

'I see,' said Harry. They paused at the car. 'Wherever they've taken her, they'll keep her until a man called Michalides comes to collect her, which will probably be when the war is over and power lies in different hands.'

'The police will do all they can,' said the colonel, 'but I must get back to my office. I am so sorry. We can at least check again whether she's returned to her room. There may be that chance. Will you come back with me?'

Every instinct told Harry she would not be in her room.

'I must do some walking, some thinking,' he said.

He plunged into the city, its unfamiliarity a complication and an obstacle. His anger with himself and his fear for the princess made it difficult to think. He was desperately worried not only by his failure but by the possibility that she was already being carried miles away, in a cab, a cart or even a car. She was not just a problem figure to him now, she was someone who had become very real and close.

He thought. He racked his brains, but every thought led nowhere. It was not long after ten, the day was young. There were queues at shops. He walked, he looked, he worried. A familiarity reached into his subconscious realm as he waited to cross a street, as his introspective eyes took in passers-by on the other side. It was a dark red costume that obtruded itself, and its familiarity clarified into recognition. He knew its wearer, the girl Nadia. She was hurrying and she did not look like the naive, breathless girl of the train. She was purposeful in her walk.

It was curiosity which captured Harry first, then a wondering suspicion. He remembered her entry into the compartment and how the official had shown her in, although the man must have known all the seats were taken. He had not left her in the corridor with other unlucky passengers. Either she had heavily tipped him or he had known her. In the compartment the occupants would have been expected to squeeze up to make room for a slim pretty girl. The farcical musical chairs being played at that precise moment had fortuitously offered her a vacancy, but no genuinely eager-to-please girl would have been brazen enough to take it in the way she did. And there had been her eyes, innocently bright, watching him and Irena.

His curiosity and suspicion melted into hope and he thought he saw a forlorn chance. He could not pass it by. He crossed the street and followed her. It was not a lonely and obvious furrow he ploughed, however, for the city was alive with people coming, going or wandering. For the busy pavements he was both grateful and uneasy. Grateful because he was one of many at her back, uneasy because among so many people ahead he might lose her.

She went across a square and turned right down a narrow street. He followed at a distance of about forty yards. She stopped midway down the street, looked into a shop window. Harry drew back into a doorway. He emerged after a few moments and saw her entering the shop. He walked quickly on, stopped and examined the shop window himself. It was a tobacconist's. Through the window the shop looked small and dark. He saw a counter but no proprietor, no customer. He counted to five to steady his nerves and went in. A little bell rang as he opened and closed the door. He saw a bead curtain on the customer side of the counter. Through an open door on the counter side a stout woman appeared. Harry looked at the shelves. He pointed to some cigarettes in lurid packets on an upper shelf.

'Kaj?' she said. What?

He pointed again and in French said, 'Cigarettes, if you please.'

Heavily and grumblingly she began to climb a little ladder. The shadow of a man darkened the dusty shop window. Harry made up his mind. There was nothing to lose except the stout woman's goodwill which, because of her climb, was minimal already. He shot through the bead curtain and found himself in a passage. At the end was a half-open door. He heard the voices of men, like an angry buzz. He heard the lighter tones of the girl who called herself Nadia. He slipped his hand into his jacket pocket. The feel of the revolver he had taken from Michalides on that first night was comforting.

From the shop the woman was calling in hoarse indignation. Harry sped quietly along the passage and into the room. There were three men and the girl. His pulses raced as he also saw Irena. She was sitting on a chair, the men were talking angrily to her and Nadia was arguing with everybody. They all had their backs to him except Irena. She did not seem frightened, but she was pale, her hands pressed to her ears to shut out the sound of the threats and insults. She saw Harry. Her blood rushed, her paleness submerged beneath the glad, surging tide and her eyes came to warm, beautiful life for the briefest moment before filling with alarm for him.

The men turned. The girl turned.

'Ah, the brave one,' she said, 'how good to see you, m'sieu. It's better to treat with both of you. There are questions, you see.'

'I hope I'm not going to be a disappointment to you, mademoiselle,' said Harry, his French a little rushed because of his nerves. He brought out the revolver. 'Stand still, please.'

But one of the men moved fast. He pushed Nadia hard in the back and she tumbled and pitched at Harry. The man came at Harry from behind the lurching girl and smashed a clenched fist down on the gun. Harry let his arm go with the weapon, keeping hold of it, and as Nadia fell on her knees and the man closed with him he brought up his right knee and made crippling contact with a highly susceptible stomach. The other men rushed, Irena held back a scream and looked wildly round for a weapon. Quick footsteps sounded in the passage and suddenly the room was swarming with plain-clothes men. They swooped and the room became a bedlam of kicks, curses, armlocks and arrests.

Irena, up from her chair, stood spellbound, staring at Harry out of dizzy and joyful eyes, warm blood suffusing her.

'Are you all right?' he asked, pocketing the revolver.

'Harry?' Because of emotion it was all she could say and the room was still so noisy.

'Have they hurt you?' He was intensely relieved.

'Oh, no, and I am quite all right now.' Her colour would not go. She wanted to kiss him. Oh, how wonderful that he had found her. The police were cuffing and subduing their still resistant captives. Nadia was spitting like a robbed young tigress. She was bundled out with her comrades, all of them advised they were under arrest for abducting a citizen of Austria.

'Austria, Austria? You are fools,' she cried, but it made no difference. The orders of the police were to hold them all for twenty-four hours and allow them to communicate with no one.

Irena and Harry were escorted back to the railway station, where Colonel Gebert was delighted to see them. He had asked the police to keep track of Harry, confessing that he felt Monsieur

Rokossky had his own undisclosable methods of finding things out, but that for his own good police protection had never been far away. Irena and Harry were both warmly grateful for this piece of foresight. The arrival of the plain-clothes men had resolved a very tricky situation in their favour.

'But I had no methods of any kind,' said Harry, 'only an immense piece of luck.' He recounted how his feelings and suspicions concerning the girl, Nadia, had led him to Fräulein Strasser.

'My friends at police headquarters have already telephoned to give me the names of the four people involved,' said the colonel. 'The girl's full name is Nadia Jovanovic. Does that mean anything to you?'

'Nothing,' said Harry. 'Except for the man Michalides they've all only been faces to me. But then,' he went on casually, 'in this business one's adversaries are often anonymous figures until the moment of truth arrives.'

'Really?' The colonel nodded as if he understood that that was something not open to general discussion. He informed them they would not be required to stay in Zagreb, the matter would be settled quietly and Nadia Jovanovic packed off back to Belgrade. Therefore they still had time to catch the noon train, especially if it did not quite leave at noon.

'But I have still not been to the shops,' protested Irena.

'My dear young lady,' said the colonel, shaking his head and shuffling papers about on his desk.

'It's one thing to be remarkable,' said Harry

severely, 'it's another thing to be careless.'

Irena made a little face. She had not been careless, she said, she had simply been carried off by ruffians. She told the colonel what she had already told Harry. She had been stopped by that two-faced girl when she left the building. Three men had appeared, all with nasty-looking knives, and she had been bundled into a waiting cab right outside the building. She had been taken to that shop and held in that unpleasant room. They had threatened her with all kinds of things, none of them very comforting.

'That is the way of people whose god is dark politics,' said Colonel Gebert. 'You are lucky to have escaped them, Fräulein Strasser. And you, M'sieu Rokossky, have a very fine aptitude for your work, whatever it is.'

Irena said, 'Colonel Gebert, we–'

'No, my dear young lady, I wish to hear no more.' His smile was tactful. 'I wish to remain satisfied with things as they are. Might I suggest you find some coffee and food, then meet me again in thirty minutes? You will not miss the train.'

Harry took her quietly but firmly back to her room. He followed her in and closed the door. Irena turned, glowing and alive, glad they were alone at last and she could tell him how wonderful he had been in rescuing her. Their eyes met and held, hers brown and big and warm, his dark and withdrawn. She felt a little shock that he looked grim rather than glad.

'Your Highness–'

'Oh, no,' she said in protest at such formality.

'I want you to know I'm not forgetting your position,' said Harry stiffly, 'but now that I'm able to talk to you without others listening, I'm going to give you an order, whether you dislike it or not. You–'

'Oh, what are you saying?' She was distressed. 'Why are you so cold when you have just done something wonderful? You are trying not to let me thank you. I thought you could never find me and when you did, when you came into that room, I was so happy – oh, I was a little afraid too–'

'It was my responsibility to find you.'

'Your responsibility?' Irena felt frozen.

'Yes.' Harry was forcing himself to be brutal. The intensity of his relief at her rescue had made him realize he was developing feelings that could escalate to an impossible level unless he re-established the impersonality of their original relationship. 'I am telling you, Your Highness, I am insisting, that you are not to go wandering about again.'

She was pale with shock.

'What are you doing, why are you like this? What have I done?' She had never been so distressed. 'I was not wandering about, I was going straight to Colonel Gebert.'

'That was a mistake that was almost fatal. You should have waited for me.'

Aghast, she wanted to weep. Instead, she drew fiercely on her pride. She flung up her head.

'Then it was a mistake by both of us,' she retorted, 'you did not tell me to wait.'

'I know I didn't.' He turned and faced the

window. 'I was an infernal idiot. I'm so damned angry with myself for letting you take risks. I should have known Michalides wasn't going to be fooled as easily as that. My God, I thought he'd got you for good.'

How intense he was, how dark. She stared bitterly at him, then her warm blood began to rush again. He was not angry with her, only with himself. She desperately did not want him to be angry with her, but she did not like him being so terribly angry with himself. Not when his arrival in that room had made her so giddy with happy relief.

'Please, Harry,' she said.

He looked at her so strangely, almost as if seeing her for the first time. He was silent, she was distressed. The moment was emotional. She dropped her eyes, her heart beating a little painfully.

'I'm sorry,' said Harry. He found it impossible to sustain brutality. Her distress made him wince. 'I really had no right to talk to you like that. But I'd hate to have Michalides drag you back to Rumania. So shall we decide not to make any more mistakes? Frankly, I wouldn't like to have to look Major Carlsen in the face and tell him I'd lost you.'

She had turned her back. She was unfastening her coat. He helped her off with it. She removed her hat. Those men had been irritated by its little veil and had ripped it off. They had not ripped the hat, thank goodness. She turned it over in her hands, looking at it but not really seeing it. She had wanted to thank Harry, to show him her gratitude, but he did not want her to be demonstrative.

She heard him say, 'Your Highness?'

That was it. He did not think she was entitled to be demonstrative, to be an ordinary woman.

She said muffledly, 'I understand. But you are being unfair to yourself. How could you have known that that dreadful girl was an agent for Michalides? You have done so much for me already. Perhaps it was a mistake for me to be on my own, but we are allowed one mistake, aren't we?'

'I think we've made more than one, but we've been lucky, we've survived them. We can't take any more chances.'

How formal he was, how polite, how logical. The adventure, which had been so dangerous but so exhilarating, had suddenly become a matter for cold common sense.

She turned to look at him, spots of colour tinting her cheeks.

'Captain Phillips,' she said, 'we knew it was going to be difficult, but we are ahead of them now, aren't we? It was something special, your work this morning and getting them locked up. I may say that, may I? You do not realize how depressed I was, how unhappy, and they were shouting at me–'

'Yes, why were they shouting at you?' asked Harry, thinking about it. 'They had you, all they needed to do was to keep you quietly out of sight until Michalides was able to come and collect you. So why were they shouting and looking so annoyed when they should have been feeling pleased with themselves?'

Irena went to the dressing table and began to

tidy her hair. It was easier to talk in this changed atmosphere when she was doing something.

'Oh, they were very pleased,' she said, 'but they are naturally abusive people and dislike me for all kinds of reasons, and so of course they had to shout and use dreadful language. Oh, and yes, they were angry because I would say nothing about you. That girl did not come in the cab herself, she stayed to find out what you would do. She came later, just before you did and told the men you had gone somewhere with Colonel Gebert, which made them more abusive. They wanted to know why you had gone with him, but I knew nothing and said nothing.'

'But what interest would they have in me once they had you?'

'I think perhaps they knew you were not the kind of man who would simply sit and do nothing,' she said, 'and they were right, weren't they? I am glad they were.'

Harry was thoughtful. He remembered the rifled case.

'Tell me,' he said, 'are those diamonds and your other jewels anything to do with all this?'

'Oh, how silly,' she said, 'of course not.'

'Are you sure? Jewels of that value do bring their own troubles.'

That upset her. Did he think it was the jewels he was being asked to protect? She became as cold as he had been a few moments ago.

'Thank you, Captain Phillips, for being so frank. It is always better to know exactly where one stands. I realize I am a problem to you and my jewels a trouble. What shall I do to make it easier for you? Throw myself or the diamonds out of the window? Myself, of course. The diamonds are much more manageable.'

'Stop talking nonsense,' said Harry.

'I am not talking nonsense.' She whirled round on him. It was better, yes, it was better to be like this. It did not embarrass him as her desire to be grateful did. 'I am quite serious, Captain Phillips. But as I am rather a coward perhaps you would help me by opening the window for me and giving me a push?'

He laughed. That was better for him too.

'Shall we see if we can find that coffee and some food?' he said.

'I am too upset,' she said frostily.

'That's understandable after what you've been through this morning,' he said, 'but I must contradict you on one thing. You are not a coward. You are a princess. Major Carlsen is proud of you. So am I.'

She stared wide-eyed at him. She was back on the rack of emotion.

'Harry? Oh, I know I'm a little trouble to you, and there is Elisabeth to think about, but I am not quite a disaster, am I?'

'Not yet,' said Harry.

They got some coffee and a little food, during which she was quiet. When they had finished they collected their things, vacated their rooms and went to find Colonel Gebert. He was in his office, immersed in the insoluble problems created by the news that the Austrian forces were withdrawing completely from the Balkans. He would have to find transport for all those who reached Zagreb. But he insisted on escorting Irena and Harry to the Trieste train. He took them to a compartment not only reserved for them but guarded by a soldier from his staff.

'You should not be disturbed,' he said, 'the man has orders to this effect and will be going all the way to Trieste.'

'How do we begin to thank you?' said Harry. He felt guilty at his deception of this courtly Austrian, but also he felt that if the colonel did find out he had helped an escaping British officer and a Rumanian princess, he would accept that it could not then be undone. Colonel Gebert was a man who would be philosophical about a fait accompli and the fortunes of war. Harry hoped he would have something more than his memories to live on when his more gracious world had disappeared.

'You've been so very kind,' said Irena, giving the colonel her hand. He gallantly kissed her fingertips.

'Kind? I've been very intrigued,' he said, 'and I shall always find it difficult to believe you are just a young lady from the Tyrol.' He turned to Harry and said something that sounded extremely foreign and incomprehensible.

'Pardon?' said Harry, asking for enlightenment.

'Young man, whoever you are, I've just said goodbye to you in Russian,' said the colonel, and pressed a slip of paper into Harry's hand. He smiled, and turned in the doorway of the compartment on his way out. 'By the way, trains run on steam. To make steam you need water. You arrived here with not more than a few litres in the boiler. It was very narrowly timed and typical of a man who takes risks. There's something in each of you two which makes for a compatible partnership in all that you do. When the war is over live in peace and with courage. I hope you will not have to wait too long before the train is on the move. Meanwhile, I must go and attend to the impossible again. Goodbye.'

When he had gone Irena looked hard out of the window, her eyes moist. Harry, his back against the closed compartment door, unfolded the slip of paper the colonel had given him. He said, 'You know, with a man like that one wonders what all the shooting has been about and why. And I don't think he ever believed I was Russian.'

'He is the kindest of men,' said Irena in a muffled voice.

'A friend,' said Harry. He read what was scribbled on the slip.

'Yes.'

'It's confusing my loyalties, you know.'

'Then it is making you think.' She sounded upset, accusing, her eyes on the platform scenes. 'Perhaps that is good for you. Perhaps it will make you understand that only the Bolsheviks will get anything out of the war. People like Colonel Gebert will lose everything.'

'You'd like me to join the Austrians and fight the Bolsheviks? I'm sorry, I can't do that.' He was calm, unaffected, and that upset her more.

'I'm not asking you to,' she said, 'I'm only thinking how nice Colonel Gebert is. You are only thinking of winning the war so that England can tell the rest of us what to do and what not to do. Well, England will see what happens when she tries to tell the Russian Bolsheviks what to do. She will find then that she has been fighting the wrong people.'

'I see. Those are your politics, are they?'

'Those are my feelings,' she said, her face still averted.

'Well, damn me,' said Harry. He stared at her. She did not care to return his look, it seemed. 'Thank you for that observation, ma'am. But at the moment, before I can return to blowing the enemy to bits, I'm committed to getting you to England. You might now prefer Colonel Gebert to do the job, but since I've given my word to Major Carlsen you'll have to continue putting up with me.'

'Yes, it's a nuisance for you, isn't it?' she said.

'Look here, I can't stand this,' said Harry, 'what the devil is happening?'

'Nothing,' she said in a suppressed voice, 'I am just upset, that is all.'

'I see.' He didn't see. He was aware of his own feelings. He was not sure of hers or precisely why she was upset. He looked again at the slip of paper. It contained the address of the Austrian-Lloyd Steam Navigation Company of Trieste, and a name, Josef Halder.

'Look at that,' he said in a matter-of-fact way to ease the atmosphere, and he passed the slip to her. She bent her head, hiding her eyes, and after a little while managed to read it. 'Colonel Gebert passed it to me,' said Harry.

'What does it mean?' she asked.

'That he suspected our reason for wanting to

get to Trieste may have had something to do with arranging a sea passage to somewhere. After all, would you go to Trieste in order to get back to the Austrian Tyrol? He must have thought about that. Now he's indicating that if we want to go to sea we should call at these offices in Trieste and ask for a Josef Halder. Do you think perhaps that he did recognize you?'

'No, how could he?' Irena was recovering.

'How? Your pictures and your person.'

'Do you think so? Well, perhaps,' she said. 'He was so very helpful, wasn't he? And he did not like Bolsheviks.' She drew a breath and said with a little air of formality, 'Please sit down, Captain Phillips. There is all this room, it isn't necessary for you to stand.'

He sat down opposite her. He needed to re-orientate his feelings, to complete his mission on a detached and impersonal basis. But there was this new and highly disturbing awareness of her. She had removed her coat. She sat in her good-looking brown costume and the brown hat she had managed to clean. The veil was missing, and her unprotected eyes looked as if they had just been softly washed in their absorbed study of the platform. She had so much charm, so much swift life.

The fact was, she was extraordinarily lovely.

He realized how damned difficult the rest of the journey was going to be.

There were the usual masses of people in the station, some there to say goodbye to others, some in search of others and some who, in the depression of the moment, wanted nothing to do with anybody. Croats, Slovenes, Austrians, Hungarians and Germans mingled, separated, pushed and shouted. Irena at the compartment window was a striking visibility.

'Where's your veil?' asked Harry.

'Somewhere in that room,' said Irena, 'they tore it off. But we are quite safe now.'

'Are we?' he said.

'I mean,' she said a little confusedly, 'I mean we are at least safer, aren't we? It is going to be much more difficult for Michalides to trace us with his friends here locked up.'

'I'd like to think so,' said Harry.

'You know, I've only the things I've been travelling in and you have only what you are wearing. Does it matter about trying to hide our faces when our clothes are so familiar to people who are looking for us?'

'They're familiar to Michalides and his friends, ma'am,' said Harry, 'but I was thinking that any member of the public in these regions might recognize you. I admit I wouldn't have known who you were myself, but you're very recognizable in most of the Balkan countries, aren't you?'

'Oh, not really to many people,' she said.

'But perhaps it's a good idea to get some different clothes,' he said, 'we'll see what there is for you in Trieste.'

'Yes,' she said.

'Are all these people looking for trains?' he said as she turned her eyes on the platform again.

'Perhaps they aren't sure what they are looking for.' She cast a quick glance at him, her nerves and emotions betrayed by the sweeping cast of her lashes as he returned her glance.

'No, perhaps they aren't,' he said.

She felt so upset. Things were not the same between them. He was keeping himself at such a distance and she had said such unfair things to him. Something had happened between them, it had happened when he had swept into that room to deliver her from political ruffians and make her dizzy with joy, and when she had wanted to thank him and he would not let her. Now he was being terribly polite and it hurt. He was even calling her Ma'am. It was making her live on emotions far too finely balanced. She wished the train would start. They would be able to be natural again when it did, when there was movement and scenery and Trieste lay ahead. It had always been easy to talk to him, even when she had been standing on her dignity and he had been making a little fun of her or ordering her about.

The silence too much for her, she said lightly, 'When we are on our way, I do think Michalides will give up, really.'

'Give up?' Harry was astonished. 'Don't you realize that when he receives nothing but a blank silence from his friends here, he's going to arrange for some new frenzy of activity?'

She was quite glad in a way to be able to say, 'Well, there's no need to scowl at me.'

'I'm not.' He wasn't. 'But Michalides is a hungry bloodhound, not a fat cat, and if you think he and his friends are ready to let you go now, what was Major Carlsen making all the fuss about in the first place?'

Oh, that is better, she thought. He is back to

bullying me and worrying about me. Anything was preferable to having him silent or polite.

'Oh, you are right, of course.' She managed a smile. 'I think my escape this morning has gone to my head a little. See, I will do everything you say from now on, I promise.'

Those eyes of hers. So hugely bewitching, thought Harry. They could charm the boots off Hindenburg. No wonder the Germans thought she might induce a mood of defiance in their ambivalent Kaiser.

'Just let's do everything the safe way,' he said.

'Yes,' she said. 'Please, I am sorry I said silly things just now.'

'No,' he said with the glimmer of a smile, 'you must speak your opinions. They're very illuminating, ma'am, I assure you.'

'Captain Phillips, please don't call me that.'

'Queen Victoria accepted it as appropriate,' he said.

'I am not Queen Victoria.'

'If you were, I'd be frightened to death,' he said.

'Please, we are friends, aren't we?' She was making an effort, finding the strain unbearable when everything only a few hours ago had been wonderful. 'It's nice that we have the compartment to ourselves and can talk. Tell me about Elisabeth.'

It came out impulsively. Compulsively. Elisabeth was far more important now than she had been. Before she had been a shadowy factor, meaning something to Harry but not to her. Now it was necessary to know all about her, for Harry to talk and not be withdrawn and formal.

'Elisabeth?' he said, while the train stood and the people outside got in each other's way.

'Yes. Your fiancée. You have not forgotten her, have you?'

He thought about Elisabeth. She was as fair and honeyed as Irena was dark and vivid. His mind's eye pictured her in portrait, investing her with the soft, serene beauty of Gladys Cooper in those postcard photographs soldiers put up on the walls of their trench dugouts. He had known Elisabeth for twelve years, ever since his father, a bank manager, had taken charge of a branch in a Hampshire market town. He had been fifteen then, Elisabeth twelve. She lived close by and followed him about, having a calming influence on his boyish recklessness. He liked to scrump apples. She would never let him take more than they could eat, say two for her and three for him. They had become the closest and most affectionate of friends through the years. To be friends as well as lovers was to promise the best of marital relationships.

'Elisabeth is really much too good for me,' he said.

'Is she? You are being too modest, aren't you? Is she pretty?'

Harry smiled.

'She's a woman,' he said. 'Girls are pretty. Women are lovely. There's a difference, isn't there, when they come of age?'

She knew he did not simply mean when they became twenty-one.

'She will be so glad when the war is over,' she said.

'She'll be wondering at this moment what the devil's happened to me,' said Harry, 'I'll have been posted missing weeks ago.'

'Perhaps, if she has come of age in an imaginative way and is very lovely,' said Irena, 'she will decide to marry someone else.'

'Imaginative way? I would be too dull for her, you mean?'

'Oh, no!' She was shocked at his inferring she meant that. 'Oh, you are not at all dull. I meant she will attract men whom she can see each day – oh, I am saying quite the wrong things. No one who is engaged to you would marry anyone else.'

'Oh?' said Harry with a smile.

Doors slammed then. Whistles blew, officials took command of the platform and the crowds drew back. The train began to move. It was not much after noon. Colonel Gebert, thought Harry, would be pleased about a train almost leaving on time when the empire was in such chaos.

Chapter Ten

Trieste. It had been governed by Austria since 1382 when it placed itself under the aegis of Leopold III and secured protection against the aggressive ambitions of the Venetians. But it was a city Austria had never been able to separate from its extrovert Italian origins, and the more Austrianized its façade became the more rampant grew its underlying florid Latin exhibitionism.

Austria, claiming it an integral part of her dominion, pursued an uneasy relationship with the Italian community during the war for the simple reason that Italy herself was on the Allied side.

The evening was dark, the wind from the Adriatic cold and damp, as Irena and Harry emerged from the station. But the seaport's wintry chill crackled with the overtones of Austria's imminent plunge into the abyss. The Emperor Charles was conducting independent peace negotiations with the Allies and Austria was within twenty-four hours of her Armistice Day. The Italian irredentists of Trieste were celebrating in advance. Carrying burning torches, they were dancing and cavorting in the steep, narrow streets of the old town and conducting a noisy prelude to the act of separatism.

Harry was not inclined to be drawn into these premature festivities and he supposed Irena's pro-German outlook was hardly likely to make her want to dance. He suggested they go immediately to the steamship company, find Josef Halder and make enquiries of him. If the offices were closed they would have to look for accommodation and try again in the morning. Irena wondered if that was not hurrying things, but said that as she had promised to be amenable she could not very well be otherwise now, could she?

'Not without being a disappointment to both of us,' said Harry. He put his hand under her elbow as roistering Italians surged by. His touch made her impulsively responsive. She put her arm through his.

Her speech was just as impulsive. She said, 'Oh, you aren't angry with me any more, are you?'

He was a little astonished. They had left the memory of that scene behind them hours ago.

'I know I sometimes sound as if I'm giving orders,' he said, 'but I'm not allowed to be angry with one of your high state.'

'Please don't sound as if you are making a speech,' she said.

She kept her arm through his. The streets were cold and dark in places, bursting into torchlit tides of revelry elsewhere or bringing rowdy running students out of junctions, and it was natural for Harry to give her his arm and for her to take it. She was close to his side. He felt her warmth. He tried to think of Elisabeth waiting at home for him. He smiled wryly at himself. A woman who was waiting was a far more logical comfort to have on one's mind than a woman who was a princess.

Some shops were open. So were the offices of the Austrian-Lloyd Steam Navigation Company, which looked besieged. There were queues and clamour, people desperate for passage on ships which either did not exist or were blockaded in, but which might exist or might be free to sail because of the news. Harry forced his way through with Irena and spoke to the first harassed shipping clerk he saw.

He asked in French if he could see Josef Halder.

The clerk, unresponsive, said in German, 'What is it you want?' Harry let Irena answer, telling her to mention Colonel Gebert.

So she said, 'Do you know Colonel Gebert of Zagreb?'

'No,' said the clerk, preparing to shuffle off. He had had a thousand people all asking questions he could not answer.

'Herr Halder does,' she said, 'please fetch him.'

'Impossible, impossible, do you think liners are suddenly sailing?'

'Please,' said Irena with her loveliest smile, 'please will you fetch Herr Halder?'

He could not resist that smile. He disappeared. He returned a few minutes later.

'Come with me, please,' he said and they followed him through a maze of corridors. They met Josef Halder in an old office that looked as weatherbeaten as he did, with his white hair and thin, nut-brown face. His white moustache was tipped with brown from cigarette smoke, his hair tufted above his ears like white wings.

'We are closing in a moment,' he said, lifting a large watch from his waistcoat pocket and consulting it. 'You are friends of Colonel Gebert?'

'We count him as one of our best and kindest friends,' said Irena.

Harry was not going to be able to follow the German conversation, but he laid the slip of paper on the desk. It had been signed by the colonel.

'Humph,' said Herr Halder, eyeing it suspiciously.

'The Herr Colonel wishes you to put us on a boat,' said Irena.

'Boat? Boat?' Josef Halder looked at her in comical disgust. Then at Harry, who in his blue peaked cap and black jersey did not seem unlike a seaman. 'Do you mean a rowing boat?'

'I mean something that puts to sea,' said Irena.

'Something?' Herr Halder was gravelly. 'A ship, perhaps?'

'What is the difference?'

'I would not put to sea in a boat myself, but then I am a cautious man. Where is it you wish to go?'

'Where do we wish to go?' asked Irena of Harry in French.

'To the nearest Italian port,' said Harry.

'Ah, he's French?' said Herr Halder ominously.

'I am a White Russian,' said Harry, producing his papers.

'And you, Fräulein?'

'I am Austrian,' said Irena.

'So,' said Herr Halder, curling one of his tufts, 'he's a White Russian and you are Austrian, and of course you both have identification documents and all you want is passage to Italy. No doubt for the purpose of seeing Hungarian relatives who are unfortunately dying but who don't mind passing into the merciful hands of God as long as they first see you and exchange a few last words with him. Are you married?'

'Colonel Gebert did not ask that question, why should you?' said Irena.

'Because you have come to coax a favour from me, because ten thousand other people are trying to do the same,' he said. 'They all want a passage to somewhere, anywhere, as long as it resembles the Garden of Eden. Day and night I'm accosted, bullied, cajoled, seduced and battered by people I've never seen before and never will again. And what rogues, vagabonds and miscreants most of them are, looking over their shoulders the whole time and not a respectable relationship among any of them or a single truthful eye. It would be a welcome change to look into the face of truth and virtue again.'

'Herr Halder!' Irena was biting, frosty. 'Really, you must count yourself lucky that my Russian friend doesn't understand you or he would certainly have the fiercest words with you. How dare you suggest that I'm not virtuous and he isn't truthful?' Her brown eyes were scolding. 'The fact that we may not be married today doesn't mean we shall not be married tomorrow.'

Herr Halder caressed his moustache, his deep-set eyes thoughtful beneath his shaggy white brows.

Harry said, 'What's going on?'

'He's concerned that we're not respectable,' said Irena.

'Name of a name,' said Harry with teeth-grinding effect.

'I've told him,' said Irena, 'that though we may not be married now we may be tomorrow.'

'Quite right,' said Harry.

'There, you see,' said Irena to the hard-headed company manager, 'my friend has just pledged himself to me in the most respectable fashion.'

'Humph,' said Josef Halder. He searched among some papers on his desk and found a note he had scribbled. 'You are lucky. Colonel Gebert has spoken to me on the telephone. Otherwise I'd have had you arrested.'

'He has taken the trouble to telephone? Why, then,' said Irena, 'are you conducting such an unfriendly interview with us?'

'Ah, we all have our ways of discovering what people are like. My good friend Colonel Gebert said you were not quite like other miserable people who come hammering on my door.' He chuckled. 'You have a laudable tongue, young lady, and your Russian friend is a saviour of trains, I believe.' He turned over more papers. He peered at one. 'Well, go to the Porto Franco at midnight, to the gates. A man will meet you there. A Captain Sabata. He'll take you to Italy.' He chuckled again. 'But not in a rowing boat. It will cost you money.'

'How much?' said Irena.

Josef Halder turned his peering eyes on her.

'Captain Sabata will tell you that. Do you imagine that I wish to make myself rich in such a way? The Austrians may go, the Italians may come, but I am interested only in the sea and ships. Men will never make of the sea what they have made of the land, and every ship afloat sails only on sufferance.'

'You are a good man, Herr Halder,' said Irena. She informed Harry of the arrangement, adding that if they were to leave at midnight she would like to find time to buy some new clothes.

'Agreed,' said Harry, 'but the important thing is to leave.'

'Yes,' she said. He was thinking of Elisabeth, of course, who did not know what had happened to him. 'My friend is very grateful,' she said to Herr Halder, 'and immensely in your debt for arranging things so quickly.'

'Ah, the Russians, they are very intense,' said Herr Halder, 'and with them such things as going to Italy for the sake of love are a matter of life and death.'

Deeply the pink suffused Irena's face.

'Now what has he said?' asked Harry.

'Nothing,' she said.

They shook hands with Josef Halder, thanked him and said goodbye. Like Colonel Gebert, Josef Halder wondered why when so many other events were far more important, far more doom-laden, he had chosen to give time and help to these two young people. Perhaps because he saw in them hope for the aftermath, perhaps because he felt they were inseparably committed to life and adventure, and each other.

Shops in the Italian quarter were open, cafes were full. There was not much to sell in the shops, not much to serve in the cafes, but who wanted to close when the war was coming to its end and the future was going to be Italian? Trieste would return to the warm embrace of Italy, for the Allies had promised it would. And one could celebrate on a feast of words and orations, while adding water to the wine to make more of it.

Irena and Harry sat in a cafe. The coffee was awful and Irena could not understand why the fish they were eating, baked in sauce, did not taste fresh. It smelled, she said, like a trawler's deck drying in the sun.

'Eat it up,' said Harry.

He was more relaxed. He was not terribly, awfully distant any more. They were able to talk again.

'Yes, eat it up, my child,' she murmured, 'or

your guardian and protector will stand you in a corner.'

'Then we'll see if there's a dress shop open,' said Harry.

'Oh, I have your permission? You will let me shop?'

'You've been a good girl this evening,' said Harry, 'you deserve a small treat.'

'Oh, Harry, you beast to tease me so.' It was a little burst of delicious reaction because he was smiling again, teasing her again. She knew she must be very careful all the same, they each had to be careful in their own way.

But as they looked at each other they laughed.

They went in and out of shops. There was nothing, simply nothing, Irena said. It was bad enough the war costing so many lives and forcing people into near starvation, without taking away from women the means to dress decently. No, she was not getting things out of proportion, she insisted, anyone who had studied the effects of war on the civilian populations would know it was the morale of women which was of the greatest importance in helping nations to survive.

'But what we've seen so far seemed decent enough to me,' said Harry.

'Something which covers one is adequate, it is not necessarily decent. It must have some style or one might as well go around in sacks.'

'Quite so,' said Harry tolerantly as they avoided fervent Italians wanting to embrace them, 'but something adequate, warm and practical would really be a better buy than a silk morning dress.'

'Practical? Are you crazy? I would rather die.'

'I now understand,' said Harry, 'why when they put the princess into a bed of twelve mattresses she couldn't sleep because there was a pea under the bottom one.'

'How ridiculous,' said Irena. She laughed in the cold night air. 'How funny,' she said.

People surged over the cobbles and a girl linked her arm with Harry's and a man helped himself to Irena's hand. In loud and amorous Italian they issued invitations to love and excitement.

'Parlez-vous français?' said Harry.

'Oui,' said the young Latin lady.

'Good,' said Harry, 'I'm trying to find a shop where my wife can buy a decent dress. By decent I mean something to make her mouth water. *Comprendre*, mademoiselle?'

'Ah, you're the right kind of husband to have in times like these,' she said. 'M'sieu, go to Merlini's. Even now, they're still able to dress the very best people, though not every week. It's for the celebrations you wish your wife to dress well?'

'Yes,' said Harry, 'but even on ordinary occasions she wouldn't be seen dead in anything practical.'

'Such a good principle,' said the girl. She instructed Harry on the location of Merlini's, then she and the man disengaged themselves and went to look for people more interested in amour than fashions. Harry explained to Irena about Merlini's.

'I heard everything, thank you,' said Irena, 'including the revelation that you are an exceptional husband and I am an impractical wife.'

They found their way to Merlini's, which did not look much on the outside but was very elegant inside. There were no creations on view, only some imposing chairs of blue and gilt selectively residing on a blue carpet. And a madame, who did not seem very accommodating at first. Merlini's did not specialize in receiving customers who came in company with someone who looked like a seaman and carried a battered case only good for housing bombs. Irena, cool and gracious, put matters right with the information that her companion was an eccentric acquaintance of Victor.

'Victor?'

'Who else?' said Irena, sweetly urbane and convincing.

'The Italian K–'

'Hush,' said Irena.

Madame was not completely taken in but she was amused. And this was how many of the best people did behave, as if they were slightly off their heads. She called an assistant and from the coffers of fashion buried unseen beyond the salon came dresses and coats. Irena wanted one dress and one coat, nothing more, she said. Harry hoped she was not deceiving herself.

As far as dresses were concerned there were no silks. Silk was tragically unobtainable. Irena went into a room and tried on a selection of dresses in other materials. That selection was of three only. Each dress was exquisitely styled and stitched, and to her delight one in speckled grey and white, so unusual, suited her beautifully. At least, she thought so. So did Madame, who would never let any client leave the shop with a Merlini creation that did not. No one else's opinion was needed. However, perhaps Harry should see she was not wasting her money.

'I think perhaps my eccentric friend might like to see it?' she suggested. Madame's opinion, which she did not voice, was that husbands allowed price to prejudice them but men friends did not. She preceded Irena back into the shop and presented her to Harry with a flourish. He took in the sweeping, slenderizing lines of the dress and the willowy look it gave her. She wore a quite shy smile with it and the faintest flush. 'What do you think?' she asked shyly.

Harry thought it enchanting.

'Is it warm?' he said. He could have said much more. He knew it was better not to.

Irena, bitterly disappointed at such an unimaginative response, said, 'Warm? Warm? Oh, Philistine!' She swept back into the dressing room to try on coats. She settled on a long, waisted black one with a white fur collar. She insisted out of sheer heartburning that Harry see her in this too. He thought it made her look like a warm winter princess.

'Excellent,' he said, 'that should keep the cold out.'

She could not bear it. She swept up to him and whispered fiercely, 'You are supposed to tell me how it makes me look, not how it will resist the weather!'

'It makes you look like a princess,' said Harry as lightly as he could manage, but that made up for everything and her eyes shone.

Madame stood aside in smiling satisfaction, judging their whispers to be romantic. It was a good time to be romantic, with Italy and Italians looking in the face of oncoming victory. Irena, her feet taken from under her because of what he had said, wanted to hug him for being so nice. Harry, caught by feelings he knew he should guard against, wondered whether Her Highness should be kissed courteously for being what she was, or generously for being so beautiful.

'I shall now buy a new hat,' said Irena a little breathlessly. Madame said they did not sell hats as separates and there was only one she could offer, which was that belonging to the coat, a black-and-white one. It was quite perfect, so much so that Harry took only one brief look at sheer enchantment and then studiously regarded the carpet to bring himself back into the realm of common sense. Irena went back into the dressing room to change, to pay for her purchases and have them packed in a large cardboard box.

Harry waited. A woman came in, a woman wearing furs, who was so obviously aristocratic that naturally she thought Harry, in his seaman's black jersey and dark grey suit, was someone who carried furniture about. She looked around, faintly surprised that a furniture man should be in sole occupation of the salon. Madame emerged with Irena, Irena carrying a long white, gilt-lettered box. The woman stared, Irena caught her stare. The woman smiled in delight and gushed.

'Sonya Irena! I–'

'You are mistaken,' said Irena and walked

aloofly by, leaving the shop in company with Harry.

'What was that all about?' asked Harry in the street.

'Nothing important,' said Irena.

'She recognized you,' said Harry.

'It's nothing to worry about.'

'Yes, it is.'

'It is not! And we had better hurry.'

'There's plenty of time,' said Harry. 'She did recognize you. Well, it was bound to happen sooner or later, I suppose. Who was she?'

'Oh, some insignificant countess,' said Irena, 'and who would think that after four years of war she would walk around in all those ostentatious furs?'

'She'll gossip about you all over Trieste. The sooner we get away the better.'

'Yes, I have just said that.' She was a little agitated.

'Did you buy a veil?'

'No.'

'Hmm,' said Harry.

'Please don't hmm,' she said. He was carrying the case. He took the long box from her and put it under his arm. She thanked him. He was silent, thinking about her vulnerability. She said in a small voice, 'Harry, please don't be cross again. I will not need a veil once we are in Italy, we can both be ourselves.'

'I'm not cross,' he said, 'but even in Italy there may be comrades willing to do Michalides' work for him. Comrades throw bombs, you know.'

'You are still worrying about me,' she said.

'Yes,' he said.

They got away from the increasing night revelry, away from singing and dancing Italians and out of the damp cold, whiling away the next hour or so in a cafe illuminated by tall candles. Harry drank brandy and Irena drank wine. The place was crowded and warm.

'Do you really think we shall be able to get on a ship?' asked Irena.

'You're not thinking of a P&O liner, are you?' he smiled.

'P&O? What is that?' She was wearing her plain coat and brown hat again. He did not think she looked any less attractive.

'A shipping line, very well thought of in my country.'

'Oh, yes, I think I know.' She smiled. She was happy that they were so companionable again. 'They have ships that go sailing into the sun and are also very well thought of for honeymoons, yes?'

'If you're rich,' said Harry.

'And if there's no war. Yes, that would be nice, do you think?'

'Oh, very nice,' he said casually. 'Well, perhaps you'll meet an exiled Russian Highness and try it with him.' Irena winced. 'And unless the war is over when we get back I shan't have time to go anywhere with Elisabeth, I'll have to return to my regiment.'

'But Major Carlsen said the war is bound to be over soon.'

Harry wondered if she needed a Bible when she had Major Carlsen. That correct, persuasive German had landed him with more than the original problem. He looked at Irena, at her earnest, brown-eyed beguilement. She was always earnest when she was quoting Major Carlsen or talking about him.

'The war looks like being over for Austria, perhaps, but Germany is a different kettle of fish. In spite of Major Carlsen.'

'Yes, you are right, of course. You are always right.' She was sweetly stinging. 'You are quite an oracle.'

'Well, you can get Major Carlsen to wrap me in plaster after the war, turn me into a monument and mount me on a piece of marble somewhere in Ancient Greece.'

'I would like to know what I have done,' she said a little bitterly, 'you have been grumpy on and off with me all day.'

'Grumpy again? Where did you get hold of that word?'

'Isn't it right, grumpy? Oh, is it gruffy?'

He couldn't help himself, despite the necessity of keeping at arm's length. He laughed. She felt relieved. But she simply wasn't going to be able to stand it if he continued to say things that made her feel he didn't like her.

'I'm sorry, did I sound grumpy?' he said. 'It must be things on my mind. You put up with me very well.'

'Oh, I have a temperament quite angelic, you know,' she said.

'Have you?'

'No,' she confessed.

He laughed again. The cafe was cosy because of

all the people there, everyone cheerful because the war was nearly over. Irena was looking at him from under her lashes. He thought her resilience as endearing as her courage. She was going into exile because people considered she had been too pro-German. It was not going to be easy for her, whether she stayed in England or went elsewhere. She was facing the loneliness and bitterness of exile, but she was not crying, she was not complaining. She had just bought herself some brave and beautiful new clothes.

He supposed that in new clothes young women like Princess Irena could face up to all kinds of disasters.

How the devil could one supply a purely impersonal service to a woman like that?

Chapter Eleven

They arrived at the harbour of Porto Franco just before midnight. It was black, it was chilly, and the Adriatic looked menacing. The gates to the shipping berths were locked and guarded. They waited, growing cold. It was a little after midnight when a short, tubby man in a thick coat and peaked cap loomed up out of the damp darkness. He had eyes like a cat and came straight to them.

'You're Herr Halder's friends?' He spoke in German.

'Yes,' said Irena.

'Good. This way.' He took them away from the gates, round a corner and into an empty warehouse. Harry, carrying the case and the box, was aware of the easy target he made in the cold, unfamiliar surroundings, but he did not think Josef Halder a man who rubbed shoulders with assassins.

Captain Sabata lit an oil lamp, lifted it and showed his prospective passengers his honest face, which was round, bristly and amiable.

'I am Captain Sabata,' he said.

'Do you speak English?' asked Harry.

Captain Sabata could but did not ask why that language was preferred. He stated in so many words that he was in business to help those who needed it and could help defray the overheads. He was the soul of Italian amiability and his round, fat smiles induced refugees to pay up with much less heartbreak than if he had been a stony-faced bargainer. He had been running the gauntlet in his fishing smack for many months now, ferrying people from Trieste to Italy under the noses of the Austrian navy, which never ventured very far because of British and French warships. The war, yes, that made things difficult and expensive, but when one was in business for the good of people one had to take risks.

It was understood, was it, that he could not afford to do it out of pity or sympathy alone?

Harry said it was completely understood.

Where did they want to go? To any port in Italy? Well, he could put them ashore wherever they liked as long as it was close to Chioggia, south of Venice. It would be costly but not prohibitive. That was understood too?

Harry said it was and wondered how much he and Irena could produce between them.

How much was it understood? Captain Sabata's lamplit smile was a beam of encouragement. Harry had a little money left, and pooled what he had with Irena's residue of German banknotes. Captain Sabata took them, flipped through them and handed them back with a fat smile. He was sorry, excessively so, but there was some paper money which he did not regard as a good investment. Perhaps English pounds? No? What could be done then?

Irena asked him to compose himself for a moment. She vanished into shadows. She came back and showed the captain two shining, lustrous pearls. His sigh was an exhalation of happy relief for all of them. However, they would permit him? He took the pearls, examined them under the lamp, tried them between his teeth and then said with the utmost cordiality that when understanding was mutual between people nothing less than mutual satisfaction came of it. No more need be said. They could come fishing with him.

'We're to go now?' said Irena.

'But yes, signorina, sure we go now. What is it you think, that with Captain Pietro Sabata you stand around?'

Harry was glad to move. The warehouse seemed full of rustles and whispers. That could be because of rats. But Michalides had pressed so close on them that it was difficult to believe they would simply walk out of this place and on to Captain Sabata's smack without hindrance.

They followed the Italian through the warehouse. He unbolted a door and they stepped out on to the dockside. Irena shivered a little because of the cold sea wind. It was so quiet that they heard the soft slap of water against moored vessels. Captain Sabata's vessel, the sloop *Antonia*, was a dark mass of masts and tackle, hugging the jetty as if loath to be parted from its solid, landrooted security. Two crew members, awaiting the captain, helped Irena aboard. Below, in the low-ceilinged quarters, she and Harry found the captain was not doing business with them alone. There were at least twenty people, men, women and children, crammed into a space designed for six. They were on the bunks, around the clamped table and on the floor. They were quiet but anxious, patient but impatient. A sigh went up as Irena and Harry descended into their midst to take up what little space was left.

The old tub coughed, the engine dully hammered, and the *Antonia* reluctantly divorced itself from its berth. With chugging heaviness it nosed towards the harbour mouth. The wind was cold but light as Captain Sabata put to sea with other vessels of the Trieste fishing fleet, but when they veered south for the fishing grounds he kept to a south-west course. The crew doused the lights.

It was cramped, uncomfortable and dark for the passengers, all of whom had their own reasons for risking the trip. The silence was compulsive, as if each of them was listening for the sounds of pursuit. It was tense for nearly an hour, when any coastguard cutter or naval launch, lurking around to pounce on just such a runner as Captain

Sabata, might have made an interception and blinded the *Antonia* with light. But nothing happened and there was a perceptible relaxing of nerves and bodies, although they had hours of chugging progress still in front of them.

It rained. They heard it pattering insistently on the deck, but no one mentioned it, no one talked about anything, and the few children who snuggled close to parents did not raise a sound. It seemed that everyone had secrets to keep.

Irena and Harry sat on the floor, backs against a lower bunk. They were silent too, Irena with her arm in his and close to his warmth. She did not think Harry minded this, it was just her natural need for feeling secure, and she hoped Elisabeth would not mind, either. He was probably thinking of Elisabeth. In these crowded quarters, in this silence, only one's mind could be busy.

A swell developed. The *Antonia,* known as a drunk, was a roller, a wallower, and several people, including two children, were sick. Included in the price, however, were basins. Everything began to smell, but no one complained, and the seasick sufferers did their groaning in the basins.

Harry thought that Italy should see the beginning of the easiest and safest part of the journey. It was an Allied country. All they had to look out for in making their way to France and through France were the comrades Michalides might be in touch with. Harry had no idea whether the Socialist ramifications were as internationally widespread as Major Carlsen had implied. If they were he supposed an extremist French comrade would be as hostile to Princess

Irena as a Rumanian one. He was sure of one thing. Michalides did not want to lose her.

He felt her move. Her head came to rest on his shoulder. She was actually composed enough, even on this wallowing old tub, to close her eyes and sleep. She had taken off her hat and her soft hair caressed his cheek. As the *Antonia* slugged a rolling way through the heavy sea to Chioggia, Irena achieved a modest series of catnaps, as she had on the train to Belgrade.

Apart from the seasickness among some, the crossing was uneventful. An hour before dawn, with the *Antonia* standing well off from the Italian coastline, the passengers were rowed to a beach south of the island of Chioggia. Captain Sabata said a round, smiling goodbye to them. Having cheerfully skinned most of them he invited all of them to come back when the war was over.

There was a long walk, a trudge, ahead. Irena and Harry made light of it and that afternoon reached Padua by train. There Irena begged the comfort and rest of an hotel for a day or two. Padua of ancient fame was beguiling, and Italy, although torn, bewildered and impoverished by the war, was in a state of sudden headiness. Austria had this day concluded an armistice with her. The Habsburg Empire had collapsed and the picturesque city of Padua was as delighted as the rest of the country. Women, resuscitating the best that they had in their depleted wardrobes, were out wearing feathers and boas and hats and colours again. And everybody was kissing everybody else.

'Hotel?' said Harry. 'Hm.'

'Oh, hm, hm,' said Irena.

'Your papers. Austrian. Perhaps it won't matter now. I think the Austrians are probably being kissed too.'

'Oh, I no longer need those papers,' she said, 'I'm myself again. Sonya Irena and so on. And so are you.' She laughed as they walked. 'Also, we are married, yes? There is the marriage certificate which I have. I have kept it very carefully hidden. We are supposed to be husband and wife from now on, aren't we.'

'I thought the idea was that we weren't supposed to be that at all, that it was merely an arrangement to get you safely into England.'

'I am only saying,' she said calmly as they crossed the Piazza del Signori, 'that if anyone makes a fuss about who I am, or if I'm required to answer fussy questions, I shall simply point out I'm your wife. As you are a British officer who has just made a marvellous and heroic escape no one will wish to make things uncomfortable for us then, do you think?'

It simply wasn't possible to resist her. Harry smiled. The day was dull and wet but Irena was delightfully indifferent to it. She was responsive to life, to people, and rain or sunshine were only important in as far as they governed what she should wear. Rain could not depress her.

'Well, we'll look for an hotel,' said Harry, 'and then I must see if there's a British consulate here. I'd better show myself if there is.'

They managed to get a cab. They asked to be driven to a good hotel. The cabbie looked at

Irena and said he would take them to the Victor Emmanuel. Bowling choppily along through the wet but festive streets, Irena had the opportunity to delve into a tiny pocket in her handbag.

'There, you see?' she said and showed him a gold wedding ring. She took off her glove and slipped the ring on. 'It is necessary to wear it now, isn't it?'

'I suppose so,' said Harry. He remembered the ritual of the ring at the ceremony in her Bucharest house. She had removed it after finishing her role as a widow. Now it was on her finger again and she was viewing it with a wry smile. Harry wrestled with unreality and found it rather an unsatisfactory contest.

The Victor Emmanuel Hotel was imposing. Harry in his crumpled suit and common jersey was obviously not the greatest catch the establishment had made, but Irena, for all her signs of travel and travail, was obviously not just somebody who had come in out of the rain. At the reception desk English was spoken. Harry asked for two adjoining rooms.

'Or a suite,' said Irena, with visions of lots of space and a huge bath. 'My husband is Captain Harry Phillips, it is no good giving us something pokey.'

Ah? They looked at Harry's clothes. Well, there was a family suite available but–

The 'but' concerned Harry's workmanlike look and their combined luggage of a small, shabby case and a long cardboard box. The clerk and the manager eyed both items unenthusiastically. Irena did not bother with the clerk. She looked the manager up and down. He recognized then the air of a personage. Personages mattered. It was persons one discouraged. The luggage, such as it was, was taken up.

The suite was commodious. It included a large sitting room and two bedrooms, one bedroom with its separate dressing room. They would not be thrown together too closely, but an awareness of the unconventional and imprudent existed the moment they took up occupation. Irena thought back to the small apartment in Belgrade. Circumstances and necessity had been the only conscious factors there. No sensitive, personal aspects had disturbed the common-sense nature of the situation. Belgrade had been a practical stepping stone. Zagreb should have been another. But it hadn't been. Something had happened there.

And Padua was going to be so trying to her emotions.

Harry took his bath first, so as to lose no time in presenting himself to the nearest British authorities. He shaved while the bath filled. Irena came knocking at the door.

'Harry? Excuse me, please.' She sounded worried.

'What is it?' he called, turning off the loudly rushing bath taps.

'What am I to wear this evening?'

He looked at his half-shaven face in the steamy mirror.

'Good God,' he said in amazement. Was it possible that a woman who was also a princess could be so pricelessly feminine? 'What?' he called, thinking he might have misheard her.

'Harry, I have nothing to wear.' She sounded worse than worried.

He swept the razor over the unshaven half, rinsed off lather and dabbed his chin with a towel. He opened the door. There she was, looking sincerely desperate and lovely.

'What do you mean?' he said.

'Mean? Is it possible you can accept my going down to dinner looking as if I am dressed for afternoon tea?'

'I'm not sure whether hotels still serve dressy dinners, or if they even serve dinners. Look here,' said Harry firmly, 'we've been through all this. In any case, what's the point of dressing up and looking like Your Highness? Please, Your Highness, I entreat your wisdom and your sense of caution. Put on the dress you bought last night in Trieste.'

Irena staggered around in despair.

'Are you crazy? That dress is simply something to wear, it's not an evening gown. Harry, it's their armistice today, everyone will dress like heaven tonight. If I wore that dress to dinner I should look like an old maid.'

'Good,' said Harry.

'Good?' Irena could not believe her ears. 'Good?'

'Yes, good,' he said with straight-faced candour. 'After all, in my clothes I look like Captain Sabata's second mate. I think you should do your best to look like a second mate's wife. I daresay you could adjust the old-maid look a little. That would fill in the picture very well for outsiders and lurking comrades. Looking like a princess simply won't do, ma'am.'

'Oh, how terrible you are,' she cried, 'you are condemning me to death by slow mortification.'

'If they do serve dinner,' said Harry, 'we can have it up here.'

'But we shall miss all the excitement,' she cried.

'Is it exciting for you?' he asked in curiosity. 'Are you pleased, then, that the Austrians have surrendered? That doesn't help your German friends, does it?'

'Oh!' From whimsically pleading an indulgence she leapt into angry resentment of injustice. 'That is too much! Now I know what I have done, I have said things! Because you are helping me escape and putting me in your debt, I must say nothing, I must not have opinions and I must think the same as you do about my friends!'

'Your German friends?'

'Yes! Yes!' She stood up to him, proud, bitter, fuming. 'I have German friends and Austrian friends, I have Swiss friends, Italian friends and Hungarian friends, and what has happened to most of them I don't know! But I am glad of one thing, I have never had any English friends! I would not want any! I am sure they are all like you! Odious!'

'Your Highness, nothing will have happened to your Swiss friends. They've been wise enough to stay out of the war.'

'Oh!' She was outraged. 'You are doing this deliberately, and I know why! Yes! You wish to be rid of me! I am a trouble, a nuisance, and you have had enough. So you are making it impossible for me to continue with you. Well, I will go, then!'

She stormed away. He went after her. She began to throw things into the long cardboard box. In seconds it was madly overflowing.

'I'm sorry, I can't let you do that,' he said.

'Go away!'

'I've a promise I must keep.'

'You can discuss that with Major Carlsen.' Her bitterness was cold now. 'I hope he is old-fashioned enough to call you out and run you through. Please go away.' She turned on him as firmly he took things out of her hands, out of the box, and put them aside. 'I don't need your services or want them.'

'I'm sorry,' said Harry grimly, 'but that is irrelevant. The arrangement is a matter of honour. I shall get you to England whether you need my services or not. And please don't think, because I'm curious about you and ask questions, that I'm trying to insult you. You must not be so sensitive. Please, put those things away. I'm not going to let you leave.'

She was breathing hard, her face flushed, her eyes big.

'You would dare to stop me, to lay your hands on me?'

Harry's expression was regretful but resolute.

'Yes,' he said, 'I would have to commit the unforgivable, Your Highness, even if only to save you running headlong into the arms of your enemies.'

She stared, her flush deepening.

'You would seize me, bundle me about, throw

me down?' she gasped.

'It would be a matter of my honour and your safety,' he said gravely, 'but I should actually tie you up.'

'Tie me up?' She looked incredulous. 'Tie me up?'

'Only if it were unavoidable,' said Harry.

'Oh, I cannot believe it,' she gasped, 'you are a monster in disguise.'

'Will you promise to behave?'

'Never! Never!' She turned and ran. She darted from the bedroom and through the living room. As she reached the door Harry caught her, lifted her and carried her. She did not scream, but she kicked furiously, legs a shining flurry amid a cloud of white petticoat lace, and she beat at him with clenched fists. 'Monster, monster! Put me down!'

'I warned you,' said Harry, and carried her back to her room and spilled her on to the bed. She lay there, staring up at him out of enormous, outraged brown eyes, her breathing fast and agitated. 'I must have my bath,' he said, 'and you must calm down.'

Speechless, she watched him take the key from the inside of the door lock and transfer it to the outside. He closed the door and she heard the key turn. He had locked her in. He had laid his hands on her, thrown her about and locked her in. She sat up, gave one tight little scream, then fell back again. Oh, how magnificent. No man would do such desperate things as he had, taking hold of her, bundling her about, making dire threats and actually locking her in, unless his deepest concern was for her. She lay there in exhilaration.

It was forty minutes before the door was unlocked. This was followed by a knock. She made no response. She watched the door. It opened a little and Harry put his head in.

'Your Highness?'

'Yes?'

He came in.

'I must apologize, Your Highness,' he said, 'but all the same, I meant what I said.'

'Oh,' she said as she saw him. He was in khaki. His tailored uniform fitted him so well. He should have had it pressed because of the creases, but the warmth of his body would ease them out. He looked so impressive to her susceptible eyes that her thoughts flew again to an evening gown. She must have one, she must be complementary to him at dinner tonight. 'Oh, how splendid you look,' she said impulsively.

'I don't want to lock you in–'

'Oh, Harry, we are so silly, aren't we?' she said.

He thought that was the least of it. She was still lying on her bed, and in her cream blouse and brown skirt, with ankles and lace peeping, much more of an endearing young woman than a troublesome princess. He had decided on an attitude of restraint. In her vulnerability, in her smile that was asking for a restoration of harmony, she was a bewitching threat to his good intentions.

'It's the strain,' he said, 'and I should remember it's much more of a strain for you. I'm used to roughing it a bit. All the same–'

'Yes, I understand, it is a matter of honour,' she said swiftly. She slipped from the bed and came up to him. 'You need not lock me in, I shall not run away, I promise.' Almost shyly she said, 'How could I manage on my own and without you now?'

'Well, we'll manage it together,' said Harry.

'Oh, you are very good to me,' she said. Since he had laid hands on her a short while ago this made him smile. 'But you must not have the wrong impressions about my loyalties,' she went on, 'I am a Rumanian and I love my country. I simply meant to say I was glad the war is nearly over for everyone, not just for the Italians. I was silly to be so angry with you, but never did I think you would be so angry with me as to throw me about.'

'Ah,' said Harry, not sure of his depth. 'Unforgivable,' he said.

'Oh, I do forgive you,' she said graciously, 'but there is still this terrible problem about what I am to wear tonight. Harry, please, the waiters, the maître d'hôtel, they will never believe it if I appear at dinner in a day dress. They will not come near us. I must go out and buy a gown.'

'I'd rather you didn't,' said Harry, 'and we agreed you shouldn't.'

'Very well.' Irena drew herself up. There was a way out but she would keep it to herself. 'You are awfully stern with me sometimes.'

'I know,' said Harry, 'but most monsters are tyrannical. I'm going to look for the consulate now. You'll stay here until I get back?'

She said yes, she said she would not go out, she would take her bath and perhaps try to get her hair done in the hotel salon. He was not to hurry on her account but on the other hand he was not to be too long. Her smile and her manner were so engagingly warm and open that he wondered if she was up to something.

When he had gone she sat down at the dressing table. She looked into the mirror. She mused on an emotional problem becoming more insoluble by the hour.

'Elisabeth,' she said, 'I'm sure you're very nice but I do wish you would marry someone else. You're very lucky that life is so uncomplicated for you, that you only have to sit and wait for him.' She smiled ruefully. 'And he is in a hurry to get home to you.'

She requested the manager to come up five minutes later. He, visibly impressed by her looks and charm, quite understood her desire to celebrate Italy's armistice with Austria by acquiring a creation. He would have Signor Carletti of Padua's leading fashion house call on her. To be frank, it was the only fashion house because of the shortage of materials, but Signor Carletti would not disappoint her. As for the celebrations, she might care to know that at the university they would be dancing until dawn.

She did care to know. Dancing. How wonderful.

Signor Carletti arrived with a model, a dresser and an array of gowns. Considering the ravages of war and the gargantuan appetite the warring nations had developed for all raw materials, Signor Carletti had triumphed superbly over his difficulties. There were actually silks. Irena did not ask where they had come from. She had an entirely delicious time simply looking, followed by a rapturous moment of purchase. Signor Carletti departed in a state of artistic fulfilment, leaving Irena certain that to look, to consider, to decide and to buy beautified one's soul when it happened after four terrible years of war.

She would have her hair done later. She suddenly felt tired. The crossing on the *Antonia* had been as exhausting as other stages of their journey. She would rest for a while before having a bath. She slipped off her shoes and lay on the bed. The feeling of drowsy pleasure was immediate. She closed her eyes. Harry would be back soon. Could it be true that he had actually laid hands on her and thrown her about? If Major Carlsen had seen it happen he would almost certainly have shot Harry. He would not have understood.

She slept.

It was dark when she woke up. The winter had drawn its cold night veil over the ancient city. She felt dreamy but refreshed. She turned. There was a lamp on the bedside table. Where was the switch? She reached, then stiffened as she heard a noise. Not from inside the bedroom. Outside it. It was like a slither, a shuffle, and with it a faint clicking.

Harry? She found the light and flicked the little brass knob. The lamp glowed. The red velvet curtains hung darkly. The clock said ten to six.

'Harry?' she called tentatively. She got up and went to the door. 'Harry?' She realized she was frightened. How silly. There was no need to be. She heard the noise again, like someone trying to slide open a badly fitting window. Her heart began to hammer. She opened the door quietly and looked into the darkness of the sitting room. She listened with goose pimples icily searing her skin. Harry's room, opposite hers, showed no light. Even so, she called his name again.

The response was a little rushing slither of sound, as if someone had rapidly moved. She froze, a sensation of exquisitely cold and rarefied air attacking her back. She simply stopped breathing. The deadly silence which ensued seemed to scream at her. The service bell, the light. The light. She forced herself to feel for the light switch on the wall beside the bedroom door. The polished brass plate with its knob slid smoothly under her fingers. She clicked on the ceiling light of the bedroom. It transmitted life to the bedroom, gave light to part of the sitting room. Outside the November wind blew in a sudden gust and rattled a swinging sign. The bathroom door, ajar, quivered and slammed. Irena jumped, screamed and stood paralysed. The bathroom door, it had been closed when Harry had gone, hadn't it?

Again came that slither of sound. It plucked like a sharp, tearing bow at the frayed strings of her nerves.

'Who is there? Who is there?'

She rushed into the sitting room, switched on the light. Where was the bell? No, the door, the door. She must get out. Blindly she found the door and reached for the white enamelled knob. Before she could touch it the door opened. The scream that was locked in her throat leapt free, only to choke on itself as she saw Harry. The strangled sound shocked him.

'What's wrong?'

'Harry – oh!' She flung herself into his arms and clung. The warmth of his body and the reassurance of his presence equalled the rapture of the awakener who realizes horror has only been a nightmare.

'What's wrong?' he asked again. She was trembling violently.

'There's someone in the bathroom,' she gasped against his shoulder.

'In the bathroom?' He was dubious about a cry of warning that seemed to carry a hint of farce with it. But he was very aware of her frightened state and she was not a young woman who lost her nerve easily. He was also aware of her slender, rounded warmth, the pressure of a quivering body seeking security. Had Michalides traced her already? 'Are you sure we're invaded?' he asked quietly.

'Yes. There is someone there. I heard him.'

'Well, we'd better have a look,' said Harry.

'Are you crazy?' She lifted her head. 'Get the manager, call the staff. You don't have to go in there yourself.'

'Somehow,' said Harry, 'I don't think anyone would pick a bathroom to hide in, and I'm sure Michalides' Italian comrades aren't on to you yet.' He put her gently aside and walked to the bathroom. Irena shivered at his recklessness. As Harry opened the bathroom door she heard the sound again, a slither and a clicking. Harry heard it too. He went in. The bathroom was empty. But he saw the small window he himself had left latched wide to clear the steam. The curtain on its line of small brass rings was moving, the wind tugging it. He called Irena, and showed her the moving curtain. The rings slithered and clicked over the rail. 'Is that what you heard?' he asked.

'Oh,' she said and became pink with mortification. Imagination had played its unkind trick and shattered her customary coolness. Harry was smiling. Her facile mind laid rescuing fingers of quick thought on her, plucking her from total demoralization. 'Oh,' she said, 'who would have believed anyone would have climbed out of a window as small as that?'

'And then fallen three floors to the ground without cracking his head,' said Harry.

'Incredible,' said Irena, full of beautiful relief and rich absurdity. 'But of course you have heard of a proverb of ours. Those who leap with courage draw kindness from the earth.'

'No, I haven't heard of it,' said Harry, 'I think it's not so much a proverb as a piece of quick thinking.'

'He must have been a very thin man,' said Irena, shamelessly avoiding the question posed by the comment. They returned to the sitting room. 'Why were you away so long? See what happens when you go wandering about, some strange man finds his way in and nearly stabs me to death.'

'Your Highness–'

'You know there's no need to call me that.'

'Yes, quite so.' Harry was guarded. She had taken her hairpins out before lying down and her spilling hair, dancing softly around her, made her look so young. He took his eyes away from enchantment. 'Was I a long time? Perhaps I was.' He took off his peaked khaki cap and tossed it on to a chair. 'But there's no consulate here, so I took a taxicab to Venice. It's not far. Now I've answered all the questions and re-established my identity. I received an advance, otherwise I couldn't have paid the cab off. I'm expected to rejoin my regiment as soon as possible. I'll rejoin it via England. We leave here tomorrow.'

'Tomorrow?' She did not seem rapturous.

'The sooner the better for both of us,' he said, 'and I imagine you won't feel really safe until you get to somewhere like America.'

'America? I am not going to America.'

'But it's a nice long way from Michalides and they look after princesses there. You'll like New York. It was built for princesses. Young ones, anyway.' He was taking the conversation along lightly, casually, and Irena was stiffening, and they were heading for another clash of nerves. 'I went there for a short spell when I was at college. It's what they call dynamic and it's made for the young and the free. And there aren't any anarchists.'

'Really? How very informative. What do you have in mind now, tying me up and putting me on a ship to New York? Thank you,' said Irena with her nose in the air, 'but I am going to England.' With just a slight note of regal triumph she added, 'It is a matter of honour, you remember, to get me there.'

'Oh, I thought America worth a mention,' he said.

'Well, you have mentioned it, so now it is done

with. But must we leave here tomorrow?' England and his reunion with Elisabeth seemed alarmingly close, so did the awfulness of being on her own.

'You must remember I'm still on active service,' he said.

'But it's so nice here,' she said, 'and you are entitled to a few days' rest. It's unfair you should have to go tomorrow.'

'It can't be all that nice,' said Harry, 'not with thin men slipping in and out of the bathroom window with knives between their teeth.'

'Sometimes, you know, you are quite horrid,' said Irena. He laughed. He was apt to laugh a lot with her, and she did not know why just lately he had taken to being so stiff or stern or distant. But he was laughing now and she seized the chance to ask him to take her after dinner to Padua University, where there would be dancing until dawn. The university was the foundation of Padua's history and culture. They ought not to miss the chance to go there and she dearly wanted to dance until dawn herself.

'But are you really in the mood with the Central Powers collapsing?' he said.

'Oh, we are not going to argue about that again, are we?' she said. 'Are you happy to know that no one will really win except the Bolsheviks? Germany would have kept them out of Europe, but now, you will see, they will swarm all over it.'

'I see,' he said, 'what you really mean is that you're anti-Bolshevik.'

'So should everyone be who has any sense,' said Irena.

'We must find a platform for you in Hyde Park,'

smiled Harry, 'at a place called Speakers' Corner.'

'Oh, I would speak, yes,' she said defiantly. 'Harry, please let us go to the dance. The manager will arrange it for us. I have been good, haven't I? I stayed in while you were out. Oh, I would so like to dance.'

He could not resist her.

But he did say, 'Won't it be risky if the nobs are there?'

'Nobs?'

'Ducal personages and so on.'

'Oh, no, I have never mixed with the dukes of Padua and it's to be masked and very festive, but all very informal, to celebrate peace.'

'All right,' said Harry. He wondered how it had come about that this young woman of exalted position allowed him to lay down the rules. He supposed it was because he bullied her so much.

'Do you mean it? We can go?' She was not sure if he did mean it. But he did. 'Oh, how nice you are to me,' she said, and the faint flush came to her face. 'To dance will be fun, won't it?'

'It'll be a nice change from boats and trains,' he said, 'but for heaven's sake, don't go wandering about dancing with furtive villains. Make do with dukes or doges.'

'I'm not going to dance with anybody but–' She stopped, and blushed vividly. 'I mean, you must approve my partners for me, of course. You will let me know if you wish to dance with me yourself, I should not want to go off with dukes all the time if you did not care all the time to go off with their ladies.'

'Hmm,' said Harry, working thoughtfully on that

one. He wondered what dancing with her would do to his dangerously heady state. For his own sake and Elisabeth's it would be better to stand in a corner and keep his eye on Irena. Elisabeth drew a man into a context of calm. Irena, so colourful, was far more disturbing. 'When I'm not a soldier I'm a farmer,' he said, 'and I'm not the world's best performer at a ball.'

'It isn't a ball, it's a masked frolic,' said Irena, 'and I'm not a very good dancer myself, I have an imperfect sense of timing. So we will be two dunces together and will suit each other very well. Yes?' She was almost shy again in the flicker of her lashes, the hesitancy of her smile. He nodded. 'Well, now I shall have my bath,' she said, 'then have my hair done, then have our meal sent up and then I shall dress. We need not go down to dinner, after all. I have spoken to the manager. Oh, and he will send up masks for us.'

'Great overworked pumpkins,' said Harry helplessly, 'how long is all that going to take? I'm starving.'

He was so like a man, quite unable to understand how she would enjoy every moment of all the time it would take to make herself look beautiful. He did not even understand it would be for him. She had a wrench of conscience, for she knew she was beginning to fight Elisabeth. She simply could not help herself.

She had her bath. Then she went down to the hairdressing salon and returned an enormous time later with her crowning glory a rich chestnut brilliance. It made Harry look away, it made him study a painting of Venice on the wall. Their meal was served. The Victor Emmanuel was still managing to excel in its preparation of food without being able to disguise the fact that quantity was limited. So was the menu. It did not matter. Irena and Harry enjoyed what they had. It was ten o'clock when Irena retired to her room once more to dress for the festive frolic. The manager sent up masks, a black one for Harry, a silver and red one for Irena.

She made her entrance as coolly as she could, saying casually, 'I am ready now, Harry,' as she came out of her room. Harry turned in his chair. He had been thinking, but not about what she was going to wear. He had vaguely supposed she would wear something nice, like the dress she had bought in Trieste. He was quite unprepared for her visionary effect. She shimmered. She was gowned in silky white with gold brocade. It rounded her figure and sheathed her hips, it gave her a regal richness. It had a collar, turned up and studded with tiny gold stars. It had flowing sleeves. From beneath the hem peeped gold and silver slippers. She wore no jewellery except a ring and the gold wedding band. Harry blinked. She laughed a little nervously and said, 'A Signor Carletti from a dress shop came, and this was the best he could do for me. There's a shortage of things because of the war, you know. Do you think because of the war I should not be gowned like this? But there is the armistice between Italy and Austria to celebrate, isn't there?'

'Oh, good God,' said Harry.

'What is wrong?' Irena's nerves showed a little. 'Doesn't it suit me? Is it gaudy?'

'Tell me,' said Harry, 'is this how you look when you're entertaining crown princes?'

'No,' said Irena, 'it's how I look when I am celebrating an armistice with you.'

'I'm overwhelmed,' said Harry.

'That is a compliment?' Her eyes danced. 'Well, I think you are quite nice too.'

They took a cab to the university. Padua had the lights of peace on, even though no armistice had yet been signed with Germany. The university hall was an ageless wonder and tonight was alive with colour, revelry and music. With a feeling for the appropriate, an Italian military band had been engaged to play. In uniforms of red and blue, and their brass instruments gleaming, the soldier musicians produced music full of martial melody through which ran the infectious panache of Italian nuances.

The youth and the men and women of Padua, masked and dressed in anything that had individuality and colour, danced and galloped as if at the birth of a new and beautiful world. The students were bizarre in what they wore, nerveless in all they did. Irena and Harry stood watching for a while, Irena's eyes big and brilliant through her mask, her foot tapping. It was so exciting, so colourful in its gay pageantry after so much sombre death. They were so lucky, she and Harry, they were alive.

A man, slim and dark and playful, leapt clear of the swirling mass of dancers and alighted at the feet of the radiant Irena.

'Enchantress! Goddess! Diana! Venus! Fly to the stars with me, I am Hermes!'

'Alas, I am totally engaged to Jupiter,' said Irena. She said to Harry, 'He says he is Hermes, but I think he's a little drunk and it was never Hermes who was drunk, was it? It was someone else, yes?'

'Bacchus,' said Harry. 'But I think he means well and is obviously taken with you. So dance with him if you wish, I'll keep an eye on you.'

'Oh, you beast,' she whispered, 'I am not going to be pulled around by an intoxicated Bacchus.'

'What are you saying, O heavenly body?' cried the smitten young man.

'That I can't fly away with you, Signor.'

'Ah,' said the young man woundedly, 'that's how it always is with Venus. Mortal men can never get near her. But be warned, I may descend more purposefully on you and carry you off to my garret and my gramophone.'

'I'll turn you into a cheese if you do,' said Irena. She whispered again to Harry. 'What are you doing? You are letting him accost me.'

Harry resigned himself to a night of emotional turmoil. He took her hand, and they became part of the riotous mass of dancers, part of the joy and exhilaration of peace.

She had lied. She danced vivaciously, rhythmically, headily. She was so warm, so vibrant, so intensely committed to revelry. It was as if she was snatching all she could from life before the loneliness of exile enclosed her. She swam, she floated, she spun. Vitality, eager and extravagant, poured into her and from her. Her teeth glimmered between her breathless, parted lips, her eyes shone through her mask. She was superbly gowned and it made her feel like a queen. Eyes were on her, a hundred eyes, her silver and red mask hiding her identity but not her vivid appeal. Harry in his British khaki was acclaimed like a conquistador from time to time, couples breaking apart to lift their hands high and applaud him as he danced by with Irena. She laughed at that.

'That is nice, isn't it? They would not be like that with Major Carlsen.'

Wondering about her feelings for the handsome major, Harry said, 'Well, he has others who love him, I suppose.'

'Oh, yes,' laughed Irena.

There were speeches and orations in between dances, and periodically intrigued and animated men swarmed around Irena like magnetized galaxies. They sought with Latin verve to separate her from Harry, to discover who she was and whirl her away. Harry, always conscious of who she was and what she was, adroitly contrived to pluck her free of every imbroglio before the outrageous Italians could outmanoeuvre him. One was not to know how dangerous some of the more radical students might be if they recognized her. After what had happened in Zagreb, he did not want to let her run the faintest risk.

So periodically he rescued her from gallants who wanted to carry her off.

'Harry, what is the matter with them? Are all of them drunk?'

'Not really, dear Princess. Dazzled, I think. You've made yourself the belle of the ball.'

She was having the loveliest time, being with him and dancing with him. She coloured at being called dear Princess. She said lightly, 'Well, I am lucky you are keeping your head. I should have been torn to pieces if you had not stood up to them. Isn't it wonderful to dance? I haven't done so for ages, you know.'

He took the hint and they went in a crazy, flying polka, the music of the military band racing the dancers into a gallop. Joyfully, Irena went hand in hand with him, then into his arms, and away and away with him. She knew he had been too modest about his accomplishments.

She was breathless at the end of that. They withdrew from the hall to find a seat in a corridor, and Harry brought her a tall glass of sparkling white wine.

'Oh, how good,' she said. Excitement had made her more vivid. He took his eyes off her. He leaned back and looked at the brown stone of the vaulted corridor. 'What are you thinking?' she asked.

'I don't often dance with princesses,' he said.

'Nor I with English farmers,' she said, then gave a little gasp of dismay as she realized how awful that must sound, and she hadn't meant it to be awful at all. 'Oh, I mean–'

'No, you're right,' said Harry, 'few English farmers must have come knocking on your castle door. I count my luck exceptional. Actually, I was thinking of Elisabeth. I have to.'

Irena looked into her glass.

'Do you mean because you are here, because you are dancing and she is waiting and wondering?'

'Well, yes, that and because I'm going to have

to explain things, because I'm going to arrive on her doorstep with a wife.'

'But you will give her the reason for that,' said Irena, 'it was all discussed by us. She will understand. Oh, I have made things very complicated for you, haven't I?'

'Yes,' he said unequivocally. It took some of the life from her expressive eyes. She did not realize he was answering a question much more comprehensive than the one she had asked.

But they danced again. Irena said he had lied about his ability, he was very good. At which Harry said she had lied too, but whereas he had done so out of natural modesty he was surprised that with her impeccable upbringing she could lie at all.

'But sometimes it simply isn't possible to tell the truth,' she said, 'and I wish that when you were being so nice to me you would not be so horrid as well.'

That made him laugh, which in turn made her wish there was no Elisabeth.

She intrigued an Italian officer. Through his mask his eyes watched her, followed her. Once or twice he seemed tempted to approach her but held back, perhaps because he did not want to compete with so many others.

He spoke to his companion, a young woman.

'Do you know who that lady is?'

The young woman was not exactly enchanted by the question. She had a natural disinclination to share any interest he had in other women.

'I have no idea, except that she is making quite an exhibition of herself.'

'No, she only seems to be enjoying herself, it's the young men who are exhibitionist.'

'If you are terribly interested in her–?'

'I'm curious, that's all. I feel I either know her or have seen her before.'

'Well, everyone says there are few women you aren't on some terms with, Alberto.'

'Everyone is you, silly girl. Come, dance with me and stop looking put out.'

But a little later his eyes were drawn to Irena again. She had come off the floor with her escort, a British officer, and she was laughing, her white teeth sparkling between her warm lips, her eyes animated through her mask.

'I do know her, at least I think I do.'

'I am thrilled for you,' said his companion, then went into a huff as he excused himself and approached Irena. He nodded politely to Harry, and Harry thought him different from the rest. He was more sophisticated, more self-assured and, perhaps, more of a danger.

'Signorina?' he said and bowed to Irena. Irena glanced at Harry, giving him a rather rueful smile. One could tell when it was not going to be easy to discourage an advance.

'Signore?' she murmured. The Italian's eyes glinted. He did know her.

'Alberto of Brabanti at your service,' he said with a smile.

Irena stiffened and a flush deepened her colouring. Harry sighed a little. Someone had recognized her, despite her mask. That had been on the cards all along. They had been lucky up to now.

'Signore?' said Irena again.

'I'm not mistaken, am I?' said the Count of Brabanti. The conversation was in Italian, one more language that was all Greek to Harry.

Irena, recovering, said lightly, 'You wish to dance? Of course. I shall be happy to.' She turned to Harry and murmured in French, 'You will excuse me?'

'Certainly,' said Harry.

He watched her enter the whirl of movement with the Italian. He did not think she would panic. She was a resourceful princess.

Irena was still a little flushed as she danced, her eyes coyly averted. The count looked at her, happy to have resolved his perplexity about her.

'How unexpected, how delightful,' he said.

'Signore?' she murmured innocently.

'Come,' he said, 'we know each other, confess it.'

'Do we? The advantage is yours.'

'The luck is mine. I swear, despite that mask, that you've grown even more beautiful. How long is it since we last saw each other? Four years? Yes. It was at Castle Elau on the Danube. A magnificent house party. Do you remember?'

'Castle Elau on the Danube? Where is that?' Irena was coolly enquiring.

'Sonya Irena, it is I, Alberto, who holds you. Alberto, your most devoted one.'

'Alberto? Oh, Alberto – yes, of course.' Her eyes simulated surprised recognition. 'Please forgive me, but four years is a long time, and your mask, your uniform–'

'It's been far too long,' said the count, smiling. 'We were so young, I was so earnest, you were so haughty.'

'Never,' said Irena, 'I'm not made that way.'

'Oh, you were always devilishly on your mettle.'

'Not as devilishly as you were on yours,' she said.

She made light conversation with him, but began to let her eyes run all ways in search of Harry, who would be watching her every move. She sighted him and he was not watching her at all. He had been seized by a gloriously shapely creature in red, who was dancing with him. The gloriously shapely creature was shamelessly close to him. Irena burned. Oh, how dared he be so – so – yes, irresponsible. Why, for all he knew, anything might be happening to her. Alberto of Brabanti might be someone in the pay of the Socialists, ready to sweep her back into the fatal embrace of Michalides, instead of a charming Italian count whom she had known before the war.

If Harry was making up to that woman...

'This is enchanting, to have found you again,' Alberto was saying. 'But the last I heard you were trapped in Rumania and having to endure hordes of German conquerors. How did you get out?'

'It wasn't easy, but I'm here now,' she said.

'Mysteriously so,' said the count. He ran on. He was a smooth, polished dancer, an effortless talker, and his conversation flowed in easy confluence with his physical rhythm. Irena circled in his arms but the exhilaration was not the same. He was only one more of many young men who had danced attendance on her because at seventeen and eighteen she had been called Rumania's loveliest flower. But he had recognized her. Harry would be angry with her. He would adopt his bullying 'I told you so' attitude or be frowningly dark and hideously English, making her feel he would be only too glad to see the back of her.

'You still haven't told me how you did get out,' said Alberto.

'Oh, it's very secretive,' said Irena, 'and yes, darkly political.'

'Darkly political?'

'You know how it is.'

'No, I don't.'

'Where is my escort? Can you see him?'

'He's closely engaged,' said the count. 'Sonya Irena, you're being very mysterious. Why is it darkly political and how did you escape the Germans?'

'Who is closely engaged?' Irena, following Alberto's rhythmic flights, glimpsed Harry. The shameless configuration of red was so close to him that she quivered in outrage. Oh, he was horrid to dance like that with such a woman. Had he forgotten he was supposed to be taking care of her? 'Oh, how indecent,' she breathed.

'What is that?' Alberto peered at her, observing the warmth in her face, the heat in her eyes. 'Tell me, Sonya Irena, tell me your story.'

She was on dangerous ground. Alberto had always had a charming persistence.

'Oh, it's far too long,' she said, leaning back against his arm as he deftly flighted her to escape the exuberance of other couples, 'I will tell you when I next see you.'

'But tomorrow I must be in Rome.'

'How lovely,' she said and meant it.

'It isn't lovely to be in Rome when I've just found you here in Padua. Who is your escort, the British officer?'

'Oh, he is all part of it being political and secretive,' she murmured conspiratorially, 'and there are others who have managed to get away.'

'Others? King Ferdinand? Queen Marie?'

'Hush,' said Irena. She was a little breathless, Count Alberto so tireless. And she was shocked to see that Harry was now actually seated beside that creature who looked like a hothouse bloom with her gown a scarlet undulation over her white bosom. Oh, she thought, I am in terrible trouble with my emotions.

The music stopped. Alberto released her, took her gloved right hand and raised it to his lips.

'Sonya Irena, that was delightful because it was so unexpected. Now, let me take you back to the man who is all part of this dark, political secretiveness.'

'No, there's no need. Thank you, Alberto.'

Count Alberto insisted. She was not a shop girl, he said. And even a shop girl would not be left on the floor. He took her hand again, drew it through his arm, looked around and saw Harry. Harry was on his feet, parting from the flamboyant figure in red.

'Please, Alberto,' she said, 'say nothing at all to Captain Phillips. He's absurdly fierce about the secrecy of everything. We are really not supposed to be here, we couldn't have come had it not been masked.'

'It's devilishly mysterious,' smiled the count. He returned her to Harry. 'Thank you, Captain,' he said, 'it was a great pleasure.'

'Pardon?' Harry groped for an interpretation of the Italian words.

'Count Brabanti is saying he's enchanted with me,' said Irena in English.

'Indeed, yes,' said Alberto, 'and I am also intrigued. Take care of her, Captain. She is priceless. She–'

'Thank you, Alberto,' said Irena, 'we will meet again in Rome, perhaps.'

'We must,' smiled Alberto, 'we have much to make up for.' He looked as if he would like to have lingered, but he knew that his erstwhile companion would be spitting a little now and he was also aware that Irena's escort did not seem disposed to take a further back seat. He said goodbye, kissing Irena's fingertips extravagantly.

When he had gone Irena smoothed her gloves and busied herself looking at each slimly sheathed finger.

'Hm,' said Harry, 'is it serious?'

'Serious?' It was not a bit serious now that she had avoided the brink, unless he meant the extent of her relationship with the count. 'He's just an old friend.'

'Hm,' said Harry again.

'Oh, you are not jealous, are you?' she said, and immediately could have bitten her tongue out for being so stupid. Oh, what an idiotic thing to have said. He would think her utterly childish. 'I mean, it does not really matter that I danced with him, does it?'

Harry, poker-faced, said, 'What I meant was is it serious that he recognized you? Is he going to talk about your being here and is someone likely to throw a bomb at you before we leave?'

'Harry, of course not,' she said. Dancers were galloping to music that raced. 'Nothing like that will happen. Alberto will be very discreet, I told him to say nothing.' Before he could become cuttingly English she changed the subject. 'Harry, really, that woman was very vulgar.'

'Which woman?'

'The one in the red gown.'

'In? She was halfway out of it,' said Harry.

Irena blushed for him. But he was laughing. Not out loud, but laughing all the same. Sometimes his sense of humour made her feel in delicious rapport with him, sometimes it made her want to bite. Now it made her feel weak and yielding.

She would not dance with anyone else at all, although she was still frequently besieged. In a little extravaganza of emotional sentiment she made the evening an occasion for bitter-sweet memories. It was stupid, but eventually she would have only the memories, she knew that. She was very sad when they left at last, before the unmasking took place. Back at the hotel she was not sleepy, she still felt so alive, and in the sitting room of the suite she whirled around before sinking into a chair.

'Oh, it was so good,' she said, 'I have never enjoyed myself so much.'

'I'm sure that's not true,' said Harry, who saw the necessity of keeping his feet on the ground.

'But think of Michalides, think of all we have been through,' she said in soft earnestness, 'and then think of tonight. Harry, you weren't bored, were you?'

'Bored?' He looked down at her. His eyes, dark and intense, made her heart beat a little painfully. She wished he would kiss her. But he had never stepped outside his role as her help and protector, except that he had managed to call her dear Princess tonight. That had been something.

'What is wrong, I am dishevelled?' she said unsteadily.

'No. You look very lovely. And I wasn't bored. Goodnight, Your Highness.'

She did not want to be left, not after being called lovely.

'You are not going to bed, are you?' she said. 'They will send up some coffee if we ask and you can talk to me. I'm not at all tired.'

'We're off tomorrow – no, today,' he said soberly.

'Yes, I know.' She knew he was thinking of Elisabeth again. A sudden little rush of jealousy shocked her. For a moment or so it attacked her quite fiercely. She drew a breath, calmed herself. 'Yes, you have to go home to Elisabeth. But you aren't the only one who has to think of someone else.'

She meant Major Carlsen, thought Harry.

'You've an understanding with him?' he said ironically.

'Of course.' She sat up proudly. She hoped he would not ask who the man was. She would have to lie. 'Do you think I am not as eligible as your Elisabeth?'

'I think you very eligible, Your Highness.' If that

was a compliment, it was said very brusquely. But the evening had been so lovely and she did not want it to be spoiled. So she smiled, shook her head at him and said, 'Harry, it is true, you really are a farmer? That is what you will do when the war is over, farming?'

'What I hope to do is buy a small farm of my own. I assisted in the management of a large one before the war.' He smiled at a thought he had just had. 'I must go to my father's temple and ask for a loan. My father's temple is a bank.'

'Oh, I could–' She stopped in time. She knew she could not offer him money, that he would never take it from her. 'I think I should like to have a farm,' she said.

'No, that's not for princesses,' he said.

'You think I could not work hard at it?' she said a little proudly.

'Farming is nothing to do with good intentions,' said Harry. 'No, you'll set up court for Rumanian exiles somewhere, I expect.'

'That would be chasing shadows,' she said, 'and is for others, perhaps, not for me.' She stood up. 'Oh, I will go to bed, then. That is what you wish. But I have had a wonderful time, yes. Really I have. Thank you, Harry.'

'I'm not complaining, you know,' he said and his smile was affectionate. 'Goodnight.'

She put her hand lightly on his arm.

'Goodnight, dear guardian, I am so much in your debt.'

Their eyes compulsively held.

'Even though I bundle you about?' he said whimsically.

'Even though you do,' she said. And the kiss was there, unenacted but there. In her eyes.

He lay awake for a while. Irena, who thought she would be unable to sleep, sank into beautiful dreams almost at once.

Chapter Twelve

They left Padua the next day. Their journey from there to France and through France was slow and tiring, full of delays and minor inconveniences. It took them a week to reach Dieppe. In other respects it was trouble-free, although Harry was constantly looking over his shoulder. Irena seemed quite without qualms and stood up to him when he firmly requested she buy herself a veil.

'No. We are quite safe now. And veils make me look old.'

'What does that matter?'

'Nothing to you,' she retorted, 'but everything to me.'

'Anyway, you're wrong. They don't make you look old. You wear a veil very elegantly. We may be quite safe but we'll not take chances, not when we've come so far.'

'I am to buy a veil, then?'

'Yes.'

'I will not.' She was as highly strung as a thoroughbred.

'Princess Irena – ma'am–'

'Oh!' More than anything she hated him calling her ma'am. And they were always so close to edginess, to emotional clashes. The nearer they got to England the worse became the tension between them. 'I will not!' she repeated.

'I insist.'

'No!'

'Then I beg you,' said Harry and gave her a smile, 'I ask you. I think you charming in a veil. Perhaps it's rather Edwardian but there are still some Edwardian things worth keeping, especially those relating to elegance. Will you buy a veil, Your Highness?'

'Oh!' It was almost a wail. 'Oh, I wish you would not call me that!'

He knew he should not but he said gently, 'My dear Sonya Irena, shall we go to a shop?'

She went with him, her eyes alarmingly moist.

She wore the new veil. Harry felt a little happier for her. He still looked over his shoulder, but if Michalides had friends, comrades or agents in France, none showed up.

They arrived in Dieppe tired but very fit. Irena thought Harry looked as lean and hungry as Shakespeare's Cassius, and she pictured Elisabeth falling radiantly into his arms.

The moment of nerve-racking confrontation with authority came when they crossed to Newhaven on the day of the general armistice, when the flags were out and the church bells ringing, when the day was dry but pale with winter. Irena, in her waisted black coat and new hat, elegance and composure hiding her anxieties, stepped ashore as coolly as if she already belonged. But oh, the questions, the straight-faced intransigence of uniformed officials, the suspicious scrutiny of the marriage certificate by one, two and even three of them, each passing it around as if it were as suspect as a dubious banknote. And Harry was looking grimmer and grimmer, quite tall and quite magnificent.

Where was her passport?

At which Harry said in a grinding voice that Rumanians having to run from Germans don't stop to apply for passports.

Oh, she had never had a passport?

Harry said there'd been a war on. Perhaps they hadn't heard?

He had married her in Bucharest? How did that come about?

Harry said he had been a hospitalized prisoner of war and she had been a ministering angel who had brought him flowers, at which Irena, for all her hidden anxieties, wanted to gasp with delight. But the immigration officers did not seem amused.

'Well, sir–'

'Never mind that,' said Harry ferociously, 'do you see this lady?'

'Yes, sir.'

'Well, this lady is my wife. Fetch my MP. I'll wait. We'll both wait.'

How superb, thought Irena. Oh, dear heaven, how was she going to manage without him, without having him there to laugh at her?

The officials scrutinized the marriage certificate again, they scrutinized Irena again. In her black coat with its white fur collar and the matching black-and-white hat, she was worth a second look. She smiled tenderly into inquisitive, interrogative eyes. Her smile, her clear brown eyes, combined with Harry's muttering ferocity, created the longed-for rapport. The possibility of being anything but cordial in the face of such a combination was coughed away.

'Welcome to Britain, Mrs Phillips.'

It was with a feeling of climactic giddiness that she discovered in the customs shed that she was not required to open a single piece of luggage. Customs men looked at her, looked at Harry and his uniform, and said, 'Your wife, sir?'

Harry said, 'Yes, I found her on the other side of Salonika. She wasn't doing anything else at the time so I married her.'

They slapped cheerful chalk marks on the luggage. And she and Harry walked out of the shed to the waiting London train. They had done it.

'Well, here you are, then,' said Harry. 'Now you simply live quietly incognito for a while. Is that the idea?'

'Yes,' she said. 'Thank you, Harry, you have been quite marvellous. Isn't it nice to hear the bells ringing?'

'Someone must have known royalty was arriving,' said Harry.

The train took them to London and they deposited their luggage at Victoria Station for the moment. She was fascinated as they emerged from the station and she saw the festooned buildings and flag-waving crowds. They had seen Padua on Italy's armistice day with Austria, and to be in London on Britain's day of peace and victory was another excitement. They queued for a cab so that they could drive to the Strand, where Harry thought she might like to see the celebratory spirit of the West End.

The Strand was choked. They left the cab before they arrived there. Buses were almost at a standstill, their open-top decks packed with people, up on their feet, showing the flag and singing 'Tipperary'. On the pavements and in the roads people swung along arm in arm, hats tipped and voices hoarse. Army khaki and navy blue threaded through the pattern of colour. The day, overcast but dry, was itself shot with colour.

They moved towards Trafalgar Square, Irena keeping close to Harry because of the crush and, she thought, the imminence of a frightening riot.

'Harry, so many people! Is everyone in England here?'

'Haven't you ever been to London?' asked Harry.

'Never,' she said.

'Not to your distant relatives at Buckingham Palace?'

'Oh, they are very distant,' she said, 'and I'm not on their guest list. Harry, look, those women are trying to take off the policemen's helmets.'

'All jolly fun,' said Harry, 'nobody will get shot.'

As they struggled through the crowds Harry was repeatedly seized, hugged and kissed by women with hats askew and hairpins dislodged. He explained to the slightly overcome Irena that the women were a bit tiddly and would kiss anybody.

'What is tiddly?' she said.

'A little drunk.'

'I should like to get a bit tiddly, then,' she said.

'And kiss anybody?'

'No, not anybody,' she said with a faint smile.

On the edge of Trafalgar Square she herself was embraced by an American doughboy. It startled her, made her blush crimson. Harry laughed. Then he was almost swept away from her by a group of khaki-uniformed WACs, who knew that on Armistice Day they could get away with any breach of discipline providing no guns were fired. The WACs, on the prowl for forbidden fruit, were happy with their capture.

'Come on, sir, come on, dance around Nelson with us. I'm Cecily.'

'Don't have anything to do with her, sir, she eats even sergeant majors, and I'm Freda.'

'Come on, sir, come on, oh do!'

It was a wonderful day. Harry kissed them all. Some clung tightly to get more than their dues. Irena was shocked. Certain that if they made away with him she would never get him back, she stamped her foot.

'Let go of him!' she cried. They were pulling him all ways, utterly delighted with his kisses, and Harry did not seem disposed to resist the partitioning. He was laughing. 'Harry, stop this!'

'Hello, ducky,' said a rich, ripe voice, and a large sailor gathered her into an expansively fond embrace and kissed her with gusty, naval good-will, then gave her another for luck. Irena's hat went awry and she sucked in astonished breath. 'God bless yer, love, even my Aunt Mabel would like you and mostly she can't stand no one except her parrot,' he said and pinched her bottom. Irena shrieked, jumped and blushed to the roots of her hair, all composure gone.

'Harry,' she gasped, 'save me!'

Harry was roaring with laughter. The sailor had passed on in search of similar beauty. There was a lot of it out and about today. Irena looked utterly incredulous. Harry rescued himself from the adventurous WACs and moved to her side, cautioning her against her predilection for careless wandering. Irena drew herself up, straightened her hat and delivered her pink-faced riposte.

'What do you mean? It was nothing to do with me, I am not responsible for the outrageous behaviour of others, and you did not tell me English people were like this. Oh, you are a fine one to shake your finger at me when you are kissing every woman you see and leaving me in danger of being trampled to death!'

She was delicious. He could have told her she was in much more danger of being kissed to death.

'Come along,' he said and steered her firmly through people massing by Northumberland Avenue. He put his arm around her. It was protective, only that, but it made her quiver a little. And it was very upsetting that he could kiss those girls so amorously and not kiss her at all.

A linked line of soldiers, sailors and young women spilled from pavement to road, singing and dancing, the girls with legs kicking and petticoats whipping.

'What are they doing?' asked Irena.

'It's a ritual enactment of tribal joy called "Knees Up, Mother Brown",' said Harry.

'It is very – oh!' Irena went hot as in seemingly abandoned vulgarity the young women revealed undergarments that one simply did not reveal. And Harry was looking. And laughing again. 'It is not a bit nice,' she said.

'Don't the Rumanian girls dance like that at harvest time?' said Harry.

'Well, I do not,' said Irena.

Harry, slightly intoxicated by the uninhibited gaiety of the day, and quite entranced by discovering that Her Cool Royal Highness was really deliciously shy about some things, said, 'I wish you would, this is just the occasion for it.'

'Oh, you are terrible,' she said and went resolutely on. Harry took her arm. 'You would wish me to kick my legs about with everybody looking?'

'No, not everybody,' said Harry. He was laughing so much. And then she was laughing too.

'It is nice, isn't it?' she said.

'What is?'

'Oh, to be just a little bit naughty sometimes,' she said in a rush, 'but only for– I mean–'

'Yes, I know,' said Harry and felt very tender because she was blushing again. They watched other revellers for a while, with Nelson turning his blind eye far above, and then they made their way to the War Office. Harry did not want to waste time or opportunity. He would report to the top and let the best red tape sort it out.

Inside the building the air of celebration was

more polished, more disciplined, and it took Harry quite a while to break through it. Eventually, however, he was taken to see a Colonel Smithers. He took Irena with him. She was quite willing to accompany him anywhere, to darkest Africa even, but she did not say so. She did, however, ask him not to disclose her identity. Harry did not want to provoke loud and pompous reaction in Parliament and said the last thing he had in mind was disclosure. She was not to worry, he said.

Colonel Smithers was an extremely decent type and charmed to meet Irena. He peered keenly at her. She smiled. He listened to Harry, asked questions, requested him to fill in a form, congratulated him on his escape, even if it had come a bit late, and on his gallant venture into matrimony when things had hardly looked as good for orange blossom as they did now. Altogether he obviously considered Harry had got far more out of the war than most. Irena could not quite understand why he did not wring Harry's hand, clap him on the shoulder and decorate him there and then. But Colonel Smithers, of course, could not be expected to see through the limited details Harry gave him of his escape. Only she knew of the blood-tingling magnificence of their charge through that ambush. That was something Harry had to keep to himself. Otherwise Colonel Smithers would want to know why he hadn't handed the train and its complement of German troops to those Croatian insurgents.

There was a fairly friendly humming and hemming as Colonel Smithers wondered exactly what to do about the matter. It being Armistice Day, he felt there was no immediate urgency to do anything except decently celebrate. The location of Harry's regiment must be looked into. Meanwhile, Harry could take indefinite leave and wait to hear.

Harry did not quarrel with that.

'And then there's your wife.' Colonel Smithers smiled at Irena. 'I hardly think it's been a honeymoon since you slipped out of Bucharest, what? Have to arrange the adjustment of your pay. Did we get the date of the marriage? Good. Well, highly commendable effort, Captain. Highly.'

When they were on their way out of the building Irena murmured, 'Do you think he meant your escape was highly commendable or your marriage?'

'I think he meant you were quite the best part of it all,' said Harry. 'I'll probably get a different reaction from my regimental colonel. He'll want to know why I didn't try getting back to my battery instead of gallivanting across Europe with a wife whom I married without his permission. His mind works rather like a pair of crossed swords. On the other hand, I'm not a regular officer, I only hold a wartime commission. Now, let me see,' he went on matter-of-factly as they emerged into Whitehall, 'I'd better catch a train home tonight, but first do you think we might dine together if we can get a table at the Trocadero or the Criterion or some other place fairly decent and lit up? No, before that I must find you an hotel. Let's try the Northumberland, it isn't far.'

Irena, paling, said disbelievingly, 'An hotel?'

He drew her aside from the thumping surge of people, sheltering her against the wall of the building.

'I assume this is where we go our separate ways,' he said, 'we have to do that sometime.'

She looked as if she had been struck in the face.

'You mean now?' she said numbly. 'You are going home and leaving me here in a strange hotel?'

He was unable to explain why this was so necessary and what it would do to him. His one chance of saving the relationship he had with Elisabeth was to break with Irena now. If his association with Irena went on longer he knew he would be totally unable to do justice to any marriage with Elisabeth. He would be hopelessly in love with a personage, and personages might dance with farmers, but they would never marry them.

'I thought,' he said, 'that you intended to stay in London once we reached England. You're safe now and you have your own plans, I imagine. Perhaps you also have some way of letting Major Carlsen know you're safe, I think he wants to know. I presume you and I have to meet again when the question of the annulment comes up, but I did think we might have dinner together before we say goodbye. You know, don't you, that I am proud of you, that it's been a privilege to be with you. You do know that?'

She was pale, incredulous, stricken. London in eruptive revelry was not exciting now, it was a noise that beat at her. She could not look at him. Instead her eyes were on the choked traffic, the blur of people and waving flags.

'Captain Phillips?' Her voice in a strange way did not seem to belong to her. 'You are going to leave me in London? Here, by myself?'

He did not think that that in itself was a great problem to her. She walked into hotels as if they belonged to her. And she had a way with her, a way that charmed people into serving her and helping her, and she had courage and aptitude. London was confusing to her now. She would have it at her feet by tomorrow.

'Isn't that best?' he said.

'I don't understand.' Her brown eyes, frozen, were fixed on nothing. 'What have I done? Is it that you don't like me? We – we were supposed to stay together until the annulment.'

'Were we?' He could not precisely remember when that was arranged. He was torn by her stricken look, but governed by the necessity for common sense and by all he owed Elisabeth. 'I'd assumed you would be in London, at least for a while.' He held off pressure from a new surge of people. He tried to do what he could for Elisabeth and his peace of mind in the gentlest way possible. 'Elisabeth will accept my story, I hope, but I'm not really sure she would accept the necessity of you and me living together. I've a small house in a Hampshire village which is hardly suitable for a platonic relationship, even in the eyes of the most charitable people, and it's less than suitable for Your Highness. What do you think it would do to a straightforward annulment if I took you there? It's better, surely, that we don't live together.'

'An annulment is only affected if–' She swallowed. 'If we had loved each other.'

'I know that isn't likely to happen, but–'

'I see.' She had expected the break to come eventually, but not now, not today when they had only just arrived, now at a moment when everyone else was celebrating. It was shattering. She had only her pride with which to face up to him. She spoke quietly, as oblivious as he was to the waving flags. 'I do understand about you and Elisabeth. I will go to the hotel and get someone to collect my luggage from the station.' She was very proud but so pale, and he felt sick with himself because in his insistence on common sense he knew he had hurt her. She had been so unafraid, so stimulating in adversity, so endearing in her little moments of temper. She had stoked the fire and held off the throat-cutting bandits of Croatia. 'Yes, you must go home at once, of course you must,' she said. 'I am sorry if I did not see that just now, but it has been so – so–'

'Yes, I know,' he said, wondering if he would ever forget how bravely beautiful she had looked through her soot.

'It was all so splendid, so magnificent. Everything.' She was drawing on every reserve of desperate pride. 'We will say goodbye now? That would be better. I have your address, I will write to you about the annulment.'

He found it unendurable. He had known it was going to be difficult. It was far worse than that. Here, in Whitehall, with processions of people hampering real communication, parting from her was impossible.

'Oh, damn and blast,' he said, 'I'm making such a mess of this.'

She put out a gloved hand. 'How am I to thank you, how am I ever to thank you?' she said.

'We did it together,' said Harry. He did not take her hand. 'Oh, hell,' he said. She winced. 'Well, how the devil can we say goodbye here, in the street? It's not so much that I feel I'm leaving you alone. You're not a penniless nobody, you've got distant relatives at the Palace and personages in high places who are supposed to be worried about you. And failing their hospitality there's the Ritz. You'd fit into a suite there as naturally as any royalty. But that's not the point, is it, I'm damned if it is.'

'I don't wish you to get angry or to swear,' she said, 'I'm sure I shall be quite safe from anarchists, if that's what you are thinking about.'

'No, I'm not thinking about anarchists at all. You should be safe enough in London.' He muttered under his breath. 'Look here,' he said.

'I do not want to be a worry to you,' she said.

'Well, you are. Look here,' he said again, 'the war's over, everyone's having a high old time and you don't deserve to be left out of it.' He took her by the arm and moved her back into the entrance to the War Office, where they would not be jostled and inhibited by the thickening crowds. 'Would you like to spend a few days in London with me? We could both wind down a little.'

'Wind down?' A faint ray of hope brightened her.

'Relax. Forget all the tensions and simply celebrate. I'm not sure we both don't deserve a few days off. I'll say nothing to Elisabeth or my parents about being back yet. I can't leave you to cope with Armistice Day on your own, I owe you more than that.'

'Harry, you owe me nothing, it is I who–'

'I owe you for being on that train with me, for using that rifle, for other things. On the other hand, you've had to put up with me for quite a while now, and you may not want too much more of me. It's just that–'

'Harry!' She was distressed. 'Oh, how could you even think that!'

'Well, look here, then, shall we celebrate for a couple of days? Then we can talk about your future again.'

'We will stay at the hotel together?'

He rubbed his chin. Her eyes were big, ready to brim if she lost control of herself.

'Not quite together, as we were in Padua,' he said, 'not now we've arrived. We have to be careful about these things now, don't we, in view of the annulment? We must get separate rooms.'

'Yes, of course. Oh, I'm sorry, I've made such a fuss, haven't I?'

'No, not at all.' Harry finally reduced the dialogue to an easy conversational level. 'Now you're sure you'll like this, a couple of days seeing London with me?'

'Oh, yes,' she said gratefully, 'it will give me time to get used to it. It is very foreign to me, you see.'

'Yes, that's a point,' said Harry matter-of-factly. 'Well, we'll see how we go.'

'Yes,' she said, managing to sound quietly restrained. He did not know what an effort it was for her not to be demonstrative in her relief. It was easy for him. Distaste for showing one's emotions was born in the English. She wondered if English babies cried like other babies when they came into the world. They probably did not dare to. To be demonstrative, to show blissful relief that he was not going to leave her yet, would never do. And it would make things worse. She said, 'Thank you, Harry, it will be nice to celebrate.'

They managed to get rooms at the Northumberland. From her window Irena looked down into the avenue and saw flags flying in a thousand hands. There were so many different uniforms, Allied as well as British. The passage of countless people strung across the width of the street merged with the tides sweeping into Trafalgar Square. The noise was tumultuous, it affected one's blood. The windows of buildings were open and filled with the heads of people. Beer bottles spouted foam from one window as tops were twisted off. There was a heady deliriousness about the mood of the people. They sang and they danced. Irena thought of Rumania, its conquest and its passive resilience under German occupation. She thought of Major Carlsen. At the moment he would be bitterly aware of an outcome he had at one time never envisaged.

It hardly seemed possible that his great nation, for so long Europe's greatest military power, lay broken in defeat, that the Kaiser Wilhelm had lost his throne, his empire and his people. Major Carlsen would need all his nerve and courage to live with the fact that Germany, which had promised so much, lay in greater ruins than any other country.

Irena sighed. But she watched fascinated from the hotel window, opening it wider to look and to listen. How bright the celebrations made the grey November day. The clouds swept low over the capital, running before a light wind, scattering a few drops of rain which counted for nothing as the people surged and danced through streets and avenues to mass in Trafalgar Square or to force their way through to Piccadilly Circus. No one had ever told her that the British danced in their streets on occasions like this one, that the girls and women of London kicked up their legs and showed their petticoats, that they lost their hats and hairpins, that their hair ran free and wild and that they behaved like laughing gipsies.

And there were even some American soldiers, with their boy scout hats and their wide shoulders, picking up girls and throwing them high and throwing their hats up after the screaming girls and catching both on the way down. And there was so much kissing. All this time, all the way from Bucharest, and she had not been kissed once, except by a large sailor she had not even been introduced to. She had been harried and carried and bullied, but not once had she been kissed. Not even today, when it was his victory day. Naturally, there was Elisabeth, but surely–

'Oh, I am so stupid!' she cried out loud.

What with the emotional impact of the people, the soldiers, the victory, and Harry, the hot tears pricked her eyes as she stood at the window.

Someone saw her, someone able to distinguish her vivid beauty even from the street below, but not her tears, and he called, a soldier of the King's Own Light Infantry, a man of Flanders.

'Come down, love, come down!'

She laughed at him through her tears and she waved and he waved back, a young and thin-faced veteran of the trenches, in his peaked khaki cap and his uniform of blue, the uniform of the convalescent wounded. His left sleeve was empty but his eyes were full, enraptured by the vision of a beautiful young woman laughing down at him from the hotel window.

'Come down, sweetie, come down!'

She could not hear him above the noisy exultation, but she saw his empty sleeve and the smile eager and encouraging on his face, and extravagantly, still crying, she blew him kisses with both hands. He kissed her back in the same way, but with one hand, then was swept along and away by the flowing mass of revellers.

It was so emotional, all these people singing and dancing because the war was over and won. Here in London they surged through the streets, they rode on the open tops of crawling buses. Yet in Berlin, Irena couldn't help remembering, the women walked dazed and bewildered, in Vienna they wept.

Irena, watching victorious London, could not help weeping herself.

There was a knock on her door. Hastily she banished her tears, dabbed her eyes and face.

'Come.'

She thought it would be Harry but it was a

pageboy in uniform and pillbox. He handed her a white oblong box. She thanked him. She could not tip him, she had no English money. Expressively, with her eyes and her smile, and a little shrug, she indicated her deep regret. The pageboy grinned and said, 'Don't you worry, madam.' He could smell generous tips when she had English coinage.

She closed the door and opened the box. It contained a dozen late autumn roses, perfectly budded and all a deep red. Their scent was a fragrant reminder of summer departed. There was a card.

'For bravery. Harry.'

'Oh,' she gasped and sat down in new emotion. With the box on her knees she gazed numbly at the blooms. *For bravery*. She wanted to cry again. She knew flowers from Harry really belonged to Elisabeth. She knew she was keeping him from his fiancée, that she was making a terrible mistake. He would think about it and begin to resent it. But for the moment he had thought to send her roses. She sat very quietly for a while, the tumult of London pounding in on her through the open window. She got up and closed it. She hesitated, then went along to room 27. She knocked. Harry answered in his shirt, tie and trousers. He looked a little sleepy.

'I had my feet up,' he said.

'The roses,' she said, trying to sound delighted but not intense, 'oh, they are lovely. Thank you so much.'

'Oh, yes. The roses.' He smiled. 'They were overdue.'

He did not invite her in. She understood. They had to be very circumspect.

'No one has ever sent me flowers because of my bravery,' she said.

'Well, I have,' said Harry.

'They are nicer than a medal,' she said, 'thank you, Harry.' And she hurried back to her room. He called to her and she turned in the corridor. He came up to her.

'Princess, will you dine with me at Romano's tonight? I've managed to get them to squeeze us in. I think you'll like it there.'

'Oh, I am sure I will like it anywhere tonight,' she said breathlessly.

'I'll call for you at eight and we'll look at London first,' he said.

She was ready at eight. She looked beautiful. Harry had had his uniform pressed and she would have liked to have said how proud she was of him. When they walked through the lobby the pageboy bowed to her and outside the commissionaire saluted them. They were able to get a taxi and it took them around London. Harry said she must see the Palace, the residence of her distant relatives. The taxi skipped and flirted around revellers who claimed the roads as well as the pavements as their right this night. In front of the Palace the people thronged, the façade of lighted windows a magnet and a hopeful sign that the royal family would appear yet again. They drove down the Mall and into the heart of the West End. There traffic moved at a walking pace, hemmed in by rivers of people. The lights were on, the theatres brilliant with flashing bulbs, and there was a special charity performance of *Chu Chin Chow*, the musical which had dominated London's entertainment throughout the war. Irena peered and looked, entranced and exhilarated, a gossamer scarf around her piled hair, a coat over her shoulders. Dearly she would have liked a stole, a rich, soft, warm fur stole. She had not thought of victory night in London when buying things in France.

The noise was of horns, bells, songs and cheers. And triumph. Peace would come later, a bewildering peace. Tonight they were still dancing, soldiers, sailors and girls. There were so many girls, so many women, scores of them, hundreds of them, haunted by the men who had gone, who lay in Flanders, in Mesopotamia, in Salonika, in Gallipoli and in drowned iron battleships. The British Empire had prevailed, but it had lost a million of its finest men and it had seen its most brilliant and exciting era during the Edwardian years. Edward and Alexandra had given it gaiety, colour and an almost blinding splendour, had matched it with the magnificence of Ancient Rome, and few realized that the flame lit by Victoria's gregarious son had burnt itself out in a consuming war only a few years after his death. Piccadilly Circus, the hub of the empire, did not cast any mantle of darkness, it was ablaze with its multitude of lights, and the men and women who had served the empire and survived did not know they were dancing around a heart that was dying.

'Harry, I did not know it was like this,' said Irena as the cab eased its way into the brilliance. The lights were like running, flashing fire. Hats waved, flags flew, and the girls were laughing at the moment and forgetting both the past and the future.

'What didn't you know was like this?' asked Harry.

'London,' said Irena, 'you never told me a thing about it, yet look how exciting it is.'

'It'll be cold and cluttered at dawn,' said Harry, 'and probably foggy.'

'Please don't be so gloomy. Harry, aren't you proud? Look at everything and everyone. Oh, I should be very proud.'

'What of?' said Harry. He was aware of her warmth, her scent, her excitement.

'Of belonging here, of knowing I had done something to make London and the people proud of me.'

'You're inebriated,' said Harry.

'Inebriated?'

'Ah – drunk,' said Harry.

'I am not!' She took his English very literally at times. 'I have not had anything. Harry,' she said, 'can we go and see – what is it now? – a clock, yes? Big Benk, isn't it?'

'Big what?'

'Isn't that right, Big Benk?'

'Big Ben?'

'Yes, that is right,' she said, pleased with herself.

'I'll see if the driver can get us there.'

The driver said he'd do his best, but if they got squeezed flat, taxi and all, he wouldn't half have something to say about it. But he got there and they sat in the cab and looked up at the huge, shining face of the illuminated clock. They waited until it struck nine o'clock. The strokes boomed out over the inky Thames, darkly flowing, and the haunting, lingering echo of each stroke filled Irena with wonder. Westminster Bridge was a tideway of people, the Houses of Parliament and Westminster Abbey etched against the black sky, and Irena could not think why Harry was so quiet, why he was not stirred. She glanced at him. The lights reached into the cab. His eyes were still and reflective. And she knew he was not thinking of victory but of men he had known, men who had not been as lucky as he had.

Involuntarily she reached and pressed his hand. He squeezed her fingers.

'Let's go to Romano's now, shall we?' he said.

'Yes. But thank you for Big Ben. It was very stirring.'

'Just an old clock,' he said.

Romano's was beautifully warm and welcoming. Its plush red and gilt and its Edwardian opulence reminded her a little of Maxim's in Paris. The tables glittered with glasses and silvery buckets of crushed ice glittered with condensation. Miniature flags of the Allies formed the table decorations. There were Allied officers crowding in, French, British and a few American. The French seemed to arrive with a woman on each arm, the Americans came as a party and in uninhibited possession of a bevy of girls. The British officers, who were, of course, playing at home, seemed in a state of correct bonhomie with one lady apiece. Other men arrived in toppers, tails and cloaks, a splendid pre-war style.

Younger women, girls, came in modern 1918 style, in evening dresses whose lines were straight. A number of the maturer women arrived in striking defiance of straight lines and wartime austerity. They wore plunging, off-shoulder gowns bravely lifted from wardrobes they had put aside, and they looked as if they were Edwardian beauties brilliantly reborn. What other fashions could do justice to Armistice night? What was there of imaginative flair in November 1918 that matched even the most modest of Edwardian styles? As far as these women at Romano's were concerned there was nothing, and they left every trace of a tired 1918 at home. They declared for the sumptuous, exotic and banished Empire lines, they declared for Queen Alexandra, for Alexandra was the inspiration and arbiter of all Edwardian grace and style, and had refused to clothe herself like a shapeless neuter. They retraced their steps on Armistice night to bring back the recent, the glorious past, as if they knew that the present was synonymous with drabness and the future would offer them nothing memorable. They had been young when Edward was King and this was their final flamboyant salute to the world which, in retrospect, seemed hauntingly and excitingly beautiful. So they came to Romano's, these women of London, the society figures, the actresses and the paramours, and for one night they brought back the splendour of Edward and Alexandra and their mighty Empire. And they made anonymous figures of the girls and the women who declared for the shapelessness of 1918.

Irena did not disgrace their challenging appeal.

She came in the beauty of the silk gown she had bought in Padua, so different with its long flowing sleeves and its studded collar. Preceding Harry, she followed the head waiter to their table. Her gown shimmeringly clasped her body, her dark hair was piled high, her vivid beauty enriched by the lights and the luminous quality of her excited eyes. She wore no gloves and no jewellery, none at all, except for a plain gold wedding band, but in her dark hair was a single red rose. She turned heads, she drew eyes, and she walked, thought Harry, as he imagined all princesses did, in graceful, inherent obliviousness of everything but her own regality.

My God, he thought, what am I doing here with her? What the devil would Elisabeth say?

The plush red embraced her as she sat down.

Romano's crowded them with warm, vibrating excitement. Irena sparkled, adoring it all, the magnificent colour to which every gown, every dress and every uniform contributed, and every white tie seemed like a neatly outlined shape on the glowing canvas. Harry avoided looking at her. She was a warm radiance. He felt extremely proud of her but he was very aware that to look at her was no help at all. So he kept his eyes elsewhere. She was sensitively quick to realize this. He did not even look at her when he spoke to her or when she spoke to him.

'There is something wrong with me? I have not powdered my nose?'

'Why do you ask that?'

'You're not looking at me. I mean, you are looking as if I am not here.'

'I've got something in my eye,' said Harry.
'Let me see.'
'It's a mote.'
'What is that, what is a mote? Isn't it water round a castle?'
He laughed. That made her happier. They ordered from a menu that seemed surprisingly varied considering the shortages. But considering also that the food was secondary to the privilege of being here on Armistice night, what they had was excellent. Tiny chicken vol-au-vents which melted in the mouth came crisp and hot. They followed with little strips of fish in sauce which were delicious, although Harry said they were dismembered pilchards.
Above the hubbub Irena said, 'Pilchards? They are fish?'
'What do they sound like to you, Bulgarian policemen?'
'I hope I am not eating dismembered Bulgarian policemen,' said Irena.
Harry, in the midst of swallowing a piece, put a hand up to his mouth.
'Oh, good God,' he said muffledly.
'What is wrong?'
'Nothing. Just very funny.'
'You are making a joke?' she said.
'You made the joke.'
'Bulgarian policemen? That was a joke?'
'Wasn't it?'
'I was very serious. Would you like to be eating–'
'No, don't, not again, Princess.'
Their eyes met. She coloured. He smiled. She

laughed nervously.

They drank champagne. The war had reduced supplies but not shut them off completely. It was prohibitively expensive but Harry had no intention of settling for less on such a night, with such a woman. And the champagne would do for him what his resolution could not, it would cast a glow over his problems. Irena loved the champagne and enjoyed the food. She ate the main course with relish. It was a roast. The English translation on the menu said rib of beef and indeed it had been carved for them in front of their eyes. Irena thought it delicious and said so.

'It's very eatable,' said Harry, 'but I'm not sure whether it's beef or horse.'

'Horse?' She was beginning to have a warm, delightful evening. She knew he was not being serious. 'Horse?' she said.

'Did you see the shape of that rib? Very round. Horse, I tell you.'

'But beefs are round too.'

He let her get away with beefs.

'Beefs are squarer,' he said.

'We are eating horse? Because of the war? Well, horse is very nice,' she said.

'No, it's my joke this time,' he said, 'I don't want you to have a dull evening.'

'Dull? Dull? But, Harry, it's wonderful, isn't it? Everyone looking so grand.'

She was looking so vivid, so alive. The champagne was casting its glow. Over both of them. Over others. A French officer at a nearby table raised his glass to Irena, winked at her and drank to her. Irena acknowledged the gesture with a smile. Corks popped, girls shrieked. The Frenchmen stood up and sang the Marseillaise. Everyone else stood up and joined in. That brought on the cabaret star, a flame-haired woman wearing a flag as a sash over her black satin dress. She began to sing the songs of war. She sang 'Tipperary', 'Home Fires' and 'Soldiers of the Queen'. She did not sing alone. They would not let her go, nor did she wish to with such an audience as this. She sang on.

Irena was watching Harry. He was sitting back, not singing. He was remembering the guns, the belching, recoiling guns, the limbered guns, the sweating horses, the mud of Flanders and the heat of Mesopotamia. And the German guns, the German shells, the savage, straining effort to bring the battery clear, the carnage when horses were blown to bits. Despite the golden aura of the champagne he did not find the singer uplifting. Her songs were not meant for cabaret, they were the songs of the men of war, of men marching to entrain for leave, of recruits marching for the first time into the line. They were the songs of the infantry, and they belonged to these men.

'Harry?' whispered Irena.

'Send her home,' he said.

What was he saying? She thought the songs so varied, some haunting and some heart-quickening, though she did not really know them too well. Harry was odd and had said odd things this evening.

Streamers ran through the air and balloons sailed like light colourful ships. And still they would not let the singer go. She was looking at

Harry, the only man who had not been responsive to her rich voice. He sat there, not far from her, she bathed in the spotlight, he dark in the shadow. She saw Irena watching him. She turned to her pianist and spoke to him.

She sang 'Greensleeves', a ballad not about war but about a lady, attributed to Henry VIII. At which Harry smiled and the singer smiled back. And the women clothed in Edwardian splendour listened and they too had their memories.

People merged, tables merged, and Harry and Irena found themselves drawn into the midst of women who wanted to kiss Harry and men who could not take their eyes off Irena. She watched flamboyant women kiss his mouth and she fumed, although she laughed. To men who wanted to kiss her she offered her hand. The French, British and Americans drank and celebrated, the cosmopolitan factor adding its own international excitement to the atmosphere. Irena seemed to put aside all her pro-German sentiments and lose herself in the evocative exhilaration brought about by a long war grimly fought and well won.

Champagne bottles came and went.

'More, please, Harry.' Irena held out her glass. She was flushed, excited, her eyes softly brilliant.

'You sure?' Harry looked into the lambent eyes. Her dreamy smile embraced him. 'A victory's a victory, an intoxicated princess is a defeat.'

'Oh, pooh,' she said.

'Chérie?' A French officer gallantly filled her glass for her. She gave him her sweetest smile. He was on his feet, leaning over her shoulder. Just as gallantly he kissed her. She was too dreamy to escape that one.

'Hm,' said Harry.

'Hm?' Irena, her flush deeper, turned to him. 'What is hm for? Everyone is kissing, you are kissing, so I am kissing too.'

'So there,' said Harry and laughed. She was an irresistible princess.

It was late, so late, when they left Romano's. The Strand was quietening, although there were still some revellers about, still some soldiers and girls swinging along. The sky was black but clear, the Strand shining like a dark river.

'Shall we walk, Harry? I am not tired, are you?'

He gave her his arm. She was grateful for it, drawing close to him, for it was cold after the warmth. But she wanted to walk, to feel the air on her face, and what was the cold of a London night after the bitter cold of Trieste? She was, despite the temperature, full of dreamy well-being. They did not have far to go, but the pavements were damp and she hitched her gown with her free hand.

'Are you cold?' His voice had well-being in it too.

'Oh, no. Harry, thank you for taking me there, I am still so excited. It was lovely, wasn't it?'

'Well, better than beans in Belgrade,' he said, conscious of her warmth, her nearness. The gossamer scarf stirred around her head, caressing her hair and the red rose. 'I'll take you round the shops tomorrow. I'd like to have you meet some lords and ladies, but I don't know any–'

'Why should I meet lords and ladies?'

'To make you feel more at home. Your Highness, I–'

'Oh!' That incensed her, she felt a deliberateness about it, as if the cold night had already swept away the lovely warm excitement they had just shared. 'I am Sonya Irena, why don't you call me that, why don't you? I'm not too proud to call you Harry, you should not be too proud to call me Sonya Irena.'

'I intend to behave with perfect decorum from start to finish,' said Harry, as they crossed the road in front of Charing Cross station.

'Perfect decorum?' Irena had her chin in the air. 'What is that, some stupid English name for starch?'

'Starch?' He knew what was coming but he had to invite it.

'Yes, starch.' She was almost disdainful. 'That is what I've heard about the English, they are all stuff and starch. You are all stuff and starch.'

'Well, my father's a bank manager,' said Harry.

'How ridiculous.' She was superbly lofty. 'What is it to do with your father? He is probably a very nice man.'

'Yes, quite so, but–'

'You are a snob. I have heard that about the English too.'

'Haven't you heard anything nice?'

'No,' she said and wondered if the tall slender pedestal on which Nelson stood was swaying in the night or whether she was not quite steady herself. 'No, I have not.'

'Then it's damn lucky for you I didn't turn out an absolute bounder and sell you to the highest bidder.' He helped her avoid carousing sailors as they turned into Northumberland Avenue. 'Now look here, Sonya Irena–'

'Oh, that is better. What do you mean, highest bidder?'

They were not really quarrelling. They were fencing, and a little recklessly because of the evening they had had. In an acutely sensitive relationship it is better to strike sparks than to show warmth.

'Some of the French have money,' said Harry, 'and a very fine appreciation of beautiful women.'

'I am a beautiful woman?' said Irena lightly.

'I don't think I'd have had any problem selling you to a French millionaire.'

'Now who is drunk?'

'I'm not.'

'Then you are disgusting. Harry, isn't it a lovely night?'

'No, it's damp and cold. You should exile yourself to the South of France.'

'Oh, there is no need to give me any pushes,' said Irena, 'you will be rid of me soon enough.'

'Don't be silly,' said Harry.

That hurt her. Her arm stiffened through his and her chin lifted high.

'You are forgetting yourself, Captain Phillips.'

'I see. Very well, Your Highness.'

'Oh!'

'I like to know where I stand.'

'You are walking and being stuffy.'

They laughed at each other then and at themselves. They entered the hotel. He said goodnight to her at the door to room 21. It was early morning. Her eyes were soft, dreamy, a message lurking.

Please kiss me. Just once, won't you?

'Goodnight,' he said again and went on to room 27.

Chapter Thirteen

She slept very late. In the afternoon Harry took her out to the shops, which delighted her because she loved the shops of any capital city and the London shops were festooned with the flags and banners of victory. And because he took her to places like Bond Street, Oxford Street, Regent Street and Burlington Arcade.

But, 'I have no money, I can't buy anything.'

'Good,' said Harry, which made her laugh. She had her arm through his, she was warmly wrapped up in coat and hat, and she falsified reality and let herself belong to him.

'Oh, I am quite happy just looking.'

'You'll amaze me if you are. If there's anything you really want I'll pay for it by cheque and we'll add them up and charge them to Major Carlsen as expenses. I presume we'll hear from him sometime.'

'But I have my jewels,' she said, 'I can sell some.

She was earnest, soft, lovely. Oh, my God, he thought, oh my God. For all her moments of putting her nose in the air, for all the difference in their positions, they both knew that what counted most was the risks and the hazards they had shared. He knew she regarded him as a close friend, would always accept him as such, would speak of him as such. She walked on his ground now, as if there were no differences, but by doing so, by coming down from her castles, she was making things the more impossible for him. Better by far for her to be what she was. He was an idiot. He hadn't even told Elisabeth he was back.

'Well, look here–'

'You are so sweet, Harry. Each time you say look here I know you are going to be nice to me–' She stopped, realizing how she was talking. It was affectionately proprietary. But that was how it was, and getting worse each day, and not wanting to face the awful moment when he would have to go back to Elisabeth. 'Oh, it doesn't matter, really. I don't want to buy anything, I will wait until I am more settled. I will buy all the wrong things if I shop now, yes?'

'All the same, you must have some money. Come on, we'll go and cash a cheque.'

They went to a bank. He drew fifty pounds and gave her thirty. She looked at the crisp, white five-pound notes with their fine black script. It was not something to get emotional about. They knew each other now, trusted each other, and she would pay him back. The gesture was a practical one, but she still felt emotional. He only had a captain's pay, that hardly made him rich.

'Harry–'

'It cost you pearls to get us out of Trieste, remember?' he said.

'Oh, that was nothing,' she said and led the way out of the bank, wondering in distress how she was going to manage without him. Not because she was a useless or helpless person. She wasn't.

'Where the devil are you going?' Harry's hand took her by the arm, pulling her back from the kerb. The street was a maelstrom of horse-drawn traffic and motor vehicles.

'I am all right.'

'Yes, I daresay, but don't get carried away. Princesses crossing a London street incognita are in as much danger as ordinary people. If you want to stop the traffic wear your tiara.'

'Oh, you are so ridiculous,' she said but she was laughing.

They went on with their window-shopping, their walking, their strolling, their peering. Irena rubbed shoulders with the people, except that she hung on to Harry's arm and wondered desperately from time to time if any woman had more problems than she had. There was so much that separated her from Harry, and being arm in arm with him neither eased the problems nor made them go away.

The afternoon darkness of November descended. This brought on the shop and street lights, and after the dark years all over Europe, illuminated London seemed to glow with warm triumph. The people about were still in a mood of cheer and buoyancy. When, at closing time, some of the shops began to put shutters up Irena felt it to be an affront to the spirit of the Armistice. She did not want any of the lights to go out, any withdrawals from the bright arena of celebration or, for that matter, any suggestion that she and Harry should leave it. But they had to return to the hotel eventually.

They dined quietly in the hotel restaurant that evening. Irena had no objection. She thought it would be cosy and it was. They talked, and freely. They talked about their journey, about Michalides, and laughed. Irena was loquacious, reminiscent. Do you remember, do you remember? They both remembered. Her eyes shone. She felt she and Harry had shared dangers and adventures that set them apart, that whatever else happened they would remember each other very specially. She did not want to think about what was going to happen, for the future in all its facets compulsorily embraced Elisabeth.

Harry was such good company. They communicated so easily and they spent the whole evening being together, talking together and laughing together. The hours sped so swiftly, midnight rushed at them. He escorted her up to her room. At the door she said, 'Oh, I have talked so much, I have not been boring, have I?'

'Quite the reverse,' said Harry, 'and it's a time for talking one's head off.'

'Yes, the war is really over, isn't it?'

'And we can have some peace now.'

'Yes,' she said. They looked at each other and suddenly there were no more words except those which were easily spoken and did not mean anything.

'Goodnight, Sonya Irena.'

'Goodnight, Harry.'

Chapter Fourteen

At lunch next day Harry said, 'I ought to go home now, you agree?'

Irena put her hands in her lap and looked at her plate.

'Yes,' she said. 'I don't wish you to worry about me any more, you have worried quite enough. I shall stay here for a little while and think about things. You must go home to Elisabeth.'

It had gone, the two days' respite.

'Yes, I must,' said Harry. The restaurant was almost full but they had both gone beyond using atmosphere to minimize their problems. 'But I still don't think much of my idea of leaving you here. I think now that Major Carlsen meant for me to look after you until the annulment or until he turns up, which I'm sure he will do. Will you come home with me?'

She kept her eyes on the plate, hiding the hope that was sometimes dormant and sometimes alive. It was alive now.

'No, it would not be fair to you,' she said.

'But would you rather come than stay here? You must understand it's not a palace, it's very ordinary.'

She knew she was fighting Elisabeth again. It did not make her feel very happy. But she could not bear the thought of being left. It would be like an abysmal plunge into nothingness.

'I'm such a problem, aren't I?' She tried to smile. 'But may I come? And it would not be a bad thing, would it, if I met Elisabeth and told her everything myself? You see, some women– I mean she is going to look at you when you begin to tell her about our marriage, it might not be as easy as you think.'

Her brown eyes were earnest. Harry knew that if he took her home he might be doing the worst possible thing for Elisabeth, for himself and even for Irena. She needed a week of quiet, gracious living in a first-class hotel, a week which would relax her, refresh her and bring her within the context of her own special kind of existence again. He had kept his distance as much as he could, he had given her the help he had bargained to give. But if she came to live under his roof, even for only a few days, he frankly did not know how he was going to trust himself. But he could not walk away from her, he could not leave her alone.

'We'll pack this afternoon,' he said, 'and catch a train from Waterloo. We can explain together to Elisabeth. Yes, that might be the best thing. But,' he said with a faint smile, 'do you think you could try looking a little drab and dowdy when you meet her? It'll be difficult enough as it is, without you turning up looking like the awakened Sleeping Beauty.'

Irena wondered how much it would matter if in the middle of her lunch in this busy hotel restaurant she had a little cry.

Instead she said lightly, 'Oh, it is quite easy for any Sleeping Beauty to make herself look dreadfully unappealing.'

'I'll believe that in your case when I see it,' said Harry.

They checked out of the hotel after lunch and went to Waterloo. There, because he remembered he ought to use the telephone, he left her to make her first astonished acquaintance with the oddities of an English railway buffet, where yellow wartime buns, with hardly a currant between a baker's dozen, were served from under a glass case. And tea was tapped from an urn into a cup containing a measure of milk so that what one received was not tea as she knew it, but a fait accompli of an obstinately English kind. One hardly liked to complain when one was still a newcomer. All the same, she thought she would get Harry to write to someone about it. He would be very good at ordering someone in the railway hierarchy to do things properly.

Harry phoned his parents' home first, using a telephone in the public house. His mother was rapturous to hear him. He talked to her affectionately but guardedly, saying nothing for the moment about Irena. She talked to him in exclamation marks. Then he telephoned Elisabeth. Her mother answered. She was delighted to know he was safe and actually in London. Elisabeth, unfortunately, wasn't in. She was working in the library at Portlington, she had taken the job three months ago and was quite in love with it. She adored books. Of course, now Harry was home he must not let that sort of thing go on. Harry said he would talk to Elisabeth about it. He said he would telephone again, he had a long story to tell. She said Elisabeth would be off her head with relief and happiness.

Harry, putting the phone down, thought Elisabeth would show her happiness with a warm, sweet kiss, not by turning cartwheels. Curiously he realized if anyone would jump over the moon in a moment of excessive happiness it would be a princess he happened to know.

He sighed a little. Thoughts and things kept coming back to Her Irrepressible Highness.

He found her looking quite incredulous at the vast amount of milky tea being drunk in the station buffet. She was happy he had returned and began to tell him that perhaps something could be done about people who gave you milk with your tea when you did not want it–

'I know how you feel,' said Harry, 'but do you mind terribly if we leave that for some other time?'

'No, not at all, I was only–'

'Come along,' said Harry.

They caught a train which took them southwest into Hampshire. She was taut with nerves and he was quiet. The restraint imposed by the presence of other passengers was not unwelcome in its way. It was teatime and dark when they arrived at the village of Amblestoke. The station gas lamps flickered as old Bill Parkin took their tickets, recognized Harry, welcomed him home and blinked with candid interest at the woman he had brought home with him.

He looked, he blinked again, Irena smiled and he said, 'Well, I'm blowed.' And Harry knew it would be all over the village before lights went out that night.

'How are your chickens?' he asked.

Old Bill looked as if he wanted to know how Harry's were. Irena, coat tight around her, the cold a wintry embrace, smiled again and old Bill reckoned afterwards that she fairly lit the place up, fog and all. Harry enquired after the possibilities of a cab.

'Ain't been no cab for months,' said Bill, 'but lend you a handcart for them bags if you like.'

'You're on,' said Harry. Irena loved him for that. That was how he was, he never made a fuss about the unimportant things, he simply got on with them. He would make a fine farmer. She thought of warm, golden corn and of watching him reap it.

They piled the luggage, which had grown by two more cases, on to the handcart outside the station, and Harry pushed it home. Irena walked by his side and reflected on what it was all about. It was all about simple living after a dreadful war.

They did not have far to go, no more than a mile, and the walk warmed her. They reached houses. Lights showed behind curtains. There were small houses and country cottages, some with low wooden fences, others with little hedges. She could smell the smoke of coal fires and wood fires. Harry trundled the cart up against a grass verge and stopped. She saw a little wooden gate about three feet high. There was a path leading up to a small house, which was in darkness.

'Stay there,' said Harry, 'while I get the key from Mrs Sawyer. She's been keeping an eye on things for me. It's been lived in, a soldiers' billet, so it shouldn't be too damp.'

She wanted to say something absurd, such as she wouldn't have minded if it had only been a tent in a wet field and that she wished her name was Elisabeth instead of Sonya Irena Helene Magda.

But all she said was, 'After everything else, do you think I would care about a little damp?'

She waited at the little gate. He was longer than she expected, although Mrs Sawyer was only in the next house about thirty yards away. But Mrs Sawyer kept him gassing, he said. Mrs Sawyer liked a good gas. Irena asked what a good gas was.

'A very long chat,' said Harry and let her into the house. He applied a match to every mantle in the place until all was bathed in cheerful light. Mrs Sawyer had been conscientious since the last soldiers left some months ago. The rooms looked clean and tidy and only the kitchen felt a little damp. Irena turned on the brass tap over the sink. Water gushed.

'Oh, that is good,' she said, 'in Rumanian villages houses have no running water.'

'Here,' said Harry, 'we're full of civilized amenities. There's even a bathroom upstairs. Mrs Sawyer brings her children in to use it on Fridays. She has six.'

'Six children? How lovely,' said Irena.

'Don't tell her that.'

'But six *is* lovely,' said Irena, forgetting that in Rumania she had always been able to recognize what was admirably practical about romance and what was cloud cuckoo land. She was excited, intrigued, exploratory. He told her to look around if she wanted to and she did. It was only a small village house but it was Harry's, and she put her lovely nose into everything while he brought in the luggage and took it up to the bedrooms. Upstairs there were two bedrooms and the bathroom. The beds were not made, the linen and blankets were in the landing cupboard, which was heated by pipes running up from the kitchen range. The range was laid and he lit it. The balled paper flared. He also lit the fire in the sitting room. The sitting room was wallpapered and cosy. The fire, when it began to burn, made it cosier. Irena, still in her hat and coat, was wandering about. She roamed upstairs. She roamed down again. It was such a nice little house. It wasn't at all grand. It was just right for two people.

The fire in the kitchen range was crackling and leaping, already warming the room and the hot-water pipes. Harry put his head round the door and said he was going down to the village store to try and get some food. If it was shut he would knock them up. 'You forage around,' he smiled.

'Forage?' She puzzled over that. 'Forage is for horses, isn't it?'

'Yes. But foraging around is for princesses who leave their castles and come down to look into the mysteries of rustic dwellings.'

'You mean poking my nose in. That is right, isn't it?'

She went upstairs again when he had gone. The bedrooms had latticed gable windows and low ceilings. The brass of the bedsteads was polished and there were small bedside rugs on the linoleum-covered floors. She could smell the faint, clean tang of furniture polish. She went down to the sitting room and sat in an armchair in front of the fire. The flames licked up from the glowing coal. It was quiet, so quiet. She felt sad, lonely. She was here but she did not really belong. She was in Elisabeth's chair. It was not right to have come, it made things so much more complicated for Harry. Perhaps when she had first seen him she should have said to Major Carlsen, 'No, I do not want him, find me someone else.'

Harry came back with food. He had half a loaf of bread, some cheese, margarine and pickled onions, the onions wrapped in stiff brown paper. He also had plum jam, two tomatoes, two pounds of potatoes, some greens, some milk and a bottle of Camp coffee. And a small lemon, which looked with its dry tough skin as if it had lain forgotten for a year. She could not quite relate each item to the next as far as a meal was concerned. Harry said he wasn't going to throw them all into a stew together. What was the lemon for?

'Ah, yes,' he said. He fished out the last item. 'That's a packet of tea. The lemon is for your tea. You'll have to make it last, I'm afraid.'

'Oh,' she said, and there was a dreadful lump in her throat all because of an old lemon.

Was she hungry? She was famished. He prepared a simple meal, cooking potatoes, mashing them and creaming them with margarine and milk. He sliced the tomatoes while the dish of creamed potato was browning under the grill of the gas stove. Then he put the sliced tomatoes on top of the creamed potato and when they were hot covered them with grated cheese and grilled the whole dish some more. The cheese softened, spread and turned brown. The aroma was delicious. Irena looked on, fascinated. The kitchen was beautifully warm, Harry so efficient. She told him how good he was.

'You should see Elisabeth at work,' he said, 'this is very rough and ready.'

'Elisabeth is a fine woman, isn't she?'

Strangely, he did not answer that.

'I'm afraid it's not much of a meal,' he said, removing the dish, 'but it was impossible to get any meat. We'll see about ration cards tomorrow.'

They ate in the small dining room, off a small refectory table of mahogany, and when they had finished the hot vegetarian dish Harry made some toast, which they had with margarine and plum jam. They were still hungry. So they finished up what was left of the cheese and bread, except for what was required of the latter for tomorrow's breakfast. Irena watched Harry crisply munch a pickled onion with his bread and cheese. She distrusted them herself, but his munching spoke of such enjoyment that she asked if she might please try one. They had been a little careful with each other, just a little constrained even, but when she attempted to cut her round, slippery onion with a knife and fork and it skidded off the plate and landed in her lap, Harry made no bones about what he felt. He roared with laughter. Irena flushed and put her chin up a little.

'Oh, it's a stupid thing,' she said, placing the onion back on her plate.

'Pick it up and bite it,' said Harry, 'that'll bring it to its senses.'

She did so. Her white teeth crunched it. It was juicy and delicious. She was so pleased at having brought it to its senses and found it so good that she laughed. It eased the constraint and brought the little dining room to life. Harry made coffee and they had it in front of the sitting-room fire. Harry was quiet, staring almost frowningly into the flames. She was keyed up. She should have stayed in London. In that hotel she could have managed very well. It would not have been like this, too intimate, too tense, too uneasy. Elisabeth would not like her being here. In Elisabeth's place she would not have liked it at all and would have wanted to scratch.

'Are you warm enough?' asked Harry. She was sitting with her arms embracing herself.

'Oh, yes, the fire is lovely.'

'Would you like more coffee?'

'Thank you, no.'

The constraint burdened the atmosphere.

'It's a little more humdrum here than it was on that train,' said Harry.

'What is humdrum?'

'Dull,' said Harry.

'No, that is not the word,' she said, 'it is peaceful. Oh, you are not thinking of palaces and servants because of me, are you?'

'That has crossed my mind,' said Harry, 'but just then I was thinking of the train ambush and how you shot those Croats to pieces.'

'Oh, but I have been on hunting trips with my father, he taught me how to use a rifle.'

'What, when you were a child?' said Harry.

'A child? Oh, yes,' she said and blushed. 'I was a very precocious child, you see.'

'Were you?' He had discovered modesty in her and shyness, but she could also be a little spirited and haughty. He supposed that it was not uncommon for young princesses to be a bit wilful.

'Harry,' she said quietly, 'perhaps it would be better for me to be in London. I will go back tomorrow. I am sorry – oh–' She was horrified because tears were so close. He saw them in her eyes and wanted to kiss them away.

'I don't know whether you should be alone,' he said. 'It can't have been the easiest thing in the world for you to have left your country and everything that means so much to you. I'd suggest you return to London when you're feeling better about that. It doesn't matter to me that you have German sympathies. I suppose you could say we met some very likeable ones. You're very likeable yourself, quite the most likeable princess I expect to meet. It's a privilege to have you here. I'll nail a plaque to the front door when you've gone. You know, Princess Irena of Moldavia slept here.'

Her eyes brimmed.

'Harry – oh, I am in such a mess,' she said and bent her head and stared unseeingly and moistly at the fire.

'You do need more coffee,' said Harry sympathetically, 'I'll go and make some.'

She had recovered by the time he brought the fresh coffee in. She wondered why, when he was so self-sufficient, he needed a wife.

'You are so good at everything that when you

are married you will leave Elisabeth nothing to do,' she said.

'I've only learned how to do a few things for myself during the war,' he said, 'I haven't learned how to do without marriage. Don't most people like to share their lives with others? To have families? Royalty must have its courts and its responsibilities, we must have apple trees in our gardens and kids to play in them.'

'Yes, how wonderful,' said Irena.

'But not six,' said Harry, stirring his coffee.

'Four would be nice,' said Irena.

'Not in this place, but on a farm, yes.'

'Yes, how wonderful,' said Irena again.

They sat before the fire until Harry said good God, the beds had to be made. She went up with him, insisting that she helped. The airing-cupboard was hot as he took out the blankets and bed linen. Together they made the beds, and suddenly she seemed so competent and domesticated that it made him ask questions.

'Harry, I am not as hopeless as that!' She was indignant. 'When I was at school in Switzerland we all had to make our own beds and learn domestic science.'

'Domestic science? You should be able to cook, then.'

She blushed.

'Oh, a little, perhaps, but I am very modest about it.'

'But in Belgrade,' he said as they tucked blankets in, 'you didn't even know what a green bean was.'

'Yes, I did, I said it was for eating.'

He shook his head at her. She blushed again.

'Your Highness,' he said severely, 'you can cook breakfast in the morning.'

'Oh, may I?' It was said impulsively, happily.

'I wasn't serious, I can't have you–'

'Why can't you?' She had burned a boat and was willing to take the consequences. 'I would like to, it's only fair.'

He shook his head again, smiling. She was full of surprises.

'Just toast, then,' he said, 'and coffee or tea, whichever you prefer.'

They said goodnight after that. She was quite tired. But she lay awake for a while, wanting what she knew she could not have. She had never realized love made one so terribly hungry emotionally and physically.

The sun was pale and wintry in the morning but the light was enough to let her see, as she stood at the bedroom window, that the village was in the heart of green farmland. Everything looked quiet, peaceful, and moist with November damp. But it would be lovely in the spring and rich in the summer.

Harry slept even later than she did. When he came down to the kitchen she was making toast, the slices of bread sitting neatly under the gas grill. The kitchen table with its covering of green and white oilcloth was laid. She had put out the margarine and plum jam. She had stirred the embers of the range fire and it was glowing. She was slightly flushed. And very nervous.

'Good morning,' she said. She was in a neat cream blouse and dark skirt. Her hair was soft and loose, the slide holding it only at the back of her neck. Harry felt strange twinges. She looked as if the bright, warm kitchen was hers.

'You're managing?' he said.

'Yes, except where is the coffee?'

He showed her the bottle of dark chicory and told her she needed a spoonful in each cup with hot water.

'That is English coffee?' she said.

'Not very good?'

'It was what we had last night? It was better than some we have had, wasn't it?'

'There's a brave girl,' he said. 'No, I'm sorry, that was–'

'Harry, that was very nice,' she said, turning the toast. 'I would rather be called a brave girl than Your Highness, although I am not a girl, you know.'

'Yes, I do know,' said Harry.

They breakfasted on the toast and coffee. He said he would try and get some marmalade and eggs. They became careful and polite with each other again because of the intimacy of breakfasting together, with Elisabeth in the near background. He complimented her on the excellence of the toast. Afterwards be told her he was going to the library at Portlington.

'Elisabeth works there. I must see her.'

'Yes, of course,' she said, 'I shall be quite all right. You must see her and explain. I will also see her if you wish me to. Tell her we will arrange the annulment quickly.'

'I'll see a solicitor,' said Harry.

Her heart plummeted.

When he had gone she tidied up. It was quiet and she felt so alone. She was so used to having him around. She bit her lip because she did not like being without him and because there was nothing to take the place of his companionship. Someone knocked at the front door. It confused her. She stood for a moment and composed herself, then answered the knock. A young woman in a dark blue coat and matching hat stared in amazement at her. And Irena knew that this was Elisabeth.

Elisabeth, grey-eyed, slim and very fair, said, 'Oh.'

Irena braced herself.

'You are looking for Captain Phillips?' she said. Her accent was a further mystery to the bemused caller.

'Yes, I thought he was back– Oh, are you renting the house?'

'Please, will you come in?'

Elisabeth entered in something of a trance. Irena drew on more reserves. It was going to be terrible. She smiled.

'Captain Phillips is out,' she said, 'he has gone to Portlington. I think that was the name of the place he said. It was to see you, I think. You are Elisabeth, yes?'

'Portlington? Oh.' It was a soft little exclamation of disappointment. 'But when he telephoned my mother yesterday he said nothing about–' Elisabeth broke off, not disposed to launch into a trying conversation with someone who was not only a stranger and foreign, but whose presence in the house was highly suspect. 'I'm sorry,' she said, 'but I'm completely at a loss. May I know who I'm talking to?'

'I am someone from Rumania,' said Irena. 'I met Captain Phillips in Bucharest. He has spoken so much about you. Please, won't you sit down?'

'I think I must,' confessed Elisabeth, 'my head is suddenly spinning.'

They sat down. Irena was at the crossroads. Harry's fiancée was quietly formidable under her bewilderment. Some women would have been inclined to scream and some to faint at the appearance of another woman in a fiancé's bachelor establishment. Elisabeth, however, was perceptibly pulling herself together. Irena admired that. It would make things easier because Elisabeth would listen. She would not have tantrums and stamp about. She looked very English. Fair and clear-eyed and dreadfully lovely. Dreadfully. Irena knew she had to talk to her. It could not be avoided. But perhaps it would help Harry. He would then only have to add his own words, the reassuring ones, the affectionate ones.

'There are things I must tell you,' said Irena.

'Obviously,' said Elisabeth.

At which Irena took a deep breath and told the story from the beginning, leaving out only the incidents which might make Elisabeth draw the wrong inferences. She said nothing, for instance, about how she and Harry had shared the tiny apartment in Belgrade or the hotel suite in Padua, or how they had stayed in London to celebrate. She spoke of Harry as impersonally as she could, referring to him always as Captain Phillips, although she could not hide the fact that she considered him a quite exceptional man. She could not make light of all he had done.

Elisabeth, listening with a stunned expression, did manage to find her voice at one point.

'He actually drove that train?'

'We both did,' said Irena a little proudly, 'but without either of us having any real idea of how we were managing it.'

At the end Elisabeth came out of her trance to say, 'You'll forgive me, but am I to believe all this?'

'It is all true,' said Irena.

There was a long silence, with Elisabeth deep in thought. Consciously, the implications and impossibilities were staggering.

'You're saying you are Princess Irena of Moldavia?' she said at last.

'That isn't easy to believe, is it?' Irena smiled. Elisabeth regarded her in wonder and curiosity. She was not angry, she was not shocked. She was intelligently aware of one obvious fact, that few men could have refused to help a woman as vividly attractive as this one.

'It's not too difficult, either,' she said. The compliment surprised Irena. 'What is difficult,' Elisabeth went on, 'is trying to take it all in. It's so incredible. I had no idea Harry was such a Don Quixote. He has really been quite mad. He's actually married to you?'

'Oh, you must believe what I told you,' said Irena, 'it was arranged only to get me into England.'

'Was it?' Elisabeth was not sarcastic, she was calmly enquiring, although underlying incredulity was still there. She looked around the sitting room. She even smiled. She is telling me, thought Irena, that a marriage of convenience could easily become a lot more than that under the roof of this small house.

'Believe me,' said Irena.

'Do you mind if I take my coat off?' said Elisabeth. 'It's warm in here with the fire.'

'Please do,' said Irena. She had flutters under her friendly smile, for Elisabeth was beginning to be quite dangerously calm, divesting herself unhurriedly of her coat and laying it over the back of a chair. Her dress was royal blue, with white collar and cuffs. It was most suitable for a librarian, it was charming, it was right. She would be at home amongst literature, thought Irena, she is probably much more intelligent and well-read than I am.

'Let's have some tea,' said Elisabeth.

'Tea?' Irena was slightly taken aback by that piece of coolness.

'If it's not too much trouble. I think I need a stimulant.'

Not at all confident that she could prepare tea satisfying to the highly critical taste of this poised Englishwoman, Irena said, 'There is coffee, if you prefer.' She patted her hair, striving for a naturalness.

'Coffee? Ground coffee? No, it can't be.' Elisabeth was definite. 'I'm certain it could only be chicory. It's not what you like, is it?'

'It is better than what we had to drink in most places.'

'Then let's have some,' said Elisabeth, 'I don't

mind chicory in the least. Shall I make it or will you?'

'Perhaps you would like to?' said Irena, conceding Elisabeth's prior moral right.

They were both so polite that they both suddenly smiled.

'It's no use pretending the situation isn't very odd,' said Elisabeth as they went into the kitchen, 'but there are worse things to have come out of the war.'

She made the coffee. It gave her time to think. Irena stirred the range fire which did not need stirring.

'I'm not sure,' said Elisabeth as they sat drinking the coffee at the kitchen table, 'what I am to call you?'

She really was quite the calmest person, thought Irena, she would fight all her battles without ever raising her voice. She would tranquillize a marriage.

'I am Sonya Irena and so on,' she said, 'please call me Sonya. I should like us to be friends, I should not simply want to go away and forget all Captain Phillips has done for me.' She drew patterns on the green and white oilcloth with her finger. 'I could not forget how correct he has been.'

'Correct?' Elisabeth smiled. 'Well, he has principles but I've found him rather devilish at times. I'm not a princess, however. When is the marriage to be annulled?'

'When we are sure nobody knows I am here and it can be done quietly.'

'Nobody does know, do they? Except me,' said Elisabeth.

'Then it can be very soon,' said Irena. She got up and looked at the range fire again and poked it again, then flushed because her action was that of a woman in possession. Elisabeth, indeed, was regarding her very curiously.

'I really must go.' Elisabeth consulted her watch. 'I arranged to take the morning off to come and see Harry, I must catch the next train to Portlington. I live fifteen miles from here, near his parents. I hope he'll wait in the library and not go to my home, otherwise we'll be running around in circles. If I miss him perhaps he'll call on me this evening. I wonder,' she said with a smile, 'what he'll say to me? Extraordinary man.'

'You must believe,' said Irena, 'that there's nothing he has done to affect your relationship with him.'

'Except that he's married to you,' said Elisabeth. 'The cool cheek of the man. I didn't realize he was as adventurous as this. I mean, it was rather more quixotic than climbing a mountain. And one can climb a mountain without having to marry it. Goodbye. It's been a little head-spinning but I think we'll all calm down in the end.'

When she had gone Irena wondered how it was possible to fight someone who neither cried nor screamed, neither kicked nor scratched.

She had lost the fight before she had ever begun it.

Chapter Fifteen

Elizabeth arrived at the Portlington library just before twelve thirty. Two minutes later she was at her desk. Ten minutes later Harry came in. She looked up from her careful cataloguing work and there he was, uniformed and healthy, but with the air of a man on tenterhooks. She was sweetly happy to have the advantage.

'Harry? Why, how lovely.' She stood up. They were unable to embrace because of people around. The most intimate gesture he could make was to lightly brush her lips with his finger. 'I thought you might have called to see me last night. I was in a state of very happy anticipation.'

'I couldn't, so I came here this morning.' His smile was wry. 'I was told you'd taken the morning off. If I'd known I'd have called at your home. I've just come back from seeing my parents. Your colleagues told me you'd be here about now. Is there somewhere we can talk?'

She spoke to the chief librarian, then retired with Harry to the little staffroom. She turned to him as he closed the door, her action deliberate, intrigued. He hesitated. She noticed it. Then he kissed her. She let him. Her mouth was soft and warm, his firmly affectionate. Hm, she thought.

'My dearest Elisabeth,' he said.

'My dear Harry,' she said. They had always been good friends, always understood each other.

She knew they could have a good marriage. 'I'm so glad the war is over, so glad for you and all the other men who have managed to survive.'

'You look just the same,' he said.

'I hope you can do better than that.'

'Do I have to? I like you looking the same.'

'But my dress is new.' She was lightly teasing. 'Tell me about yourself now that you've won the war and the right to a future.'

'Elisabeth–'

'Oh, I'm very proud of you,' she smiled, and she was, 'you're an exceptional man, aren't you?'

'You won't think so when I tell you what's been happening.'

She could have punished him a little, let him tackle the awkward problem of finding the right way to tell his story, but she was not like that. She said, 'I know what's been happening. I called on you this morning. My state of happy anticipation wouldn't let me wait for you to call on me later. You weren't home. But Princess Irena of Moldavia was. Harry, a princess. You did fly high, didn't you?'

'Damn,' said Harry.

'Damn?' said Elisabeth.

'What else? That was the one thing you should have been protected against, seeing her there before you knew anything about her. I wanted you to know all there was to know before you met her. Damn it. But it means nothing, nothing at all, the fact that she's there.'

'It means you're married to her.' Elisabeth seemed more curious than anything else. 'Harry, my dear sweet man, what on earth possessed you to become involved in an escapade as mad as that?'

'She's told you about it?' said Harry.

'I've had the most extraordinary story from her,' said Elisabeth, 'but naturally I don't know if she's left anything out. Anything important, that is.'

'Important to you and me? There was nothing,' said Harry.

'Harry, what made you do it?'

'In simple terms, pressure of circumstances, I suppose,' said Harry. 'I was in German hands at the time and she was being harassed by gangs of bearded Bolsheviks who wanted to cut her throat.'

'Yes, I think I've heard all that,' said Elisabeth, as smooth as her neatly-parted hair. 'What I'd like to know is this – was the prospect of adventure too irresistible or was she?'

'Now wait a moment,' said Harry. 'Let's make it clear, shall we, that that aspect never entered into it.'

'Which aspect?' asked Elisabeth sweetly. 'The prospect of adventure or beauty in distress?'

'Elisabeth, look here, it's not been a picnic, it's been damn trying.' That was true, by God. 'So stop making me jump through hoops.'

'Harry dear, you have no idea how intrigued I am.' Elisabeth brushed a fleck from his jacket. 'You simply could not resist the challenge of it all, could you? I'm quite bowled over by your dashing gallantry. No praise is too high for you. And princesses are no more immune to valour than ordinary women. You realize what has happened, don't you?'

'What?' said Harry, feeling her cool good humour was a little suspect. He had known she would not have hysterics, he had not expected her to take it as calmly as this.

'She's fallen hopelessly in love with you.'

'What?' He was shaken by that and by the placid way it was said.

'I think you heard me, Harry.'

'Are you out of your mind?'

'Now, Harry.' She was sweet reason personified.

'Look here,' he said grimly, 'you're too cool by half. Damn it, you're having me on.'

'Indeed I'm not, that's not my style at all. You, my Don Quixote, must take the consequences of your romantic tilt at the windmills of adventure. If a man did for me what you've done for her, he'd be my lifelong Galahad. Oh, feckless Harry.' Elisabeth wagged her finger at him. 'Why didn't you think of that? She may be a princess but you've spoiled her for any other man. That was very unfair of you, since in me you already had your Guinevere. You should have let that German officer carry the responsibility–'

'That German officer, if you must know, is the man she's sweet on.'

'Oh, my poor pet, you are confused, aren't you?' Elisabeth thought back over the years. She had known him as a devilish boy, as a comforting man. She had never known him confused. 'But you have the coolest cheek, you know, coming home to me with a wife on your arm. Wait till the newspapers find out who she is.'

'That mustn't happen,' said Harry, 'it'll cause havoc. The marriage is due for annulment. The radical politicians will crucify her, they'll shout their heads off that she used me merely to get into the country.'

'Which is true, isn't it? Well, that's what she told me.'

'I know, damn it, but she was running for her life, and even here she could be in danger if there's too much publicity. Elisabeth, keep it under your hat, there's a sweet.'

'You propose to be her shining knight for ever?' said Elisabeth with accrued interest.

'No, of course not,' he said decisively, 'I've got you to think about.'

'And her. She loves you, Harry.'

'Don't be silly.'

'And far more than I do, I think. Do you mind me saying that?'

'I mind you talking nonsense.'

Elisabeth put cool fingers over his lips to stop his muttering.

'It isn't nonsense, my sweet,' she said. 'You weren't there listening to her, watching her as she talked about you. I thought her very natural and calm at first, then I began to realize she was quite emotional underneath. Her hands were never still. She's all nerves, and desperate about something. About you and me, I think, and our engagement. Harry, my dear, we've been such good friends, you and I, we've liked each other tremendously, and we've grown up thinking we should marry eventually, probably as much to please our parents as each other. But is there a grand passion? Oh, I'd be quite happy to marry you, but listening to your Princess Irena this morning I knew I wouldn't feel desolate if your marriage to her weren't annulled. She's hoping, you know, that you'll go to her and tell her it won't be. I suppose she can have a commoner for a husband. She's not in line for a crown, is she? Harry, do you love her?'

'This is madness,' said Harry, guilt discomfiting him, 'and I'm not going to continue with it. This is the right place to thump you with a good book, if that's the only way to make you see sense.'

'Here is a very good book,' said Elisabeth, picking one up from the table. '*The History of Mr Polly* by H.G. Wells. Thump me with it and I shall know you love me very much. I might be cross at first, as I don't like violence, but later I shall feel thrilled–'

'You're off your head.'

'No, not a bit.'

'We're talking ourselves into a crazy condition,' said Harry firmly, 'and it's got to stop. We'll all sit down when we're clear-headed and discuss it rationally.'

'Rationally?' Elisabeth laughed softly. 'Do you expect a woman madly in love to be rational?'

'Well, you tell me,' said Harry, walking about, 'what's more irrational than a rich princess thinking of herself as a farmer's wife, if she's thinking of that at all? Can you see Her Serene Highness in a farmhouse? I'd have to hang it with chandeliers and hire a butler.'

'Harry,' she said gently, 'you aren't very convincing.'

'The right kind of love is what you and I have,' said Harry.

'I must say,' said Elisabeth, 'you're doing your very best for me and you're doing your very best by all your principles.' She smiled affectionately. 'That's sweet, but I don't know whether it's right or even sensible. It depends, doesn't it, on whether you love her. Do you?'

'Elisabeth,' he said, 'have you met someone else?'

Elisabeth looked a little shocked.

'I've met other men, yes, a lot of them during my charity work at the military hospital. But I haven't fallen in love with any of them. However, if you've fallen in love yourself, with your house guest, I shan't stand in your way, I'd be happy for you to tell her so. I think her reaction will surprise you. I think she'll cry.'

'Madness,' said Harry again, and walked around and muttered.

'Go and talk to her,' said Elisabeth, 'you owe her an awful lot of your time and understanding for making her fall in love with you. I don't think you can send her away, my sweet. Rumanians aren't noted for being stoical, for stiff upper lips. If you make her terribly unhappy she's quite likely to jump out of a high window. So go and talk to her. You're not to think of our parents, you're to think of her. And me.'

'Damn it, I am thinking of you,' said Harry, convinced that he had let her down and she was making the grand gesture.

'I know, but I'd not want to marry you if you were more in love with someone else. Why did you bring her to your house?'

'Elisabeth, I couldn't leave her alone in London.'

'There, you see?' said Elisabeth coolly.

'Oh, women,' said Harry raggedly.

'We are God's sweeter creatures,' said Elisabeth with her most tranquil smile.

'Look here,' said Harry, 'I'll do this much, I'll think things over. But I know you haven't considered the impossibility of it all, and I have.'

'Have you, sweet? Then you've considered the possibility as well, haven't you?' Elisabeth's laugh was soft, forgiving and very affectionate. 'You know, it's all so terribly intriguing and quite splendid in its way, and I think your princess very likeable. Harry, we'll say nothing to our parents for a while. You and I, we are the best of friends, aren't we? I've always known that. So have you.'

'I still think you need thumping,' said Harry.

'What on earth did you say to Elisabeth?' They were his first words to Irena when he got back.

Irena rose up from her chair by the fire. The fire was glowing brightly. A little pulse beat in her throat.

'Oh, have you seen her? She thought she might miss you. Harry, I only told her what you would have told her yourself.'

'Oh, the Lord help the unanointed,' said Harry helplessly. He knew how expressive she was, how she would have embellished the part he had played. He ran his hand through his hair and looked at her with some of Elisabeth's words drumming in his mind. She had changed into a soft green dress, something else she had bought in France, and he wished that sometimes she would put on rusty old black and not look so lovely. 'She's got some bee in her bonnet that there's more to it than there is.'

'What is a bee in her bonnet?' she asked, and he thought the whole endearing quality of her appeal was in the way she put that question.

'An odd idea.'

'She is suspicious, she is cross?'

'No. As calm as you like.'

'Oh. That isn't an awfully good sign.' She took up the poker and moved a piece of hot coal. 'Oh, she will come round, you will see.'

He noticed the coal bucket was full.

'Who filled that?' he asked, pointing.

'I did,' she said, 'I found where it was kept in the little shed in the garden. And there were some old gloves–'

'My God,' said Harry, 'you don't have to carry coal in.'

'Why not? I am to let the fires go out?' She was quick, nervous, putting the poker back on its stand and straightening the cushion on a chair. 'Harry, come and see what I've done in the kitchen, I've polished everything twice over and you have never seen such a shine.'

'What the devil have you been doing?' He was brusque.

'I am here, so I've been helping. I am not going to just sit and do nothing. Harry, you aren't cross, are you?' She glanced anxiously at him. He wasn't dark or scowling, he had the oddest look on his face. 'I told Elisabeth everything so that you would not have to explain it all yourself. I was very nice about you, wanting her to be proud of you.'

'Oh, she's very proud of me.' He sat down. He picked up the poker and jabbed the coals. 'My God,' he muttered, 'I'm at it now.'

'Harry? Elisabeth is not very happy?' Irena was tentatively enquiring. 'Well, how could she be at first? You did not expect her to laugh about it, did you?'

'No,' said Harry, 'but she did.'

'She laughed?' The little pulse fluttered again. 'Harry, she laughed?'

'Yes,' said Harry ironically, 'I think you can say that.'

'How very odd,' said Irena.

'You think so, do you?' he said.

He sounded, she thought, as if he intended to provoke a quarrel. That was unfair.

'Yes, I think it very odd,' she said. 'In her place I would have kicked and scratched.'

'Kicked and scratched?' He was mildly amazed.

'But yes. If I were your– If we were– Well, I mean, yes, I would pull another woman's hair out.'

'Good grief, is that how the Rumanians bring all their princesses up?'

'It's nothing to do with being a princess,' said Irena. 'Harry, I had to explain to her when she came, I could not simply say nothing. But I should not have thought it would have made her laugh.'

'Well, it did. What did you tell her about me?'

Irena managed to reorientate herself and sit down. Her slim, silk-clad ankles peeped, her pointed black button-up shoes toed into the fire-side rug. She smoothed her dress, then clasped her hands in her lap.

'Harry, I told her you had been quite marvellous–'

'Marvellous? Didn't you mention that I'd been bumptious, that I'd ordered you about and bullied you?'

'No, of course not.' A little heatedly she said, 'She probably knew, there was no need to tell her what she would be aware of. I expect you have bullied her at times.'

'I haven't had to. She's never been as obstinate as Your Highness.'

'Oh, that is not fair.'

'I apologize. Did you tell her we spent two days in London together?'

'No. That would have been silly.'

'I appreciate that,' said Harry. 'You know, to do the right thing by Elisabeth I think we should arrange an immediate annulment.'

'Oh.' She swallowed. She smoothed her dress again. 'Yes, of course,' she said with an effort.

'We have to convince her that ours is a relationship due to circumstances, not emotions,' he said woodenly, 'or she'll insist on making sacrifices.'

'Sacrifices?' Her knuckles whitened, her heart began to pump. 'What do you mean?'

'Did I say sacrifices? Perhaps that's the wrong word. I mean she'll make gestures, and she'll begin by breaking the engagement.'

'What are you saying?' She could not keep emotion out of her voice. 'Does she think that we – that you and I–'

'Yes,' said Harry, 'she does.'

She looked up. Their eyes met. Colour rushed into her face.

'That is silly,' she breathed, 'we have done nothing. It isn't as if we have those kind of feelings for each other, as if there was anything that mattered in our marriage.'

'Yes, what could be more impossible between us than a real marriage?'

She winced and said, 'Mostly you don't even like me.'

'What rubbish,' said Harry.

'It's true–'

'It's rubbish.' Abruptly he got up and went into the kitchen. She was not equipped at that moment to react philosophically to such cursory behaviour and she knew she was either going to cry or kick. Pride and spirit triumphed and she stood up, threw her armchair cushion to the floor, hitched her dress and kicked. The cushion flew. Its short flight coincided with a thudding crash from the kitchen. She jumped, then stood transfixed by the awful silence. Oh! The polished kitchen floor, the floor that shone, the blue linoleum that gleamed. Oh, no! She rushed from the room. In the kitchen Harry was lying on his back, his head close to the kitchen range, and he was quite still.

'Harry! Oh, my darling!'

She was down on her knees, distraught, and Harry was opening his eyes. Her colour became fiery red. He had heard her anguished endearment, he must have, for he was looking at her so strangely.

Lightly, courageously, covering her mistake, she said, 'Oh, you silly darling man, there's no need to throw yourself about, Elisabeth will feel better about it tomorrow.' He lay there saying nothing, just looking up at her. Anxiety returned and she said, 'Harry, you aren't hurt, are you? Please?'

He smiled in a rueful way.

'You silly darling Princess,' he said in reciprocal lightness, 'you waxed it.'

'Waxed it?' Everything was thumping at her.

'The floor.' He got up. He helped her to her feet. He rubbed his head. He winced. She was in such a sensitive state that she felt the hurt herself.

'Please let me see,' she said. She did not know what to make of what he had called her, except that it did not seem right for him to have said it without then kissing her.

'It's nothing, just a slight knock,' he said.

'I'm so sorry, I polished it too much.'

'Never mind,' he said. 'I'd better go down to the shops.'

'I will come with you,' she said.

'No, I think not, if you don't mind,' said Harry.

She knew he meant that it would not do for them to walk out together, but she was here, and people in the village were aware that she was, so it could hardly matter if she went shopping with him. His attitude dismayed her.

It was no better during the next day or two. There was so much constraint, tension and terrible politeness, a politeness so civilized and English that at times she had a wildly primitive desire to shock him out of it. She knew they could not go on like this. He caught a train to Portlington immediately after breakfast on their fourth morning together, saying he was going to see Elisabeth again and also a solicitor. The annulment had to be taken in hand. Elisabeth could not be left to face the curious questions and pitying glances of friends, neighbours and relatives.

He left her in a state she had never experienced before. She recognized the stranger as sheer misery.

'What have I done?' she asked herself. 'What have I done to make him like this? It isn't just Elisabeth. I should never have come, I am in the way and he's beginning to hate me.'

Harry returned ninety minutes later. He had got off the train midway to Portlington and waited thirty minutes to catch one back. He walked, or rather stalked into the sitting room like a dark, athletic priest who had come to conduct a dialogue with a graceless heretic. The room was empty. The kitchen was empty. The silence was empty. He went to the foot of the stairs.

'Your Highness?' he called, his voice biting.

There was no reply. He climbed to the landing. The bedrooms and the bathroom were unresponsive. The room she had used was neat and tidy, but her clothes were gone, her cases gone.

She was gone.

'Oh, my God,' he said.

He would never find her. He must go back to the station and find out if she had taken a train to London.

He heard the back door open and close. Swiftly

he descended the stairs. She came through the kitchen and into the sitting room. She was wearing the black coat with a white fur collar and the matching hat, bought in Trieste, and she looked just as she had when she first tried them on. Like a winter princess. Subconsciously he admitted himself prejudiced because of his feelings for her.

Irena, not expecting to see him, stiffened. And his grim, unsmiling look made her shiver a little.

'What d'you think you're doing?' he asked.

'I am going,' she said.

'I think not,' said Harry, 'at least not yet.'

The front door shook to a loud knocking.

'There is a trap outside which has taken me trouble to find,' said Irena, 'and that is the driver to collect my things.'

'Is it? Is it indeed,' said Harry and went to the door. He saw the trap waiting. He paid the man off for his time and his lost fare. He returned to the sitting room. Irena stood in proud aloofness but trembling perceptibly.

'What have you done?' she asked.

'Sent him away.'

'How dare you? You cannot keep me here. If I wish to go, I will go.'

'Incidentally, where are your things?' asked Harry.

'In the dining room. I am quite packed up, thank you, and I intend to go.' She was at her proudest. It cut no ice with Harry.

'I didn't look in the dining room,' he said, 'but never mind that for the moment.'

'I do mind. I am going.' She attempted to sweep past him. He put himself in her way. 'Captain Phillips, you are forgetting yourself.'

He returned her proud look with one of uncompromising grimness. It sent new shivers down her back. What terrible thing had she done now?

'Until I find out whether you're an out-of-work Rumanian actress or Mata Hari's most promising pupil, you're staying here,' he said.

And suddenly Irena had a dreadful feeling that an earthquake was about to engulf her.

'Oh, no,' she said faintly, 'oh, no.'

'Oh, yes,' he said, 'I've something here I want you to see.' He produced a newspaper he had bought on his way to the station. 'I was reading this on the train. It made me get out before I'd reached Portlington. I caught the next train back. Would you care to glance at it?' He showed her a small paragraph on the second page. She saw the headline.

ROYAL EXILE LEAVES FOR AMERICA

There was a photograph, a portrait of a young woman not unlike herself, a formal portrait similar to the one Major Carlsen had shown Harry, although it had lost something in its coarse-screened newsprint reproduction. The paragraph under the headline referred to the departure of Princess Irena of Moldavia from Cherbourg to New York, the princess stating that certain circumstances were forcing her into exile in the United States.

Irena prayed desperately for an earthquake to happen. She read the item twice, taking time to adjust herself to the tearing, shattering quarrel that was utterly inevitable. She prayed again, for salvation.

'I am ill,' she gasped and sat heavily down.

'Ill?' Harry's eyes glinted. 'No tricks, madam. Stand up and look me in the face.'

'Oh, how can I?' She was in despair. 'You will strike me.'

'Fortunately for you I've gone past that. Did you and Major Carlsen enjoy making a fool out of me?'

Indescribably wounded by that, she gave a tragic moan. Harry sensed her performance was going to be riveting.

'Oh, God forgive you for even thinking that,' she gasped.

Harry responded with a look which to Irena was doom-laden. She shuddered.

'You witch,' he said.

'Harry!'

'You've had me on the end of your string since we first met. By God, the nerve of your major. What a cool pair of lovebirds the two of you are.'

'Oh, how can you say such things! You are making me die!'

'I'm sure you'll expire very realistically,' said Harry. She moaned again. 'Why not tell me who you really are, why not be sincere with me for a change and tell me your story? Are you an actress?'

Irena, pale with guilt and despair, was not sure just how hard he was going to be on her, but to be called an actress!

'How dare you think that!' Her spirit flashed.

'Madam,' said Harry, sitting down opposite her and tapping her knees with the rolled-up newspaper, 'kindly realize calamity has struck and that you're poised over a yawning gap. No more lines from your field of drama, if you please. Just the truth.'

'Oh, Harry, this is awful, awful,' she gasped, 'I've been dreading it. Oh, please don't look so angry. I would have told you, I wanted to so much, but I promised Major Carlsen never to breathe a word to anyone until it was known that Princess Irena was safe. And at least I really *am* Sonya Irena Helene Magda Ananescu.'

'How touching,' said Harry. 'I count myself fortunate in nipping your sly little getaway in the bud. I ought to get some satisfaction from cornering you, my flash young flyaway.'

'Oh, that's a dreadful thing to say, and I was not going because of this but because you dislike me so.'

'Really?'

'Yes.' She was in sheer unhappiness. Never had she seen him so cold. She prayed again. 'Harry, I will tell you.'

'Proceed, madam.'

'I am Sonya Irena, truly,' she said earnestly. 'I was at school in Switzerland when I was seventeen and I met Princess Irena there. We are the same age. My father is a Rumanian banker. Irena and I became friends. She is a brave person, very outspoken, never afraid to say what she thinks, and if she was mistaken about some things, well, we all are at times, aren't we? She truly believed the defeat of Germany and Austria would be the worst possible thing for Europe, and she said so. I think I believe that too. She has not been a traitor to Rumania but she has been made to look so, to sound so.'

'Go on,' said Harry impassively.

'Yes, I will.' She cast him a quick, nervous glance, her long lashes agitatedly fluttering. 'Oh, you are believing me, aren't you?'

'You haven't said anything yet,' observed Harry.

'In Bucharest she and I met Major Carlsen. He admired her at once and she admired him. He was sure she would lose her life unless she got away, far away, and so he thought up the idea of having me pose as the princess and going off with you, and having her enemies chase after us. Because her enemies said she loved the Germans they would think it natural for her to run from Bucharest with a man they thought was a German colonel. They watched Irena night and day and were suspicious of Major Carlsen, thinking he would be the one most likely to get her away. So you see, he had this idea of making Michalides and others think it was the princess who left the house with you that night. I was afraid it had gone wrong the moment Michalides spoke to us, but you see, he was so sure I was Irena that he did not bother to pull me out of the cab and take a good look at me. It was very dark, you remember, yes? In the cab even darker, yes? And I am quite like Irena in appearance.'

'I see,' said Harry, 'you were the decoy very neatly paired off with the dupe.'

'That is unkind.' She was more controlled now and just a little proud, even. She was sure she was going to sink without trace, but she was not going to go down crying her eyes out. And it was a relief to confess it all at last. 'Yes, I was the decoy. But no, never once did I think of you as the dupe. And Major Carlsen may have deceived you but he admired you very much in the end.'

'Impressed by my simple charm, no doubt.'

'Harry, I am so unhappy, please don't make it worse for me.'

'Forgive me if I sound unreasonable. But please go on.'

'Major Carlsen did admire you, believe me,' she insisted. 'But he did not completely know you, he would not risk telling you everything. He made me promise to say nothing about the real Irena. I kept that promise. After you and I had taken that cab to Chitila, he got away in his civilian clothes with her. By then Michalides and his men were running about looking for you and me. When Major Carlsen met me in that cafe in Belgrade–'

'By arrangement?'

'Yes. He told me then that he had Princess Irena safely out of sight for the moment, and he wanted you and me to stay in Belgrade long enough to keep Michalides occupied until he received orders which would enable him to take Irena out of the city. He received them quite soon. She was on that train to Zagreb, disguised as one of the peasant women. Those poor women did not know what it was all about. He did not risk getting on the train at Belgrade, but at that little station. He had seen those women on his way there and had simply placed them under arrest, telling them they were to go to Zagreb. But, of course, it was so that he could hide Princess Irena among them, and when we reached Vrycho he put them off there. The ambush was a dreadful shock and worry to him, and you can imagine how he admired you for getting the train through. He got off at Vrycho too, with Princess Irena.'

'No wonder he didn't appear when we reached Zagreb,' said Harry. He pondered while Irena's heart went up and down. 'Yes, it's making sense,' he said, 'I felt there was something too obvious about that flashing torch and standing cab. He wanted Michalides to suspect that something was up. He had to take the risk that you'd be found out. That would have been a disappointment, but nothing would have been lost and he'd have tried again with another scheme, or a different version of this one.'

'Yes, that is right,' she said, 'but Michalides was taken in and began to chase us. And, you see, when you knocked him out in the cab that was the best thing you could have done to convince him I was the princess, especially after making him think it was something to do with your Secret Service. You were very good, Harry.'

'I'd been sucked in myself by that time. Carry on.'

'Well, you see,' she said, flushed and still earnest, 'it left Major Carlsen free to go off with Irena, except that he disliked it when he found us on that train to Zagreb. It put us too close to him and Irena, and it was close, wasn't it, because Michalides had that awful girl Nadia watching us. Major Carlsen got over the danger of that by slipping away at Vrycho, though he did not know about Nadia. He only suspected someone might be on board, keeping an eye on us. He was right.'

'What a Prussian fox,' said Harry. 'Now I

understand why you were never recognized. You weren't the princess. No wonder you didn't bother to hide your face at times, and why you were never in a hurry. You knew I was the man Michalides had marked as the princess's escort, and while I was around the comrades were around too, and Major Carlsen was getting farther away with the prize.'

'You are terribly angry?' she said unhappily.

'I'm sick,' said Harry, 'that neither of you confided in me.'

Her flush deepened.

'Oh, I am sorry–'

'Go on, you haven't finished yet.'

'At least you do not have to be angry with yourself,' she said. 'You see, you did help Princess Irena, even if not in quite the way you thought. Yes?' She tried a desperate little smile. It evoked a look of dark suspicion, as if he thought she was about to be devious. It made her heart feel painfully squeezed. 'Oh, the woman who saw me in the shop at Trieste, she knew who I really was, of course. So did Count Alberto in Padua. I had such awful moments then, not because of the plan but because of what you would think and say if either of them had made you realize I wasn't Princess Irena, just Sonya Irena. And you would not have taken me to England.'

'Would that have mattered?'

Her mouth trembled and her unhappy eyes dropped.

'Harry, I have had terrible times wondering what you would think. I–'

'Would it have mattered, my not taking you to England?'

'Oh, please, I can't answer that,' she said.
'Continue,' he said.
'You saw Irena once, though you did not know. She was the housemaid who let you in that night and witnessed the wedding. When Michalides at last realized I was not her, he must have guessed Major Carlsen had tricked him.'
'Yes,' said Harry, 'his friends in Zagreb found you out and would have informed him. That was why they were shouting at you. Damn it, of course. They knew you weren't the princess, they wanted you to tell them where she was. Is that right?'
'Oh, yes. You have been right so many times. You are maddeningly clever, Harry.'
He received that little piece of soft soap without comment. He was damned, all the same, by the hold she had on him. Elisabeth was right. Affectionate friendship was satisfying, but it was not enough.
'What am I going to do with you?' he said.
She perceived a little ray of hope.
'Oh, please forgive me, won't you?' Her brown eyes begged him. 'I told you the other evening I was in a mess. I knew you would find out in the end and I was praying to hear that Irena was all right so that I could confess to you first.'
'Wait a moment.' Harry had a new dark thought. 'There's something not quite right. Damn it, yes. Once they'd found you out in Zagreb, what was the point of you running any farther? They weren't going to be after you any more. You could have remained there.'
'No,' she said emotionally.

'Why not?'
She searched desperately for words.
'You see,' she said, having found some, 'they would have wanted to get hold of me again and made me tell them things.'
'In Padua, then? You could have stayed in Padua.'
She had to engage in another search.
'Oh, it was lovely in Padua, wasn't it?' she said with tremulous irrelevance.
'So why didn't you stay there instead of coming to England? Damn it,' said Harry, 'we didn't even have to get married.'
'But we did,' she gasped, 'how could I have got into England except as your wife?'
'Look at me,' said Harry. She lifted downcast lashes and looked at him. He had never seen such guilt. 'Shall we have all the truth? We might as well, don't you think?'
'Oh, please, I can't,' she said.
'You can and you will,' said Harry.
'But you will never forgive me,' she breathed.
'I'll try to be Christianlike,' said Harry.
'Oh, you are going to be so angry and I am going to be so miserable.' She took a deep breath. 'You see, Harry, you see, Major Carlsen said that once we reached Trieste – he was sure you would go there – I did not need to go any farther. He said you would be able to make the rest of your escape easily from there, and that by then he should have had Irena well on the way to safety. All the real danger for me was between Bucharest and Trieste. He said that from Trieste– Oh, Harry, please don't make me say any more.'

'Tell me,' said Harry mercilessly.
'No,' she gasped.
'Tell me.'
'Oh, you are giving me a dreadful time. Harry, Major Carlsen said I would be able to get back to Rumania from Trieste without too much difficulty if I wanted to. I did not have to be an exile myself.'
'So?'
With an effort she whispered, 'I was to leave you in Trieste.'
'I see. To slip away? No goodbyes?' He was smiling at last, but it was a smile that made her shudder. 'You'd have left a note, I suppose?'
'Oh, please don't look at me like that, I am enduring an awful time, and you are hating me for deceiving you.'
'Why didn't you slip away, may I ask?'
The crimson suffused her face.
'Oh, how can I tell you that? You must know why.' She put her gloved hands to her hot face. 'I could not help myself, I had to come with you, even though there was Elisabeth.'
'Why?'
'Oh.' She shook her head, then plunged into admission. 'Did you think that after being with you on that train, after that wonderful moment in Zagreb and after being with you in Padua, I could simply turn round and go back to Rumania? Oh, Harry, please be kind, I am so in love.'
'You're grateful, I expect–'
'Grateful? No!'
'...and we both have Elisabeth to think about.'
'Yes. Yes, I know. But you see,' she said in her

desperation, 'I thought when she knew how we had been together, all the way from Bucharest, and that we were married– Harry, I thought she would kick and scream and have nothing more to do with you.'

'Good God,' said Harry and wondered if this was the way the minds of all Balkan people worked. If so, that would account for their fractious politics and irrational behaviour.

'But she isn't like that, is she?' Irena's clasped hands were trembling in her lap. He felt completely and incurably in love with her, he felt pangs for her. He had given her a hard time. 'Harry, does it take very long to fall out of love?'

'I don't know,' said Harry, 'but my parents are still known to hold hands occasionally.' He wondered if he had had all the story. He felt something still had to fall into place. Something that nagged at him but which he could not put his finger on. 'Whose jewels have you been carrying?'

'Irena's, truly. Except the pearls. They are mine. You see, if they had caught her they would have taken everything from her. Major Carlsen knew that if they caught me they would only be angry, they would not have suspected I had her jewellery. I'm to keep it until I hear from her. She will get in touch with my parents in Bucharest.'

'Why your parents?'

'But you see it was supposed I would return to Rumania from Trieste sooner or later, but not go to Bucharest until it had all died down and her enemies did not wish to bother with me any more. I was to go to our country house in Moldavia and keep in touch with my parents from there.'

Harry's dark look finally faded. She was a remarkable young woman. She had taken tremendous risks in helping Princess Irena. It had put her on the wrong side of the extremists. They would have put her name on their lists.

'You've been carrying more than those diamonds for her?'

'Yes, much more,' she said, turning her eyes on the fire and seeing only miserable pictures in the flames.

'You lost two of your pearls to Captain Sabata.'

'Yes,' she said, 'but I would have given him all of them as long as it meant I could still be with you. I am sorry, I know I must not be in love with you. But I am.'

'There's something still not quite right,' said Harry, 'I still can't see why we had to get married. Sonya Irena, are you sure you've told me everything?'

She kept her eyes on the fire as she said, 'I have tried to. It was Major Carlsen's idea that we must be married. He was sure it would convince you of the desperate danger Irena was in, that it would make you commit yourself like a true officer and gentleman.'

Harry hid a smile.

'Heavens,' he said, 'mine is only a wartime commission. There's a difference, as any regular officer will tell you.'

'Major Carlsen did not seem to think so. And the marriage really was necessary if things went terribly wrong and I did have to continue on to

England with you. He said there was always the risk the extremists would still come after me. Oh, Harry, it is right, isn't it? I am in such a mess. It is awful to be so much in love.'

'I've found it very trying,' said Harry. 'Tomorrow I'm going to look over a farm I'm interested in. It shouldn't be too long before I'm out of the army. Would you like to come and look it over with me? Perhaps, if you don't mind being a farmer's wife, you'd better come. I wouldn't want to make an offer for it unless we both liked it.'

Irena lifted her eyes. They were huge in their disbelief. Harry was smiling.

'Harry?' she said faintly.

'You were beautiful at Romano's, Sonya Irena, did you know that?'

'Oh, something is happening, isn't it?' Her heart was hammering. 'Something wonderful? Oh, I could not bear it if you were joking. You are saying you love me, aren't you?'

'I think the happening occurred when I saw you through all that soot.'

'Oh, say it, Harry, please say it,' she begged.

'That I love you? Well, I love you, don't you know that? Why do you think I brought you here? I couldn't part with you, but I didn't know what the devil I was going to do with you. Good God, I thought, what can any ordinary man do with a princess except keep her in a glass case?'

'Oh, Harry!' She was rapturously emotional. 'You aren't joking? I am really to be your wife?'

'You are my wife, and as Elisabeth and I have discovered we're just very good friends, it sounds serious to me. A princess would have been impossible, you'll be lovely.'

He stood up, took her hands and brought her to her feet. Her brown eyes were swimming. She fell into his arms. Her hat lost its bearings and the kisses were very erratic until the communication of warm love prevailed.

'I am being kissed?' she gasped, pausing for breath.

'I think so,' said Harry.

'It is not before time. Oh, it's lovely, isn't it?' She was richly alive in her delight. 'I mean, after being so dreadful to me, now you are being wonderful. I am losing my head.'

'That's your hat,' he said. She laughed, flung her hat off and hugged him. 'Now,' he said, 'if you're really sure you've told me everything?'

'Oh, yes,' she said with feeling, 'except have I told you I love you? Oh, you have no idea, I–'

'Hold on,' said Harry. The nebulous, nagging something had suddenly crystallized into being. He held her at arm's length and looked into her shining eyes. 'There is something else, isn't there? Tell me, young lady, if you had decided to slip away at Trieste, what was going to happen to the annulment? I'd have been left in a fine fix trying to get myself unmarried to you and married to Elisabeth. And just how would you have got on if you'd met someone else?'

Lashes swept down to cover the last guilty secret, but the telltale flush was all too visible. She pressed herself back into his arms and hid her face in his shoulder. She took her deepest breath and rushed muffledly into ingenious confession. 'Darling, I was just going to say I should be so glad if we could be married soon. Do you think tomorrow?'

'Oh, my God,' said Harry.

'Harry.' She pressed closer, as desperate now as she had ever been. 'Oh, you must be forgiving, darling, this is my most terrible moment of all. You see, we aren't really married. It was all done to impress you and to make us look married if I had to go to England with you, and I did have to, I could not bear you leaving me. But I would not have risked marrying a man I did not really know, not even for Princess Irena. So they faked the ceremony and the certificate. But wasn't it wonderful that they did? I should not have got into England, otherwise–' She stopped, not because she had no more words but because Harry seemed so frigidly unreceptive. She held on frantically to him, certain that if she let him push her away she would never get close to him again.

'I'm speechless,' said Harry.

She shivered. She said, 'Harry, it was all for Princess Irena, and Major Carlsen said there would be times when it would be easier if I were your wife.'

'But you never were.'

'No, oh, I know, but I was supposed to be. We had the marriage certificate and your people passed it when we landed. So we were almost nearly married. Harry? Oh, please don't be angry, please don't send me away.'

Suddenly he was laughing. She unwound herself and looked at him. And she knew he was not going to send her away. The blissful relief drowned her.

'I'm damned if this doesn't beat everything,' he

said. 'You witch, you'll get me hanged.'

'Hanged?' she gasped, but he was still laughing. 'Oh, how was I to know what would happen, that you would make me fall in love with you?'

'Make you?' Harry was beginning to realize she had her own sense of logic.

'Yes,' she said. 'Well, you should not have been so gallant, so masterful.' Her return to rapture made her teasingly imaginative. 'You should not have bundled me about. It is dangerous to bundle any woman about, it makes her feel she is the object of special care and devotion, and she simply will not let you go. When it happened to me–'

'Just a moment,' said Harry. He could not let her ride on clouds, she must be brought down to earth. 'Sonya Irena, do you want to be a farmer's wife?'

'Oh, more than anything, as long as the farmer is you.'

'Then I should tell you it's not going to be like dancing at Padua or Romano's. It's going to be very hard work. For both of us. I'd like to have you with me because I love you in a way I don't think I could love another woman, but I wonder if I'm asking too much of you.'

She became intense in her reaction to that.

'You think I have never really known hard work?'

'Have you?'

'No. My father is rich, you see. But then I have never really known life, either. I did not begin to live until I promised to help Princess Irena and met you. You are not going to ask me to stop living because you feel it would be nicer for me in a glass case, are you? Or because you feel I could not work hard? You know I could, you are just trying to say to me, "Sonya Irena, take care, think seriously if this is what you want." Well, it is. It is. Oh, perhaps I will kick and scream sometimes, but please please don't have doubts about what I want. I want you.'

He remembered her courage, her resourcefulness. He smiled.

'I think you'll do very well,' he said, 'I think we'll both do very well, but you won't have time to kick and scream.'

'Harry, of course we will do well, we shall be together.' She looked very intently at the top button of his jacket. A little breathlessly she said, 'And we can't farm night and day, darling, there has to be time for some other things.'

'Ah,' said Harry. 'I'll do my best,' he added.

'You had better if we are going to have four children. And we have time now to kiss again, yes?'

'I think so,' said Harry, 'I think there will always be time for that, Sonya Irena.'

'Oh, it's wonderful, isn't it?' said Sonya Irena after only a short time.

It was emotional as well. So much so that she was crying her eyes out, as Elisabeth had known she would.

The publishers hope that this book has given you enjoyable reading. Large Print Books are especially designed to be as easy to see and hold as possible. If you wish a complete list of our books please ask at your local library or write directly to:

Magna Large Print Books
Magna House, Long Preston,
Skipton, North Yorkshire.
BD23 4ND